Leaving

Cynthia Krause

Also by Cynthia Kraack:

Minnesota Cold
Ashwood
Harvesting Ashwood

Leaving Ashwood

Cynthia Kraack

North Star Press of St. Cloud, Inc.
St. Cloud, Minnesota

Copyright © 2014 Cynthia Kraack

ISBN 978-0-87839-721-1

First Edition: July 2014

All rights reserved.

This is a work of fiction. Names, characters, places, and incidents are the products of the author's imagination or are used fictitiously. Any resemblance to actual events or persons, living or dead, is entirely coincidental.

Cover art by Terrence Scott.

Printed in the United States of America

Published by
North Star Press of St. Cloud, Inc
PO Box 451
St. Cloud, MN 56302
www.northstarpress.com

For Grace.

Chapter One

IN THE DEEPEST YEAR of the Second Great Depression, I became a statistic. Widowed and bankrupt, I lost our home when my mother passed away. She'd left me with only her debts, including too many years of unpaid mortgage payments and overdue property taxes. I joined the millions of homeless.

Before the sheriff nailed the front door shut, though, I gathered what could fit into three boxes and paid a year's rent on a storage locker. Hoping the housing authorities were as overburdened as the rest of the government, I stayed another week, then dressed in as many layers of clothes as I could manage, packed a suitcase, strapped a sleeping bag to my back and began walking. In two days I covered thirty miles to St. Paul where I slept on the sidewalk outside a regional housing agency while awaiting placement. The next ninety days I slept in the former walk-in closet of a private house lost to the city.

Where once I was powerless to protect my family and home, the passing decades brought opportunities to start over, to build financial security and earn the power needed to keep those I love secure. Some feel I have worked too hard and worried too often about Ashwood, with its gray stucco residence and productive acres. Those scarred by the Second Great Depression know that isn't possible.

THE SKINHEAD BOY kissing a frizzhead girl under the early June moon had no idea their passionate interlude would upset their employer's breakfast. Street-savvy teenagers don't think of cameras in an apple orchard miles from the city, much less understand why the owner of a large enterprise would be concerned about a few squeezes and kisses.

Above all our heads an invisible power canopy hid our identities from the air force of drones sent by corporations, government agencies, media groups, and anyone with a nosey personality and money to burn. Opaque netting tented much of the surrounding land to keep giant mutated insects and birds from damaging crops, bothering livestock, hurting residents. These two lusty sixteen-year-olds were amazed by the illusion of open skies, ignorant of what protected them as well as the monitors that captured their actions.

Before a zipper could be unzipped, a night supervisor had arrived on the scene, encouraged them to break it up, to not mar their records on this fifth night, to get a good night's sleep before another day of physical labor and academic work.

Leaving Ashwood

They were just two teens doing what boys and girls have done in the dark of an orchard for centuries. That they were able to slip from their dormitories and pass undetected into Ashwood's orchards was the problem. Our problem.

The skies changed from feeding our bodies to threatening our lives gradually. For children playing four square in the estate's plaza, a protected environment was normal. For a man born eighty-seven years earlier on the open plains under the blue canopy of South Dakota's sky, the changes ate away at what was good about life. As each breath placed more stress on his failing heart, my father-in-law grew to accept his invalid condition.

Had I mentioned it, he might have teased me out of thinking about last night's video. He'd told me recently that bright June mornings tickled memories of cookouts, softball games, tulip gardens. But we didn't talk much anymore about those summers. Better to pretend the world maintained a predictable pattern with a man tired by the struggle of eating breakfast.

"You'll call the other kids today?" His words came out whispery. He cleared his throat, coughed, raised a thin hand to his lips. A cultivator accident claimed a half finger before we met. Paul Regan, my father-in-law and business confidante, was waiting for congestive heart failure to finish its course. At his age, he was too old to benefit from current cardiac procedures. "Anne, you'll be honest and tell them I'm dying."

"I'll call this morning." I held his other hand, so cool and boney. I would ask them to come home, to say good-bye. "I promise I'll be honest."

He sat back, one eye closed and gave me the look he'd once saved for his late wife, Sarah. The look that implied he trusted me to carry the family through his dying process. "The kids' lives should be easier after everything we went through during the depression. I hoped they'd be settling down, getting married, and living like people used to live. Those damn multi-corps." Paul coughed, a weak sound against phlegm collected in his throat.

I handed him a tissue. We had this conversation most days. The last time my stepdaughter Phoebe was home, Paul was still working with the field crews. His reunion night with Noah, her brother, had been emotional, both seeing the changes etched in the other's face. Talking about farming was the highlight of Paul's visit with Phoebe's half-brother, John.

"I really enjoyed talking with John. That young man's got a good head on him." Paul pulled in a rattle-like breath. "He reminds me of David as a boy. When he isn't acting like you."

My ear bud buzzed to let me know of a seven o'clock conference. "Time for you to rest," I said as I stood. "Let me get rid of your tray. Any plans for this morning?"

Paul cleared his throat again. "You gotta make the most of the good days. I might sit outside for a while and admire the roses."

Chapter Two

Lately when difficult work and family matters demanded simultaneous attention, I thought about how I might have been a retired schoolteacher if not for the Second Great Depression. Born in the Millennial generation, I spent a happy childhood living in a suburban house, and came to maturity in a world teetering between the great recession and what media hucksters call G2D, or the Second Great Depression. A bureaucrat decided I was worth more to the nation as an agricultural business manager than a teacher. They were right. I was so ridiculously good that when the first century of the twenty-first millennium passed its halfway point, Hartford, Ltd., was named one of the top 100 privately held companies in the United States.

Eating breakfast with Paul cut into my morning office time. We had not told him about a hostile takeover effort on Hartford, Ltd., by Deshomm, one the world's largest multi-corps. Our company could be a boutique agricultural producer and marketing brand within the gargantuan multi-corps. A very profitable boutique. It was no secret that Paul's shares would change ownership within the family when he died, but with no means for public trading of Hartford's stock, Deshomm's aggressive stance was perplexing. Nine family members and a handful of management employees owned one hundred percent of our company. I knew the details of my father-in-law's will. My husband, David, and I thought we knew that none of our children would open Hartford, Ltd., to such risk.

As assured as I originally felt, managing the Deshomm threat dwarfed everything on my agenda as Hartford's chief executive officer. Somewhere I'd find time to make the calls Paul requested. Phoebe, my stepdaughter through David's first marriage, promised she would be available. My son, Andrew, was traveling.

"Anne." Clarissa joined me for the walk from the family residence to Hartford's executive business offices, a structure built decades ago by the Department of Energy to house David's research group. "A group representing ELH appeared at the main gate at seven claiming they had a meeting scheduled with you. Nothing's on your calendar. They insisted on parking along the road until we ironed out this misunderstanding."

A few years older than I, she wore her gray hair short and her standard business outfit tailored. Clarissa earned my respect and trust. We would never be warm friends, but over seventeen years of working together she had become the one critical person every executive needs—half assistant and half chief of staff. Her relationship with Andrew was less successful. Sister to Andrew's father, Clarissa brought my son to Ashwood after her brother's death.

"They've caught wind of Deshomm's shenanigans and want a piece of the action," she said. "I suppose if you don't give them time they'll jam communications again."

"No time to meet with them today and no interest. Let Sadig know there could be security interference." We walked side-by-side making the most of the very short distance to Hartford's executive suite. "I'm surprised Deshomm hasn't tried more serious communications tactics." We stopped for security scans. The office doors opened. "They're like little boys showing interest in a girl by putting a worm in her desk."

"How is Paul?" Her voice softened.

"Holding his own for another day. I need time today to call Phoebe and Andrew. They have to know how he is doing. And about Deshomm." I knew my schedule had no breaks until after dinner that evening.

"I cleared time with Phoebe's communicator. If we push back morning assembly for a half hour, you could call her. Andrew is traveling. When you're available I'll initiate contact."

"Tell them to hold the assembly without me, Clarissa. I'll contact Phoebe right away."

She headed for her workstation and I poured myself a cup of coffee before going to my office. Not even seven thirty and every staff member was at work. To play against the multi-corps, we had to be on top of the market around the clock.

The Second Great Depression created the need to develop a different world financial model. As the United States lurched into an odd socialist structure to keep people fed and safe while rebuilding its economy, we couldn't fathom returning to the old private market system. The government became employer, producer, and marketer. We were confused, but grateful. When big businesses re-opened, they were colossal in size with global investors pooling funds. They nudged governments out of the market place and recast their former regulators into providers of educational and social systems. Common people saw only good as the multi-nationals exerted their power to force the shut down of terrorist organizations that threatened global business. The price for living in a safer world hasn't been determined.

Phoebe liked to say she was a woman with three mothers—the surrogate who carried her, the blood mother who died, and me, the one she calls Mom. Perhaps the passing of Phoebe from surrogate's womb to her mother's arms, into my care in only eight weeks foretold the complex life my stepdaughter would lead. At twenty-five years of age, one of the nation's Intellectual Corps, Phoebe was a brilliant, beautiful, genetically engineered woman. Raised on a Minnesota farm, she proved to be ill-equipped to live the grueling lifestyle chosen for her by our government's Bureau of Human Capital.

Although she hadn't been here for more than a few days in five years, Phoebe called Ashwood home. She referred to her eight-hundred-square-foot apartment on Chicago's Lake Shore Drive as an "upscale holding cell were cares took care of her basic needs." Meals were brought to her, housecleaning services just happened, clothing appeared. Cares were always watching, always keeping the outside from disturbing Phoebe's productivity. Family ranked high on the cares' list of annoyances. My attempts to contact her were frequently blocked.

While the holo request made its way through IC loops, I looked out my office windows and thought of the large windows in Phoebe's place. The beauty of the ever-changing waters of Lake Michigan are soothing for me, but frightened Phoebe who had no history with a body of water bigger than the ponds on our estate. Shortly after we moved her to Chicago, we once waded knee deep into Lake Michigan and the sand washing out from under her toes convinced her she might be swallowed alive by the water. Her hand gripped mine as a child's might, and tears rolled down her cheeks.

Waiting for Phoebe, I wondered how she might look today. Physically her father's child, tall and graceful, her face was beautiful with a noble-looking broad forehead and elegant trim nose. Phoebe's curly dark hair and green eyes came through her mother. We'd watched all kinds of odd behaviors pop up during Phoebe's Intellectual Corps lifestyle, so many possible signs of her mother's emotional instability. I'd had such faith in nurture over nature. Until parenting Phoebe.

My hologram appearance caught Phoebe in the middle of collecting her boyfriend's athletic jerseys from shelves and chairs. Her hair, curls pinned up in random clips, captured light like a finely built halo. My picture faded as she moved in and out of sunbeams.

"Phoebe?"

She stood still, some unknown passion drained from her face as she pulled on the look adult children show when talking with their parents. "You're looking good, Mom." Sitting down on a low-slung upholstered bench, she dumped Ahlmet's shirts on the floor. "If you've been trying to find me the last few days, I was in a secured lab. No connectivity allowed." Her breathing slowed. "How is everything? I wasn't expecting to hear from you."

"Someone told Clarissa this would be a good day to talk." The same comment made to a staff member wouldn't sound scolding. "Things are happening here you will want to know."

"Go ahead." Transparent with her feelings, I heard irritation. "Is this about Deshomm?"

"Partially. Interesting you'd say that. What do you know?"

"Noah said something was going on a few weeks ago. And my communicator is pissed about the distraction at this time in my project."

"It's a complicated story. To be blunt they're attempting a hostile takeover of Hartford, Ltd."

"Who would sell out? You've been thorough with all the legal junk." Her eyes slipped to the windows. "Did you mess up when they wanted to purchase Dad's herd? This would kill Grandpa. I hope the field workers aren't talking about it when he's around them."

That she could chose to forget that her grandfather was ill, very ill, annoyed me almost more than the blatant blame of the herd sale fiasco. I brushed a hand through hair that had been unwashed one too many days because of time spent with Paul, pushed a strand behind my ear.

"Let's talk about Grandpa first." Behind her head I saw her apartment windows, wished I could see the lake.

"Everything's okay, right?" I heard sleepless nights under her voice and a request for assurance to give her permission to head back to her lab or to Ahlmet or whatever she does when she isn't working. "What's up, Mom?"

"Grandpa isn't doing well. He wants to see all of you soon. If you can arrange to be away from the lab, this is the time to come to Ashwood."

Her hands quieted as she sat upright. She turned to me with intensity, wanting to be told this wouldn't be like her grandmother Sarah's passing away. No one here had ever asked her to drop work.

"How about a holo-gathering, Mom? Maybe two or three hours this weekend? I'll make all the arrangements with Noah and John. I'll even contact Andrew. Would that make you feel better?"

My youngest daughter, Faith, popped her head into my office. For a few seconds I was distracted as she tried to ask me a question. She left without an answer.

"Work is calling me," Phoebe said. The problem with her work was that she could be telling the truth or protesting my intrusion. "Figure out a schedule for getting together. I really have to go."

"This is when you wanted to visit." My breath caught in my chest, but I barreled through before Phoebe could sign off. "Noah arrived last night and John is here to finish his research."

Amber, Ashwood's residential manager, knocked on my door. I held up a hand to hold her off. She walked away.

"Life doesn't change at Ashwood, huh?" Phoebe distanced herself from our conversation. "You're always the one everyone wants." She reached up and unpinned her hair. "Is Grandpa really that sick? You're making it sound like I'm the only one out of the loop. I'm at a very critical point in the water clarity project."

A wheezy cough escaped before I turned my head to pop a suppressant.

Phoebe, hypersensitive to the slightest issue in David's or my health, interrupted her protest.

"Are you okay, Mom?"

If we had a more adult relationship, I would have told her I was tired from caring for Paul, worried about how her father will deal with losing his father, frustrated about the parade of multi-corps demanding meetings or calls, nearly fed up with the difficulty of managing Hartford, Ltd., in the crowd of big guys. But Phoebe, an intellectual removed from reality, lived in a world where relationships were about caring for her needs.

"I'm fine, Phoebe. Just trying to get through a difficult time." Suppressant now under my tongue, I slowed my words. "About your first question. There aren't a lot of eighty-seven-year-olds left in the country. His medical advisor says he might have two weeks, maybe six, but not a lot more."

Tears appeared. She turned her head back toward the windows and the lake. "No one tells me any of this stuff," she mumbled as she turned back toward me. "Grandpa sent me a fruit and vegetable pack a few days ago with a note about staying away from store berries because of a new preservative that could give me a rash. You know the rash I get from chemicals. I don't understand how he could be so sick and remember my rash."

It wasn't the time to tell this brilliant woman that Amber did the weekly food shipment and brought notes to Paul for a signature. I hoped she'd say something to remind me of her former gentle-hearted self. I wasn't comfortable believing in Phoebe's willingness to accept all the little deceptions we'd taken to create an illusion where Ashwood remained constant.

"Are Dad's labs still secured?"

"The Department of Energy just certified them. We won't have any researchers onsite until late August."

"I'll do my best." Her voice flattened. "I'll send information about my plans."

"Dad and I have never suggested you interrupt your work, but this is important."

Sadness dimmed the animation that made her so unique. "It's been years since I came home. I'm so wound up in work that I didn't even think about that until right now. I love you, Mom."

"I love you, too." A slight buzzing interfered with our images.

"Are you okay, Phoebe? You seemed distressed when we first connected." The buzzing became more constant. "Something's bothering our holo."

"It's Ahlmet."

"I'll let you go."

"No bother, Mom."

"He can come with you if that would make you happy."

"It's over." She glared toward me. "I'm getting rid of his stuff."

So Ahlmet was history. The intense young engineer who had introduced Phoebe to the things young people with money did in Chicago was gone. I hoped he had anticipated the ending.

She wouldn't tolerate sympathy so I didn't ask for details. "Take care of yourself, sweetheart. I'll look for information about your plans. Love you."

"Love you, too, Mom."

Our flawed holo disappeared. Maybe in the lives of my grandchildren, someone would invent long-distance communication that could include a hug. I sat back in my chair and coughed. Many times.

Chapter Three

The square footage of Phoebe's Chicago apartment equaled the minimum space required to house a family of four by Minnesota statute, one of the most generous housing allowances in the nation. High rises in every concentrated living area were built off the same plans with two small sleeping rooms, a bathroom, and one large space to serve all other needs. Communal dining areas often occupied parts of a few floors and residents could cook in these kitchens or bring their families for the meal of the day.

The holo with Phoebe made me late for one of my least favorite monthly meetings, the local branch of the Federation for Faith and Peace. Organized religions helped keep many people alive during the Second Great Depression. In return, for almost a decade, the government required weekly faith sessions at residential worker settings like Ashwood. Decades of court decisions were swept aside as the nation turned to God for relief from hunger and disease. I believed in God, even prayed, but hated the artificial marriage of religion and government. Then came the Federation for Faith and Peace.

Incorporating the world's twenty largest religions into a huge for-profit structure whose operating budget rose or fell on its success in maintaining peace seemed like a politician's pipe dream. No holy wars, no forced mergers of shrinking religions. The politicians couldn't make it happen, but the capitalists did. Suicide bombers and chemical weapons interfered with production and distribution. Now, with world hunger again increasing, the Federation assumed responsibility for local feeding programs.

Food in all its simple, natural forms had become a middle class staple and lower economic class treat. Children in high-density living centers received two meals a day and two nutritional units appropriate for their age and growth needs. Adults might eat only one meal of real food and rely on processed, pre-packaged units for all other nutritional requirements. Protein sticks, sweet o's, dried milk, or juice dusts and vitamin-infused daily bullets were distributed in colorful, edible wraps from machines on every block and at work.

Trapped at my desk while FFP representatives reviewed numbers and reports and recommendations about food resource centers locations drove me crazy. This month, like every month, the appeal to sponsor new centers came without time for analysis.

Unlike other months, silence followed the FFP nutritional chair's request. She cleared her throat and leaned toward her camera. "We have dire needs in the north metro and southeastern traffic corridors. Is there data that anyone would like repeated?"

Committee members from Deshomm, ELH and other multinationals checked the time. Smaller food producers assigned to the group, already taxed generously to supplement feeding programs, wore neutral faces. Whatever was said in this meeting about this topic would be on the news boards immediately. Hartford, Ltd., already managed a dozen nutritional sites, employed people to teach food preparation in those locations and stocked their shelves and refrigerators.

Finally a multinational volunteered to supplement a number of sites serving children if allowed to test new nutritional products. I bit my tongue as the FFP chair accepted. God knows what will be fed to unsuspecting families with FFP absorbing full cost of providing market testing. Instead of speaking what would be an unpopular opinion, I signed myself out, claiming a conflict in my schedule.

"Anne, do you have a minute?"

"For you, Amber." Her name choked into another cough. Discretely I felt around my top desk drawer for the case of suppressants. "I've got to get us off the board of the local FFP or at least its emergency feeding advisors. Between the graft and corporate games some mess will be exposed and implicate everyone."

"That's an awful wheeze. Are you okay?"

"I thought my office had a musty smell when I got here this morning. Or it could be allergies."

"When I helped Paul settle in the back screen porch, he wanted me to remind you about calling Phoebe and Andrew. Clarissa said you spoke with Phoebe, and I wanted to save you from calling Andrew because I just heard from him. He'll be here tomorrow." Her beautiful black hair fell in loose curls down her back and made it hard to think her thirtieth birthday would be in this summer. She was the first person I met when I arrived at Ashwood. Then she was a tiny five-year-old worker adjusting to being away from home.

"Wonderful. Phoebe said she'd try to get away."

"We'll get rooms ready for everyone. How amazing it will be to have the whole family together."

"Don't say anything to Faith right now." Our youngest daughter, born seven years after the youngest of her siblings, loved being with any combination of her brothers and missed Phoebe. Amber, adopted by us in her early teens, had been Faith's closest companion for many years.

"By the way, Sadig says they've completed a work-around to bedevil the multinationals' jamming of our communications. We're still in security status limiting visitors and vendors."

I sensed weariness with the corporate situation and tried to make a light joke.

"Does that mean a certain medical technician won't be wandering up the drive to look at the lilacs?" David called Amber the kind of woman whose beauty stopped conversations and wondered how the poor tech would find enough courage to talk with her.

"You're behind on estate gossip, Anne. That's been over for weeks." Her shoulders rose and lowered. "You might have at least one spinster daughter."

In the urban areas people still met and married in traditional ways. On the estates, work left little opportunity for causal socialization. Amber never shared why she returned to Ashwood after a few years in California and France. We thought she'd find someone, and never expected her to come back and ask to work at Ashwood.

"Ahlmet is history also." Amber would find her way. Phoebe might not. Ahlmet seemed most likely to bring regular life to our daughter's world.

"No surprise. Nothing outside the Intellectual Corps really holds that woman's attention," Amber said before she left my office.

Hartford sucked ninety minutes out of each hour I gave it. Facing the takeover threat shoved every business meeting off my calendar. Dozens of small incidents throughout Hartford revealed that Deshomm was gaining toeholds in our corporation that might not be reclaimed. My communication tools vibrated in a pattern that indicated trouble in our systems.

"Sadig." Using a very old-fashioned pager unit I told him I wanted to talk face-to-face. As I waited for him to walk from the business building I found a note from Phoebe with details about plans to arrive late that afternoon. She'd received clearance to work in David's former DOE labs for some undefined period of time.

Instead of approving copy from the consultants working on the Deshomm crisis, I turned my chair to look out the window at Ashwood. I could only wonder how Phoebe would fit into this world. Like the fickle waters of Lake Michigan, Phoebe may look calm while a constant undertow threatened her hold on reality. She might be bright sunlight during the darkness of Paul's decline or add more stress.

Bringing a member of the Intellectual Corps to Ashwood required adherence to a higher level of government protocol. Our daughter was a national treasure protected by people and technology every minute of her day. As Sadig entered I finished sending a note to David and Amber about Phoebe's plans and asked one of them to assume responsibility for fulfilling the Intellectual Corps' requirements for the place she called home.

"We've cleared the communications issue, Miss Anne." Sadig began speaking as he walked in the door. He continued with details as he shut it. Pure Somali ancestry showed in his tall, lean body and sharply chiseled face. He was the grandchild of immigrants whose motivations I did not always understand. His mother, a woman soured by many disappointments in her life, had worked in our kitchens until her unreliability forced Amber to change assignments.

"You told Amber it was corrected an hour ago. And there's this whole episode of the two kids making out in the orchard after lockdown last night. If we need outside expertise during the next few weeks we'll roll the expenses into our defense costs." My coughing started again. Again my fingers searched for suppressants.

"I was distracted from giving approval to the patch. We have a log of calls or messages that you may have missed. The supervisor has been disciplined about incomplete procedures. It was not really a big deal." He lowered himself into a chair. "Are you okay?"

"Doctor Frances says smog from the cities is giving many of us with environmental asthma some troubles." The suppressant didn't ease my spasms. "Timing is bad."

He tapped on his pad. "Dr. Frances knows you are in distress?"

I shook my head. "You are the one who might be in distress. Phoebe will be here late this afternoon. That means a lot of security activity. Maybe the Intellectual Corps already contacted you?"

"Just now. Is this why you wanted to see me?" He didn't wait for answer. "Don't worry. Hartford security meets Corps protocol. I have heard a lot about her and look forward to personally meeting one of our nation's elite. You must be proud to have parented her."

The careful turn of words displayed Sadig's multi-corps experience. No sloppy "proud to be her mother" or awkward "proud to have your stepdaughter so recognized." I waved him to my conference table, hoped to catch my breath while moving from my desk. The morning was almost half gone.

Chapter four

THE BEST SECURITY PROFESSIONALS say little that is unnecessary. A suggestion to sit and talk suggested a call to danger.

"You have my full attention, Sadig."

"You should have that cough checked at the Mayo, Ms. Anne. It might be something in your environment that Doctor Frances cannot detect." He sat, back perfectly straight, long hands resting on the chair's arms as if testing it for size. "I have reason to believe the air quality of this office has been compromised to cause you discomfort. We will be installing a new micro-scrubber later this morning. I don't know who has caused this tampering, but I will. Soon."

John's address displayed on my communicator. I tapped once to let my son know I would be with him soon. "That's one of the creepier invasions we've experienced. Just my space?"

"You're the one with the power to make decisions."

"We have family concerns that make the Deshomm challenge particularly difficult."

"Hartford, Ltd., is most vulnerable if something happens to you."

Giant Pines, one of our livestock and traditional grain operations, had been hotly pursued for at least eighteen months. Our private-labeled organic foods had a few suitors. More than one multi-corps had made offers for our educational services branch. Deshomm executives from around the world had flown to Minnesota specifically to convince me that all of Hartford, Ltd., should become a satellite company within their business web. Large money and stock were the lure. Subtle threats, security breaches, communication jams suggested what our existence might be like if offers were ignored.

"Ms. Anne, there is no issue more important to Hartford, Ltd., than your safety." He spoke slowly as if delivering news to an uncomprehending child. "Not one."

The man across my table had been a toddler during the Second Great Depression, too young to experience that everything could be taken away—family, land, money, hope—if unprotected. In a quarter century our world had transformed from protective governments to dominant multi-corps. Money ruled. Governments served those with the power, not those in need.

"That it is why you report to me. And why I bring up the undetected kids in the orchard. Outside my office window." David and John walked past my inside office window. David sent a small smile in my direction. He had a stately air, with his salt-and-pepper hair, broad shoulders, and the padding of a man his age across his chest.

"That man," I pointed to David, "doesn't feel comfortable with security around me. He would have choice words to say if he knew of this breach."

Sadig gave the impression of being fully engaged in our conversation and fully distanced, as he monitored an ear communication piece, a data pad, and whatever other security monitors he carried. Either he didn't hear my displeasure with his performance, or ignored the message. Not for the first time I wondered if he didn't listen as carefully because of my gender.

"In the past it made sense to have security and engineering management together. In light of the intensity of the multi-corps, maybe it's time to reconsider that structure." This caught his attention and I continued without hurrying a word. "Perhaps directing security for a corporation with installations in multiple states is a big enough job?"

A work crew, all young people who arrived at Ashwood unprepared for the agricultural life, rode past my outward facing windows, heading toward the ginseng growing buildings. Some proclaimed their metro roots with bald heads, one wore braided locks and facial hair. All were trim, muscular, healthy after a few months of regular meals and exercise. Once I knew the workers' names and stories and would be able to call those teens something other than boy and girl.

"What are you saying, Ms. Anne?"

"Deshomm's timing is critical because my father-in-law's passing will lead to changes in shareholders. Changes in who might control key votes like changing our articles of incorporation." It was time for him to show he had control of our physical safety. I threw a fairly basic fact into the conversation to test his knowledge of Hartford's structure.

One eyebrow raised above Sadig's coffee black eyes. "This is confidential?"

He had not wondered about the possibility of upheaval when Paul passed. Sadness slowed me, the memory of discussing this plan with my father-in-law. "There could be challenges. The South Dakota Regan family ranch is not as prosperous as Hartford, Ltd., and we think one of David's brothers might ask for consideration. And there is a slim chance one or more of the surrogate offspring could be demanding."

Finally Sadig ignored his communication tools, but his answer was disappointing. "I do not understand this last item. These surrogates were compensated by the government, signed legal documents to relinquish rights to the Regan name. What worries you?"

David's nagging about Sadig worried me. When Sadig joined Hartford, Ltd., we temporarily contracted with ABF, a national intelligence specialist, to give him time to become familiar with the breadth of issues. Two years later, Sadig hadn't grown beyond the narrow vision nurtured as a specialty manager for fifteen years in a multi-corps' security force. He focused on technology, laws, and physical property. As David predicted, Sadig's incompetence had become a liability.

"Have you read ABF's report that suggests a family member, or someone in a close relationship, provided Deshomm insider information?" Wheezy compression caught my breathing, stopped me from saying so much more about his lack of insight. Sadig pushed a glass of water toward me, but I stood up to get to the suppressant tablets. He stood as well.

"You need to return to the residence, Ms. Anne, until we have the air filtration system cleansed." He opened the door. "Come." One hand, long fingers and pink palm, extended my way. "Now."

My eyes watered, the suppressants failed. Holding on the table, I coughed like a seal.

David joined us. "Everything okay? You sound terrible."

"Sadig says . . ." I tried drawing a deeper breath, swallowed, anything to gain control and finish the statement. "Sadig . . ."

"She should go to the main house." My security chief finished the statement.

We moved as a trio, stopping once for me to cough in the long glass walkway between the executive offices and our residence. I felt panic, tried harder to fill my lungs.

"You sound like one of the metro smoggites, Annie." David rubbed my back, massaged my neck. "Stop trying so hard. Just pull in a sip of air."

When solar panels had become more efficient, we'd replaced the heat-retaining tiled floor with a recycled product capable of muffling noise. Nothing muffled the sounds of my breathing. Looking for an external distraction, I gazed toward the rear of our residence at the gardens our family planted near the backyard pond. My eyes settled on Sarah's shaded corner where she could rest away from a crowded house. I wished life had given me the time to move slower.

"I'm better." My voice cracked a bit. "You both need to get ready for Phoebe." The smile I expected crossed David's tired face. "Have you seen your dad?"

"He's having a good day." We began walking again. "He sounds better than you. Maybe you should knock off for the day."

"I'm okay." Then coughed in contradiction. "I have Deshomm documents to review."

"Use the desk in our bedroom. The guys and I are heading to Giant Pines. No one will bother you."

With a quick nod, Sadig left us. He spoke intensely via his communicator while heading out of the building. I kept my worries about him confidential for the time. "What's interesting at Giant Pines?" My question ended in a whisper.

David kept us moving. "John would like to leave the university research team and begin running part of Hartford, Ltd."

"He hasn't said anything to me. Why didn't you?"

"Until he had a plan, it seemed premature." David walked like his father, long steps learned on open farmland, uninterrupted by curbs or other people or the baggage of city life. For a quarter century, we'd walked side-by-side.

"Isn't a smallish agribusiness a risk for his career?" More than David, I followed the brutal treatment of young talent in the big corporations. They looked for people with single purpose.

His arm settled across my shoulder. "If John is really interested in agribusiness, there's plenty within Hartford to keep him satisfied."

"I want more than this for him, David. He's smart."

"You've been married to the son of a rancher. To a man who traveled the world for work, but never felt alive unless he was here. I don't know that I want our son to have the hellish life of a government intellectual just because he's pretty damn smart."

Sadly I never grew to love the earth like the Regans, didn't feel sad about growing food under domes or in multi-story greenhouses. Hartford's breadth hardly interested them. They were farmers who were never as pleased about a cutting-edge distribution system as new tillable acres.

Hartford, Ltd., hadn't invested in new agricultural property for many years. I've approved selling small acreage to diversify our holdings, to invest in gold—as a safety for my family's future if the multi-corps drive the global economy back down. My family will not know poverty again.

"This isn't about the business being too simple for John. We agree that Hartford, Ltd., might not be large enough yet to support diverting his contract from the research agency. Are we ready?"

We walked into our residence, a building constructed by the government during the early post-depression recovery period to house up to a couple of dozen people. We changed its footprint to accommodate more, then reconfigured the space to fit a small family and one of Hartford's food research kitchens. As much as we've tinkered with the place, we'd never completely eradicated the clumsy original design that was more federal post office than family home.

"Sadig wasn't kidding about that wheezing." Doctor Frances and her son waited in the central hall. She and her husband, Terrell, were our closest friends. But at this moment she was all physician. "Tablets not helping?"

I nodded, aware of an odd mid-morning fatigue. "He thinks someone is compromising my office air."

"Your health records are in the Bureau data. It wouldn't be a surprise if an info merchant mined the system." Right there, she ran her diagnostic wand up and down my body. "Jeremiah, go to my office and ask Pia to send you back with a nebulizer and one C5 unit." Her son ran off, a boy with his father's height and his mother's temperament. "Where are you heading?"

"To our room. David thinks I should work from there while Sadig does his environment assessment." A cough began, accelerated to a whooping sound with a trailing wheeze. I turned slightly, covered my mouth with my sleeve. "Damn," I moaned.

All I could do was watch Frances and Jeremiah outfit the bedroom study with a supplementary portable air filter, a humidifier, and nebulizer. She squeezed a giant dose of antihistamine up my nose. Hot tea and a pitcher of cool water arrived from the kitchen.

"Could someone let Clarissa know where I'm working? My schedule will be impossible."

"No need. I just checked." Clarissa entered as the kitchen worker left. "One of the kids mentioned you were sick. Quite the news on Ashwood when Ms. Anne needs special attention." She seldom made me laugh, but the comment inspired a smile. "I hear my nephew will be joining the family gathering."

I nodded, breath too precious for words. She placed a pile of documents, each carefully earmarked for my review, on the desk.

"He's truly my brother's son, but you transformed him." She looked around the room at the nebulizer and medicines. "These things belong with Paul, not you. I'm going to stay on top of Sadig's staff, but promise me you'll stay here until your office is clean?"

Not a physically affectionate person, Clarissa's slight squeeze of my shoulder as she left was surprising. When the door closed, I felt like a kid on a sick day with an extraordinary amount of homework.

Chapter five

THE CHANCES HARTFORD, LTD., could outrun Deshomm were not unlike those of our large herd Australian shepherds facing an uncontrolled large pack of aggressive Rhodesian ridgebacks. As I studied our intelligence consultants' materials in the concentrated quiet, inconsistencies began to surface. They provided us with critical information as we shed or acquired any business asset, but not thorough information. In ninety minutes, I traced how three small plots of land acquired for easier access to Hartford acres were purchased with various contingencies to Deshomm-held subsidiaries.

"Mom?" John's deep voice outside our bedroom door interrupted what might have developed into a major executive blow up. Any breathing problems at this point were from frustration, not environment.

"Come on in. This is a good time for me to take a break." I pushed away my notes.

John stood inches taller than David with thick wavy brown hair that hung slightly shaggy above his collar. He was a large man, packing close to two hundred pounds on a body of toned muscles. The deep voice that surprised everyone when John was a boy had developed an interesting slow cadence.

"How about a hug, Mom?" Before I could stand, he bent to squeeze my shoulders and kiss the top of my head.

"The crew did a good job cleaning the old engineer's house. Thanks for letting Noah and me use the space."

"Are you kidding? Dad and I are so grateful the two of you are able to be here."

"There's nothing to be grateful for, Mom. In fact, I'd like to make being here or at Giant Pines permanent." He tucked his hands into his pants pockets. "Is this an okay time to talk?"

"Sure. Seriously, are you sure you want to be tied to a rather national agribusiness, John?" I gestured toward David's reading chair. I could see the lower back lawns and remembered how often our son set up the badminton net as a child and persuaded people to play.

"Not exactly. I am interested in part of Giant Pines for a different use." His voice sounded no disrespect. "I've got a co-investor and substantial government grant that could make Giant Pines a regional center of research for agribusiness.

Leaving Ashwood

The strong, quality operation you and Grandpa and Max built is every attractive to investors." He paused. "But you know that."

As boys, John and Noah played in the orchards outside our office windows with children sent from the cities to spend years on Ashwood as light-duty workers. They chased each other through the young fruit trees David insisted we plant. Nothing quiet could be done inside during those noisy energetic games. By the time John was a teenager, workers arriving at Ashwood were often rough older kids sent to us for rescue. The orchards became off limits for many reasons. Now, machines did everything a teenager or grown adult could possibly do—prune, clear, harvest.

"A lot has changed here since you left." Unlike Phoebe, Noah, and Andrew, John is an unaltered person. No genetic intervention and more freedom in choosing a life employer, but less clout in declaring large resources. Leaving the university research group could be a disaster in the long view of his working career. His eyes followed me as I sat back in the chair. "There's so much more of the world for you to experience before you think of a commitment this large."

"I've traveled plenty for my grant research. When we finish this phase, our whole team will be contracted out to the highest bidder. I don't want to be caught up by the multi-corps and live in that whole regime. I want to make my own decisions. To have a real home, not company quarters." His words slowed. "It's important to me to start working now and to own some land." Before I responded, he delivered his greatest surprise. "Because I think someday I'd like to make a run for political office."

A dozen or more politicians visited Ashwood each year, some to see how private agribusiness operated, to be seen in the country, to meet real voters. But we had few personal friends involved in big scale politics.

"Local?"

He shook his head. "The locals don't have much muscle today. Mostly deal with street repairs and charities and school attendance. I'll start at the state level." John inhaled, placed one arm over the back of his chair. "Hell, I really want to go to Washington, D.C., but I've got to be realistic."

"Who have you talked with about this ambition?" I remembered my brother talking about this dream and tempered that with the reality of David's almost forty years working for the increasingly bureaucracy-bound U.S. Department of Energy.

"You." No smile accompanied his answer. John, being serious, was difficult to influence. "And Milan."

He surprised me with his seriousness. Confiding in my oldest confidante, a very highly placed national bureaucrat was a mature person's action, not just a young man with dreams.

"Milan makes sense." Parenting even adult children happened without advance warning. Like contaminated air in an office or unexpected power surges, your offspring brought their world to you unannounced.

"Statistics would be against you even at the state level." I felt my way through the challenges facing his dream, looking for the opportunities. "To cast a vote for the state legislature or elected officials requires two consecutive years of minimum land ownership. Most state voters are about forty years old. Federal elections have higher land ownership requirements plus a threshold of personal taxes paid for three years."

He blew air out through his nose, a low snorting sound. "You remember when a person just had to be eighteen and a citizen."

"Your father lost his federal voting rights because of restrictions on citizens in high homeland security positions. Remember that quote by one of the multi-corps chairperson about how the vote of a shareholder is a commitment to building a better world while the vote of a citizen is an uneducated guess at what liar is the most trustworthy?"

"Who can vote is just one issue on a significant list of civil rights that need to be returned to Americans." John shifted on the chair. His voice strengthened. He could be a good consultant or sales person. "I want to talk about Giant Pines. Politics is the long-view goal."

"Of course, but first will you tell me how Milan responded to your political dream?"

One shoulder raised, stayed that way. "He was honest about how difficult it is to be elected and how tough it can be to stick to your principles in office."

"I have a half hour for you to tell me about this plan for Giant Pines." I cleared the desk and motioned him to move the chair closer. "Just for the record, Noah's decision to refuse the Intellectual Corps career wasn't a huge surprise. Andrew's move from the multi-corps energy group for the consulting world surprised Dad. Your political aspiration will blow him away."

He looked so serious, so hopeful. I wanted to witness his success. "I'm proud of you, John. Dad called you and Faith our free children, not tethered to the Intellectual Corps standards. Grandpa would like to hear about your big dream."

This was one reason Hartford, Ltd., existed, to become large enough to offer our children escape from government work assignments. We'd be testing our financial model. "Maybe your baby sister will do something even bigger."

"She will, Mom." He projected a business plan onto the desk. "I've got thirty minutes to make my case to Hartford's CEO. Can we start?"

Chapter Six

WITH SECURITY INSPECTIONS of my office still underway, I took advantage of the beautiful summer day to read additional intelligence reports on our screened porch. From my table I could hear the trees rustling, muffled noises of people moving about, and machinery in the fields.

Across the porch Faith sat at her own table and studied her book. Conceived during the lowest point in our marriage, she developed as the most serene of our kids. She looked like none of us—or maybe like the most perfect blend of our genetics. Auburn hair fell thick and wavy like mine when I was young. Blue eyes, centered under naturally curved eyebrows, were the gift of some long-forgotten relative. Trailing her siblings by many years, she absorbed some of their best traits—Noah's humor, John's responsibility, Phoebe's intellectual curiosity, and Andrew's kindness—all with more balance. She's the only one of our children who ever chose to study in my office instead of our residence or the school building.

"Mom, do you think Phoebe will be happy to be home?" Her question wasn't meant as light conversation.

"What's on your mind, Faith?" I had moved from discovery to strategy in my work, a good time for a break.

"Phoebe lets me follow her network, but I haven't talked with her for the longest time. She's kind of become different than us like that whole thing of having a cares to do everything for her." Faith wrinkled her nose. "That's creepy."

"I'm kind of there with you on the cares thing." These silent laborers lurked around the Intellectual Corps night and day to keep their lives free from mundane tasks. They also supposedly listened to all conversations and reported back to the intellectual's handlers. I realized I had assumed Phoebe would come without a cares in attendance. "Her life's different than ours. People expect a lot from her and she's only nine years older than you."

One hand pushed hair off her shoulder in a natural and pretty gesture. David and I are amazed by Faith's wholesome good looks.

"Would you have let her go to the university so young if you knew how the Intellectual Corps would treat her?" She flexed a toned arm, prettiness chased aside. "Will she expect special treatment?" Lines showed on her forehead. "Grandpa doesn't need any upsetting."

I thought of the times David or I made quick trips to Chicago to calm Phoebe through rough times. She was eccentric. The trips, always unexpected, were organized by the Bureau. The summons carried national security ratings and trumped running a corporation. She could be working on social theory or the scheduling of drone invasions. We never knew.

I didn't think Phoebe was unstable, but I no longer understood what drove her. Intellectual Corps wasn't a normal path open to just any of the three hundred seventy million people living in the United States.

"I used to love talking with her about books or music or where she was traveling. Now I can't think of one thing we have in common besides being sisters." Faith voiced some of the questions David and I discussed the night before. "I don't get what she does or how she lives."

"It's possible we won't see much of her—she's not on a vacation. Like John and Noah, she'll be working. My hope is that we'll have a few meals together with Grandpa."

"I told him I'd bring him flowers from Grandma's garden." Faith changed directions without forewarning. "Do you mind if I leave my school stuff here? Do you need this table?"

"Go ahead."

I heard her talk with friends as she walked away. We'd been reluctant to approve a communications implant so she relied on a bracelet communicator. This fall as the only student accepted from our region for the metro language academy, she dreamt of taking public transit to classes. Drones would make the commute too dangerous, but that hadn't cut through her naïve belief that she's metro-savvy because she attended her first years of school in Minneapolis.

We hoped to find a way for her to leave Ashwood for a real college and not one of the big corporation-dominated schools that exist to train potential workers. Few options remained in the United States.

"You're frowning." David joined me. "I can think of many reasons for that look. Either one of our daughters, my father, Giant Pines, or the thought of having most of us together for dinner."

"I thought you left to buy new boots before picking up Phoebe."

"That wouldn't make you frown."

In summer, David wore looser cotton-blend pants and shirts. His gray-streaked hair has thinning. He tended to overestimate the physical part of his days when serving himself at meals. Or maybe he found comfort in food as his father faded away.

Leaving Ashwood

"Actually I was thinking about Faith's college plans." I steered away from Hartford and work. "I read that Argonae and Bio announced exclusive relations with Carleton College. That was the last opportunity in Minnesota for a student who isn't on employment track with a multi-corp."

"So we'll find a good school outside of Minnesota if that's what she wants." David sat down in an oak chair made by his father. "Dad hopes to be able to join us for dinner."

From the pocket of his pants, David slowly withdrew a red-enameled box the size of a deck of cards and twice as tall. "He asked me to give this to you."

Paul and I had talked about the contents of this box many times since Sarah passed away. David held it toward me, grief over the approaching loss of Paul showing in tightness around his mouth and a dulling of his dark eyes.

I took the box with both hands, my fingers searching for a small chip in the enamel on the left underside.

David sat back in his chair. "He said you wouldn't be surprised."

"I knew it would come. Just not today."

The box in hand, I cleared space to give Paul's gift full attention. David watched.

"He suggested you open it alone."

"I know." I looked up, my face soft with empathy for David. Accompaniment on Paul's slow passage tired all of us, David maybe the most. "Later."

He cleared his throat, rubbed the site of an old shoulder wound. "Dad seemed intent on knowing you had this right now, before the kids all returned."

"That sounds right." Noise in the courtyard seemed loud between us. "I will open it this afternoon, I promise."

Being David, he toned down his curiosity. "It's going to be good to have the kids all here. Dad's looking forward to spending time with them."

I couldn't bear his sadness any longer. I left my chair to put my arms around him. He rested his chin on my shoulder, his arms wound across my back.

"I've got to leave to get Phoebe." His voice, smooth and rich, had fatigue etched under each vowel as they stretched out in upper Midwest style. "I'm looking forward to having time alone with her." He straightened out of my arms, kissed my forehead and stood.

"Drive safely. Please don't take any short cuts in the estates region."

"You worry too much."

I walked with him to the courtyard. Three men trailed Amber up the main walk to the residence. Each pushed a handcart piled with boxes or suitcases.

"Jim, those go into the Blue Suite of the DOE building," she directed. "The rest of the things go into the old teachers' rooms."

David turned, eyebrows raised.

"Phoebe's things." I explained. "One of her support people sent a complete inventory this morning. Everything she would need or want, all in original packaging, to arrive before Phoebe. Clothing, custom pillows, air purification, work out equipment, favorite Chicago foods." We watched as Amber and the laborers disappeared into the residence's kitchen entrance. "Our daughter does not travel light. Nothing was specified about traveling with a cares."

"She can't carry all this when she's on research trips." David could travel to Europe with one bag carried over a shoulder.

"You can ask her about that when you pick her up. Go. Give her a hug for me."

By the time he drove through Ashwood's gates, I had gathered my things and walked to the executive offices, a game plan forming along the way. Hartford, Ltd., might outrun Deshomm. I needed every minute before David returned.

SINCE THE SECOND GREAT DEPRESSION, the Minneapolis-St. Paul metro area boundaries have not expanded even one city block. Hartford's twenty thousand acres begin at the Ashwood orchard fences, still thirty-five miles from the heart of the cities and ten miles within the estate zone.

Acreage meant little today with multi-story growing sheds producing year-round harvesting of fruits, vegetables, aquatic plants, and fish. High-yield crops and grains matured under rotating sunscreens. Cattle, hogs, and chickens were housed at Giant Pines in environmentally controlled buildings and outdoor spaces.

Beyond the courtyard area of our home at Ashwood, a small village of buildings had developed. A school, a dining hall, workers' housing, the business offices of Hartford, Ltd., a power plant, a giant garage for storage and maintenance of equipment. Behind Ashwood's fences, a half-dozen houses had been built for essential employees. A state-owned clinic opened to the road with its small infirmary technically sitting on the estate's land.

Since I arrived, we had moved buildings farther from the main residence to create a security zone with a second gate where transports must be cleared before approaching the front door. Soccer fields and a softball diamond were now behind the residence instead of outside our front windows. Each change challenged my sense of peace, but life continued without interference.

Working on the screen porch lining half of the residence's front, the air was heavy with the smells of growing plants and trees. Night and day windmills on the lands and fans in the giant growing facilities whirled. Depending on the time of year, the porch was anything but quiet.

Chapter Seven

PEOPLE WHO KNEW PHOEBE came out of Ashwood's offices and kitchen and barns to follow the transport up the drive and welcome her home. Others who could wander away from work joined for the novelty of viewing an Intellectual Corps member. With the transport making its way through the second security gate, I was caught near the back of what became a crowded courtyard.

She opened her door in a hurry, a knapsack falling to the pavers before shiny black boots could be seen, then thin legs covered by the black pants metro dwellers favored. I moved faster, the sight of those spindly legs sending warning that all was not well with our daughter. Beyond our protective canopy drones hummed like a swarm of flies approaching fresh food.

She jumped from the transport, looked through the waiting crowd. I knew she needed to see me. When I called her name, Phoebe smiled at Terrell and John, but pushed past them into my arms. With her head bent to my shoulder, a sprinkle of gray hairs could be seen running through her dark curls. Her body felt as thin as a young apple tree, her shirtsleeves pulled up on equally bony arms.

"Phoebe, I'm so glad to have you standing here," I said into her ear. "You look tired. Let's get you in the house."

"I should say hello to everybody." Under her words I heard David's gravelly tones announcing sleepless days. "It's been a long time."

She leaned against me as we walked through the gathering. Magda, a family friend and Hartford leader, and her partner stepped forward. One picked up the forgotten knapsack while the other wound another arm around Phoebe's waist. Terrell's large voice softened as he fell into step with us. I looked over my shoulder and saw David hand the transport control pack to a worker. When he looked up, a mask of neutrality controlled his face.

"We've put you in the old teacher quarters." I spoke loud enough that Magda could help me steer my daughter. Up our home's long front steps, past the large white geraniums standing in front of the tall red wooden doors, the three of us matched stride. Inside, in the quiet of the foyer, Phoebe's sigh floated across aging wooden floors. "Let's go to your room first. Amber had someone unpack the boxes your people sent ahead. Did you bring anything, or anyone, else?"

She straightened out of our loose arms. "Just my knapsack and a small bag." Her solo steps straggled, unsteady. Phoebe shrugged her shoulders then pointed at the knapsack Magda carried. "I can take that. Why not my old room?"

Twenty-five years old, many years away from here, and she still wanted the small room on the east side of the residence, a room she had shared with her little sister.

"I knew you'd like looking out at the orchards." We turned left after the dining room and walked down a narrower hallway toward a collection of rooms added twenty years earlier to accommodate the estate's teaching team.

"What's wrong with my old room?" Phoebe knew stubbornness wore people down.

"Faith filled it with her things years ago." I wondered how she had forgotten Faith's bulletins on decorating. "She still has those obnoxious English posters you sent from London."

"I met a man there who sold my mother a large mirror. He remembered all the details because Tia was so strange and shipping that large an item to the states was unusual around the depression. Do you know where it might be?" Phoebe now walked independently with a wobbly swagger.

"The big mirror that stood in the reception room?" I remembered David in front of the mirror with an infant Phoebe, how she loved to inspect her own image. "You played yoga teacher in front of it?"

Her laugh, all high notes like a soprano, filled the hall. "My God, that big old black framed thing. My mother had that shipped from England. You must have thought she was crazy."

"Actually it was here when I arrived. Your parents had a feng shui expert who placed all the furnishings in that room and it was perfectly angled to reflect the outside light." My first walk through Ashwood, the mirror captured a bleak November evening. "Now it's doing that in your grandfather's suite."

I opened the door to her temporary quarters. After decades of austerity, our ability to purchase a new double bed and modern furnishings for a guest still amazed me. When Phoebe was born the entire residence was painted government white and we stocked bed coverings in simple primary colors.

"We've made sure security has Phoebe's codes active in Ashwood's systems." Magda gave Phoebe a hug. "I need to leave, but if you'd like a tour of any of our new buildings or want to visit the greenhouses call me."

Phoebe surveyed the room, not even looking out its windows. "Someone at Ashwood has a good eye," she said. "I could stay here for a long time." Summer sun slipped through her clothes. I looked away, my feet not moving. From ten feet away, the outline of her body suggested an eating disorder, or drug abuse, or emotional distress.

"In case you're hungry." Phoebe would be with us for weeks or months so other conversations could happen at leisure. "Ashwood is still on country time with dinner at five thirty. There's still fruit and snacks in the kitchen during the day."

Gracefully she lowered herself to the bed. "I need to check in with the lab. Could someone bring a tray?" One hand smoothed the coverlet. "In fact it would be helpful if we could set up a call system. I hate eating sticks and o's. You know I never keep regular hours." She raised one shoulder, a gesture filled with womanly sensuality. "Like Dad."

Always a Daddy's girl, her words projected into the space between us like a brick thrown through glass.

"The agency sent a list of your needs to Amber. She'll go over everything with you after dinner." Phoebe eased off her boots and shed her jacket. "I'll have someone bring a tray now. Terrell's got a few of your favorite things ready."

How I wanted to kidnap my daughter, take her across the border and ward off anyone who might suggest she think of work. "I'm so glad to have you here, Phoebe. Thank you for coming."

A look, maybe annoyance or maybe discomfort, crossed her face. She turned her head away for a second. When she turned back, her words and features were out of synch.

"I love Grandpa. You just had to ask."

Chapter Eight

David waited for me on the screen porch, a glass of water in his large hands hardened by outdoor labor. Our faces mirrored the same worry. He stood.

"Your office is cleared." His hand gripped the glass as if it held a great weight. "Sadig's crew told me they found two packets of pollen stuffed into the air vents." His voice was low, conscious of how sound could carry beyond the screened area. "Do you have time to talk?"

Truthfully I didn't, but I couldn't work productively while ruminating about Phoebe on my own. "There's nothing I'd like to do more than spend time with you." I took his glass. "Industrial espionage, most all of our children about to meet under our roof and our daughter's grand arrival kind of made this a big day." I pointed toward the outside entrance. "Could we walk through the orchard?"

"If you won't start coughing. The cities' smog is blowing our way."

"I'll take the risk." We walked comfortably. "How was your time with Phoebe?" David's face melted into sadness. "Maybe one of our offices would be a better place to talk?" His stress was more visible under the open sky. "Doesn't look like a cares accompanied her. Maybe she's been freed from supervisory oversight?"

He confirmed what he knew about her work from a discussion early that morning with her research coordinator about securing lab space in the DOE building. The irony that Tia's daughter would be leading scientific discussions about clean water was bittersweet. On this day, each of the fragile bonds between Phoebe and her biological mother pointed us toward darker thoughts.

Inside my office, David walked to the windows. He worked the thumb of his right hand into the palm of his left while watching birds at a feeder. Our girls had built it for him for Fathers' Day a decade earlier. I gazed at my monitor, saw Phoebe remained in her quarters. Internal identification chips changed everything about parenting from the days we relied on kids to tell us where they were going. On the other hand, it was nearly impossible to become invisible even on an estate the size of Ashwood.

"This Ahlmet guy seems to have filled Phoebe's head with stories about roadway attacks and security issues in the estate zones." David turned, pulled out a chair and sat. "She suggested we should have a full-time bodyguard-driver and made

Leaving Ashwood

a number of comments about not feeling safe until we were inside Ashwood's second gates. Almost obsessed with the whole deal."

What he shared supported my first impression of Phoebe, now an ultra-thin, stressed-out woman. "I don't think she's happy that we put her in the teachers' suite. She forgets Faith has had full use of their old room for almost ten years."

David ruefully smiled. "I sense she thinks I'm old-fashioned and not entirely approving of her lifestyle."

"Don't be hard on yourself. Phoebe always reminds me that you understand the expectations she faces better than any of us. I suspect Ashwood will be a difficult adjustment after living in the intellectual quarters."

"True, but I think she'll work just as hard while here." He was thoughtful. "Maybe she can reconnect with regular people and discover more balance. If she doesn't, she'll crash in a bad way."

I wondered if he remembered the only time I'd traveled to Paris, to be with Phoebe in one of her darkest times. One of her cares reported that Phoebe was talking about dying. While the idea that the Intellectual Corps members had watchers always jarred me, that time I was thankful. How the Bureau of Human Capital Management would continue their watcher routine inside Ashwood unnerved me. There were no strangers within our gates. Someone we trusted had been tapped, and trained, for this possibility. David didn't need to be brought into my discomfort.

"Well, I think she's better for ditching Ahlmet. You met him the last time you visited. Was he kind of a jerk?" David was a father again.

I remembered a different response. Ahlmet treated Phoebe like a beautiful woman, like a peer. We went to a wonderful private dining club, listened to music and talked about their two short vacation trips. She relaxed at his side.

"I didn't sense that he was anything other than a respectful, fellow intellectual who found her attractive on many levels. But, I know something went very wrong. Maybe even in the last day."

My beloved David finally sat back and looked at me. Even when his mother died I had not seen the deep sadness now darkening his eyes and robbing his face of the fullness that normally made him appear younger than his years.

"When I said that maybe she'd sleep better at Ashwood, she laughed at me." His voice broke up. "Said I should know better. That the lab managers were always chopping weeks off multi-corps deadlines." He swallowed as if the words that were coming might drown him. "And that sometimes she regretted being born."

How could anyone in the early days of this new society understand that genetic engineering would produce a child as amazing as Phoebe or comprehend that her adult intellect would be treated like a national investment? Certainly not the man who called everyone from all corners of Ashwood to the front door when his first-born child was brought home. Even with the soft grief building in our home for the coming loss of Paul, Phoebe's pain carried more power. After pressing controls to close the blinds and lock the door, I put my arms around David. He lowered his head to my shoulder. While upset at a watcher existing in our home, I hoped that person was vigilant so nothing happened to her while we kept vigil for Paul.

Chapter Nine

DAVID PULLED HIMSELF TOGETHER. The DOE needed him to review a report. I had two important calls to make. The first was to Raima, the best independent attorney available in the upper Midwest. Years ago I had convinced her to represent our business interests when all I knew was that because of a government screw-up I had become a significant landowner. In the early post-depression era, the government had little to use beyond devalued money and endless land to settle wrongdoings against citizens.

Visits to Raima's offices provided tantalizing dips into a luxurious lifestyle enjoyed by few. The century-old ten-story building she owned in downtown Minneapolis served as both offices and home. She'd purchased the building from a failed creative agency when the kids and I lived in the city. We watched workers update an exclusive dinner club on the first floor, build out her law practice on the next five levels, and finally finish her home on the penthouse level including a rare rooftop garden.

Raima was shrewd and driven and bitter as hell about all her family had lost in the Second Great Depression. The combination fueled her ambition. When we were both featured in a national publication as successful female business leaders, I came off as smart and CEO-like. Raima dominated the story with confidence.

"How are you doing, Annie?" The remnants of Raima's Middle Eastern tones added power to her voice. Her athletic body and long silver hair attracted men, who were often unsure how to deal with her strength. "And how is Paul?"

"I wish we could be sitting in your living room and drinking a glass of wine while we talk about all of this." Whether the height of the building, the view of her part of downtown Minneapolis, or the fantasy of escaping my responsibilities, I spoke the truth.

"A transport can be at your gate in a half hour. Come spend the evening." She put down a pen. "We'll talk about business and family."

"Sometime soon, but not tonight, Raima." Suddenly I was aware of my unwashed hair and casual attire. The day had escaped without a shower. "The experts give Paul two to six weeks. Miracle of miracles, Phoebe, Noah, and John have come home for extended visits. We're having dinner as a family tonight. Andrew will be here tomorrow."

My father-in-law had a quirky relationship with Raima. She turned on her sexual charms around him and he loved the game. Many years ago Raima stepped in to wrangle an agreement out of a federal agency when a suit close to Paul's heart was in deep trouble. His gratitude assured that she ate well from the Regan's South Dakota ranch and Ashwood.

"Is he able to have visitors? I'm open tomorrow evening." Her manner calmed with the offer.

"He is weak, but loves talking with people."

"I'll be there at six." She pressed a tab on her bracelet communicator. "I'm on a short rein right now, so what does Hartford, Ltd., need?"

I told her of discoveries in the ABF intelligence reports and my suspicion that Deshomm might contaminate the consultants. "We've entered some minor deals that gave Deshomm access to business data through well-hidden subsidiary arrangements. Those deals can't be undone, but I need to build some internal walls quickly and find a new intelligence consultant." I paused. "As much as I hate to admit this, David made a better call on Sadig than I did. I'm not sure of timing, but I have to replace him."

"Tell me about these internal walls?"

I told her about a new governance structure, then walked through how John's Giant Pines proposal led me to consider creating a formal non-profit research foundation within the corporation with possible branches in appropriate units. "We can't afford to bid against the multi-corps for university-originated research projects, but I think we'll be able to grab our share with our facilities and expertise."

"Send me your notes. I agree that you need new intelligence support and a new chief security officer," she said. "Let me give those some thought overnight. I would suggest you have deeper personal security when you're away from Ashwood. I get nervous when you're here with just a driver and some gear attached to your clothes."

"With the armored, drone-resistant transporter and the gear, I feel safe."

"Well, you think about that as you shower, then after enjoying family dinner talk with David." A man's voice called her. "And hold off on any big decisions until we meet tomorrow." She waved and disappeared.

Reyes Milan, my long-time confidante and former Bureau of Human Capital Management supervisor, once served as a legal guardian for Phoebe, Noah, and Andrew. Now he worked less and lived in Duluth where his children had settled in healthcare careers. Global warming brought earlier springs to Minnesota's North Shore so Milan began our hologram visit with a tour of his flowering gardens. "My wife grew up on the Iron Range in Virginia. You probably didn't know that." He lifted a rose bud, barely opened, my way. "Her father was an engineer who came here to work for a mining company." Milan had executive presence even in his garden. "Not the easiest life for her mother in those days."

"I still don't understand what can keep you busy in Duluth."

"Anne, remember, in my world it doesn't really matter where I live."

From the moment Milan disclosed his guardian status for two-month-old Phoebe and her unborn brother, my husband felt less a full father. Like a bitterly divorced couple, the two still maneuvered through this tricky relationship. Milan never second-guessed our parenting decisions or changed the kids' education or service year plans, but we always knew he could. For David, Milan stood as a symbol of government tyranny. For Milan, David's emotions were not worth acknowledging. Strict implementation of Bureau protocol could have stripped David's children with Tia from our family home, but my confidante never raised that threat.

His bald head caught sunshine, shone briefly. "How's my Phoebe? And how is it to have her at Ashwood?"

It wasn't worth asking how he knew she was here. "You probably know better than I do, Milan. I'm worried."

He spoke from a garden bench. "She's not well suited for her life. I've been told her work is brilliant, but there are concerns about her stability."

"Is that on information from the watchers?"

An ultra-calm look directed beyond me told me he wouldn't disclose how he knew these facts. "I'm calling for a favor, Milan. I need to find the best intelligence consultants available outside the multi-corps or government spheres. Two or three people who can work quickly and brilliantly with Hartford."

"Deshomm's heating up, Annie?" He waited. "Going to tell me more?"

"Not yet. Do you know anyone you might recommend?"

"Madison Clark and Theo Vicktor. They're only bound to each other and not to any bank, multi-corps or government agency. Both worked in the too-big-to-fail universe and delight in helping small businesses succeed. I'll have them call you."

"What do you know about the ABF Group? They've been under contract with us for a couple of years."

"They're good at what they do. They've been relatively secure, but Hartford, Ltd., is very small potatoes in their client list." Milan stood, obviously distracted by something beyond our hologram. "Clark and Vicktor would be a better match. They work well in crisis interventions."

"Thanks." I wanted more of his attention, even a cup of tea together. "Any chance of seeing you in our neighborhood?"

"I'll be there if anything happens to your father-in-law."

Milan remained one safe haven. His words brought tears to my eyes because I didn't have to be the tower of strength for him. "It's rough to watch him deteriorate. I'll miss him." I calmed before continuing. "David's not doing well. Faith is wonderful with Paul, but then she comes to me to cry. Amber seems to be the one Paul wants around the most and she's been super." A cough started, the first in hours. "Now we'll mix in the guys and Phoebe."

"Any of the other grandchildren have plans to visit?"

"The South Dakota group visited last month. Andrew has managed to squeeze time here on his way from Alaska to Michigan."

"I have to go, Anne. Keep in touch." He tipped his head and disappeared. Abrupt departures were always his mode of operation.

IGNORING OUR WATER conservation practices, I stood in the shower longer than usual before giving myself the pure luxury of a half hour to get ready for our family dinner. I pulled on a linen dress and pinned up my hair. Paul would appreciate the effort, but in all honesty, I did it for myself. It just felt good.

Chapter Ten

Business operated twenty-four/seven so David and I chose when we took our downtime and made sure others filled the void. The tradition of an early family dinner reflected Ashwood's agricultural tradition. For Paul's sake, there was a holiday feel as we gathered for dinner.

In the dining room Phoebe stood talking with Terrell, the only man who could bring out her soft side. She had not changed her clothes and appeared strung as tight as a violin string—thin and delicate yet incredibly strong until that moment when one snaps. Terrell laughed softly, sensitive to communicating with someone who might be startled by the full sound of his voice. Ashwood's cook when Phoebe was born, Terrell once nurtured a serious little girl's silly side with singing, dancing, baking.

Amber, dressed in rose cotton pants and a white shirt, hugged Phoebe, an old world gesture almost extinct in the metro. She stepped back as Phoebe's arms did not rise. Our daughter's eyes glittered with outer-world reflection as well as the narcissism accepted in the Intellectual Corps.

"I was in Europe too long," Amber said to cover the moment. "It's so good to have you here." She laughed, a woman comfortable with life.

"I forgot that you're quite pretty." Phoebe looked Amber over for a fraction too long. She raised one hand as if to touch Amber, but instead smoothed her own hair. "I wish I knew how to pin my hair up. You taught me years ago, but I've forgotten the trick to using long pins. I should shave mine off."

Nothing announced metro resident more than unisex dark jumpsuits, boots, and bald heads. Faith with her long hair and curvy body would never be confused with young women raised in the city who were more likely to be flat chested because of poor nourishment. All slightly disconcerting.

"No Phoebs, you're not going to shave off your hair and look like unisexual groupies." Noah slid his hand through her curls, the kind of easy intimacy they had as children still visible. "You're a beautiful woman."

Watching Noah and Phoebe entertained me. They remained attractive—curly dark hair, tall bodies, and European faces. So few full-blooded Caucasians were accepted in the Intellectual Corps that Phoebe stood out with her fair skin.

David helped Paul to a chair next to Faith at the round table, and we began our meal—the most complete gathering of Ashwood's Regans in a half dozen years. Amber, our adopted daughter, sat next to John and talked easily about experiences traveling. Some found John's communications abrupt, but not Amber. I knew him to be the most like me, one who would worry about the future while living in the moment.

Paul, his voice barely more than a whisper, asked questions about their lives beyond Ashwood. I watched Phoebe and remembered all of them as youngsters. She had tried to mother her brothers, and then Faith when she came along. I tried to catch David's eye, but he was lost in the moment's richness.

Our visiting kids ate the simple chicken, fresh vegetables, and biscuits as if home tasted good. Noah slid half a biscuit with honey butter on Phoebe's plate, replaced peas and mushrooms when those disappeared.

As the kitchen staff served dessert, Phoebe lowered her head and withdrew from conversation. Had she been a child, I would have left my chair to go to her side. Some odd emotion or sensation seemed to overtake her. Noah put a hand on her arm. She shrugged it off. Persistent, he extended his arm around her shoulders. I couldn't overhear what he said to her, just saw that when she turned toward him she had tears in her eyes. I began to move, but David stopped me.

"This happened a few times on our drive home," he said with his mouth near my ear. "Like a communication device bothered her. But she had a wrist model on and it never pinged. Something is going on, but she seems unaware."

The odd grimace left Phoebe and was replaced by an expression that could only be anger. I wondered what Noah said, but noticed her lean into his shoulder for comfort. John and Amber laughed at an old joke Paul shared. David raised his glass and tapped a spoon against his coffee cup.

"I'll keep this simple." The Regan patriarch role moved across the table from father to son. "Dad, you have been a forceful role model for each of us as well as the small army of children and workers who called Ashwood home through the years." He smiled only for his Dad, a kid wanting to show gratitude. "Thank you for making the difficult decision to leave South Dakota and share your life with us." The smile wobbled a bit before David lightened his tone. "You even brought these young people home, something a whole lot of holidays couldn't do."

Led by Noah, our children stood and applauded, then left their seats to gather around Paul. Phoebe kissed Paul's cheek and left without touching the fresh berry torte prepared special for her. I followed behind her, confused at the tones of her whispers and protests as she walked toward the front door. Obviously she had an embedded communicator, but I couldn't understand who would raise such emotion.

"Ahlmet, I'll kill you if you ever come near me. Do you understand?" Phoebe's words bounced from one hard wall to the other in the front hall where wood floors met slate and tall metal doors trimmed in bullet-resistant glass. One hand, long fingers splayed, slapped a wall. She stamped one foot and then the other. "You scum." When she placed her forehead against the wall I ran to help. Her spine appeared to dissolve.

"I need help in the foyer," I blurted into my own communicator. "Now." I reached her before she made it to the floor, her eyes opened in fear, her hands grasping at the smooth plaster.

"Phoebe, lean on me." Although taller than me, she may have weighed a hundred pounds. I supported her, eased us to the floor. Already the limpness began leaving her body, but she stayed against my chest and curled her palms into fists as she cursed in a language I didn't know.

Sadig, napkin in hand, and Terrell arrived first. Phoebe shook her hands free, extended one to her old friend. "Damn bugger's got control of me," she said as he carefully helped her up. The transformation was amazing. I pushed myself up.

"Phoebe, are you all right?" As my question ended, she would have toppled once again if not for Terrell already holding her elbow. I saw her body slip as her eyes remained defiant, then frightened. "Close the dining room doors and send Dr. Frances to the front hall," I ordered.

We carried her to the family room where the odd pattern repeated over and over for the next hour. It was an excruciating performance that exhausted Phoebe while our resident doctor attended. I sensed Phoebe knew the cause, but her speech was incomprehensible.

"It's not a seizure disorder. I'm not detecting hallucinogenic drugs in her system." Frances told us. "But she's not very strong and her heart rate needs to slow. I'm going to take a chance and administer a sedative."

Phoebe's thin arm reminded me of starving youth workers, of the metros who ate only wrapped sticks and bullets or used chemicals to stay childishly thin. Frances pulled a capsule from her medicine bag. She snapped it under Phoebe's nose and held one half in each nostril.

"It's like something outside is controlling her body," I said from Phoebe's side. "Is it possible someone is using her communicator to do this?"

Sadig and Frances shrugged at the same time.

"What can we do?"

Frances checked the time. "I don't know what to expect next, but my kids are in study hall for the next ninety minutes so I'll stay. Why don't you check back in an hour. Maybe we'll know more."

A psychiatrist by training, Frances had come to Ashwood to care for young Phoebe's horrific night terrors. She developed a select group of other, never named, patients in the southern estates region. Her government-assignment still remained general medicine, caring for patient overflow from the neighborhood clinic built on our land.

Two staff still cleared the dining tables when I returned looking for family.

"Anne?" David surprised me by walking out of the kitchen. He carried a pitcher of water. "Phoebe left quickly. Did she go to the lab?"

"Where are you going with that pitcher?"

"Dad." He tilted his head. "What's going on?"

"Let's walk and talk. Dinner must have been exhausting for him." After a quarter century of marriage, David knew walk and talk to be more than a social gesture. "Phoebe went through an odd sort of collapse. She's in the family quarters with Frances."

His next footstep happened out of rhythm. I tucked my hand into the bend of his arm. "Frances wants about an hour alone with her. Where are the others?"

"Amber and John took off to look at office space in the estates' business building, Faith is giving Noah a tour of the gym." He hurried through the sentences. "We brought Phoebe home at a critical moment, Annie."

The scientist's gift for understatement in the absence of facts often amazed me. I didn't respond as I opened Paul's door. A young man Frances had identified as having healthcare worker potential helped Paul into bed. They talked about dinner and plans for the next day. David placed the pitcher on a table.

"I thank Doctor Frances every day for training Otis to be such a great assistant," Paul said while settling against his pillows. "I hope he gets enough time in her office to keep learning. Can't imagine what bureaucratic idiot thought this kid should spend his life pruning bushes."

A grayish pallor had replaced my father-in-law's rancher tan. Red lines marked his cheeks; dark circles made his eyes appear sunken deep within his face. Otis offered him a small oxygen apparatus. "What a nice dinner. Too bad Andrew isn't here yet. I'm waiting to hear about Alaska." He inhaled deeply. "Always wanted to see that state."

Except for accommodating an adjustable bed, this space had not changed significantly since I slept here my first night at Ashwood. The outer sitting room held furniture Paul and Sarah brought from South Dakota, and lately a bed for Otis. David leaned against a wall, I sat near Paul, and we chatted about dinner. I told him about Raima's plans for the next evening, sparking other stories and memories. As he tired, I stood to give Paul a goodnight kiss and suggested we leave.

"Raima's coming just to see Dad?" David appreciated our legal counsel's fine billing technique. "I know they are friends, but that's still special."

"Well, she wanted to come after dinner, but that changed when I asked her for some advice. Actually she's coming in the late afternoon for a work session."

"About Deshomm?"

His communicator buzzed with the DOE tone. "Damn. I've got to take this." I recognized the change in his voice that still happened when work called. "I'll join you as soon as I can."

Our family quarters had become a busy center. Frances sat next to Phoebe on a sofa. Amber and John lounged side-by-side across from them with Faith leaning near their legs. Noah, always our family dramatist, stood and gestured while telling a story. All appeared relaxed. I joined the gathering, sat in a wing chair, listened to them talk about work and leisure and friends.

"Grandpa looked good at dinner," John commented. "We probably tired him."

Amber patted John's knee. "He rested as much as he could today to stay up this late. Faith and I aren't nearly as exciting as the three of you. I can't bear to think of him not being here." She bent her neck, one hand covering her mouth. John pulled her to his shoulder, his chin resting into her hair.

"I love him." Phoebe put the words out without embellishment. "I still want to make him smile and be proud. With so many grandchildren, I've always had to work extra hard."

Frances pushed up from the sofa. "Your grandfather has lived an amazing life." She touched Phoebe's shoulder. "It's my night to supervise the twins' bedtime so I'd better get out of here. If you need me, call." Her eyes stayed on Phoebe. "Anytime."

She left without offering insight into Phoebe's condition. I recognized doctor and patient confidentiality, chafed at being kept in the dark. As his wife left, Terrell joined the gathering, bringing a snack of fruit and nuts and sweets.

Synapses weakened by long absences reconnected and siblings learned the language of each other's current world, I tried to stay in the moment and experience the family David and I had created. I leaned back against my chair, let go of worrying about a Phoebe relapse and heard about successes and struggles in a very different world than Ashwood. With the exception of Faith, our children had grown up in a time of scarcity and government-controlled structures, starting their adult lives in the era of multi-corps' domination.

Nations' hunger for jobs of any kind had been satisfied by industries with deep pockets as the Second Great Depression eased. Deals were struck, access to natural resources granted, citizens trained to meet employers' requirements. Economists struggled with models to right size government. Privatization was a tool, then the creed. The old game of states stealing jobs from each other looked like child's play as the growing corporations shifted operations from country to country in search of cheap labor and loose regulations.

The conversation had just turned to a wide-range discussion of which multi-corps were infiltrating others' spaces and John began sharing a story about an agricultural project he completed in Canada when the lights dimmed, then blinked before yellowing.

"Feels like downtown Chicago," Phoebe commented. "Damn power grid goes down in the summer when you really need air cooled, goes down in the winter when the wind goes through buildings."

I wondered if John still became tense when the lights dimmed, if the trauma of Ashwood's invasion by a rogue military when he was a little boy left a small scar on his calm exterior. Noah looked at his communicator, a frown forming across his high forehead.

"Mom, are we okay?" Faith asked the question we all were thinking.

My communicator pulsed, once long and twice short. Sadig's signal. "I'll go check," I said as I stood. "You all stay here. The residence will stay secure, but the drone field might erode."

David, just walking into the room, heard my voice. A frown line deeper than his son's suggesting either concern or annoyance.

"What's Sadig got to say," he asked as we met in the doorway.

"He wants me to meet him in Engineering. This can't be good."

"I'll be there in a few minutes. I want to make sure Dad's okay." He turned away like an aged athlete, strong and coordinated, but no longer graceful or swift. Watching him walk down Ashwood's central hall, I noticed the stiffness in his left shoulder.

"Wait for me, Mom." John rose from the floor. "Doesn't seem like a good plan for you to be walking alone when the security systems might be compromised."

He knew nothing of the video of two teenagers standing near my office window last night. I waited for him at the door, hoped this was just an odd coincidence.

Chapter Eleven

CLOUDS FLOATED ACROSS THE MOON in a sky clearly visible after the sun membranes had been pulled aside and drones floated unencumbered into our courtyard. We had our own power plant. A disruption meant mechanical failure or vandalism. Fortunately at this hour of the night, an electrical issue would inconvenience people more than plants or livestock.

I thought I saw irritation in the way Sadig looked at John when we entered Engineering. Jaylynn, our chief engineer, worked on a large screen, testing switches and diverting power to sensitive operations. A wall thermometer showed it was still eighty-three degrees outside.

"Anne, I thought you'd want to see what's happening." Sadig didn't look at John. "We are unable to access the back up generators. The problem is vandalism in the power head."

Jaylynn backed away from the screen. "There was an unauthorized entry into our system shortly thereafter, Ms. Anne. Simultaneous program hack and a line partially cut. The perpetrator of the physical damage is locked in a cattle stall."

"The engineering crew detected a hacker shortly before the incident," Sadig said as Jaylynn continued working. "The coding wasn't very sophisticated, but led to mechanical damage. It's going to be a long night to bring up some of the growing buildings before mid-day sun."

"First priorities have to be Paul's oxygen and the drone guard." I spoke directly to Jaylynn. "If we can't get that back to full strength, Phoebe needs to be in the safe room. What's your assessment?

She tapped on the screen. "Paul is on a portable generator. I notified Intellectual Corps staff and put our best engineer on patching the drone guard to our largest portable. We had some infiltration before the switch took place and it won't hold for more than two or three hours, but I understand the IC requirements, ma'am. We're fully capable of following security protocol."

"With the Deshomm issue, shouldn't there be more protection around my mother?" A challenge sounded under John's voice. Sadig did not respond.

"Is the vandal an Ashwood employee?" I knew the answer because no temporary laborer would still be on the estate at this time of night.

"Jake Peterson."

His surname is still common in this land where the Scandinavians settled, but John and I were both startled. "How long has he been with us and in what role?" I pressed my communicator code for David, knew he would find me.

"He is an engineering student doing a six-month cooperative work-study assignment." Sadig looked up, established unblinking eye contact with me. "He was raised by his mother in Boston and came to the Institute of Technology under sponsorship of Honeywell. They suggested he spend time in a small installation setting and our work-study engineering assistant was graduating."

"Do you know his father?" I shot the question to Jaylynn, unhappy at even the slightest revisit of one of Ashwood's darkest periods. "Have you heard of Colonel Peterson, a Marine who tried to take control of Ashwood almost seventeen years ago?"

Jaylynn, a competent engineer and pleasant woman in her mid-thirties, shook her head. "I've heard a little about Director David being ambushed and all, but nothing specifically about a guy named Peterson. Should someone have known this?"

"Why don't we do a more thorough background check on the kid in the morning." David entered the room and conversation with a suggestion that showed he had overheard us. "Peterson is a fairly common name in Minnesota. In the meantime, anything I can do to help?"

"Sadig." The voice of Max Cravileau, head of operations at Giant Pines, interrupted. "We've got power outages in sections of our grid. The property fencing is out near the main barns. Parts of the cattle sheds and milking equipment are also down. Those are the immediate concerns."

"We have a situation in Engineering, Max." Sadig sounded cool, his eyes returning to the wall screen. "How much of the fencing is out?"

"The pasture lands on the main road side near the cattle sheds and feedlot." Max didn't waste words or emotion. He was a native Wisconsinite with farming in his family since they'd emigrated from Belgium two hundred years ago. "We rigged up security lighting and will ride the fence until it is re-activated."

"Max, this is David. Any sign of strangers in the barns?"

A slight hesitation raised tension. "We're not sure. There are no lights in your herd's enclosure so we don't know if anyone's been in with the cattle. But, someone reported that we're missing a calf."

"I'll be there as soon as I can. And I'll bring John." David looked to Sadig who shrugged one shoulder.

"Wear barn boots and bring your own lights." Max sounded as keyed up as I've heard him, outside of cheering for his son's soccer team. "Keep me informed, Sadig."

"Will do, Max."

"I'm going back to the milking parlor. Anything I should tell people about using lights and such?"

"Make sure anything not needed is turned off," Jaylynn directed. "We'll control power flow over the next twenty-four hours."

A dozen or so small blinking drones buzzed around the courtyard during our walk back to the residence. Clearing the estate of the invaders would take most of the next day. We kept quiet. A part of me wanted to join the guys, a part of me was very tired.

"I need to get to work," Phoebe was announcing as we rejoined the family. "Three hours of laughing with my sibs was just the mini-vacation Dr. Frances ordered." She stretched, thin arms reaching outward, her back easing into a lovely curve. "Even though it's late and dark, I've got to see our old room first, Faith. Mom tells me you've got the eye for decorating."

"The London posters started me." Standing next to each other, Phoebe and Faith both looked older than their ages. "I can't believe you've not been home since then."

Faith stopped to kiss me goodnight. A weaker Phoebe looped an arm around my shoulders and leaned in for a hug. I wanted to follow them, to be sure Phoebe would sleep safe at home.

"Before you leave, I've just learned that protection is compromised on the estate so you both need to stay inside." Phoebe yawned, unused to thinking about personal security. Faith understood the drill. "If anything changes for the worse, we'll use the safe room."

"No thanks, Mom. You'd have to drug me to drag me into that closet."

I knew Phoebe wasn't exaggerating.

"We'll do whatever it takes to keep everyone safe, Phoebs." I didn't exaggerate either.

My own claustrophobia made the family space with windows on two walls more attractive than a dim bedroom. I straightened pillows and tables then stretched out on a sofa with my work pad. Pages from an ADM purchase contract appeared.

I scrolled through the document signed by a stranger about two hours earlier. ADM agreed to purchase David's herd of specially bred dairy cattle from a third party for an exorbitant price with a contract execution date three days out. The

Hartford, Ltd., representative's signature scrawled across the screen in an unintelligent collection of bumps. David and I held legal rights over those cattle with no one else authorized to sell or breed the herd.

"Sadig." I glanced at the clock while paging. "David." Moving toward midnight. I'd been up since shortly after four. "We have another situation."

My husband answered first, the sound of a transport's hum coming through under his voice. "We're driving alongside Giant Pines. What's up?" Fatigue flattened the vowels in his words, that Germanic influence of the Dakota farmlands teased from M.I.T. educated speech.

Sadig joined the conversation.

"Someone has sold your herd to ADM. A third party supposedly acting on your behalf. I received a copy of the purchase agreement. The livestock are to be picked up from a location off of Giant Pines in three days. I don't know who signed the contract, but it wasn't either of us."

"David, you should stop where you are," Sadig inserted. "I've contacted estates' regional security for support. This could get dangerous if we have cattle rustlers."

"That's incomplete thinking, Sadig," David said. "We're beyond the regional police on the scope of this mess. Anyone at that level could be bribed."

David would not have challenged Lao, our former head of security that way. In the morning I'd meet with Hartford's human capital leader about Sadig. But, as midnight approached, I suggested they develop a game plan. With news that priority areas of the two estates were nearly powered, I told them all to be smart and stay safe before ending the conversation.

One last note arrived as I began signing off. Andrew would be arriving after lunch. My first child, the son I carried as a surrogate when the world order we now know began forming. The family says he has a number of my features—Hartford eyes, a tendency to sidestep the emotional for the factual, gentleness with children.

From his first day at Ashwood as a preteen, Andrew's presence calmed Phoebe. In fact, one summer they both spent at Ashwood as teens, I thought he fell in love with her. I hoped his presence would still quiet her, but stopped thinking at that point. They were both adults now with their own histories of mature relationships.

Chapter Twelve

ANTICIPATING LOGISTIC ISSUES in the morning with a partially hobbled power grid, I forced myself to go to sleep. Phoebe's odd collapse brought me back to her years of night terrors and sleep walking through the halls. Tonight she worked, maybe avoiding the difficulty of troubled dreams. I slept until the sun began rising.

Repeating our decades-old morning pattern, Terrell and I poured coffee and settled in the kitchen to talk and watch the start of Ashwood's day. We gossiped about the estate, our children, Paul's health, our shared history. We set aside our business roles to start the day in the comfort of friendly conversation.

"Jaylynn tells me they need to keep all domestic and office buildings on reduced juice. She's adjusted the thermostats." Terrell waved to someone outside the windowed wall. The old small dining room area built to accommodate laborers in Ashwood's early days housed Terrell's offices with most of the test kitchen work contracted out. Frances opened the side door, her curly hair still damp.

He stretched an arm toward his wife, drew her near for a kiss. "Glad our kids got their mother's good looks." Frances shook her head and reached around his side for an empty mug. "By the way, Otis was in for Mr. Paul's coffee around five. Said he woke up feeling good." He paused, looked over his glasses at me. "And Phoebe asked for a breakfast tray to be delivered to her DOE office about the same time. Cook made up a healthy plate and had it carried over." Frances sat down, put her mug on the counter, sinking into thought as Terrell spoke. "Don't think she made it to bed last night."

"A cares will arrive today." Frances let the words settle. "Pretty shocking they didn't send someone yesterday. Someone here must be watching out for her."

We sat in silence. My thoughts shifted from acceptance of Phoebe's eccentric lifestyle to frustration with the fuss she constantly stirred. I sighed, put the coffee mug down. "As tired as she looks, I'm sure sleep might have been a better choice for her. Can you tell me anything about what happened last night, Frances?"

"Nothing." Frances offered the word softly. "Not because of patient confidentiality, but because I genuinely could find nothing wrong with Phoebe. Physically she is fine. Thin, tired, a bit anemic. Not one of those conditions would make your legs buckle or babble in other languages."

"She didn't tell you anything?"

Frances shook her head. "Why do we keep drinking hot coffee on days like this? I'm switching to filtered water." I stared into my own cup as she dumped hers, knowing that she bought time to put together some answer for a concerned mother. Frances maintained confidentiality as staunchly as an old economy physician, a treasure in the modern world.

She leaned against a counter. "I've never seen anything like what happened last night. We certainly use more implant technology to control certain physical and mental disorders. But nothing registered with a scan. It was like her thoughts were driving physical symptoms, but not in a logical correlation." Looking away, Frances checked a clock. "I have to be in the cities for a consult this morning so I'm watching my time." She raised her glass, but didn't drink. "The most perplexing factor was that the physical dysfunction would intensify each time Phoebe tried to talk about her condition." Frances surprised me as she finished. "We should be concerned. I have no idea how to form a treatment plan, but I think this is definitely life-threatening."

"Nothing's happening on my watch." I poured what remained of my coffee down the drain. "That woman is a human, not just the multi-corps' brilliant working grunt." The importance of my afternoon meeting with Raima skyrocketed. "I don't have an exact plan in mind, but I'm not going to give over my daughter's life to corporate profit takers."

"Amen." Terrell's fist pump confirmed his support. "Frances and I are with you."

"Don't doubt that, Anne." Frances hugged me, a most unphysicianly act. "I fell in love with this man and that girl seventeen years ago. I have plans to confer with a few close associates."

"Thank you."

"I'm in on it, too." Amber joined us, her beautiful hair pinned up for another hot day. On my best day, decades earlier, I never matched her natural good looks. Phoebe could be drop-dead lovely in a classic European style, but Amber was pure twenty-first century. "Sorry, to change the subject, but did David or John return last night? Paul was asking."

"I can speak for David not returning. Is something wrong with Paul?"

"He was looking for someone to sit with him by the pond this morning." She reached for a glass. "I know your schedule is a killer."

Frances waved one hand as she picked up her bag and left. While Amber didn't know about Raima's visit, her description of my day was accurate. "Not to throw stones in your day, but Raima and I blocked out from about three thirty until dinner for a business meeting. And, Andrew arrives mid-day." The sentence brought smiles to all of us. "I don't quite know where you can find him a room. He can use one of the lower conference rooms in the DOE for work space."

"This is a good problem to have, but one I don't need to be involved with." Terrell rubbed his hands together. "If neither of you need me, I'll be having a second breakfast with my kids."

"Sorry, I can't be with Paul. I have a conference at six." One of Amber's flaws was the transparency of her emotions and I saw more than one subtly flicker in her eyes as I answered. "Something wrong?"

"I was just thinking about Phoebe. She and I are not that close, but I feel protective. She was like a baby sister when I was the youngest worker here." One shoulder rose, lowered. "I saw the security loop. What was happening to her was too scary for words."

"Do you know who at Ashwood might be her Bureau handler?" My question came from impulse; Amber wouldn't fit the Bureau's profile. She was too good-looking, too visible within the estate, too much a part of the family.

Her eyes widened. "Handler? I don't think I understand what that means. She's with her family, why would someone be watching out for her?"

"Because she's with her family. And Phoebe slipping into a more normal life is counterproductive to the people who think they own her." I shook my head and shrugged. "She's not a person in the bigger world. She's like a wild animal tamed and caged by the *IC* and totally dependent on them."

"I don't want to think of her that way," Amber said. "I'm not going there."

"Good. Maybe we can change this." I picked two pieces of fruit. "Now it's time to begin another day in this great world."

Chapter Thirteen

BEFORE THE CONFERENCE, I sent a carefully crafted communiqué to Clark and Viktor, the intelligence group recommended by Milan. Deshomm would be willing to play cat and mouse until Hartford ran out of money to spend on our defense. With clever legal work, we would change the game. We might need additional partners.

David returned from Giant Pines, tired and with a scratch across one cheek. But he winked and smiled. I let that assure me the scratch had happened in a normal barnyard accident, and turned my attention to sending a note to our human capital director about Sadig. Hartford's legal counsel appeared on my secured screen.

Jay Drury, a dry Brit employed by Raima, shuffled papers and slurped at a mug. I knew he drank only Earl Grey breakfast blend tea with cream and sugar before noon. Minnesota fit him well although I never discovered why Drury showed such a solid understanding of the agricultural market. Max claimed Drury knew the exact cost of growing a covered acre of grain, but wouldn't recognize the plant if it grew in the office.

"You're early for the strategy call," I said. "By the way, I talked with Raima about some reworking of our corporate structure. She'll bring you up-to-date."

"There's a more pressing subject." Drury leaned forward, his silky shirt catching light. "Legal documents were just delivered related to Hartford failing to comply with restrictions on the sale of the Regan private cattle herd. If you refer to article seven of the purchase offer for the easement to the former Schneider farm, one of their subsidiaries was granted first right of refusal for the sale or dispersal of any businesses or activities physically related to Giant Pines for up to twelve months. I have an ADM purchase agreement through a third party for the herd."

So the faked ADM purchase order made its way to Deshomm. I beckoned for David to join me. He didn't see my gesture as he talked to someone via his communicator. His face looked neutral.

"I received the same document around midnight. Give me ten minutes." I hit the mute button on my holographic and rushed to catch David for an update on his night at Giant Pines. Closer, the scratch appeared deeper. He held up one finger.

"I took the action I believe necessary." Continuing his communicator discussion, David frowned. His shoulders stretched straight, back upright. "I told you the regional estate security folks didn't satisfy my need to protect the herd. Lao knows Giant Pines, and our businesses, and I trust his judgment. He's working for me and I own that herd. Work with him."

We had a lifetime of needing to interrupt the other's conference calls or meetings. I placed two fingers on the back of my other hand.

"Sadig, Anne is paging." He looked beyond me while finishing the connection. "John is on site. I'll be there in about sixty minutes to hear whatever you and Lao recommend." Irritation rushed through his closing words. He pulled his earpiece out, turned his attention my way. "Do you have time for breakfast," he asked.

"Drury is waiting on me. Hartford has been served legal documents over that bogus ADM purchase agreement." Beyond the scratch, David looked like a man in his sixties who had not slept. "Quick, tell me about your face and what's going on Giant Pines. I only have a few minutes."

"One of the damn regional security agents decided I was a cattle rustler and got rough trying to arrest me." After his abduction seventeen years ago, David's response to uniformed security professionals remained mixed. "They wanted to move the herd off Giant Pines to a neutral setting. That document you forwarded makes me believe someone in the region plans to steal those cattle."

"And you called Lao?" Almost nothing could rock the confidence of our current security chief more than bringing our well-respected former head of security back to the business. Sadig felt threatened when Lao's family were guests at an Ashwood social gathering.

"Yes, while driving to Giant Pines. He is on my payroll." David rocked back on his heels.

"I need to be absolutely sure you haven't entered into any business deal related to your herd in the past ninety days."

He disliked my question. "You know I have no intention to sell that herd."

There wasn't time to deal with the emotions of the topic. I put my hand on his arm. "Ask Terrell to take a look at that scratch. Your dad had a good night and was looking for a breakfast partner." He touched the scratch at my mention. "And, Andrew will be here mid-day."

"Great news. I miss him." David soothed the grief my son had carried to Ashwood fifteen years ago, and stepped into a fatherly role as Andrew allowed.

"Talk of arrivals, Raima will be here for a few hours late this afternoon and have dinner with us before visiting Paul."

My husband loved family, each piece of news provided a few moments of respite.

"We have some interesting business to discuss. Join us around five." I patted his arm, then hurried back to my office.

Our holo meeting came back to life at my direction. "Thanks for waiting, Jay." I sipped water, grateful to Tia for the plentiful clean supply. "You might not be aware that our power grid was hacked last night, causing damage at both Ashwood and Giant Pines. We are at less than full capacity this morning so I am a bit distracted. Max is joining us after spending a night without sleep."

Drury put down his stylus. "I'm looking at a picture of Giant Pines and notice two sets of guards around the northern entrance. The livestock areas."

"You're right about that, Jay. Max, here. You're looking at regional security and private security." He slurped at coffee. "We had serious damage at Giant Pines to a stretch of fencing in that general area and equipment supporting the livestock buildings."

"I wanted Jay to see what happened last night, a short time before I received a copy of the ADM purchase order. We've hired additional security to investigate what transpired. But, it looks like someone attempted to steal the cattle and do damage to our residence and business facilities. It might appear that created an opportunity for Deshomm to play this card."

"Are you tracking this, Jay?"

He switched from screen to screen, jotted notes. "Bang on."

"I confirmed with my husband that not one of his hundred head of cattle is for sale. In fact, he spent the night at Giant Pines to be sure they were secure. Believe me, David is a frugal man and would not be spending his own money on private guards to protect somebody else's animals."

"It's all bullshit." Max growled. "There's no transfer scheduled. David acts like those cattle are humans."

"Well, it's all rather official looking for bullshit, Max." Drury beckoned toward someone outside camera reach. "We're able to track the validity of the ADM signor, but not the Giant Pines representative."

"There is no one with authority to sign for this particular herd on Giant Pines except for David. We're also curious about who originated this document." I paused. "Let's move this to the top of our priorities and, in light of everything happening, push back the strategy session for a few days." Drury stayed focused on the purchase agreement. Max agreed with a sigh of relief.

"When we know more, Jay, we will bring you into the loop. Do whatever you have to do to let the Deshomm folks know that they're chasing the wrong rabbit."

Max reconnected after Jay dropped off the conference. "Well done, Anne. I'm sick and tired of the interference with our business. We've been undoing cancelled orders and correcting hacked information for weeks."

Leaving Ashwood

Sadig never mentioned these actions during update sessions. While small matters in a big company, there was a trend someone should have been noticing. "Tell me how things went last night. David and I didn't have time for a blow by blow."

"Well, we do have two security forces guarding the fences and entrances. One watching the other." He sifted through paper, handed pieces to someone out of my sight. "Not easy to be caught between your husband and Sadig. They're good men who see the same stuff and call it something different."

With the simplicity of a man who has spent his life working the earth, Max called a pile of manure just that. Sadig's tendency to avoid crossing David's path appeared to leave Giant Pines' needs less attended. Like many senior executives I didn't hear such daily details.

"Tell me what you saw last night, Max." I trusted this man and his love for Giant Pines. "David and I exchanged a few words about engaging Lao's private group."

Max cleared his throat, thought through his response. "Take a step back. The first regional estates officers arrived before the power grid failed and entered our lots. Two of the Giant Pines crew thought they saw vandals step through the fencing at approximately the same time. Turned out to be regional security. I shared all that with David while he was driving."

David's challenge to Sadig about the possibility of bribery in the regional security forces popped into my head. Corruption piled so deep in elaborate government-business relationships that the first line employees knew better than to challenge dicey directions.

"So he called Lao." For two years I spoke with our former security chief only socially, respecting Lao's need to concentrate on his son's health. I hadn't questioned Sadig's loyalties, just understood his judgment or experience fell short of what Hartford's businesses required.

"You'll need to check this out with David, but I think he called Lao before leaving Ashwood." Max raised an eyebrow. "Lao's team got here within a few minutes of David and John."

"And one of the regional crew tried to arrest David?"

"She didn't know who he was, ordered him to step away from one of her associates who was opening the gate of a holding pen. We tried to tell her she was apprehending the owner, but there was a lot of confusion. She didn't get the message. She threw him against a post and was getting ready to apply cuffs when John got in her way."

The guard couldn't know how deep those cuffs tapped into David's psyche. I suspect the guards' dubious entrance at Giant Pines kept them from slapping

David with charges for resisting arrest. I heard Max say, "Give me five minutes" as he turned away.

"We should wrap this up and take advantage of a free hour. Is there anything else I should know about Giant Pines this morning?"

"The sun is shining. All livestock are here and accounted for and everyone reported for work." Max stretched. "A good day. I hear we're having grilled sausages for lunch which pleases this German." A wonderful smile gave him a boyish look. "Forget about Giant Pines for a few hours, Anne. Lao's got the place covered and everything's normal."

Notice of Andrew's arrival time showed on my data pad. He would be early and there was an additional rider on the transport from ADM. At nine o'clock, I left my office for a walk and food.

"Mom, wait up." Noah left his temporary office. "I finished my first orientation session and have a break." Noah and John looked like brothers, which was strange because Noah also looked like Phoebe who had very little in common physically with John, her half-brother. Genetics amazed me. This young man, almost as brilliant as his sister, had a quirky sense of humor that covered some insecurities and a gentle nature.

"Are you and Dad really okay with me stepping out of the biosciences to become a physician?" His long legs moved more like a thoroughbred racehorse than a man who spent hours studying. "Phoebe thinks I'm throwing away grand opportunities. That if I wanted to bust my butt I should apply to the Intellectual Corps."

"We're proud that you're taking control of your future."

"The big question for the morning is that there is no space at Mayo until after first of the year and I need a place to stay." The words came fast.

"Ashwood is your home, Noah, whenever you need it. Personally, I'd be thrilled to have you in Minnesota. Having you here though is even better." I threw an arm around his shoulders and gave him a small hip check.

His voice quieted. "Any chance we could find a way to keep Phoebe here? There's nothing I like about how she sounds or looks." I scurried to keep up with his steps. "Ahlmet is messing with her."

We entered the residence. Cleaners worked in the front foyer. Paul sat on the screen porch. Across the courtyard, kids played outside the school building. Everything looked easy, even cozy. But, life was never easy for the intellectual offspring—a childhood filled with studies and tests, early and advanced college, then thrown into mentally strenuous jobs within government agencies or multi-corps research organizations.

Leaving Ashwood

"Let's take some food out to the pond bench," I suggested. "I'm interested in what you know about our Phoebs."

I answered a query while Noah pulled together a late breakfast. Watching him chat with Terrell and one of the teen workers, it was hard to believe that during his first year at the gifted offspring school in St. Paul, shyness had claimed his ability to say more than a very few words at a time.

Noah could work his way around a kitchen. With no help, he assembled a tray of food with visual appeal and unique combinations. He led the way across the hall and out a side door. I finished my communication as we walked through mid-day heat toward the pond. He was barefoot and stepped off the path to walk in the grass.

"I've missed this feeling," he said with a smile that softened his mouth and cheeks. "I still hate shoes, but no choice in the city. My last apartment's tile floors were always cold." He set the tray on a bench right at the edge of the pond. I knew his feet would dip into the water.

"I hung out with a guy last winter who worked in one of the labs supporting Ahlmet. He didn't know Phoebe and Ahlmet were a couple." With city-developed respect for food, Noah picked berries from the plate and ate them one at a time. "This friend shouldn't have told me what their lab was working on, but he was bothered by where the stuff could go." Another berry popped into his mouth. "Ahlmet's niche is perfecting mind-controlling technology." He flicked one foot in the pond. "That's why I'm freaked about what happened last night. I caught Dr. Frances this morning before she left for the cities. Wish I knew more."

All around us Ashwood moved at its normal pace. On the surface, this looked like the most natural setting in today's world—fruit trees, flowers, and a flock of sheep in the distance. Like my stepson, nothing was quite that truthful. Genetically manipulated, assisted, enhanced, all were a bit stronger or brighter or longer lived than if left alone. I closed my eyes, breathing air that might bring on more coughing. What multi-corps financially supported Ahlmet's work? How did mind control technology benefit the world beyond increasing the wealth of a small pool of individuals? Who controlled the moral compass behind the Intellectual Corps?

"I don't want to believe he'd use Phoebe in his experiments, but I suspect everything's fair game in their part of the world." Phoebe gave Ahlmet greater access to her life than any other lover. His stuff littered her place, and they shared keys to each other's apartments. "Can you ask your friend for more information?"

"We haven't been 'friends' for a while." Noah's meaning registered. "Anyway, he's only a lipper in the lab. No real knowledge of the final design." He pulled his feet from the pond, picked up a buttered slice of fruit bread. "Lipper is a first year data filer. Has something to do with a program name." He looked my way. "I think this is worth worrying about."

"You're right." Above us a shade wound through Sarah's arbor for shelter from the sun's deadly rays. "From what I saw last night, he could drive her insane, maybe even kill her."

The last berry disappeared while we sat with our own thoughts. Noah pushed long fingers into curly hair, his face remaining calm. This would be the face he'd show patients when news was bad.

"Could you call Milan?" His hand settled on the bench. "Or maybe I should call. He does keep an interest in us even though that whole legal guardian thing is past."

"I just spoke with him yesterday. He's living in Duluth now."

"Call him, Mom. Right now."

I looked over my shoulder at the residence a half-acre behind us, at the breakfast table window where our younger family had gathered each morning. Grandparents, an infant, two sleepy boys and Phoebe with a dream to tell everybody.

"Mom?" Noah called me back. "What are you thinking?"

"You know the Intellectual Corps are never without handlers. I wish I knew who was watching Phoebe while she's here. Has to be one of us since she arrived alone." A large fly landed on my lower arm and I tried to wave it off. So many insects were supersized as a result of genetic engineering gone awry. "Know anything?"

"Couldn't be me. Rules say blood relatives aren't allowed." His soft shirt stretched as his shoulders tightened. I wondered how he knew the rules, but sensed he had already spoken too freely about the intellectual worker contract.

"I tried to find out from Milan, but he sidestepped the question." The fly landed again, this time on my sandaled foot. I rubbed it off with the other foot, saw it fall on the pavement, and squashed it. "I was asking in order to offer support."

"Not a good idea, Mom. Watchers and handlers don't always know who pays their way or issues orders. They can be like babysitters paid by the noncustodial parent." Noah broke up the last piece of bread to fling into the pond. "Someone told me that. Not sure it makes sense?"

"Don't throw the bread," I said too late as large crows buzzed near his hand.

"Holy shit!" Noah pulled back. "What the hell was that about?"

"With most of the ag production under cover, the crackles are becoming quite aggressive. You probably didn't notice the system we use in the courtyard area to drive them away if they get inside the netting." I stood. "Something's changed about them in the past year. A handful of workers have been injured. We better go in."

"You're kidding, aren't you?" Noah gathered the food tray, glancing frequently toward trees on the other side of the pond.

"Nope. Probably another genetic engineering plan gone amuck." We walked back to the residence. "Let's call Milan together."

I hurried to the DOE building, hoping to visit with Phoebe before making the call. Luckily, she stood near the coffee station, arms held over her head and balanced on one foot in a beautiful yoga pose. Her eyes opened as I approached and she lowered her arms.

"Without all the interruptions of the lab, I've been more productive in the last eight hours than I've been in maybe three weeks," Phoebe said. "I felt absolutely safe here, no security alerts about perverts slumming in the entrances or food contaminants in the kitchens." She smiled and looked pleased. "You've got it good here, Mom. I should spend more time at home."

Torn between preserving this moment of calm and testing her state of mind, I enjoyed the moment. "You are absolutely welcome." Acting out of impulse, I hugged her. She dropped her head on my shoulder for a second. I inhaled the scent of her unwashed body and spilled foods on her clothing, and released her to turn my head to release a sneeze.

"Mom, you've got the city sickness."

Her reference to a childhood joke of Noah's made me smile as the second sneeze ripped out.

"What is wrong with you?"

"Nothing. I'm sensitive to certain smells. Maybe your shampoo tickled my allergies."

I saw a twitch catch her shoulder; fear or anger narrowed her eyes. "It's Ahlmet, isn't it?" I asked the question quickly.

"Yes." Her eyes closed, a low growling sound slipped from between closed lips. "Stop it. Stop it." She shook her head from side to side. One hand reached for the wall as she slid downward.

"We need help," I yelled while kneeling at her side. "Phoebs, pay attention to me. Listen to me." But with only Noah's brief description to work from, I had no idea what to say so I tried for pure distraction from any thoughts related to her former lover. "Sing the alphabet with me. Think of the letters. A, B, C, D." My voice warbled from lack of use, or perhaps, fear. I pressed David's code on my bracelet. "E, F . . ." Phoebe slumped and groaned.

Lowering my head to hers, I whispered my song. By Q, she joined me. We moved through the tune, slowly, as though creating an incantation against an evil spirit. David stood near and watched. If I could be in two places at once, I would have folded my arms around both my husband and daughter. The one now in my arms relaxed, the episode passed. Next to me, I felt Phoebe take in a deep breath.

"I need help . . ." she began saying.

"We'll find it, babe," David rushed to her side.

". . . getting up." Phoebe gathered strength from a tired body. I wondered how many times in the past ten hours of solo work she had fought Ahlmet's invasions.

David offered his arms, gently easing Phoebe to her feet. She leaned against him before standing on her own feet.

"What the hell is going on, Phoebe?" A scientist, David attacked difficult theoretical problems with infinite patience. His approach frequently gave our kids space to come to their own answers as they grew up. But when something threatened his family, David was Paul's son, elbowing his way to immediate solutions.

"Not now, Dad. I can't talk now. I need some rest before my next conference session." She looked around. "Is there a blanket here? I'll slab on the couch."

"I'll walk with you to your room." I held out a hand. "We'll have a tray prepared while you take a shower."

"They've been feeding me all night. I don't have time for a sleep, just a slab. Do you keep sins?"

David shook his head. "Yes, to blanket and pillow. No to sleep inducers."

"Amber needs to prep my work space. I need all my gear in place. The boxes are stacked downstairs. It should be done while I'm not there."

"Good idea. Blankets are in the corner closet." He pointed, began moving toward his office.

Phoebe remained in place, an adult-size child waiting for someone else to take care of details. She looked around, focused on me.

"Where is all the staff? I thought we had an agreement about what I need to work here?" Overly bright eyes suggested she stayed awake through the night with chemical help. "Cares are part of the deal. I don't deal with their stuff. Why didn't you staff the cares?"

In her pique she sounded like her mother. David turned, emotions building. "We live a comfortable life here, Phoebe. But we also live like regular people. It might do you good to take *care* of yourself for a few weeks or call your Bureau manager and tell them exactly what you want. Don't treat Anne like a personal servant."

They faced each other, her young shoulders held higher and tighter than the slight curve of aging allowed him. She tilted her chin upward, let her lips curve into a slight smile. David did not melt.

"I am doing work that could save the world, Dad." A prideful boast forced each word toward him. "I live with a lot of responsibility. Every day. Nothing . . ." She paused. "Nothing relieves that responsibility."

"I lived that one, too, Phoebe. Your mother felt the same way." His voice lowered. "That's why she put you in the arms of Anne. Nothing was ever as important as your mother's work. And she paid dearly for letting people in power strip her of her humanity until she did their bidding without question."

"But she wasn't like me. She wasn't genetically altered to do what I can do." Phoebe threw her hands in the air. "Isn't that the whole point of the *Corps*? Aren't we a group of super humans?"

"I can't answer that, Phoebe." Old wounds inflicted twenty-five years ago when we learned of the government's genetic engineering of the surrogate offspring, tore open once more in David. "You are human and that's what makes you so infinitely different than the machines. Protect that difference, sweetheart."

Tears formed in Phoebe's eyes as he spoke. "Sometimes, Dad, I think I hate you for not knowing what you let the government do. On the really hard days, when I'm really lonely, when every person near me treats me like some mutant freak, I want you to know how much I hate my life." She swept tears from her cheeks. "So if I want cares to bring me food or wash my hair or flush my toilet, I think I'm entitled."

If our once ultra-sensitive daughter could still see pain in others, she would know her father had never found release from the exact guilt she named.

"That's the inheritance I got from being my parents' child," Phoebe added. "Which is why you are so terribly important to me." Turning her back on David, Phoebe wound her arms around my neck, settled her forehead on my shoulder and sobbed. "Down deep, I know you'll find a way to save me. Please, Mom."

"We'll do our best, Phoebs." My hands rubbed her back, found the rhythm that settled her during childhood night terrors. "I promise you. Right now you need to rest. I do have sins and Dad will make you a comfortable place on the couch. Come with me and we'll wash your face."

"I don't want to treat you like a cares." Her head came up, she stepped back.

"I'll tell you if I feel that you are. We're family and we help each other through tough times." We made our way to the bathroom. Noah watched from the hall, didn't approach, but turned back to the residence.

Chapter fourteen

PHOEBE FELL ASLEEP within minutes of swallowing the small tablet. Her face did not relax, and one fist lay clenched next to her chin. Not a peaceful sleep.

David came to my office, closed the door and sat as if his legs were taking him down. I joined him, took his hands in mine, explored his face. Between sharply arched eyebrows, one single prominent crease ran from the half crescent wrinkles on his forehead toward the bridge of his nose. Prominent bones rose above cheeks that held taut when he smiled and hung slightly paunchy when in repose or thought. Crows' feet circulated out from the corners of his eyes in spite of wearing hats, sun block, and protective glasses. With me, nothing hid his emotional distress. Sadness, loss, anger, and the struggle to accept what was taking place in our family dulled his eyes.

"They've made her into a workatron. I signed that paper so I'm responsible. I wanted kids so badly I didn't think carefully about the small print."

"We've talked about that feeling before, love. We couldn't understand what it would mean for our surrogate children to be genetically manipulated."

"She'll die young like Tia." He freed his hands to rub at his face, to keep his eyes free from tears. "There's nothing we can do." He kicked at the thick wooden table base. "God damn it. I swore I wouldn't let this fucking government harm our children."

I knew the path of David's words, had traveled through the emotions frequently. I watched our adult children's lives develop, but played a more traditional maternal role of listening and nurturing. I visited each of them, doing a grand tour of sorts twice a year if business meetings didn't take me to their cities. David projected his own experience as an intellectual government employee on them, knew the intensity of their work and the constant demands.

"I think I have a plan that could spring Phoebe from Chicago if she's willing."

"Shoot." He brought his feet back under the chair, fought for calm.

I fidgeted, feeling my way through the facts and feelings of my half-baked business proposition. "Back when the DOE required employees to divest of potential conflicts of interests you sold Tia's water group to Hartford, Ltd., Then Raima had TW's patents classified under the Patriots Act. There is enough revenue from grants and ongoing fees to give Hartford, Ltd., financial and legal reasons to expand the business. We need to hire a chief researcher to keep it profitable. Who better than Tia's daughter?"

"Those systems are old, Anne, with maintenance subcontracted overseas. I don't think there's enough to interest Phoebe." He moved to my conference table, activated the data port, willing to follow the path even if dubious.

"I agree with you about the current business model." The vertical crease in his forehead deepened as he sorted through information. "But, that little corporation has accumulated a whole lot of cash. It doesn't matter if there's enough valid work in the corporation now to keep Phoebe busy. The point is that the corporation with a loan from Hartford, Ltd., could buy her contract under the power of its national security status. Then she can use her intellectual prowess to build it however she wants. She could contract to a multi-corps on her own terms. She could grab research grants." I had his attention. "She will die young if she stays in that Chicago intellectual dungeon, but the business Tia started is a great escape."

David clapped. "It's brilliant, Anne."

"Raima would like to invest both time and money. She suggested other potential partners."

Then quiet settled. This was how we approached big decisions. We talked, we listened, we questioned each other. My name was on the letterhead, but we built Hartford, Ltd., together to become an emotional, fiscal and physical safety net big enough for our family.

"What about her physical condition? What does Frances think?"

One hole in my optimism. "She hoped to connect with a few people today." David watched me like a terrier protecting a treat. "Noah provided a clue. A friend of his works in Ahlmet's lab and bragged they were working on some radical brain control technology."

I expected anger, the protecting father jumping into fight mode. But David was tired from spending the night at Giant Pines. He pushed away from the table as he spoke. "Double jeopardy. If the Intellectual Corps doesn't run her into the ground, the ex-boyfriend will drive her crazy." He sighed, a heavy older man sound. "So what do we do about that?"

"We're in uncharted lands. Those research labs are sacred grounds." Energy ebbed. We had a plan and plenty of obstacles.

"I need a nap. I think I pulled a muscle." He held out an arm, turned it from side to side. "What did you think of John's plans?"

"For Giant Pines?"

"For his future."

"I think I hope I live long enough to see it happen."

"That's my Annie." A yawn stopped him from going further.

"Go take your nap. I've got things to do before Andrew arrives."

"Don't let me sleep through lunch." He stood, locked his arms above his head and stretched his back. Two or three soft cracks sounded in the room. Bringing his arms down, he groaned before straightening. "Want the door closed?"

"Please."

I saw him look toward the couch where Phoebe slept and hesitate before walking away. Before I sat down I found Milan and shared what was happening with Phoebe.

Chapter Fifteen

WHEN STARS ALIGN, amazing things get done in an hour. The conversation with Milan was brief, and he confirmed his belief in John's transformation of Giant Pines into a regional research center with a solid commerce foundation. But Phoebe's odd affliction caught him off-guard, and he ended the call on a terse note.

Clark and Vicktor asked for a holo-meeting within a few minutes. They were an odd pair—Clark appeared to be in her forties with Vicktor at least ten years younger. Beyond the referral by Milan and approval of Raima, everything about their experience and suggested approach to protecting Hartford, Ltd., was impressive. We signed an agreement to transfer intelligence work to them and set up a series of daily meetings to fast track the work.

Faith tapped at my door. "Andrew's transport is five minutes out." With another day of ninety-degree temperatures, she wore a light cotton shift, her best sandals, and a huge smile. "Come out to the courtyard." While we walked, she chattered with excitement about the brother who remembered every special event and spoke with her at least once a week. We stood next to Amber, the only family members available.

A second person rode in the transport, a smallish middle-age woman wearing the uniform of Phoebe's Chicago labs. Andrew stepped out first and reached back inside to lift a large bag from the vehicle.

"Mom, I invited Hana to share a transport. She's been Phoebe's cares in Chicago." He handed the bag to her. I thought she couldn't possibly carry it, but she wound it over both shoulders. I wondered if she ever dragged Phoebe's weight in her duties.

"I have to give this guy a hug, then I'll show Hana where she will sleep." Amber turned to Andrew; their hug lasted longer than I expected. Faith gave me a big-eyed look. "Welcome home international traveler. You're bunking above the offices in the consultant's suite."

"If the space is open, I'd like to stay for the summer when I'm not traveling."

Faith gave a hoot and threw herself into her brother's arms. "My turn. I'm so glad you're here."

"You've grown another inch, Ms. Faith." He picked her up then set her down. "Still a lightweight it seems."

Finally it was my turn to stand with arms around Andrew. My firstborn child was tall like his father with blonde, wavy hair. His eyes and nose and chin were from my family.

"How are you doing, Mom?"

The title had been hard won from the skeptical eleven-year-old of long ago. "Glad to have you here." Emotion grabbed my being and sounded in the words. We stepped apart.

"And Phoebe?"

"She's here, worked through the night, and is sleeping." I noticed Amber walking away with Hana, but Andrew's attention stayed with me. "David's doing the same. We had a security breach at Giant Pines that threatened his herd. I'll tell you all about what's going on over lunch if you have the time?"

He lifted his own bag and tipped the driver before responding. "The firm's owners gave all the traveling staff a ten-day mandatory holiday to be used this month." I startled at the novelty. "My team just wrapped up two gigantic engagements so we were first out. Amazing isn't it?" His smile eased tired circles under his eyes. "This is the where I wanted to be."

Finally turning away, Andrew extended a hand to Terrell. "Does the kitchen crew know how to make your cheesecake with fresh berries? I've been thinking about that the whole trip."

Terrell shook his head and the two of them laughed together. "I might share that recipe with the cook." He lifted Andrew's second bag. "You look good. Thought you'd be limping from that fall in Vancouver."

"So Paul shares my stories," Andrew joked. "How are your kids? Cute like their mother I hope."

"I'll get him to the lunch table, Anne." Terrell motioned Andrew away. "I've got some catching up to do with this man."

We sat down to a late lunch without Phoebe. David, showered and a bit rested, leaned forward with elbows on the table as the guys swapped stories about their work assignments and travels. Faith, very much a teenager in the midst of adults, absorbed all the talk. I knew it would feed her itch to see the world. Her brothers ate great quantities of fresh foods.

As cookies were placed on the table, Phoebe appeared. She still wore yesterday's travel clothes, her hair hung in disarray from pillow and blanket. "My God, you're here!" She ran toward Andrew, eyes brightening with tears. "I didn't believe you were coming."

Andrew stood, absorbed the impact of her, and wrapped his arms around her tall, thin body. She turned her face for a kiss and he placed his lips on her cheek.

Leaving Ashwood

"Wow, let's remember this is a family gathering," Noah said at the table. "I know there's no sibling blood between you, but there is a kid present."

Faith stood up. "Take the kid's chair, Phoebs. I'll grab another one. Did you have lunch?"

She said nothing, just sat down in Faith's place, eyes not leaving Andrew. In a corner of the room I saw Hana waiting, a tiny shadow cares. I lifted my plate and motioned that she should get food for Phoebe. She disappeared.

Dynamics shifted at the table. Noah started a new discussion about planning visits with their grandfather. Complicated scheduling was built around conference calls and research timetables and classes. Phoebe remained quiet, eating from the plate Hana delivered, which included nothing that we had been served. She ate as if the food might disappear, which was uncomfortable to watch.

"Hana will know when I'm free to spend time with Grandpa and re-arrange schedules as needed," she added as Noah finished typing the schedule. "You all understand that that's the way this has to be done?"

John looked away, Noah paused. David's mouth opened, but he only licked his lips. Andrew extended a hand across the table to touch her arm. "Tough research stretch, Phoebs?"

Her chin went up and she shook back her messed mane. "I don't know. It's not so much about any one time being tough. There is a lot invested in my work so I can't really slack off for personal appointments."

"But your boss knows that grandpa is dying," Faith asked. "It's not like he's an appointment. You came home to spend time with him." Logical, in a teenage way, she was also youthfully intolerant. "I don't get it."

Phoebe stared at nothing as Faith spoke then pushed her plate away. Hana appeared to remove it and place a glass of water and a blue pill in its place. Phoebe popped the tablet in her mouth and drank water. She held the glass out next to her and released her hold. Hana caught the tumbler then disappeared. Except for Faith, the rest of us appeared to sink into our own processing of the Phoebe show. Faith melted.

"It's complicated, Faith." Andrew put his arm across the back of her chair. "Phoebe's not used to being in the middle of a lot of people. She needs time to re-assemble everything."

"Maybe she should start with a shower." Noah still spoke frankly to his sister. "I know that your lab thing is about numbers and data. But you smell like there were small animal cages involved."

Phoebe liked his joke and we could laugh together before breaking up. Andrew walked out at her side. Hana appeared from somewhere to follow them. I'm sure the cares was doing her job, but I didn't like her vibe.

Chapter Sixteen

ASHWOOD AND THE SURROUNDING agricultural estates covered land that as a young woman I had known as the suburbs of the Twin Cities. I grew up in a four-bedroom Colonial on a cul-de-sac not far from the main east-west road that ran along our front fences. During the Second Great Depression many, many suburban homes emptied as people walked away from foreclosure, from starvation, from land no longer welcoming. The government of a hungry nation pulled down miles of houses and strip malls to feed people and create work on the acreage.

Not all the land took to growing grains. David and Paul began planting orchards around half our residence after years of lackluster crop production. Apple trees did well, and apples sold well. Andrew and I walked through the original orchard after lunch under the canopy of mature, tall trees. Openings in the sun membrane allowed birds and insects to move through as well. The grackles were not interested in the orchard until fruit formed.

"You didn't know that Phoebe and I were involved," Andrew said after we'd stepped off the crushed gravel path. "It began when I spent New Year's with her two years ago. We were close for about thirteen months until someone from the Intellectual Corps came between us. I'm sure the lab handlers found it less distracting for her to connect with a lab peer."

What I remembered from last summer was that Noah rescued Phoebe during a depressive state because I was in Europe and she didn't want to see her father. Milan tried to pull me back to Chicago, but no one else could finish critical business negotiations that were just short of an agreement. One of us was frequently summoned to Chicago.

"You told us there was someone special in your life." I tried not to sound wounded for not knowing the whole story, or confused by my son being attracted to my stepdaughter. "We had no way to know that was Phoebe."

"I think I fell in love with her when I came to live at Ashwood. She was almost eight years old and freaking out over a language proficiency exam. At eleven, I had never met anyone as fascinating. Or frustrating."

Apple picking had been a fall family activity at the turn of the century. Global warming changed the timing. Ripening fruit hung within reach in June. The heady smell of apples on a warm day brought us back to being in the country far from Chicago.

Andrew picked up a stick. "You're using Mitcur on these trees?"

"Yes. Magda's impressed with it and we can meet the organically grown specifications if it is mixed with some other product." I stopped walking. "First I want to understand your feelings for Phoebe, then we can talk about fertilizers."

"It's not a fertilizer, Mom. It fights a kind of rot that develops when sun screens are installed above orchards. John could tell you all the details." He snapped the stick, sniffed at the wood. "Seems healthy."

"How are you feeling about Phoebe now?"

"She's not healthy enough to be in a relationship, not with another adult, not even with a goldfish. I'd say that tablet her little cares slid across the table keeps Phoebe in a docile state and willing to work day and night. I'd love to talk with her after she's had a few days off food or drinks provided by Intellectual Corps kitchens."

"Are you in love with her?" It felt odd to be so direct with this personal question. None of our kids had mentioned adult love in their lives, which wasn't unusual among the intellectual class. Government bureaus were available to assist in finding partners.

"You're persistent, Mom. Tough executive who doesn't let a question go unanswered." He lightly tapped his elbow against my shoulder. "Haven't been through this level of inquisition since I tried to slip a broken window into an expense report."

We walked, but didn't talk as we turned back to the residence.

"I do love her, but not the way she exists."

I appreciated that Andrew protected his emotional boundaries. "I'm afraid Phoebe's situation has become far worse than obsessively working or being controlled by her handlers," I shared. "Ahlmet, the man she just broke up with, in some way wired her with a mind control device. She's had a number of seizure-like episodes since arriving."

Our conversation had a surreal element that left me wondering how I felt about my son being involved with someone who exhibited a precarious hold on normal life. With guilt, I understood that Tia's mental illness blocked me from blessing Andrew's choice.

A bird flew directly at Andrew's head. He stepped aside, watched it fly for some unseen target. His face hardened as he thought through the news of Phoebe's seizures. "What's being done to help her?"

"Frances is talking to people in her psychiatric and neurological networks. Milan has been alerted. There's nothing else we can do because we don't know anything beyond a comment Noah's friend made about experiments being done in Ahlmet's lab."

WHERE THE MEMBRANE WAS CLOSED, the sun was still warm as we walked in silence. From the orchard, I could barely hear a popular Latin song being sung by a work crew, a quirky tune about a woman falling in love with a machine. I coughed, knew it was time to return to purified air.

"Sorry I have to head inside. The Cities' pollution is driving my allergies into overdrive."

He shared what he knew about the pollution's path up the Mississippi and some prototypes for seeding clouds to neutralize the chemicals. I checked the time, knew the opportunity to talk so personally was ending.

I interrupted his explanation. "That's really interesting. We've got enough barriers to natural sun and air already that another one to block pollutants probably wouldn't be a bother." His shoulders returned to an outside world rigidity, his eyes swept forward as if gauging how many steps until we were in the more exposed plaza area. "You had us confused with that long hug between you and Amber."

"Amber's the kind of woman who needs a husband and a kid or two of her own. When that Frenchman hurt her, she called. And I leaned on her a bit when Phoebe broke away. She's in the best friend category." He smiled, a tight small curve of lips. "Falling for Amber would have been easier. There are always timing issues and ours didn't work."

"So what are your plans for this time off?"

"Be with Paul." Andrew looked away and cleared his throat. "Try to stabilize Phoebe. Those are my top two." He put his hand under my elbow. "Those coughs could scare a bird or two, Mom." We approached the residence. "I didn't understand Paul when I was a kid. He was always so busy that I looked to David for fathering. After I left Ashwood, Paul kept in touch, called and wrote. He's been a powerful influence during tough decisions."

Faith waved across the courtyard as she walked to the school building. With even one small motion, I knew she'd run to Andrew's side.

He waved back, an indulgent smile replaced seriousness. "Hopefully there'll be time to hang out with the guys. Maybe I can help Faith think through her future." He stepped up to the office building's door first. "And I want to spend time with you, Mom. Catch up on what's happening in the life of Hartford's big cheese." He opened the door, an old-world courtesy.

"I love having you here." We stopped at Clarissa's desk. "Visit with your aunt. Paul will wait."

Leaving Ashwood

Business issues screamed for attention, but first I removed Paul's red box from my desk. After Sarah passed, he asked me to be the executor of his estate and told me what I would find in this box. Sending it to me said Paul felt his days were dwindling. I closed the blinds and activated the do not disturb sign.

The security code for his will was engraved on a thin piece of metal tucked into the lining. The name of their private matter attorney was inscribed on its other side. To my surprise, Sarah's engagement ring lay loose in the box with a ribbon and note in her old-fashioned script that said, "For Annie, with my love."

I removed the beautiful white diamond on an old-fashioned platinum band. She'd worn it to our wedding. Paul told us they considered selling the ring to save their family ranch during the Second Great Depression. A buyer for two bulls appeared in time to cover a final mortgage payment. The ring slipped over my knuckle easily and rested against my simple wedding band. My hands with their raised veins and dry skin didn't do the beauty justice. I slid it off, touched the precious metal to my lips and thanked God for taking me into the hearts of the Regan family.

Before Raima arrived, I activated the will's code. I knew everything on the first pages--completing transfer of the South Dakota ranches to David's brothers, a trust to administer funds to David and his siblings and the grandchildren, small cash gifts to each daughter-in-law. In separate language, he gave a small piece of land and a house to Amber. Recent changes gave an outright cash gift to David, a token compared to the large spreads his brothers inherited.

Paul's shares in Giant Pines reverted to me after handsome allotments for John and Faith. Because Phoebe, Noah and Andrew had trusts from their deceased parents, he gave them each a small cash gift and something personal. I didn't expect the codicil bequeathing a significant number of shares of a multi-corps to the creation of the Sarah Regan Environmental Research Foundation under the direction of John Regan. If the foundation did not become operational in five years, the funds were to be divided among a number of charities.

Sarah's ring was mentioned in special gifts with kind words about the twenty years we shared a house and life. Another surprise was the gift of a furnished condo in Minneapolis and all its contents to me. I didn't know that they owned their city hide-away. Closing the document, I repacked the small box, refastened the seal, placed it in my office safe, and planned to talk with Paul later.

The best business news of the day waited in a message from Sadig who offered his resignation, citing shame over security failures of the past thirty-six hours. I suspected he expected me to assure him the failures were not his fault and convince him to stay. We had played that routine one other time. This time I called Lao, who was at Giant Pines.

We spoke about his family for a few minutes, about his son's special needs. Instead of asking for an update on the security of David's herd, I moved to the heart of Hartford's needs.

"Come back, Lao. On your terms—for six months, twelve months or longer." Twenty years of working in tandem stripped away the traditional recruiting dance. "Sadig will be gone. We need your expertise and sophistication and network."

He laughed, a companionable sound that suggested interest.

"My wife wants to return to the estates regions. But we want to own some land, to be voters."

"What can you afford?" Land prices froze middle-income people out of the market as rumors grew that legislation might be passed establishing a minimum acreage for future national voting eligibility. He mentioned a realistic amount.

"Would you be happy with two acres in the Ashwood housing area? We could work out a salary, housing allowance and bonus arrangement. Maybe you buy the land on the day you start work and the housing allowance serves as something like a mortgage over a five year period?" I knew his wife missed her friends on the estate and having their children in our school.

"If you allow me to retain my private company with a commitment that it will not interfere with my responsibilities to Hartford, Ltd., we could have an agreement." The details were worked out quickly as well as plans for a face-to-face meeting with Sadig that day. As we spoke I changed internal systems codes and sent alerts about a change in leadership to the required web of public protectors.

"You should know, Anne, that Sadig isn't incompetent, but his pride stops him from digging into questions he won't be able to answer." Under his words I understood Lao was not pleased with what he was uncovering at Giant Pines. "It will not take a lot of change to bring security back to best practices. I can begin today if you'll keep my staff in place at Giant Pines."

"Makes sense. There is another challenge for you, and it concerns Phoebe." I shared what we knew and asked him to talk with Frances. For the first time, Lao did not assure me that he would find a solution. "I finished setting you up in all your former access points and registered the change with the authorities. There are new people in Engineering managing the partial power down."

"Good to be back, Anne. Thanks."

I raised my blinds, unlocked the door, and worked throughout the early afternoon until David, smelling like a farmer, wandered in.

"You've been closed up in here for hours."

"And you've been in the barns." My nose wrinkled at the odor, an instinctive reaction that still made David smile.

He lifted one foot. "I changed shoes and washed up. You're too sensitive. An agribusiness owner, definitely not a farmer."

"That's what I've been told." I returned his smile. "This has been a productive few hours. You'll be happy to know I worked out a deal to bring Lao back without a messy dismissal. Sadig offered his resignation."

David smiled. "Thank you. Sound decision."

"And I've been reviewing a proposal for a poison pill that could deter Deshomm's efforts that centers around John's Giant Pines proposal. Raima's group did a bang up job." I stretched my spine and shoulders. "The big family news for the afternoon—Andrew is in love with Phoebe. They had a rather long relationship that ended when Ahlmet came on the scene."

Watching David process the information was interesting—surprise, testing the thought of his daughter being in love, acceptance, and maybe dismay—brought his eyebrows upward, then lower and fianlly together. His lips straightened before relaxing.

"Holy shit. How did we miss this?" I shrugged in response to his question. David shared his thoughts in bits. "Interesting. Andrew's the only person, beside you, who can keep Phoebe centered. How do you feel about it?"

Truthfully I hadn't found my answer to that question. "I want Andrew to be happy and that seems to include finding a woman to share his life. I want Phoebe to find peace in her life. Maybe that means a man. I'm so focused on pulling her out of this mind control nightmare, I didn't want to think about a love relationship being part of the challenge."

"Andrew would be a great son-in-law. Just like he's been a great stepson." He shook his head. "Damn crazy world." But being David, he returned immediately to the moment. "I have to clean up again. Would you like to have wine on the patio with Dad tonight?"

"That sounds great."

"Can I ask about the box?" If he hadn't smelled like livestock and feed, I would have moved closer to offer comfort.

"The code key for your father's will."

Resignation chased aside the remnants of levity in David's voice. "He has confidence in you as executor, and I intend to help."

"I was surprised to also find your mother's platinum and diamond engagement ring."

"She could have been a business woman like you if not for marrying a South Dakota rancher and having a table full of sons."

Sarah dealt with a dozen hungry children, empty pantries and the responsibility to feed a significant part of the surrounding community during her first months at Ashwood. I don't know if someone raised with classic farming experience could have success managing the interface of government units, consumer demands and confusing budget systems dropped on our backs.

"I didn't expect anything special. It's beautiful and still looks new."

"You gave them a home, incredible business opportunities and a caring community."

"We did that together, David. On my own I would have sold Giant Pines and kept Ashwood smaller. I'd be a working drone in Deshomm instead of chasing them off."

"Now, if we can only reshape the business empire for the next phase of our life." His communicator buzzed. This was the story of our lives, building big thoughts on little slices of discussion. "Have a good working session with Raima."

Chapter Seventeen

O<small>N THE SECOND NIGHT</small> we gathered for Paul, our dearest friends joined the family. Young and mature voices filled the dining room. Food flowed from the kitchen, but I have almost no memory of what we ate. I do remember how Frances and Terrell sat on both sides of Lao, the stories Magda shared with the twins about how their parents met, tears in Raima's eyes as she sat next to Paul.

Phoebe and Andrew arrived together and sat side-by-side like they did as children. I sent Hana from the room with directions to the kitchen staff to keep her away from food bound for our table and out of the dining room. Phoebe showed no interest in where Hana spent time.

Stepping outside FFP protocol that assigned all faith-based activity to the senior woman in a residence, Andrew offered to lead us in a prayer. Hands reached for other hands, heads lowered, some eyes glistened.

"Lord, we thank you for this good food raised on the earth of Ashwood. We thank you for all who have been a part of our lives here, in this home made by David and Anne. This evening, with our family and friends, we ask for your guidance and grace as we leave this table for whatever path our lives might take. Amen."

Heads stayed down in private thoughts and emotions until Paul's weak voice broke the silence.

"Can always tell the ones who weren't raised as Catholics or Jews." His old-man laugh invited company. "We weren't taught to pray out loud without a guide sheet." My generation laughed with appreciation, but the younger members smiled without understanding his generational comment. "Thanks, Andrew."

For those returning from the bigger world, three meals of fresh vegetables, home-baked breads, full-flavored dairy products may have felt like life in an old world. Cook prepared many of Paul's favorite dishes using my mother-in-law's recipes. An excellent Australian white wine brought by Raima replaced our usual estate red or white. Voices grew louder as stories chased around the tables. I noticed Faith sipping at her token glass and Phoebe twirling her first serving.

"Think you can make a difference in the ruckus in Washington," Paul asked John during a lull in the conversations.

"Yes I do, Grandpa." The family quieted as John's dream was shared for the first time. "I believe the next decade will return this country to traditional democracy or give in to rule by the multi-corps. It's a critical time."

"And how would you start this transformation," Raima questioned.

"Revoke the amendments that allowed congress and the president to make permanent changes to the Constitution during times of national security without full approval of the electorate."

Terrell led applause.

"Think how many people in this room have made significant contributions to the United States, or work for the government, and haven't had the right to vote. All of us adult kids, Lao, Amber. Most of us because of the land ownership clause. Now the multi-corps are pressuring for a change in that language to make voting even more of a privilege instead of a right."

"Amen, young man." Terrell raised his wine glass. "You will have my vote."

"But only a few people here will be able to vote for you if you want to go to Washington," Phoebe pointed out. "Maybe you could try the Minnesota State House first?"

"Sorry, but I'm not interested in delivery of services and local financial management." He leaned back in his chair. Across the table I could feel his intensity. "I want to be part of policy development." Political conversation continued until David tapped a spoon against his glass.

"I'll keep this brief." There were snickers as David was known for talking until he was finished regardless of time. "Enough." He smiled and stood at the head of the long table.

"It wasn't easy for you to make arrangements to spend time at home. Anne and I thank all of you." I saw David fight emotions. "Tonight will be one for us to all keep in our memories." He tipped his head, and then raised it. "But tonight, the true guest of honor is that old guy sitting next to my lovely wife." David lifted his glass. "Dad, if you haven't heard it before, you have made our lives better by watching your example. We love you."

We were all on our feet. It was a night for laughter and tears. While we lingered over dessert, I wished Sarah could be with us. If I was the one who guided our family through a difficult time, she was the one who comforted those who were frightened, sad, unsure.

Dinner's brief holiday feeling faded when David accompanied Paul and Raima back to his father's quarters while others disappeared to their own responsibilities. I settled on the screen porch to read through documents for the next day and wait for the transport to take Raima back to the city. This had been a prime time of day for soccer or softball games when our children were young and the government-assigned workers' average age was about eleven. David organized soccer leagues including residents of neighboring estates and a softball tournament at the end of each summer. He and I played on teams, but we were younger then and not responsible for a small international corporation.

"You were thinking of something special," David said when he joined me. "You had that certain smile." He picked up a pile of business things and put it on the floor. "Dad is tired out but enjoying his visit with Raima. She said she wouldn't stay very late."

"We had a productive meeting this afternoon. I've scheduled a six o'clock call tomorrow morning with the Hartford, Ltd., advisory team to discuss strategy around this Deshomm threat. You're welcome to join." Raima's insights gave me confidence in the plan.

"Do the plans give John a chance at building the future he wants?"

"Bigger than that, my man." David tilted his head toward me. I reminded myself to have his hearing assessed as I recognized a recent mannerism he used during important conversations.

"Did you talk with Raima about Phoebe?" Something like impatience pulled under his words. "Andrew just helped her through a seizure, or whatever we're calling these attacks."

"We talked a lot about that. Why don't you come with me when I talk to Phoebe about joining a restructured Hartford, Ltd." I checked his face for understanding, saw he was pre-occupied with her present physical condition.

My hand on his knee drew his attention. "Frances, Milan, Lao, and Raima are all doing what they can to identify the root of Phoebe's problem. Maybe you can make connections through your DOE network. I don't have any other strings to pull inside the Bureau lab structure." He sank into thought, but I knew he was listening. "I want to help our daughter put together a healthier life than the Intellectual Corps if she is willing."

"For a start I suggest someone send Hana, that creepy cares, back to Chicago." I nodded in agreement with David's assessment. "Andrew believes she's medicating Phoebe. But Phoebe won't hear of being without a cares."

Knowledge of Andrew's feelings for Phoebe, influenced my approaches to her problems in a schizophrenic manner—motherly concern for her safety and happiness, and motherly concern about quality of my son's life if settling with a high maintenance woman. "Amber has staff minimizing Hana's time alone with Phoebe."

Raima walked toward us, her steps slower than in her metro environment and sadness worn on her face. "Can I wait with you for my transport?" Her voice, usually bright and staking control, was quiet.

David pulled a chair closer.

"What a wonderful man," she said. "When Anne referred him to me as a client twenty years ago, I had no idea he'd become my stand-in father."

Eight thirty was near, the sun no longer heated us and fewer workers walked the production areas. Raima leaned toward David, an unusual gesture, and put an arm around his shoulders before resting her head there.

"You would think those of us who lost everyone during the second depression would have tougher skins." Raima straightened. "Of course there are so few truly old people left that losing any of them is a tragedy. Thanks to both of you for sharing him."

"My Dad never befriended a person he wasn't interested in, Raima."

She sorted herself back into her more controlled façade. "Is there time to speak with Phoebe before I leave? I have a few questions about her contract."

"There was another episode after dinner, I'm not sure she's up to a serious discussion," David offered. "Maybe a conference in the morning."

"I don't mean to offend you, David, but I think she can pull herself together for a discussion this important." Raima kicked through David's protective parent role without emotion. "There's no reason for Hartford, Ltd., to pay my firm's very expensive hourly rate to research breaking Phoebe's contract if she is not interested. Right?"

I saw Phoebe and Andrew walking our way during the conversation. Hana followed, a catlike shadow staying close to walls. I lifted my chin to alert David and draw attention to the cares' presence. I suggested a move to my office for Raima's talk with Phoebe.

We swapped favorite Paul stories as we walked. Phoebe sounded clear-headed and calm, both firsts for this visit. Andrew said little.

As I closed my office door, Raima morphed from family friend to Hartford's legal counsel with an eye on the clock.

"Anne's team has built a re-organization plan for Hartford, Ltd., that is excellent on many levels." She sat in a chair, gestured for Phoebe to sit next to her while David, Andrew, and I settled. I wondered why we weren't all at the conference table, but trusted Raima's instincts.

"A very significant research director role will exist within that new structure. We'll use the water resources development corporation created by your biological mother to safeguard her technology patents. The Department of Energy will invest to improve the labs here if that interests you or Hartford, Ltd., will find a third party to build labs to your specifications elsewhere. We're not worried about raising capital." She paused. "The question is whether you have interest in leaving the Intellectual Corps to take on that role?"

Autocratic didn't quite describe Phoebe's manner of communicating about her work world with outsiders. High secret labs filled with brilliant solo researchers certainly didn't waste time in development of soft skills like diplomacy or tact. Dining out with Ahlmet and Phoebe had made me feel socially polished, intellectually inferior, and dismayed that our daughter had shed much of what she'd learned about being polite and cordial as a child. In the thirty seconds of quiet following Raima's question, I braced myself for Phoebe's response.

"Why wouldn't a slave grasp at the possibility of freedom?" She spoke to Raima, ignoring all of us. Or dismissing all of us. "I would do almost anything aside from being a prostitute or testing pig to get away from the lab hell hole. It would be extraordinary if Hartford, Ltd., needed either of those in-house."

David startled, too stretched by the events of the day to not respond to Phoebe's off-the-wall statement. Whole estates agreed to serve as test sites for food supplements or pharmaceutical experiments. I would never put employees of our company in jeopardy to pad our income.

"Phoebe, I can assure you that Hartford, Ltd., will never be involved in those activities." I leaned against my desk, my feet close to hers. "I have to be very honest and tell you that we might not be able to offer you the same resources and challenge the Bureau is able to structure with the multi-corps. You will be the one to define how to be intellectually stimulated." Fighting my natural instinct to fold my arms over my chest, I placed them at my sides on the desk. "You'll not have the services of the Intellectual Corps here. If you want a personal attendant, you can hire one. You have enough money to live a very comfortable life, but unless we're able to grow the water business a great deal, you'll live like we do."

She stood, took my hand and led me to the windows. Her fingers, while smooth and cool, transferred energy to mine. In her profile I saw the brilliance Phoebe brought to her work.

"Look at those trees, Mom." Her tone implied we were alone, that the connection of our hands recreated the intimacy of mother and child. "I look at the orchard, at the sun screen fields, at the irrigation systems and find myself distracted from the work that has sucked every bit of my days. There's nothing easy about preserving water and agriculture. I see this land as a great lab. All I need to start work on a new project is a half dozen research assistants, good technology support and an academic partner." Dropping my hand, she put her arms around my shoulders and hugged me. "I would start tomorrow if you put the papers in front of me."

Raima cleared her throat. "Good, but Hartford, Ltd., will have to negotiate with the Bureau for your remaining contract. They'll fight hard, even if it's only for six months. If we succeed, you'll be dropped from the Corps."

Looking past me to her father, Phoebe said nothing. Andrew shifted in his seat. We waited.

"I don't think life could be much more demanding than what your mother and I dealt with in the early post-depression years." David spoke only to his daughter. "Like you, we were controlled by the government. Then think about this—being coerced into arranged marriages, given a work assignment and placed out in housing far removed from other people."

He paused, his voice cracking. "I found out that you would be born by a text message from the Bureau of Human Capital Management. I felt like a working dog."

His story wasn't new to me, but the facts he shared were meant for Phoebe.

"Your mother and I were not compatible in any way. The Bureau probably timed your birth because someone knew I had hit the wall. I was ready to bolt to China or anywhere that gave me more space to breathe, to find someone who wanted to be together." He had her attention. "From what I see your life is worse, and I would give anything to change that."

The rhetoric slowed our flow, appeared to annoy Raima.

"Every generation of gifted people has its difficulties to overcome," she said while moving a ring on her right hand with her thumb. "As a nation we have a long history of underappreciating our intellectuals until the big guys saw a way to make a buck from their work. What I need to know before my transport arrives is what it will take to buy Phoebe a new job."

With the late evening sun highlighting her curls and blurring the edges of her clothing, Phoebe appeared more like a thin column than a living creature. She returned to the window view.

"I would buy myself out of the contract if I could, but that isn't directly allowed." One hand raised to her forehead, pressed there briefly. I waited for signs of a new disturbance.

"The contract transfer language is oddly written. Others have said that no matter what an Intellectual Corps member wants to do with their work, all the power in our contracts favors perpetual employment by the Bureau or a chosen multi-corps." Phoebe turned, leaned against the window, crossed one ankle over the other as she finished. "They say we were bred to work."

Rising from his chair, Andrew walked to her side.

"Don't go there, Phoebe." He spoke as a peer, not a lesser intellectual. They may have had this conversation before as his voice implied he was reminding her of facts already discussed. "There are thousands of us who were genetically engineered. Somewhere out there the next generation of intellectuals is being created. But you chose the status; no one did that to you. Right?"

The way she looked at him told us all that we were now privy to one of their intimate disagreements. "You were too young to understand it was a horrible decision. But you did make it. Noah and I chose a different direction."

David raised an eyebrow, perhaps surprised by Andrew's direct words. The emotion between Phoebe and Andrew held me. I read the sadness of a former lover in Phoebe's eyes. Raima read it also, her own sexuality responding to how close the two stood.

"Can we talk about what holds you to the Corps?" Raima tried once more to turn the conversation. "What do you know of your contract? How are you compensated?"

"We are paid one hundred fifty percent higher than the total compensation of the highest paid researcher, scientist, or engineer in our selected field." She shared a figure. "In addition I'm paid for speeches, milestone achievements, and something called 'hardship equities' on a semi-annual basis, which usually matches my comp. All our living expenses are covered. I don't know what that is worth." Her eyes stayed focused on her feet as she answered Raima's questions. Our daughter was paid dearly for her virtual slavery.

"I don't spend anything. Everything is in a small bank Andrew suggested. I hoped some day I might find a way to fund something that would give me a way out," she said without emotion. I understood what she meant because I'd had the same hope when I agreed to become a surrogate at the end of the Second Great Depression. Apparently those who designed essential employee compensation had not learned that the best people would eventually want their freedom and not merely more money.

David, a scientist paid handsomely during his government employment, looked at his daughter as if she spoke an ancient language he didn't recognize. I felt sheepish about the amount of money I assembled to buy out her contract. Andrew's smile told us he already knew that Phoebe was a very wealthy woman.

Raima whistled, a low foxy sound. "Woo-eee, woman, you are sitting high on those money bags. Do you have investments or is this all cash?"

"Andrew suggested I find a financial advisor and I did hire one, but typically I make my own investment decisions and use his office for administration. It's not difficult if you understand the algorithms and a few rules." Phoebe couldn't relax. She focused on Raima.

"So a lot of it is liquid, some of it is in my room here and some is invested in both short-term and long-term instruments." At which point David laughed.

"Are you comfortable sharing your Bureau contract with me?" Raima looked out the window for her transport.

Phoebe followed Raima's gaze out the window, tapped her fingers against one leg. "The Intellectual Corps agreement is confidential." She brought her eyes back to Raima. "Milan insisted I use an outside lawyer to review it, but she had to sign a confidentiality statement."

"And so will I." Raima had been present for most of Phoebe's life, provided her with a place to stay in Minneapolis during her school years, and accompanied her to Boston for one set of college interviews. "I'm asking this as Hartford's legal representative, but you can be assured that your best interests are the only reason this discussion is happening."

"Of course." Phoebe sat back, removed her data pad. "Let me transfer the documents you need. My actual lab contract is up for renewal at the end of October. They've offered extensive incentives for me to sign early, but I want a statement of continued exclusivity, which would forbid the reselling or re-assignment of my work to a third party without my consent."

I wondered how Hartford, Ltd., could claim her as an exclusive employee. We were an insignificant company globally although we had national security status on the undeveloped water reclamation patents and our labs.

Licking her lips, Raima closed her data pad. "Send me the documents, Phoebe. Tonight if you can. There's no time to waste."

"The transport is here." Phoebe held out a hand toward Raima. "Let me walk you out and we'll talk."

In the quiet, I wasn't sure what to say to my son or husband. Family dynamics were shifting.

"Andrew—" David started. While Phoebe's voice could not be heard through the windows, we all saw her stumble beside Raima and crouch down near the ground. Andrew made it out of the office building before us and held her as her body became limp.

"For Christ's sake, this has got to end," David spat out. "All her work could be rubbish."

I squeezed David's arm and bolted from my office. I would tell him later that his comments sparked Phoebe's rescue strategy.

"Frances is on her way," Raima said pointing to the estate gates. "What the hell is going on here, Anne?"

I knelt beside Andrew, hoping this crisis would be like the others and Phoebe would soon be released from whatever controlled her. She lay too still in his arms.

I touched Phoebe's shoulder, felt her breathe, felt my anxiety and anger bloom together, "This is what I was describing earlier. Can you file a medical leave of absence request on Phoebe's behalf during your ride back to the city?"

Raima, queen of self-control, looked unglued in the middle of the unfolding situation. I moved aside for Frances.

Phoebe's eyes fluttered open. She rolled to her side, hung her head over Andrew's leg and threw up. "Call my cares, please. She'll clean this . . ." Another rolling stream came from her mouth. Tears showed in the corners of her eyes as she raised a shaky fist toward her mouth. Andrew held her hand back and dabbed at her face with his sleeve.

"Raima, David said Phoebe's work is questionable with these awful seizures." I turned my back on my children, spoke low for only Raima's hearing. "We'll buy time for Phoebe. You can tear apart her contract. If Noah's information is accurate, we'll throw a wrench in the Chicago labs with the proof that at least one multi-corps is threatening national security work by supporting sabotage within the labs."

Her eyebrows arched, acknowledging the brilliance of my plan while her mouth straightened with caution. Raima raised a hand with her thumb pointed upwards toward her transport driver. "Annie, you can't dream of mixing it up in the Bureau labs. They're a political hotbed with their own rules. Only the multi-corps have more lobbying power."

Frances and Andrew helped Phoebe to her feet, but she sank again. "Everything's spinning," she said. "Vertigo."

Motioning David to replace Frances, I pulled the doctor into our conversation. "Will you stand as the physician witness for Raima's filing of a medical leave of absence for Phoebe?"

"I've started the forms already, but wanted to talk with Phoebe before I filed a report." Frances checked her monitoring equipment. "My data pad is in the bag."

Phoebe would be furious about interference with her work. She and David had been disciplined through their education into an obsessive need to solve scientific mysteries, give their best to the project at hand, and minimize personal issues. The Second Great Depression emblazoned "WORK TO LIVE" on everyone's values beyond their toddler years, but those the government choose for special status seemed even more driven to meet a higher level of achievement.

It was difficult to leave Phoebe in the arms of Andrew, turn my back, and walk with Raima to her transport. My friend and attorney hesitated about driving back at this point and asked if she might stay overnight.

"If this is like the other attacks, Phoebe will be normal in an hour or so, unless another attack happens. It's nothing any of us can change," I explained, but saw the mixture of fear and anger in Raima's eyes that remained focused on Phoebe.

"If we work this right, we can have her on medical leave within a few hours." Raima turned her back to the threesome. "If Frances has an hour, I know how to get this done." She dismissed the transport driver, then spoke to me in a low voice "And, I want to talk with you about the whole lab sabotage theory before you take a serious risk."

Chapter Eighteen

Hana became the symbol of my frustration with the entire Intellectual Corps. Never at Phoebe's side in the middle of an attack, she lurked at windows and in doorways watching others care for her charge. Knowing she existed in my home made me uneasy.

"If you couldn't find your way outside to help, I suggest you get the hell out of our way now." The front hall magnified every angry nuance of my voice. "You are to go to your sleeping quarters until Phoebe requests your assistance. And stay out of the kitchen and foods."

In Phoebe's room, I gave my exhausted daughter a sponge bath before helping her into pajamas. She quieted as if keeping her mind clear of thoughts that might trigger another Ahlmet onslaught. When Frances arrived, she ordered Phoebe to bed with light sedation, connected to an assortment of monitors. Without discussion, Andrew established his intention to stay near Phoebe. I kissed the lined forehead above her worried eyes before I left to find Raima.

I missed standing at Phoebe's side as her protector and nurturer. No one asked me to step in to those old roles so I left. Waiting for David to come back from Paul's room, I updated Lao. His news about listening devices cleared from throughout the estate including Phoebe's room wasn't surprising. Then I called Milan who still carried legal authority to make decisions about Phoebe's medical care.

The business suit he wore looked very formal by the day's standards. The hologram caught him in a hotel suite, seated at a desk with one leg extended on a second chair.

"Milan, this is a difficult call." Two days of drama layered on Paul's decline and the Deshomm attempted takeover. I wanted peace.

"Paul or Phoebe?" His expression blended into his generic surroundings. "I'm guessing Phoebe."

"There have been more serious seizures today. Frances has Phoebs sedated and monitored."

"Should I make a stop at Ashwood?"

"Raima and Frances plan to file for an immediate medical leave. I think Frances is trying to convince Phoebe that her research could be compromised while these attacks continue."

"I'll be there in an hour."

"So you are in the Cities."

"Yes." He volunteered nothing more. "With security issues on the estate roadways, I'd like to avoid a return trip to the city. Is there a spare bed at Ashwood?"

"Of course." I sent a message to Amber as I sought clarification from Milan on the next steps. "Do you need to be involved with filing this request?"

"Technically I am the one to grant it, but I won't do that without working with lab management." He checked his communication band. "Annie, don't get ahead of yourself. Frances and I have good sources helping us understand this cohort's project."

There was a knock at my bedroom door. "Nap in the transport, I have many things to discuss with you tonight—Hartford, Ltd., and the kids. Including Phoebe."

"In an hour." He tipped his head and left.

David, carrying two bottles of Ashwood ale, found me and we headed out for our favorite stroll through the orchards. With rabbits and birds and bugs, we enjoyed the uneven grassy walk. I found more solace under the leafy canopy than by the pond's side. Paul's favorite escape had been the grain fields, walking alone under wide skies like in the Dakotas.

"How is the mother of all these big, busy adults feeling?" He raised his bottle toward mine and we tapped glass.

"Like it's been a long time since we actively parented so many." Sorting through my feelings felt more like passing through a waterfall than lifting a series of cards from a tabletop. "They're all in different places—John concentrating on career, Noah in transition, Faith eager to take the next step. Then there's Phoebe."

"Annie, you have your hands full with Hartford, Ltd., Let me worry about Phoebe and Faith. I know you'll be successful with the business plan and that will give our kids options." He pulled a long drink from his ale. "Sounds like you and Frances are on the same page about the leave. Never crossed my mind. Can they convince her to do it?"

"Milan is on his way." His head turned my way. "Raima wanted him involved. He does hold power of attorney for Phoebe. Anyway, he plans to stay overnight to see Phoebe and confer with Frances and Raima. And hopefully us."

A familiar disquiet developed between us. Milan's government-appointed relationship made both of us uncomfortable. My confidante fell into that zone of a former spouse that a current spouse might not want mentioned, particularly in times of stress.

"David, you started me thinking about a way to get to the bottom of this Ahlmet-Phoebe connection. I'd like to use what we know to ignite an investigation within the Chicago labs about questionable activity among the multi-corps sponsoring Intellectual Corps research. The rules of confidentiality in each project are quite rigorous." I held back Raima's caution about challenging the labs, believing David to be more knowledgeable of internal politics in the big agencies.

His low whistle backed up Raima's skepticism. "Hartford, Ltd., could be destroyed if you piss off the wrong snake in that ugly nest."

"So we hurry our restructuring and take advantage of the medical leave to define a role for Phoebe." I dumped my ale, too wound up to enjoy its bitterness. "Then we find a communications agency willing to plant media information about tangled relationships within the lab structure. Phoebe may get some undesired exposure, but in her compromised condition with the right publicist she'd come off very sympathetic."

Passing our typical halfway point, we turned back. David stopped, wrapped his hand over my shoulder. "Don't involve the company in this until we exhaust other ways to cut off Ahlmet. And don't even consider starting a fight on your own."

From where we stood, our plain old residence could be seen in the midst of a color fan of greens, a quiet oasis in the last of the day's sun. Figures moved within the screen porch. I leaned against David, absorbing the comfort of his broad shoulder.

"I wouldn't jeopardize our future, David. But, I will use whatever strength Hartford, Ltd., carries to stop Phoebe's suffering."

He sighed, a heavy soul emptying sound. "Of course." I felt his lips on my hair. "If all goes to hell, there's always Oak Street."

It was a sweet joke reaching back to his first gift to me—an old key to the South Dakota house inherited from his aunt thirty years ago. The house had long ago been demolished by the state for public housing. Oak Street was our tribute to the woman who encouraged David to think beyond the Regan ranch before the world went to hell.

The low bullet-gray executive transport approaching Ashwood's main gate made me curious about what Milan was doing in the Cities. He generally avoided flashy transports, sometimes drove himself. Theoretically these gray transports provide the highest level of security on our roads. He was serious about his night travel concerns.

"Come say hello." I pulled David's arm. "You should be in tonight's conversations." We dropped our bottles in the recycling and waited in the courtyard for the transport.

Milan stepped out, placing his foot on the pressed rock with care. Inside the transport I saw a second person, a man somewhat younger than I was with silver-touched, faded blonde hair above a lined face. Watching Milan's slow movements, David offered assistance.

Milan shook his head. "I'll be all right. Had unexpected surgery this morning to remove an infected sliver in my calf. Afraid I'm a bit stiff."

His fellow traveler exited easier. "Marcus Twedt," he said while extending a hand to David. "Dr. Marcus Twedt." He turned to me and tipped his head. "Director Milan pulled me from a conference to meet with Senior Researcher Regan." His hand, released by David, was pulled back and stuffed into a pocket.

Milan wrapped an arm around my shoulders. "Dr. Twedt is one of the preeminent physician scholars in the field of mind control and familiar with Senior Researcher Ahlmet's work."

An odd feeling crept over me as we exchanged greetings. I turned my head, sure we were being watched. In the kitchen's bay window Hana nearly pressed her nose against the glass. If she had been sent to report back on what happened while her mistress lived away from the labs, I assumed she could read lips.

While awkward, I turned out of Milan's loose hold. "Phoebe's cares is watching us. We're working to keep a step ahead of her speed in planting listening devices. It would be better if we moved to our clean room. It's behind the small stables."

"Maybe Milan and Dr. Twedt would like to go to their room before we meet," David suggested with a questioning look about my jump into work without more pleasantries.

"David, you're a good host. Phoebe's cares has rattled my sense of security." Milan nodded, a pleasant smile forming on his lips. Dr. Twedt focused on me, perhaps unnerved by landing in the midst of an unsettling situation. "Amber tells me Hana is quite distressed about being kept away from Phoebe." We began walking toward the stable. "Dr. Frances tested remains of a cookie Hana carried to Phoebe's lab and found traces of more than one drug in the crumbs." This was news for David, but he showed no response.

We adjusted to Milan's slower steps. Dr. Twedt looked at each building as we progressed. "I know of Dr. Frances," he volunteered. "She had a promising psychiatric practice career ahead of her before the Second Great Depression. The government should not have interfered with her plans." Although his name screamed old Minnesota, Dr. Twedt's voice suggested years in the near south. "I'm pleased to consult with her."

Leaving Ashwood

"If anyone understands Phoebe, it's Frances," I said. "She came to Ashwood through referral by Terrell Jackson when our daughter suffered with night terrors."

"Jackson. That's the former CIA man she married? He had some therapy background."

"I think he was DOE." If there was anyone whose history I knew, it was Terrell's.

"No, I clearly remember he was CIA for many years." Twedt missed cues that his pronouncement caught us by surprise. At least caught David and me by surprise. Milan concentrated on his stiff leg's movement across an irregular pathway surface. "His chef experience back in Washington, D.C., was an interesting cover although I remember he mustered out after a number of years at some Midwest estate."

"Anyone capable of doing more than one thing at a time in those rugged days got caught up somewhere by the agencies," David quipped while reaching for my hand.

Twedt blew out air through his nose. "I shouldn't have brought it up. None of it matters today. Disastrous how so many of my colleagues have changed from government flunkies to multi-corps drones over the last decade."

Nothing should have surprised me living this life in this country. Terrell was my closest friend and this hidden fact betrayed a personal code of honor.

We settled our visitors' bags in a corner of the clean meeting room and waited for the others. Milan refused to sit although his leg clearly caused him discomfort. Lao entered and I remembered the first time he showed me this space. Seventeen years had robbed the smoothness from our faces. The room's unflattering light showed a lot of lines and creases. I trusted Lao with our lives, yet wondered if he might report to another influence in the snakes' den of our society or why he never shared Terrell's past CIA affiliation.

Frances and Dr. Twedt greeted each other professionally. Milan waved people to chairs.

"Under the intellectual protection language of the National Security Actions of 2025, I retain a legal guardian relationship over Phoebe until she turns thirty years of age." He shifted his weight, the strain flickering briefly across his face. I struggled to not respond to this bit of information, thinking all the work that we'd done in the past twelve hours to create an escape hatch for her might be wasted. "I care for her, and her family, deeply." Milan paused. "So, there will be no official record of this meeting," he restarted. "Here's what I need accomplished before we go on the record about Phoebe's future."

This Milan I remembered from my first months at Ashwood. Much older, he was now a grizzled executive on a rescue mission. The doctors were sent off to complete a thorough examination and prepare a report for his review before submitting it officially. Raima received access to Bureau contracts Phoebe was unable to open from her own data pad hours earlier. Milan asked for a legal outline to be ready for discussion at ten o'clock.

They left to work on his assignments. Milan grilled Lao about Hartford's systems security then Ashwood's physical plant security. He frowned when hearing of vulnerabilities left by Sadig, but Lao had people monitoring every weakness, working on corrections or developing temporary barriers. We agreed Phoebe needed to be contained within Ashwood.

I invited Lao to remain as Milan asked questions about Hartford's restructuring and the Deshomm takeover threat as related to Phoebe—financially or professionally.

"Because Lao rejoined us today, he'll be hearing this all for the first time." I covered the plan presented to Phoebe earlier that evening and elaborated on John's angel investor and two large grants waiting to fund the new research facility that would be built at Giant Pines. David helped fill in details of the TW Water Company where Phoebe would be based.

For forty-five minutes, Milan pulled apart our plans and challenged key assumptions. He was as tough as during the years I'd reported to him when estates, whether government-funded or private enterprises, were all accountable to bureaucrats like Milan. During those years estates' production fed a starving, bankrupt country and Milan knew how to dig into the numbers. He was not as sophisticated about multi-corps workings.

"Could we talk about Phoebe?" David asked, tired of Milan's bulleted queries. "Isn't that what your trip is about? Anne doesn't need your approval to put her business plan in place."

For twenty-five years I'd held Milan tight to our family, camouflaging his government-appointed legal guardianship of our surrogate-born children from them under the guise of an adopted uncle. When Ashwood was tethered to the Bureau, no one knew if Milan's quarterly visits were made to complete site inspections or our children's academic preparation.

David failed to realize that at this point Milan's actions would be taken after consultation with Phoebe. Decisions about Phoebe's status and future directions would rely on her negotiations with Milan. On behalf of Hartford, Ltd., I merely proposed an interesting work opportunity. Tonight Milan, whether short-tempered because of his aching leg or acting appropriately in a time of crisis, didn't coddle David. They sat across the oval table. David's demands irritated Milan.

"I'm doing what needs to be done, David." Milan finally sat and raised his bum leg to rest on an empty chair. "Frances and Marcus will bring her here so she and I can talk. I needed to know that Anne's business plan is sustainable and there is a valid set of work that meets the criteria expected of someone of Phoebe's potential. Our government has a lot invested in Phoebe's training and won't walk away before society has a return."

My husband stood. "If the Bureau holds her in those labs until she is thirty, she'll follow her mother and grandfather into suicide. I hold you responsible, Milan. You."

"As I told Anne a few days ago, it is known that Phoebe is not well suited to the labs' lifestyle. That info is part of her official file, for good or bad. Removing her from the labs looks logical on the surface, but this young woman is of great interest to any number of agencies and multi-corps." Milan checked the time. "If it is possible, this mind-control issue might be a bigger story."

"She's not going to be collateral. My daughter is flesh and blood and deserves a life of more than work."

"You, of all people, understand what it is to be a government intellectual worker." Milan placed the words carefully in the room. "Phoebe accepted her place in the Intellectual Corps and their expectations of performance. Andrew has also spent many years working at a faster pace than you knew, David." He reached inside his jacket for his data pad. "That's reality for our talented citizens."

"I didn't mind serving to pull this country out of the Second Great Depression. But, I'll be damned if my kids are going to serve to line the pockets of the multi-corps."

"The circle's come full around," Milan said. "From too-big-to-fail to squeezing the governments that saved them." He looked over the top of his old-fashioned glasses. "Who would have thought that this would be our fate?"

"The water company's key people currently work out of a little town about ninety miles northeast of Green Bay in Door County." Around the table, we all looked up as David spoke. I had not been to Green Bay since before the Second Great Depression. "They used to be in Chicago, but moved about ten years ago. We could set up a sophisticated lab on the shores of Lake Michigan and attract bright folks tired of metro living."

"Do what makes good business sense," Milan said while backing away from the table. "You are premature to build plans around Phoebe at this point." He stood. "Frances says it would be better if I meet with Phoebe in the residence."

The estate quieted. David and Milan both walked toward the door, neither appeared willing to step aside.

"Would it be all right if I accompanied you, Milan?" I timed my question so he would turn and David might move through the door first.

"You can fill me in on lives of the other young people who have returned to the mother estate." Milan slowed, tilted his head to invite me. As I rose from my chair, Lao checked his communicator, a frown formed across his forehead.

"Anne, we have an unexpected visitor approaching the gate."

"Hopefully no one hoping to spend the night." I quipped. We filed out of the room. David was far ahead, answering a communication.

Lao closed the door, ran his DNA coder over its lock. "The evening is about to get very interesting. Our guest is a young senior research scientist by the name of Ahlmet traveling under a false name. Estates regional security caught the discrepancy after allowing the transport through their gates."

"Unrequited passion trumps every rule set in place by logic." Milan shook his head then laughed out loud. "Damned idiot. Intelligence doesn't guarantee social brilliance." He removed his glasses, tucked them into a pocket. "First day back and you'll have two Intellectual Corps members under your protection, Lao. Few private parties will ever say that. Use the security code assigned Ashwood for Phoebe and let someone know what's going on.

"Best to let Ahlmet enter so we know where he is. Go ahead and strip him of communications devices, then bring him to this conference room. Tell him I will be back to see him in an hour. We'll let him simmer for a while. Absolute silence should be punishing for him from what I read in his profile."

David headed toward the executive office building without turning to check on us, a sign that he was needed on a call. I added instructions for Lao's people. "Don't tell David about Ahlmet." I wasn't sure David could pass on an opportunity to do his best to convince Phoebe's former lover that the implant needed to be disabled. I wanted them in separate spaces. "No one outside security should be told about Ahlmet for now."

Milan nodded in agreement. "I told Twedt this young man wouldn't be able to stay away from our Phoebe. Is there any reason to let him see her?"

"Did you know that she and Andrew were involved before Ahlmet? She seems quite comfortable letting Andrew care for her and share in decisions."

Milan huffed. "If we weren't dealing with her entire future, possibly saving her life, this could be a rather interesting twist. Actually I think I knew. Don't ask how."

Lights were beginning to take over inside for the late evening sun. In the cool, soft-colored interior there was a sense of calm that hid the life-and-death drama being played out in Phoebe's quarters, where she fought Ahlmet's devil, and Paul's suite as he slept unsure of waking in the morning. Our shoes made small squishing sounds on aged hardwood floors undamaged by Phoebe, all her siblings, dozens of young workers, and a handful of family pets. We passed the long wooden bench made by David before my time.

"If Phoebe would like you or Andrew to stay, that's her choice." Milan slowed where two halls met. "I don't have the slightest idea where to find her."

Blinds were down in Phoebe's room. She sat in an old armchair covered by a blanket shipped new from Chicago. Her head lay against the back of the chair with hair spread against its rose-colored upholstery. Andrew gently worked a brush through tangled curls with such comfort it was impossible to escape the intensity of their emotional connection.

"Phoebe." Milan's voice broke Phoebe's reverie and she opened her eyes, dilated pupils suggesting Ahlmet's siege continued through the doctors' examination. She looked exhausted, weakened, frightened in spite of sedation.

She sat upright in the chair, tried to push herself out of it.

"Stay." Concern and affection gentled Milan's voice as he took in the scene from Andrew's ministrations to her pallor. "I hear you've been having some rough times." He pulled over a wooden chair from the desk, put it next to where Phoebe sat.

"We need to talk. Mind if I share the footrest? I had some minor surgery on my leg this afternoon before I knew about what was happening with you."

"I'd trade places with you if I could," Phoebe said while moving her feet to one side.

"From what I hear, I wouldn't doubt that." He settled. "Do you mind if Anne or Andrew stay while we talk?"

"They'll have to sit on the bed or the floor unless we all move to the next room." She tried to sound light, to smile. "It's fine if you say that's okay."

"I want to hear you tell me what's happening, what you know about why it's happening. When we're through with that, we'll talk about your work in the labs and what you want to do about your contract renewal." His voice changed, still concerned yet back to fact-finding. "I need to know if anything's changed about your thoughts on that subject since we had dinner in February and who you've talked with about your contract since then."

I did sit on the edge of the bed. Andrew leaned against the wall near Phoebe's chair. I noticed how she continued to move her hand under the light blanket. Apprehension, perhaps fear of triggering another mind control siege, hovered around her eyes and mouth like a woman in labor waiting for the next pains.

"It would be easier on Phoebe if you could just read the doctors' report," Andrew suggested. "She's been through hell for the past hour and a half. Talking about the attacks triggers more."

"Lao has Ahlmet in custody." Milan spoke to Phoebe. "He's in a secure place where communications are blocked."

Phoebe looked my way and I nodded to confirm Milan.

"Why is he in custody?"

"Because he tried to enter Ashwood."

"Oh, my God." She said nothing else about Ahlmet, maybe testing that nothing would happen to her during this discussion. "I don't know if I was able to tell the doctors much because I couldn't talk through my thought disruption." Phoebe swallowed and girded herself for potential attack. "I told Ahlmet we were through about an hour before Mom called yesterday. He began communicating with me through a thread he'd inserted in my neck area while I was asleep. He wanted to 'surprise' me. Told me that every time I thought about him, he would know and control those thoughts. Gave me a small sample."

She was crying, not under siege, but angry, frightened, and exhausted. "It's an awful feeling to describe. The more I try to stop the control, the more dissonance I experience—swirling, dizziness, disorientation. Like I want to hit my head against a wall so hard I would pass out."

"Does he tell you how to feel or what to do?" Milan asked the question without inflection.

"He has made a few suggestions. I probably can't keep up the resistance long-term."

"And your work?"

"If Ahlmet is here, he has permission to travel from someone in the labs. Who would that be?" She answered Milan's question with a fact and question of her own that I wanted answered.

"I'll find out. You and I have about forty-five minutes to talk about many important subjects." Milan turned the conversation back to her. "Do you think your work is suffering? Is there the possibility of a confidentiality breach?"

Phoebe stepped back into her professional persona—careful about challenges to the quality of her work, her integrity, her reputation. Her hands moved back on top of the blanket, her face flattened into an impersonal expression. I'd seen that look slip into place during communications from her lab crew in Chicago.

"My frustration is that Ahlmet's experiment is costing my project the loss of my time and concentration. I've never missed a deadline. Never." Her left eyebrow arched as she considered her next words. "If you all think this medical leave is essential, I want my crew to know that I'll pay their productivity bonus. The work can't continue without me and the money means a lot to them." She shrugged, forced a small smile. "I've not taken one sick day in the last four years. I'm known as a hard ass."

"Learned it at home, I'd suggest." Milan looked my way. "If Phoebe doesn't object, I would like to have the next part of this discussion in private." He gave her a moment to speak. She shrugged and agreed.

"Let me give you a good night kiss." I leaned over to touch my lips to the top of her head. She grabbed my hand, pulled me for a full hug.

"Thank you, Mom." Her whisper tickled my ear, flooded my heart.

"I love you, Phoebs."

Andrew ruffled one hand across Phoebe's hair and extended the other out in an open gesture to Milan. "Listen well. This woman could help save the world if her water study continues. And you could be instrumental in part of making that happen. As part of Hartford, Ltd."

The two men exchanged a look, one that suggested Andrew's comment capstoned longer discussions between them. I closed the door to Phoebe's room behind me, followed Andrew through the residence, without a clue what to say that could comfort either of us.

"Take me to Ahlmet." Andrew spoke calmly.

"Can't do that, Andrew. Milan and I agreed to keep his location private."

"He could inflict more pain on Phoebe at any time, bend her thinking when she needs to be absolutely clear with Milan." The hand that grabbed my arm was strong yet gentle. "I have to convince him that this experiment must stop."

"That confirms what I just heard about Ahlmet from my Chicago friend." Noah joined us. "He's AWOL in the labs. So where is he, Mom?"

Our daughter had her posse of brothers, lover, guardian, family, and friends ready to offer protection. I took comfort that she wouldn't be alone like her brilliant mother had been. But none of us could block the effects of one nana chip embedded within her body. Or the power of the Bureau labs and their multi-corps clients.

"In here." I led the two into the cook's office, the closest place with a door. "Ahlmet's presence is a matter of national security. Thank God, Lao is back with us because I believe he can manage this escalating situation. You two, Milan, Phoebe and myself are the only people beyond a few of Lao's staff who know Ahlmet is here."

They were adults, aware that forces of good and evil were not always neatly identified. They would also take risks to rescue Phoebe from her situation. I wasn't sure which son was wired tighter at the moment.

"So we should volunteer our services to Lao?" Andrew's response was not what I anticipated.

"I don't think he needs help. What you should do is go about normal activities. Don't tell anyone what you know. Anyone."

Noah, the most peaceful but least predictable of our children, withheld commitment. He exchanged a long look with Andrew, the sibling with whom he shared almost nothing except for love of Phoebe and loyalty to our family.

"I'm serious," I said in response to their silence. "We could have droves of regional police and Bureau security taking over Ashwood tonight if we don't contain this situation."

"We understand, Mom. Let's take a walk, Noah." Andrew put his hand on the door handle. "I'll be back in about thirty minutes to make sure Phoebe gets to the briefing."

"What briefing?" Noah, coming straight from hours studying in the lower level of the DOE building, didn't know about the evening's visitors or direction.

"I'll share an outline of what's happened since dinner." Andrew opened the door. "If that's okay?" He looked to me.

Unsure of Noah's willingness to withhold information from his Bureau lab friend, I hesitated. "Remember, nothing happening here is to be discussed with anyone outside the three of us and Milan. Andrew agreed to that and you're bound by the same confidentiality, Noah."

He nodded his agreement as they left.

Chapter Nineteen

MILAN AND PHOEBE TALKED for more than an hour while the doctors assembled their report and Raima prepared a brief. Lao asked me to be available, but told me nothing about what was happening with Ahlmet. Additional security agents posing as members of the overnight crew or visitors filed into Ashwood in darkened transports. People familiar with the estate's daily routine would know something was happening.

I checked on Paul and found David just leaving his father's rooms.

"He's asleep. His vitals are stable." David looked tired, worried, every day of his age. I hooked my hand through his arm. "We'll probably not do a lot of sleeping tonight," he said. "Of course the DOE needs me on a 4:00 a.m., and I told Max I'd be at Giant Pines by eight." His sigh fell heavy in the empty hall. "I feel old and kind of useless—Dad's dying and I'm not getting any closer to a contact who can help Phoebe."

We walked about six steps, as I thought of what to say and wanted to tell him about Ahlmet and the extra security gathering on our grounds. My communicator came to life with the long, high-pitched screech that indicated a serious condition somewhere on the estate.

If the alarm sounded a second time, people in the house would have less than two minutes to gather in the central hall before heavy screens cordoned off windows and other residence exposures and my communication device turned to monitoring of identification codes. Standing still, the residence in the deepening quiet of farmers' bedtime, we waited.

"Anne," Lao's voice came over my communicator, "we have a Bureau situation. No need for lock down in the residence, although Ashwood is officially closed." I wondered how individuals hired by Sadig were responding to Lao's tight command.

"David and I are in the central hall."

"Have all members of your family and guests remain in the residence or executive office building until you hear from me. We'll meet in your office as planned."

"Andrew and Noah are out walking the estate, Lao. Are they in danger?"

"They are in the kitchen." Background noise filled our transmission. "And the doctors will be coming in the same entrance in about three minutes."

"Is someone on the grounds?" Of course I was asking if Ahlmet was on the loose.

"Yes. Don't worry."

"Lao, this is David." My husband's tired face had transformed into alert. "I'm sure you'll let Annie tell me what the hell is going on."

"She should do that." Lao's words finished as my communicator fell quiet.

Chapter Twenty

PHOEBE HAD AN ATTACK as she and Milan walked to the offices. He told me that they were talking about a kitten that kept the house free of mice, but also liked to drop on people from the top of shelves. She must have been using the conversation as a diversion from thinking about Ahlmet. When the disruption hit, Phoebe leaned against a wall, clenched her teeth and turned pale. Milan found dealing with the reality of the attacks very different from reading the doctors' clinical assessment.

The whole event lasted more than a minute. While Milan was shaken and Phoebe tired, she pushed them forward, attempting to treat the brutal events as little more than a stubbed toe.

Without knowing how Ahlmet initiated the attack, Lao doubled security on our home and office building. Troubled by claustrophobia, Phoebe balked at being ordered to enter Ashwood's safe room with Milan for the remainder of the night. We agreed to meet in my office with a dozen guards.

I don't remember the clinical details or legal maneuvers discussed in the two hours we built plans for Phoebe's future. She struggled through at least two attacks, and was forced to put her head down on the table during one. Frances and Twedt were by her side. We all silenced during those dreadful seconds.

For a socially awkward woman, our daughter presented facts like an experienced pro about what she required to function as a world-class researcher outside the Chicago lab. I'd hire someone with such polished speaking skills in a minute. The investments required were substantial even with Phoebe's contribution. I made a note about protocol for bringing in my chief financial person to run numbers.

When we adjourned it was to spend the first hour of the new day drawing together loose ends for the leave of absence filing. In parallel action, Raima and Phoebe began preparation to file a report with the Chicago lab for physical and emotional harm and send notice to the labs of intention to not renew her contract. Ahlmet interrupted the session twice with attempted attacks.

Phoebe could set wheels in motion to free herself from her current work, but no one had found the way to free her from what immediately mattered. When we adjourned for a few hours of sleep, all of us knew Phoebe's life was controlled by a brilliant and sadistic scientist.

David fell asleep while I washed my face, brushed my teeth and ran the mandatory monthly biostatistics from a saliva smear. A slight increase in blood sugars was noted. But at one thirty in the morning, with David's alarm set for four, bio stats were meaningless.

He dressed without a light for the DOE call. I kept my eyes closed and prioritized the first three hours of my day. Financial modeling needed to be completed for a restructured Hartford, Ltd., with, and without, Phoebe. Key players must be updated about our corporate strategy expansion. Advisors from the intellectual security agency, our investment bank and Raima's firm needed some time to respond to the plan.

David left and I sent careful instructions to Hartford's senior managers and Clarissa. I had overspent the time I could be distracted from running the company. Habit more than hunger directed me to the kitchen. Terrell sat on a high stool, reading daily updates and drinking coffee. I said good morning and set about selecting fruit for breakfast. Neither of us spoke. The man who always had something to say stared out the window without one comment.

"Have a good day, Terrell." Instead of filling a carafe with his exceptional coffee, I opted for a cup of tea.

"We've got something to talk about, Annie."

I assumed Dr. Twedt had said something to Frances about the CIA comment. "I've only had two and a half hours of sleep, Terrell, and a long day ahead. Some other time would work better."

"Not for me. I'd rather you didn't carry around bad feelings." Terrell pushed out the empty stool next to him. I heard the kitchen doors lock. "Please, sit. I got a cup of coffee ready for you right here."

Phoebe's claustrophobia wasn't entirely genetic. The clicks of our lockdown mechanisms raised my blood pressure. "I appreciate your . . ." The word "honesty" stuck in my throat. He had brought the CIA into my home and business.

The Bureau of Human Capital felt authorized to collect data on me because I was a former employee and held significant current contracts. The Department of Energy had justification to information in my office as a business vendor and in our home as the spouse of one their emeritus intellectuals. At one time the Pentagon apparently had files on Anne Hartford because her husband was ambushed by one of their branches. But Terrell bringing the CIA to Ashwood was far more invasive.

I cleared my throat, started over. "Unlock the doors. We can talk after Raima, Milan and Twedt are gone."

"It's true, Annie. I was with the CIA when I came to Ashwood twenty-five years ago."

"I remember having a discussion when you confessed you were assigned to Ashwood by the Bureau of Human Capital Management, but employed by the Department of Energy to keep an eye on Tia Regan." I didn't sit, stayed on my feet. "So how did all of that work with the CIA? You played double-agent plus estate cook?" Behind his handsome dark head, the sun was coming up. "What was of interest to the CIA in a little Minnesota estate in 2030?"

"You."

"I was a widowed school teacher turned into estate matron of an underperforming farm. Hardly a person who could threaten the security of the United States."

"Someone had big plans for you, Annie." He let the words float across empty kitchen counters. "Assigned to the estate housing one of the country's brightest scientist and her infant children. No common grunt is given that kind of challenge. CIA got interested in you when you were chosen to be the biological mother of an intellectual director's child. You were no ordinary surrogate." His musical voice wove a story from facts. "You never put the pieces together?"

"I've never taken the time to connect imaginary dots." The pull of Hartford, Ltd., tugged, the place where I could make things happen, where history didn't count as much as what happened today. Minutes were sliding away.

"You're the one Milan always lets get away. I know he tried to lure you into Bureau jobs, landed those trips to Washington, D.C., hoping to bring back the life you could have had."

"But why didn't you tell me the truth, Terrell?"

"All I did was file reports. Daily on Tia, weekly on you." Regret trolled under his words. "They already had access to Bureau info on you, but wanted more behavioral kind of stuff. I filled in boxes and wrote a few words. Good words." His hands curled around the mug. "Everybody worked for everybody in those days. Mostly worked to make a few dollars and keep our families alive. I got one thousand dollars a month from the snoops and sent that to my sister for food. She didn't believe you and me were scraping just as hard to feed the kids."

Looking over his head at the bounty of Ashwood, I felt the cold hunger of those first months and the panic that children would starve on a nearly bankrupt estate. Terrell never faltered, always found a way to make frozen fish, powdered milk, and bread into meals those little people would eat. He made oatmeal creamy, baked it in squares with nuts like some fancy breakfast muffin, fried it up to serve with jam. He'd lifted an unspeakable fear of failing from my shoulders.

"You always been the straight arrow, Annie. Made it possible for lots of people to go on to better ways." He stood and brought his hands up to his chest. "I didn't expect to ever find a decent person in this place. After a few years I talked to Milan and he made it possible for me to quit the reporting job. By that time it was pretty obvious you'd never leave this place."

"So you left the CIA?"

"Not exactly, but I became a reviewer. Watched communications from other regions for irregularities. Did that at night. Nothing to do with Ashwood. Eventually they made me leave here for an assignment before I could break my contract." Walking across the kitchen, he held out his hand. Like the first morning in this kitchen when he said, "It seems like if you're going to trust me to have my hands in the food you eat, you can trust me enough to shake hands." That day I did. "That was the hardest move I ever made after the Second Great Depression. Moving from this place." His hand didn't shake nor did his voice. "It felt right coming back, especially without government dogs watching over my shoulder."

I held out my hand then and accepted his strong arms around my shoulders. Pushed myself away, smiled, wanted to be on my way. "Sometime I want to hear more. Not now."

"Let me make you a real breakfast and have it brought to your office." Classic Terrell to offer nurturing. I hoped I could forgive and forget.

"Can you make it for two so David eats before heading to Giant Pines?"

Terrell nodded. "Breakfast for two is no problem. But no one leaves Ashwood until some mystery issue is resolved. You'll have to talk to Lao."

"Raima and Milan need to be gone by seven."

"I think Raima's gonna be sending Milan an invoice for lost billings."

Chapter Twenty-One

I COULD SQUEEZE A DAY of work into sixty minutes if left alone. Before Milan and Lao appeared, communications with my senior management team and outside advisors were complete.

"Not yet six in the morning and the two of you together suggests trouble on Ashwood." I pushed my chair back from my desk.

"Stay there, Anne. This won't take long." Lao walked back through the doorway and waved across the office for David to join us. This unnatural behavior from Lao brought me to my feet.

Milan tried to smile, but yawned. "I suspect Phoebe slept even worse than me. I'm told I snore and your safe room doesn't have the latest in acoustics." Another yawn started, but he clenched. "When I was awake, she appeared to be sleeping. No attacks during the night."

Closing the door after David entered, Lao delivered three short sentences. "Ahlmet is on the loose within Ashwood. A guard found Hana in the clean conference room. I assume she released him."

"Shit." Muscles tightened around David's mouth. "Where's my daughter?"

"In the safe room." Lao checked his communicator. "And will be until we have Ahlmet under guard." His voice gentled, alerted me to something more sinister.

"How did Hana gain entrance to a room that isn't on estate maps?" Milan watched David as I spoke. That one action tipped me off that another member of our family was in danger. "You haven't told us everything."

"Ahlmet has Noah." David stared at Lao as if trying to decipher the meaning of his words.

We lived in violence-free peace on the estate. Occasionally metro turf wars came to Ashwood with new workers, but our screening processes were so complete that street weapons didn't make it beyond the front gates. Now one of the most intelligent men in the nation held our son as a living shield.

Noah held black belts in karate and taekwondo. He would walk in front of a speeding transport to save a kitten or jump into a bad situation to defend a victim without thinking of himself.

"You're following them on monitors?" Emotions threatened to override an internal mantra that Lao was in charge, Lao would get this right.

"Ahlmet's using blinders so we have sketchy visibility. We're conducting a thorough search. Each building is sealed as we finish." Lao checked his communicator even as he spoke. "We're moving to the residence now and will be sending everyone to the main conference room. Anyone without clearance will be escorted to the staff dining hall."

"Where's Hana? Is she still here?" I hoped she was on a transport to the cities.

"She is being detained according to high security protocols of the Bureau." Lao looked toward Milan as if checking for approval. Milan tipped his head slightly. She could be stripped and chained in a horse stall or stowed in a food storage container for all I cared.

The morning work crewmembers that lived in town arrived between five and seven. From the quiet view out my office window, I assumed schedules had been cancelled. "You've spoken with Amber and the school team?" I wanted Faith at our sides, not wandering the estate.

He nodded.

"And Paul? I don't want him stressed by this news or moved if it isn't absolutely essential." David said nothing as I spoke, but his face told me there were deep memories of his own captivity decades ago pushing against the urgency of today's situation. Seventeen years without experiencing any situation similar to that time. Seventeen years without the flashbacks we knew could happen.

Milan waved Lao out and spoke for the security agents. "Paul's suite was the first place searched and sealed. He remained asleep so his attendant was briefed. They have food and supplies for the day, including packed meals. Apparently Hana may have had access to the kitchens."

"Great," David finally spoke, giving me relief. "Anne and I ate hot breakfast about forty-five minutes ago."

"If the food had been tampered with, you'd know by now." Lao tipped his head in the doorway. "I need to leave. Milan, you need to stay here."

"I'd like to keep Phoebe company," David volunteered. "Could you alert your people that I'm on my way to the safe room?"

"We'll go part way together."

With the men gone, Milan and I stood in a quiet office. I remembered the only other time we had a hostage situation at Ashwood and the resulting firepower of the military and security forces that brought this building's predecessor down. The only time someone was killed at Ashwood.

I sat, a giant wheezing cough forming, an excuse to turn away from Milan's caring eyes. I fished around in a desk drawer for a suppressant tablet. The cough escaped as a loud sneeze, then another, and a third followed by a soft wheezing sound.

"Bless you," he said. "Are you okay?"

With the tablet melting on my tongue, I nodded. "I'm allergic to a few of the grasses and molds that are everywhere on a farm. Just annoying." I sniffled, drank water. "What do you know inside the Bureau about this Ahlmet?" While asking the question, I turned on my estate monitor. Security professionals roamed the grounds, weapons on their belts. David and Lao walked down the back stairs to the lower level and safe room.

I knew the answer, that anything not included in Ahlmet's official biography was confidential. As Phoebe's mother I probably knew more than most citizens could request—that he was born in Maine, entered boarding school at five and attended Harvard at thirteen. He liked playing rugby, driving fast boats, rebuilding vintage guns and pampered his pet guinea pigs. Almost eccentric, almost like Phoebe.

Milan changed the subject. "I suppose Raima will want to recoup her billable hours for this time. Don't suppose you have some way to use her time?"

Of course, he knew I would laugh at this feeble attempt to save his multi-billion dollar section of the Bureau thousands of dollars. Raima knocked on my door before I had to smile.

"Good morning." She reached for a clean coffee cup on my conference table. "Or at least, let's hope it becomes a good morning. This feels like a convict lockdown in the metro. At least we're not dealing with some drug-crazed idiot."

She filled a cup and held it high. "Good news—we have tentative approval on Phoebe's leave of absence including a hold harmless if she is unable to complete contracted work. I've also received the most complex confidentiality statement that binds us to not talk about her peer who I understand is running around the estate with her little cares at his side."

Milan's shoulders went back. "Lao told you that?"

I watched a small gaggle of guards surround an out building used for tool storage. The door was opened, interior inspected, then an invisible tape placed over the door with a signal to the command central.

"Hell, no. My chief administrative office heard it on a news wave when he was dressing for work. Media are six deep outside the gate." She sipped at her coffee, looked over the top of the cup. "Is that report correct?"

"Partially." Willing to trust Phoebe's fortunes in Raima's legal abilities, Milan withheld the information about Noah and didn't correct where Hana might be found.

"If we can locate an office with a good hologram, I can finish work for another client and catch up on office notes. Interruptions like this are too common downtown. Or I can drink coffee and charge somebody for the hours."

Clarissa set her up in a neighboring space. Milan sat down at my table to review his communications. We could see the large conference room begin filling with an assortment of people from the main residence.

Faith broke from the group, studies bag over one shoulder. I ushered her into my office after she grabbed a protein bar and juice. At my desk I watched the security monitors.

Settling her bag on one chair, she looked for guidance about how to behave around Milan. Being so much younger than the others, she wasn't familiar with him as a visitor.

"This is creepy," she whispered toward me. "Where's Dad?"

I gestured her to bring her chair closer. "With Phoebe, in the safe room. A lot happened after you went to bed last night." As her eyebrows suggested her next question, I continued. "Someone who might want to harm Phoebe is somewhere on Ashwood."

"That Ahlmet guy I'd guess." Faith looked for confirmation.

Milan completed his communication. "Good guess, Faith, but that's confidential."

With teenage disdain she lowered her chin to look down her nose. "Well, it isn't a secret to anyone following local reports. They're making it sound like he's playing the big jilted." Faith waited for Milan's response. Bureaucrat and father of girls, he managed to maintain no expression. "I think the only thing they don't know is that he's planted a chip in Phoebe." She ripped open the breakfast bar. "By the way, he is mercury."

Faith saved her small doses of metro slang for me because David acted like a schoolteacher hearing "ain't" in a sentence.

"When the Bureau and regional security forces tally up the expenses for this uninvited visit and manhunt, Senior Scientist Ahlmet will also be shoeless." Milan winked at Faith. "You don't want a shoeless man, even if he is mercury."

Slang fell from Milan's lips with the same ease as a column of numbers or farm production categories. Faith and I were impressed that this man, close to seventy, assimilated common talk.

"I don't know about that. Senior Director Milan, in case you don't know much about estate life, there aren't a lot of eligible guys around. Look at my brothers—way into their twenties and not one of them has a woman in his life. They're all mercury and well off."

Leaving Ashwood

He laughed, the father in him tickled by dealing with a teenager once again. My communicator called.

"Annie, what are you seeing on the monitors?" David's voice was neutral, almost flattened. "Phoebe's dealing with waves of Ahlmet attacks. Lao needs to get Frances down here."

"I'm going to put you on speaker. There's a lot of noise here with folks waiting out the residence search." I gestured for Milan to come closer. Faith stayed at my side. My connection with Lao was immediate. "What do you mean by not getting through to Lao?"

"Just that. He's not answering." His voice remained tight.

"Could I talk with Phoebe?" Lao responded, I clicked him through to David.

"Not right now." The line went silent.

"The search is near the main residence now with activity in the storage sheds." I heard sounds behind Lao's voice.

A hushing kind of sound came from the safe room.

"David?" Lao spoke. I sat forward in my chair.

"I was fiddling with the controls. I should have paid attention to the last security update."

In code I tapped a message to Lao that David's words signaled a problem in the safe room. We'd changed the safe room security programming in early spring, which resulted in a gigantic blowout between David and Sadig when the outside vendors replaced our system with an older version. The mistake was discovered during our first safe room drill weeks later and David personally hired a former trusted vendor over Sadig's protests.

"Just get Frances down here," David continued. "I've got to pay attention to our kid who may need medical attention. Tell Frances to bring white socks."

Milan quirked his head at David's last direction.

"Take care, David. Lao will get you help. I love you." I muted my system, but left the safe room's end on audio. "Noah's in the safe room."

"I'll go find Dr. Frances." Faith pushed away from my side quickly.

"You won't leave this room," I replied. "The agents need to know exactly where each of us is situated, especially family members and guests."

"Anne." Lao's voice stopped Faith's response. "What was that about?"

"Fiddling is David's code to signify trouble. He personally supervised the system updates in the safe room and there must have been a breakdown. White socks is a dumb nickname he and I called Noah."

"Got it. Stay tight."

104

In the outer area I saw Andrew circulating through the small group, offering refills of coffee or water. The absence of John made me nervous. I pinged his communicator for a location and he pinged me back from the estate offices with a simple message that said, "lockdown." I pinged Andrew and he looked up. I beckoned for him to join us.

"Do you know anything," he asked as he closed my office door. "I heard from Phoebe about five thirty that you," he looked at Milan, "were leaving to meet Lao. What's up?"

"Sit down and we'll update you." Milan gestured toward a chair.

"The safe room still isn't visible on my monitors," I shared and Andrew startled. "David alerted us to a possible situation there about two minutes ago and security is on its way to investigate. It doesn't make any sense that Noah is there."

"How can I help?" Faith volunteered like she did for any other task on Ashwood from rescuing a child caught too high in a tree to cleaning out the most odious storage bin. "We shouldn't just sit here all safe." I would have warned Andrew to block the door if the building's doors were not locked.

Milan supplied activity. "You can do some research for me. I'm too slow on this little tool and don't have my data pad with me. Give me a piece of paper." I tossed a notebook toward the table. Faith caught it and passed it to Milan. He withdrew a sleek silver pen from his pocket. "There are four people I want to send info to about this situation, but I don't have their level-four addresses. I'll give you a secure code so you can look for them."

I saw her mind and body conflict about the task. Part of her accepted that sitting in this room was the only action possible while Lao's crew searched, but another part struggled with desire to be involved. She dug her data pad out of her book bag and got busy while Milan wrote down names and codes.

Andrew stood behind me to watch the monitors. He pointed to the lower level of the residence where a half dozen security agents approached the safe room. I recognized the leader as one of Lao's hires who had survived the Sadig years.

Security agents passed the entrance to the former sick bay that now housed unused furniture then the first two food storage areas. Part of the wall adjacent to the second storage unit's door moved sideways to uncover the entrance to our safe space. I saw agents hesitate, understood the door's operation had been initiated from inside.

Andrew moved closer. His breath, heavy with coffee and the scent of apple butter, teased at the air by my face. I felt his hand on my shoulder as he knelt next to my chair. I sensed Milan joining us, heard Faith push away from the table.

Leaving Ashwood

Visions of the one clash of forces that destroyed this building played through my head as I kept the faith that this time all would be okay. The safe room's door opened slowly on carefully controlled mechanicals. Agents pulled weapons from their uniforms. Faith gasped and moaned "no" as Milan took her hand. The same word resonated in my mind and heart.

One agent, weapon readied, slipped through the opening, then another and another. My eyes switched from the hallway view to the blank screen that should display the safe room. The hall was replaced with a grainy picture inside the room captured by an agent's camera.

"Who is that?" Faith leaned over my shoulder to squint at the outline of a tall, dark-haired man standing in the middle of the room with his hands held up above his head. Two agents focused their weapons toward the man. With the door now open, light brightened the images. David was easily identifiable blocking Phoebe behind outstretched arms. Noah struggled to his feet behind the stranger.

Only I recognized the man as Ahlmet, one shoe missing, his trademark white shirt ripped open at his left shoulder. A dark circle surrounded the torn fabric.

"That's Ahlmet." Andrew filled in the name. "I didn't remember he was that tall."

Agents quickly contained and handcuffed the invader.

"Now the interesting negotiations will begin," Milan said and stepped away to answer his communicator. Faith stayed at my shoulder, watching for a signal that our family was safe.

"Annie," Lao's voice came through clearly. "Noah has an injured ankle. David and Phoebe are fine. We have Ahlmet, and Sadig was taken into custody as he tried to exit an employee entrance."

"You say they are fine, does that mean they are fully okay?" Words not said mean as much as those used in a crisis.

"Agents are bringing Frances to the safe room. She'll check out Noah, Phoebe, and David before caring for the invader." Lao appeared on the monitor.

My anxiety slipped down a few notches. "Thanks. Will you issue an all clear?"

He flipped switches on the safe room control panel, the monitor image became clearer. We could see Phoebe move next to Noah. David, clearly agitated, spoke with an agent. "Not yet," Lao said. "Not until we have our unwanted guests secured."

Ahlmet struggled against agents attempting to place cuffs on his wrists. Obscenities flowed over the monitors. Phoebe sank to her knees, hands covering her ears. This time she did not moan, but shrieked as his mind control dominated her will.

I turned off the monitor, but Andrew flipped it back on. Living on an agricultural estate, Faith had seen a fair share of messy accidents, but this was the first time she witnessed violence against people she loved.

"Andrew, let's get down there." Faith grabbed his arm.

He didn't smile, didn't minimize the situation. "Until Lao issues the all clear, we're contained in this building." Phoebe struggled to sit up, brought her knees to her chest, and rested her head. The agent examining Noah's ankle turned and asked her a question, but Phoebe brought both hands over her head and rocked.

"Twedt's recommending tough psychological training to minimize the impact of these attacks." Milan rejoined us, shared the only intervention anyone suggested through the past twenty-four hours. "If Ahlmet or his sponsors don't volunteer to neutralize the implant, nanotech surgery may be an alternative. Possibly at Mayo or in Washington, D.C."

As Phoebe continued rocking, Faith grew agitated. Although too mature for easy comforting, I put my arms around her, nuzzled a kiss into her hair. She inhaled deeply, accepted my touch, then pulled away.

"Lao, where is Ahlmet?" In the safe room, Lao walked to the monitor to answer.

"On his way to a containment environ near the lower cherry orchard. Sector 128 of the monitor network. We've set up an electron field. Anything else?"

"Can we join you? Me, Milan, Andrew, and Faith."

"Bren is at the building walkway. He'll escort you. Follow his directions."

Before we left I entered coordinates for Sector 128. Ahlmet, naked except for briefs and a bandage on one shoulder, was being led into a circle of beams. Guards stood in a square around the virtual cage. At the edge of the monitor a second circle entrapped Sadig who lay on his stomach, hands still bound behind his back. Hana sat apart. Ants, nasty biting types we had not seen in Minnesota before, had been troublesome in that section of the orchard this growing season. I didn't want to think Lao knew that and had purposefully set the three in such a place, but said nothing.

Our steps, even in indoor footwear, sounded noisy through the empty halls of Ashwood. Minus people and activity, the smell of Terrell's morning coffee floated through more rooms than usual. The cats raced from sunlit perches, loud meows suggesting something amiss. We walked past Paul's door, a security beam still blocking entrance.

"Mr. Paul asked what the hell is going on," Bren shared. "Otis says your father-in-law is having a good morning, but worried about what he isn't being told."

"Best to leave telling of the story to David," I answered. "Paul knows when I am skipping details, but David knows how to work his father."

Faith gave me a look that suggested this information was unnecessary at this time. Andrew moved ahead, anxious to be at Phoebe's side I suspected. Down the back stairs we flowed, Bren leading at a comfortable pace for all but Milan, whose stiff leg made him trail even farther behind than usual for an elderly desk-bound bureaucrat. Through the sunny lower level hall we moved. Andrew passed Bren as we entered the underground section and sprinted to the safe room's entrance. We passed Lao who gave clearance for David, Phoebe, and Noah to move into the residence after Frances completed her assessments.

In a now familiar scene, Frances crouched next to Phoebe administering a sedative. Andrew knelt, his arms encircling Phoebe. From her stiffened back to locked arms and clenched jaw, she appeared more wire-like than human.

Noah leaned against a wall, the pallor of his face hinting at serious discomfort. Faith rushed to her father for the assurance of a hug. I smiled at him over her head.

"How bad is it?" I asked Noah. A temporary splint offered minimal protection. "Worse than the soccer injury when you were a teenager?"

"I didn't pass out this time." His voice, a more polished version of David's, was reedy. "Could still do that at any moment. I think it's broken. Dr. Frances wants a scan to be sure."

"Want the wheelchair brought down from Grandpa's room?"

The fact that he considered the idea told that his pain was deep. "I can't do steps."

"We'll do a human lift," Bren offered.

Phoebe settled against Andrew's chest, her mind no longer in control of her body's response. Frances checked Noah, asking broader questions about his time held by Ahlmet as she manipulated the ankle. Fortunately the only physical contact the two had was a savage rugby style kick to Noah's ankle once in the safe room. She administered a strong painkiller then checked David's upper shoulder where he absorbed a solid right slice while charging at Ahlmet. The area would be tender for days, but merely bruised.

Andrew and I supported Phoebe who moved like a zombie, her thin body heavy against ours. Frances, confirming the possibility of broken bones, approved Bren's human transport for Noah. No one spoke as we traced our way back to the residence.

Twedt and Raima left after giving Phoebe the news about her leave, but Milan took over the clean conference room for intense negotiations concerning one of the nation's brightest citizens who sat in Sector 128 of our cherry orchard until a high security containment unit could be brought to Ashwood. The Bureau sent a transport for Hana who, while morally despicable, had done nothing illegal by releasing a citizen held by estate security.

Ironically, a medical expert in mental manipulation to support Phoebe waited for entrance to Ashwood while the security containment unit team's credentials were reviewed. Ahlmet's attacks increased regardless of the precautions placed around him. Access to her suite was limited to a few of us in small time segments.

Frances was requisitioned from Community Health to spend the majority of her time monitoring Phoebe's treatment, and treatment of Noah's ankle. By noon, the daily work of Hartford, Ltd., was back on track including reports on Deshomm's latest tactics and our counter actions. In the background, Paul began a new phase of his slow fade by asking to remain in bed.

My mother would have called this multi-tracking of life crazy making. No other words better described how the daily trek of agriculture marched forward regardless of the life or death of its caretakers. No better description could be used when David and I looked out at where Milan maintained one of the nation's Intellectual Corps in a small cell surrounded by regional guards on the land surrounded by ripening fruit. I negotiated the issues facing my corporation in marathon hologram meetings until late afternoon, muting the sound for updates on Paul's status every half hour.

When I went to bed, my mind traveled over convoluted trails of mis-remembered history and current events to hold me in the middle of wakefulness and sleep. David settled between the sheets and began gentle rhythmic snoring before I could find a firm place in my pillow. Counting backward from eight hundred fifty six, a number chosen randomly, I lost track of my place over and over. After an hour, after the third useless mental exploration of what might happen to Phoebe if Ahlmet's tyranny continued, I pushed back my covers to get up. Hot tea, a boring book, staring at the moon were better alternatives than trying to sleep with an over-stimulated mind churning all that was frightening in my immediate world.

"Where you going?" David's hand settled on my ribs, the first snooze of the night slowing his words. "You're too tired to go wandering around. Nothing you can do for Dad or Phoebe or anything in your busy brain."

His palm, almost the size of my hand, rested atop my shirt. When he was away, I missed the comfort of that touch. Tonight I felt more restrained by the weight, the stretch of his fingers around my side. I lay still, hoping he'd fall back to sleep and lose track of my presence. Instead he tugged me closer, moved his hand to rub my back then widened his circle to touch my breast. In the new quiet of my mind I settled as he nuzzled my neck then kissed my ear.

We made love in a quiet, slow way that comforted without words or groans or serious dissembling of the covers. In the midst of all that disoriented the immediate world, love's rhythm of chaos and calm brought us back to the simple reality of David and Anne. Letting go of worrying about Milan's high level negotiations, Ahlmet's presence, Phoebe's terror, Paul's dying for those few minutes gave me permission to rest and be ready for the next day.

Chapter Twenty-Two

I SLEPT FOR A FEW HOURS, the top of my head touching David's shoulder, until a communicator pulsed me awake. David rolled away, clutching covers in one hand. I eased from the bed. Milan's voice propelled me from dull to full alert.

"Sorry to wake you." Milan sounded more like Paul. "Not a lot has been done for Phoebe, but the Bureau is sending a transport for Ahlmet. He'll be back in Chicago for his breakfast."

"Dr. Twedt said direction via Ahlmet's implant would eventually destroy Phoebe." I paced our closet floor, four steps one direction and back. "With him here, Lao has been able to minimize the attacks. The Bureau is willing to put her life at risk."

"Annie, keep a cool head. There are big outside players pushing against the Bureau's decision makers." A door opened, china clinked on his side of the conversation. "I missed dinner so I'm eating before Ahlmet's transport arrives. Mine will be close behind."

Suddenly I couldn't face him leaving, knowing I wouldn't see him again until Paul's memorial service. The regular breezes of change had become threatening, straight-line winds tugging at the roots of our family.

"Stay until breakfast and tell me what you've learned. You can go back in the estate's transport." Unprotected from my daylight filter words came out rushed, emotional. "Please, Milan, just a few hours."

"It's too late to cancel my ride."

"Lao told me Sadig is going to be processed by the regional police instead of the FBI. We'll use the transport sent for you to deliver him to their offices. They'll be pleased to pull their officers from Ashwood early."

"Anne, the transport is being sent for me. It's not equipped for a prisoner."

"We've provided a safe haven for you. You can find a way to spend another two or three hours. I'll be at your door in five minutes." I pulled clothes from the shelves as I spoke, hung up and carried everything to the bathroom for a quick clean up.

On my way light shining out from beneath Phoebe's door stopped me. I knocked quietly.

Leaving Ashwood

Frances opened the door, her hair squashed from a pillow, a long jacket covering pajamas. She did a double take at the sight of me wearing daytime clothes at three o'clock in the morning. "Is everything okay, Annie?"

"I'm on my way to see Milan and noticed lights. How's Phoebe?"

She stepped back into the room and gestured for me to follow. Phoebe, curled in the fetal position, lay still in the middle of the bed.

"I gave her a sedative." Frances rubbed the back of her own head. "The consultant's techniques are helpful, but she's exhausted. The last hour was pretty horrific. I sent Andrew to bed and I'm going to nap here until Amber relieves me."

"You've got a family, Frances. After I talk with Milan, I'll stay with Phoebe."

A yawn stretched her small face as Frances shook her head. "We've got a plan. If anything changes, I'll call you." She shooed me toward the door. "By the way, I was in the residence to make an adjustment in Paul's oxygen when Phoebe called me."

Moving through the night security protocols to Milan's command post, I wondered if the time to move Hartford, Ltd., from Ashwood was approaching. We could move to the metro and spend weekends here. Or, I could move to the metro weekdays and let David manage Ashwood.

Paul's slow disintegration opened the emotional suitcase where I kept the memories of what was lost or past. At just after three in the morning, the darkened heavens held more assurance than dawn's unknown. The heaviness of my soul's age slowed each step and thought.

Milan, wearing the loose tie-waist pants and long-sleeve shirt of Ashwood's field staff, looked like a man who had not slept for many days. A pair of wire-frame glasses balanced across his skull. Grooves on the bridge of his nose suggested these also were borrowed. When I looked into his face, I remembered Milan as an early middle-aged man in a dark blue suit, felt the strong arms of my father-in-law surround me on my wedding day, heard my children laugh in the sweet tones of youth.

"Come in." As he stepped back, I looked at his feet expecting his usual well-crafted shoes and saw instead a pair of sandals made this winter for Paul that arrived too late to be needed. "Would you like a cup of tea or glass of water?" Milan asked unaware of painful windows opening and closing in my heart.

"Nothing, thank you." I noticed he had tidied the room and packed his briefcase. The dress suit he wore on arrival hung in a garment bag from David's old travel gear. "Not many have seen you dressed in field worker clothes." Had the circle moved another quarter turn during the depression either of us could have spent our years dressed in similar uniforms.

Milan, the executive bureaucrat, didn't respond to the comment. Despite the hour, this conversation was business.

"Ahlmet's transport arrives in approximately twenty minutes. The second one will be fifteen minutes later. I won't leave until he departs." He pushed aside his plate and utensils before pulling out chairs at the room's small table. "Lao is handling Ahlmet's transfer to the Bureau crew, which leaves us a half hour to talk." The glasses slipped, settled an inch above his silver eyebrows. He pushed them back to the crown of his head. "That's time enough for me to update you and talk about what is on your mind."

We sat. Milan drained a glass of water. City dwellers treasured the sweet taste of our unpolluted drinking water.

"This is a story as old as the hunger for power in our country. Ahlmet has become the brain trust of the defense sector. Imagine armies implanted with brain controllers to overrule basic survival instinct. While Phoebe is a possible savior of the world with her work on water, the men with missiles still trump our environment."

He held out his glass, looked at water droplets instead of me. "The military industrialists are rich and feel certain they own everything necessary to protect themselves and their people from impediments like continued global warming. They have bunkers the size of mansions in places off the maps of most governments and underground growing sites protected from tornadoes or drought. They will defend the government bankrolling Ahlmet's work on technology U.S. citizens would protest."

Milan's assessment presented no surprises. I declined most business opportunities with military ties. Our organic vegetables and high quality grains were not raised for officers' tables. It was a tricky strategy in a more robust world economy where corporations bought up other corporations and few raw goods moved directly from farm to consumer. Dodging the five-hundred-pound gorilla called Deshomm could have serious business implications. Our fields could suffer mysterious overnight rot, our financial accounts become unavailable, key managers might disappear.

"Do you ever want out, Milan?" He danced with more gorillas and devils in his career than I could imagine. "Don't you want to have lunch with your wife and enjoy what's left of life? Navigating through this corruption must get old."

"That's a separate discussion. We need to talk about Phoebe." One hand tapped the table, short imperfect nails topping fingers wrinkled with age. He could have used anti-aging creams, one of my indulgences. I told myself I needed to stay more youthful as Hartford's leader in the commercial world where executives freely used surgical, medical or chemical means to defy age.

"Frances described Phoebe's last few hours as pretty horrific. How do we save David's daughter? Isn't it possible to disable this implant or remove it? Would that damage Ahlmet's research?"

We were both wired and tired—not the best state for people of our ages in a serious discussion. Milan leaned his elbows on the table, extended one hand to touch my arm. I knew he had bad news.

"There are complications." In the old economy, doctors had these kinds of conversations with patients' families in small rooms away from the treatment areas. "Ahlmet's device is in a very early experimental stage. The only implant he's attempted is the one in Phoebe, which violated every human testing protocol. His sponsors are reluctant to have it extracted before more data is collected. A surgeon could damage the device."

"So Phoebe sues for violation of the human testing protocols." I raised my eyebrows. "The media will have a field day. Mind control always riles the crowds."

"It's not that simple, Annie."

"And I'm asking you to be Phoebe's guardian, not just a Bureau rep, and make it that simple."

"They'll say she agreed to the implant. That they were lovers and supported each other's work." He paused, waited for me to accept the story. "Phoebe is her biological mother's daughter and has a reputation for mood swings and some unusual behavior. That will become part of the discussion."

The sound of transports in the courtyard distracted us. I moved to the window to watch Ahlmet, surrounded by security agents, walk from the business offices to the largest vehicle.

"Interesting," Milan said in the quiet. "An armored transport. They must believe communications were intercepted and Ahlmet is at risk traveling. I wonder why they didn't air lift him."

The other vehicles waited. "If one of the other transports is for you, at least your ride back would be safe."

He checked his communicator and shook his head. "My ride is thirty minutes out."

"If you don't have a jet to catch, please let us send Sadig back on your transport and stay a while." I sensed consideration. "Shouldn't you talk personally with Phoebe?"

Ahlmet looked back at the residence before ducking into the transport. His hands were still bound in front, an odd security contraption snugged up to his throat. Unpleasant words appeared to be exchanged between Ahlmet and an agent approaching him with additional restraints. An Ashwood guard escorted Hana to the convoy from a sleeping dorm.

"He's being treated as a criminal. Horrid to think that all will be forgiven when he gets back into his lab. Glad to see that cares leave as well. Strange person." I turned away from the window, hoped Ahlmet hadn't disturbed Phoebe's rest during his exit. "Stay. Phoebe needs your guidance."

"There's an event in Minneapolis that has leased all licensed transports later in the day."

"Andrew or David will drive you." I hugged him when he capitulated then contacted Lao about sending Sadig in the next vehicle.

Back at the table Milan rested against his chair. "To be honest, Annie, I'm stumped about where to push next. There are key federal contacts who can influence decisions more than the outside players. You didn't hear this from me, but the lab structure needs a shake up. This might be the action that causes change."

We talked about staffing issues facing the Intellectual Corps and the possibility of the government re-instating mandatory assignment of a small set of genetically managed children. The Stolen Children case started by Paul and Sarah abolished that, but bureaucrats and research-driven multi-corps hungered for a captive resource. Buoyed by coffee and fatigue, we found our way back to Phoebe.

At four forty, Frances called to ask if Milan could visit with Phoebe. As we left, the transport originally scheduled to arrive a half hour earlier pulled into the courtyard. The driver got out to stretch and explain the delay.

"There was some problem with the vehicle before I left Minneapolis and they replaced something. Then the regional police kept me from making up time." He spoke with a slight Chinese accent. "Some big criminal had been dragged out of the estates so the squads are trying to get back to their coordinates. Had to watch my speed."

The guy had no idea he was talking to one of the top regional Bureau executives as he ran his mouth to a man dressed in common clothes. Lao shook hands with the regional security agent riding with Sadig. They climbed into the transport. Milan, Lao and I walked to the residence. Clouds moved across the sky, the air had a heavy feel.

"We'll have someone ready to drive you back at seven." Lao tipped his head before speaking, still respectful of old estate protocol. "I'll walk with you to Phoebe's quarters. Frances had a concern about lights flickering."

"I'll come along." I wasn't expected in the office for hours.

Milan smiled, a slight lifting of tired lips. "Give me a half hour with her. If Phoebe stays at Ashwood for the medical leave, we'll need both of you to talk about logistics."

"But I love her and want to offer comfort," I wanted to protest. "Of course," is what I did say.

A look passed between the two. Milan placed an arm around me. "Phoebe does ask for you. While Ahlmet was close and, until this consultant could work with her, there were security issues that limited access." He released his hold. "Family, particularly you and Andrew, keep this woman holding on for the future."

"Thank you." I stepped aside and watched them head to Phoebe's quarters. There were days I thought of all the children and adults who walked this hall and felt the satisfaction of creating a safe haven. With Paul's decline, there were more days I saw the ghosts of children and adults who no longer walked on this earth. My mother had called this the growing awareness of those who had passed the curse of middle age.

An old Bible remained on the main foyer shelves along with a ledger listing the dates every child and adult arrived and left Ashwood. My mother-in-law kept careful records including each resident's birthdates and day of death. Throughout her Ashwood years, Sarah would bring a new worker to the foyer table on their first day and enter their name and data. Her ledger served as the estate's family tree when completed with babies and marriages. With labor now a commodity contracted by governments to corporations, Sarah's personal touch had an antique quality.

"Anne, are you all right?" Terrell surprised me as the old grandfather clock that once chimed in David's great-grandparent's home began chiming five times. "Frances says Paul and Phoebe had rough nights. How long have you been up?"

"I was thinking of Sarah. I spoke with Frances about an hour ago." Tired as the real day started, I hooked an arm through his. "Let's have our morning coffee. We're taking Frances from your house. Who is watching the twins?"

"They spent the night with Magda and her new puppy."

"I remember when our boys convinced Paul that we should have a dog." Terrell puttered with mugs and cream while I talked. "Remember Rufus as a puppy? I swear Paul found that dog in a cornfield. Oddest looking mutt."

We settled at the table. Laborers already milked cows, began the day's crops work. We talked about our past, Terrell countering my sad mood with positive stories and easier memories. The conversation moved to the coming day, but as I responded to Terrell's suggestion about hiring of a new food marketing person, my communicator began pulsing emergency with a rhythm that could only be stopped by one action.

"Get to the safe room." Terrell took my coffee. "Go."

"We don't have a drill planned for this week." I hesitated, but he led me from the kitchen, through the empty hall, down the stairs. Ahead of us, Lao accompanied Milan and Phoebe.

"Wait for Anne." Terrell's voice carried along the tiled corridor. "Anyone else you need?" We hurried to cover the distance.

"The transport sent to pick up Milan exploded minutes ago at the end of the estates regional roadway." Lao activated the safe room entrance. "We have orders for maximum protection of Milan and Phoebe. Anne can join them or return upstairs."

"If I go in the safe room am I in for the duration?"

Lao nodded. "Orders will come from the Bureau. Could be hours or days."

"You have Grandpa and Faith to think about, Mom." Phoebe sounded like a research director making a key staffing decision. "Milan and I will keep each other company. I'll stream some of my research and do quiet work." She reached for me around Terrell. Her father's daughter looked out through calm, if tired, eyes. Neither of us supported the other as we hugged.

"I love you, Mom," she whispered then placed a kiss near my ear.

"And I love you, Phoebs." I squeezed her once more. "I'll know you're safe." I hugged Milan as well. "You, too."

Chapter Twenty-Three

THEY DISAPPEARED BEHIND a blank false wall. Terrell, Lao, and I turned away.

"Now what happens?" The threat against Milan surprised me. If it happened before, he never mentioned the risky side of his life.

Lao stopped for a communicator conversation. Terrell and I gave him space by walking to the first window. Once trees filled this area, but a security audit recommended returning to grass and low flowers. David had jokingly suggested a moat.

Minutes passed and I had the patience level of most executives. Lao held up a hand, signaling we should wait. I hoped he had permission to open the safe room. Terrell and I talked about Sadig and the regional security agent in the transport. I told him about the driver's comments to Milan including his original delay about something wrong with the vehicle. We thought of Sadig's wife and children. Finally Lao joined us.

"Tell me that was an all clear." I said.

"No such luck." Lao checked his communicator. "Bureau protocols need to be implemented. Security specialists should be in the courtyard by the time we get upstairs." He glanced at his communicator. "Bureau staff are talking with Sadig's family."

Our former security chief's wife, children, and mother were moving out of a small house on Ashwood. Their children would finish the quarter and regional competency exams in the estate school before they fully transferred to Minneapolis.

"I'll visit them later this morning. Maybe we can be of help." Used to problem solving, I moved to thoughts about extending their residence.

"Stay away." The two words from Terrell came with a harsh warning. "That family was bitter about the dismissal. They say you didn't respect Sadig's corporate experience and wouldn't listen to his ideas. In his brothers' opinion, you were wrong to let him go."

"I understand they only know Sadig's side of the story, but surely his arrest with weapons on Ashwood's property proved we'd made the right decision."

Terrell looked forward, not at me, as he responded. "His brothers say Sadig accepted Ahlmet's offer because he was desperate to make money to pay the kids' tuition for private school in Minneapolis." He cleared his throat. "Something showed up in an employment check. Nothing related to Ashwood, but bad."

"We scrubbed every part of his background before Ashwood hired him," Lao interjected. "He had a clear record and solid recommendations. He was hacked."

"Shit." My response wasn't subtle. Three people were dead because of malicious data, probably a scribbler paid by Ahlmet who would be stepping back into his lab with the full protection of corporate investors or the U.S. military within a few hours. "Can you find out more, Lao? I'm not sure what I want to do with the information, but I'd like to know."

"We really did do a thorough screening routine before hiring him." Lao answered.

"I'm curious who might have wanted to trash Sadig's future. Maybe they're connected to the transport explosion." Milan's cautions about the power of Ahlmet's supporters didn't stop me from wanting to know the extent of the scientist's transgressions. He posed a number of threats to my friend, my family, and our business.

"What actions do we need to take to secure Hartford, Ltd., and our families?"

As we climbed to Ashwood's main level, Lao shared the plans formulated during the last fifteen minutes including the Bureau's protocols.

At the top of the stairs, the normal early morning activities had started, except this morning my sons walked to the dining room shoulder-to-shoulder, a sight not witnessed at Ashwood for many years. Noah leaned on crutches.

"Good morning, Mom," John said. "We're on our way to meet Dad and Faith for early breakfast. Dad needs to be out of here by seven to drive Milan back to the cities. If we can find Phoebe, we can have a grand gathering."

Lao tipped his head before leaving. "Tell them what you know. Everyone will need to sign confidentiality contracts. Nothing goes beyond immediate family." He promised to keep me in the communication loop then left with Terrell.

"Tell us what?" Noah asked.

"Wait till we're together." Walking in with my sons raised conflicting feelings of the comfort of their nearness and worry that they were in danger by being at Ashwood. The men would accept the tough news of the transport's explosion, but I worried about Faith. Sadig's death would upset her terribly. She sat next to David, his arm wrapped over the back of her chair as they spoke. Faith smiled when she saw her brothers and jabbed David with an elbow.

"Good morning." One night of good sleep restored David's energy. "Grandpa had a rugged night, but ate a decent breakfast." He stood, pulled out a chair next to him. I shook my head and pointed to the chair next to Faith. "I told him you'd visit later. What time did you get up?"

"Three. I will visit him right after we eat." The guys waited for information about Lao's warning. Andrew picked up the coffee carafe and offered to pour. His brothers accepted. I noticed an artificial brightness in Noah's eyes and assumed his injury required pain meds.

He caught me looking his way and asked, "So what's up? You and Lao are dirt serious for this hour of the day. Maybe all those transports coming and going kept you awake?"

"Actually two awful things happened before you were awake this morning. I suspect they might be connected." I took a breath. "The first transport Noah heard took Ahlmet to the cities then back to Chicago. He left here in restraints, but will be freed at work. Milan faced incredible resistance from defense corporations supporting Ahlmet's work and was forced to release him. That brings no relief to Phoebe." I stopped at that point, saved the fine points for a private conversation with David and Andrew.

Faith raised her right hand to her mouth, the gold of David's mother's sixteenth birthday ring gleaming against her faintly tanned skin. Blue eyes, narrowing in thought, announced the gesture was not to be confused with timidity or fear.

"God damn frigging idiots." Noah exploded as he sent a spoon across the table.

"Keep your voice down," I cautioned. "This is not for widespread knowledge."

"It will be when I leave this room. I'll get it to the media." Noah began pushing away from the table. "Can't you see what Ahlmet's discovery could be in the wrong hands? A world of those who control and those are literally controlled."

"There's more." John stood to encourage Noah's return to his chair. I waited. David's communicator pulsed. He looked down then back to me. "A second transport arrived shortly after four thirty for Milan. Because Phoebe wanted to see him, we sent that vehicle out with Sadig and a guard. The transport blew up before leaving the estates region shortly before five."

None of the adults expected survivors of such an explosion. The reality that it could have happened within Ashwood shook me. Many people could have been hurt or killed.

"Milan and Phoebe are in the safe room and under Bureau protection. Obviously there is suspicion that someone connected to Ahlmet wanted Milan out of the way."

"How badly were Sadig and the others injured," Faith asked.

"They didn't survive." I put the words in our midst with respect.

"What about his children?" Tears sharpened the surprised question of the one still living as a child. "We need to go to them."

"We're advised to stay away from Sadig's family. His brothers have let it be known that they feel he was wronged by Hartford."

Our daughter leaned forward. "Why did you fire him, Mom?"

"Sadig resigned after the sabotage that shut down our energy system along with the break in at Giant Pines and hacking of our communications systems. I accepted his decision."

"I heard you let him go because Lao came begging for his old position and Hartford didn't want to pay two big salaries." She remained focused on my face.

"Actually I had to talk with Lao for hours to convince him to return. He, in turn, helped Sadig locate a new position, but clearance issues still developed. That's about all I know." I returned her focus.

"Faith, your mother was faithful to Sadig for two years," David said. "The job was too big for him. He left your mother unprotected and Hartford, Ltd., vulnerable. I would have fired him."

"But Sadig didn't have to be treated like a criminal or die," she protested. "Aren't you upset?

"Yes, I am upset," I said. "The hard truth is that he became a criminal when he joined Ahlmet in attacking Hartford and Phoebe. He injured two regional security agents, which carries federal penalties. But, I agree with you that the men who died were good people."

I stopped, picked up my water glass and noticed my hand was shaking. Others noticed as well. "Which is why I'm even more angry that Ahlmet will be back in his lab this morning as if nothing's wrong. And the people who support him will walk away with blood on their hands, but no punishment."

Faith pushed from the table. "I'm going to their house to help. They're my friends."

David put a hand on her arm. "No. Sadig's wife will want her own family." Faith looked doubtful. "Trust me. That's human nature. Family first."

Settled back in her chair, Faith's eyes filled with unshed tears. I turned in my chair to move closer. No one at the table spoke as a young worker delivered toast, fruit, and scrambled eggs.

"I suggest you all eat," David said. "This could be an unpredictable day."

"Will we have school?" Faith shook her head as each food passed. "We're supposed to have practice exams."

Her brothers served themselves and passed each item back to Faith. Andrew reached across me to place raisin toast on her plate. "Nothing interfered with course schedules when we were in gifted school. You can do well on those exams if you narrow your focus. Some day you'll be facing bigger issues with only a wrapper of artificial food to fill your stomach. Eat."

With parents who once knew starvation, our kids knew the value of food.

Chapter Twenty-four

THE TRUTH OF THE TRANSPORT EXPLOSION remained confidential for twenty-four hours and a society with a reputation for media transparency believed faulty vehicle repair triggered a dramatic fireball that caused one fatality.

Those of us who knew the truth understood the oaths of confidentiality we signed carried serious penalties. Sadig's family left in a Bureau transport while we were at breakfast. Hired packers removed the last of their belongings long before lunch. Faith was excused from school and spent the morning with Andrew. No communications were allowed to Milan or Phoebe in the safe room except through Lao. David and I prowled the residence and offices like relatives outside an operating suite.

My visit with Paul added to the day's darkness. His bad night sparked minor dementia. He asked about Sarah, then corrected himself, then asked again. I steered our conversation to talk about Phoebe and Andrew, but Paul couldn't remember that his granddaughter was at Ashwood. Then we began talking about restructuring Hartford, Ltd., and he reached for my hand.

Folding my fingers around his, as thin as lilac twigs and much more fragile, I remembered his hands pulling a calf from a laboring cow, muscle and tendons showing under weathered skin. He could fix anything with those strong farmer digits or gently clean a child's scratch. I resisted my natural instinct to rub my thumb over the back of his hand so as not to irritate the tissue-thin covering.

"Never let land get away from the family, Annie." Birdsong could cover the sound of his voice. "Governments may come and go, but new land will never be made. Hold on to what you've earned."

I used to challenge him with the legal reality that the very right to own this land had been given by the government. Unlike my father-in-law, I knew the government could take land. The suburban acre my parents once owned had evaporated into farm fields without a penny changing hands. When the depression deepened, the government gave each landowner a choice of shelter in the cities. Nobody stayed in the suburbs because nobody was allowed to stay.

"Giant Pines will be under John's direction when we are finished with restructuring." I told him a half-truth. "Don't worry."

"If you want to go over your plans, you can use me as a sounding board." Another miscued loop began in Paul's lost sense of time. "Maybe you need to get back to the office and Phoebe could visit. She was too busy yesterday to stop in."

There was no reason to point out that he hadn't seen Phoebe for almost three days. "Let's hope she'll be able to sneak in a visit later," I offered. His brow creased as if concentrating on the meaning of my words took full attention. "I do have to get back to work." I lightly closed my fingers around his hand, as much physical pressure as he could stand. "You could use a nap."

He nodded, eyes closing and lips pressing together. This time when I kissed his forehead, I truly thought it might be the last. "See you later. I love you."

Chapter Twenty-five

THE MULTI-CORPS WORLD crawls through all hours of all days, grabbing small pieces of all that is vulnerable while the lights are off. The professionals Hartford, Ltd., engaged found every minuscule crack to stage lightning attacks and diminish Deshomm's hunger for our business. While armed guards and virtual agents protected the lives of Milan and Phoebe, Hartford's hired professional forces built brilliant virtual offensive and defensive strategies against our corporate enemy.

Deshomm's global reach, while almost impossible to untangle, played to our advantage. A number of Hartford's businesses carried national security status that required no entanglement with foreign governance. Obscure and outdated policy prohibited acquisitions that could shrink market competition. Reviewing the risks of building our strategy on a handful of similar significant legal barriers to Deshomm's hostile takeover and exercising careful message management about their involvement in the energy grid vandalism, I set Hartford's hired guns against Goliath.

With blazing speed, Deshomm offered to drop their action in exchange for the opportunity to purchase Giant Pines including all livestock and lands as well as technology or expertise necessary to maintain production at the current levels. Jaws dropped at the purchase price offered.

Including transfer of all technology and expertise in their offer indicated Deshomm's intention to shut down Hartford, Ltd., Raima and I hooted at the terms of the deal that displayed our opponent's ignorance of the change in status of Giant Pines from agricultural production to a protected research foundation twenty-four hours earlier.

Celebration of the first success ceased when our communications consultants discovered a Deshomm press story scheduled for release shortly before the midday news cycle announcing acquisition of Great Pines. A Hartford, Ltd., "manager," a supervisor in the egg washing facility, was quoted as the source that announced that Max would be presented as the new general manager. Such brassy misrepresentation edged up the stakes. Customers could be spooked, employees willing to accept competitors' job offers. The multi-corps frequently drove small business owners to bankruptcy through deal negotiations before purchasing whatever they wanted at ridiculous prices.

Our staff at Giant Pines deserved to know the truth before the media carried Deshomm's story. I needed assurance Max had not abdicated from Hartford, Ltd.,

"Everything still locked down?" Max skipped the nicety of a greeting. "Lao came by early this morning. Don't know that either of us had seen the Bureau put down that many restrictions. I've got a team working just on vendor deliveries and local suppliers' access. Not easy."

Regular work crews were busy in the orchards outside my office window. Young men with shaved heads, young women with elaborate braids on one part of their skulls and bare skin on other parts. As far as I could see, laborers wearing our field gear dotted the trees. The morning looked normal.

"We're doing our best to keep a normal work day here, Max." I tried my communicator and found some bands blanked out. "Has anyone from Deshomm invited you out for dinner lately?"

"There've been a number of invites, but I'd rather eat with rats. What's it all about, boss?"

I swiveled back to my desk. "I'm letting the Bureau take care of the security situation so I can keep my eye on Hartford, Ltd., A lot is happening and I need to speak with you and critical staff members this morning."

"Bring me up to speed."

Max had a right to know, but I wondered if our communications lines had become porous. "Let me get back to you after I talk with Lao."

"Before you go, how's Paul? We got guys here who ask about him every morning."

"He's holding his own, Max. I was just with him. Weak, sleeping a lot, but talked with me about the importance of Giant Pines this morning."

"Tell him we pray for him every night." Max and his wife, old-fashioned Christians, led an evening prayer service at Giant Pines. I was surprised that many of the crew participated. Ashwood's meditation session drew few young people from the same workforce.

"Thanks, Max. Give me five and I'll be back." For once, I didn't ask for information about production. Crops and animals would continue to exist without my attention.

"Lao." I searched for him across our communications lines, but met only silence.

"Anne, there is a coded message for you on your communicator." Clarissa's calm tones broke through my concern about Lao's silence.

"Have you seen or heard from Lao," I asked. "I've tried every available line."

"He'll tell you more." She paused. "You have a few minutes now if you'd like to meet?"

"Yes. In my office." I heard her tell someone she was speaking with me. "Anything change in my schedule for the day?"

"I heard you had a very early morning so I pulled your end of day conference with Mr. Milan to immediately after lunch followed by the exec team. Materials you need are in your information file."

She would have continued, but I took her back to the conference with Milan. "I don't remember a conference with Milan. What's the agenda and who is the scheduler?"

"He requested the meeting personally around midnight. I spoke with his assistant this morning to confirm."

"Thank you, Clarissa."

In the doorway David waited for my attention. "You've been busy. Thanks for keeping me in the loop on Deshomm's games. I'd like to go to Giant Pines with you. I suppose it's too early to include John?"

"We're not ready to talk about organizational changes." I motioned for him to close the door before continuing. "Lao's on his way here. Communicators aren't working."

"That doesn't make sense."

"And Clarissa just confirmed a change of time in a conference with Milan who is supposedly in blackout in our safe room."

Lao knocked on the door and David let him in.

"Let me explain what's happening." He appeared hurried. "The Bureau closed all our middle band communications because they're vulnerable to outside listeners. They claim this is to monitor any chatter about Milan while keeping his escape confidential. Anyone who knows he is alive is virtually quarantined—not allowed to leave Ashwood—until more is known about who wants him dead." He stuffed a hand in his pocket, dragged out a small ring and handed it to me with a note: "Secure until the agencies clear out."

"Of course, the FBI would take charge of an investigation into the attempted murder of a federal official." David rolled his shoulders. "Not great that we're caught in the middle."

I slipped the ring on a finger. David watched, each reminded that government agencies frequently monitored our conversations.

"You were looking for me?" Lao finally asked.

"David and I need to talk with people at Giant Pines about a Deshomm story that will break on late-morning media. Is that possible?"

He shrugged. "I'll know better in the hour. Right now the FBI lead agent is telling the Bureau how Milan is going to be kept secure." Like kids we snickered at the thought of two such government titans in conflict. "I suspect the Bureau is talking about Phoebe's security as rationale for controlling Ashwood. I think we'll be free to carry on regular activities with the understanding that we not say anything about the transport explosion."

"Amen. I've got a few things to put together before we leave." David walked toward the door. "When do you want to leave, Annie?"

"Whenever Lao and Clarissa say go."

"The most powerful woman in Hartford, Ltd., is the one who controls this woman's calendar." David winked. "Let me know. If I'm not in my office, I'll be with Dad."

Lao moved to a chair after David left. "Milan will soon move to an FBI safe house. Ahlmet's corporate sponsors might not be privy to how high our friend sits in the federal world."

"What about Milan's wife? Isn't she in Duluth?"

"They haven't lived together for years. Of course they're still married, but work is his mistress." Lao sat back. "The wife works for an art studio in the metro area. They do share a family place in Duluth, but Milan lives in a Bureau apartment in the cities."

"That's sad. They were married before the economy tanked. I like her a lot."

But Lao never looked back unless seeking clues about the present. As I aged, I envied his pragmatic nature. He cut back to the present. "If you want to see Milan before the FBI moves him, you should go now. Phoebe is in her quarters."

"Thank you. Do I need clearance?" *In my own house*, I thought.

"You're on his approved contact list. I'll walk with you part of the way."

Amber coached a young worker on cleaning technique in the residence foyer. I recognized the boy as one pulled from gardening because of college potential. Attitude seemed to be blocking his ability to take instructions from an attractive woman. Dining room staff worked on lunch. Sounds of kitchen preparations carried to the central hall.

The door to Paul's rooms stood open, which suggested he was open for visitors. Beyond his quarters, the back stairs were seldom used. Twenty years ago child workers frequently ran up and down these steps with food supplies, laundry, to a quiet study hall or sickbay. Milan, wearing clothes I didn't recognize, leaned next to a window on the lower level and appeared lost in thought.

He was listening to a conversation, but smiled when holding up a hand to ask for silence.

Leaving Ashwood

"That's not going to work. You've got a difficult situation to resolve or others will find a solution."

I wouldn't want to hear those words from a man with a voice that challenged winter ice for coldness.

"We've covered all runway allowed for negotiations. Unless you relish charges of accessory to an attempted assassination behind your name, the next move is yours. You can finish these discussions with my appointee." He bent, rubbed at his healing leg.

I assumed the Bureau lab executive in Chicago wished he or she had not risen to quite this level where internal politics and external patrons rubbed together to ignite explosives under a vehicle hundreds of miles away. The vehicle supposedly carrying a higher-level government executive, someone that big people in Washington, D.C., valued higher than a lab executive.

"I'm sorry we dragged you into Phoebe's issue," I said when he turned to me.

One eyebrow rose. "I've never been out of Phoebe's life. Our nation's need for success of these bright young people is one of the president's priorities." He leaned back against the windowsill. "Supporting removal of Phoebe from the Bureau lab system has put me in a tough place. You don't need to understand all the ramifications. Just be aware that Phoebe's prediction that breaking her contract would be difficult is accurate." A yawn formed, he pressed his lips together tightly. The urge passed. "There's a middle ground, but you'll have to be open to government presence in Hartford, Ltd."

"Will you be okay? You seem more annoyed than concerned about this attempt on your life. How do your wife and girls feel about the danger?" I opened the door for him to talk about his family, to be truthful with me about his life.

"My daughters are married women with their own families. They care as much about my daily work as they did when they were teenagers. Unless this hits the media, they'll never know." He checked for time, looked puzzled. "My wife is safe. She worries because she is an anxious person by nature."

Nothing in his face suggested their lives were different than he wished. Governments could create legislation and economic incentives to force continued marital relationships, but the post depression world challenged such inventions.

"Your stability makes you a successful person, Annie." Milan looked up at Lao and nodded him away. "Paul and I have never talked about your kids or this bunker you made into a decent home. We talk about how Anne Hartford has the brains and resources to keep building this corporation into a more powerful entity closer to the top of the world where the air doesn't stink as much." The face he turned toward me demanded attention, his entire stance displayed cold dominance. "You fight like a survivor assuring no one pulls the rug out from under your cozy home. That's small-thinking behavior. It's time you leave Ashwood and take on important fights in the world."

Crossing his arms over his chest, Milan lowered his voice. "You and yours will never starve again, so after Paul passes, give your husband reins of this company and let him rule the family. This government is highly invested in your success. Don't be surprised if you're called to run something outside Minnesota."

Framed from behind by the arbor gate to our family pond, Milan epitomized a powerful executive. Although he rested against the window's sill, he didn't lounge but carried energy. Someone not involved in this conversation might think that he was snapping an order to an underling. Milan's dissatisfaction with my defined ambition was never so personal in the past.

"You have different ambitions for me than I do. Look at the Regan kids or the hundreds that have graduated from our school or the hundreds trained in Hartford's facilities and I call the government's investment repaid many times. That doesn't touch on the thousands fed by our production."

"Annie, you don't have ambition for yourself." He paused. "You only have one desire—keeping yourself and your family safe." He became the manager-teacher of our early years, and I felt like a star pupil unfairly chastised. "When you called for help with Phoebe, you didn't worry about how her mess could interfere with the Deshomm attack. You called as a mother. The whole Giant Pines re-incarnation isn't about growing Hartford, it's about making a logical safe haven for John and Phoebe. You are an excellent business person who frequently stops short of the fantastic deal because of your family."

"At least I had purpose in my life." Sight of the first food-deprived child in Ashwood's residence kicked me from emotionally numb to almost manically driven. "I'm not a government employee. I own a significant business. You don't get to make decisions about my future."

One hand rubbed at his chest as Milan listened. Concern toned down the annoyance or frustration that put me in an alert mode, knees locked and shoulders drawn back. I watched him rub a bit harder with his fingers, opened my mouth to ask how he was feeling.

"Annie, you just did it again. I'm pushing you to take a big step and you clicked into that caregiver mode as you watched my hand."

"What's your point, Milan? Why right now? You're under attack and you call this the right time to challenge me about what I've done with my life?"

He turned away, began speaking to another contact. I walked away, my time equally as important. Clarissa spoke in my ear; "We have clearance for a ten thirty meeting at Giant Pines. I'll notify Max. Do you want refreshments or is this a headlines only set up?"

"The latter, Clarissa, except for Max. I'll talk to him from the transport then need time with him after the employee meeting."

"Where are you now? Andrew's been waiting in your office. He asked for fifteen minutes." Her calm voice never questioned what she was telling me or implied she should know more.

"Tell him I'll be back in five minutes."

"Annie." Milan caught up. His hand settled on my shoulder. "We're not through talking."

I turned. "I have five minutes. Giant Pines employees need information. I have legal counsel reports to review for my afternoon." We were both tired and frustrated. "Is there something specific you want to say?"

"In the next few months I have promised a prominent investor the name of one person I think can transform his business. I'd like it to be yours. But, you have to want the challenge because it will be nothing like Hartford, Ltd."

"I need to know more than that to make a decision that would change many lives."

"You will. Think about it." He shrugged, once again an aging senior government official in borrowed clothes with too much to do. "And tell Lao he was partially wrong. Cheri and I are still very much married, even if this job is my mistress. Ugly as hell and totally dominating."

We laughed at the reality of everyone listening to everyone else's conversations. "I try not to be angry at you or whoever passed on that tidbit." My arms extended around his rounded shoulders. "Take care of yourself. You're welcome to our safe room any time."

"I'll try to return if Paul passes, but that might be out of my control."

"Milan, I doubt that much is truly out of your control."

"We'll be in touch about Phoebe." Milan patted my arm. "Keep David in on the discussions just in case."

"In case?"

"He becomes the new head of Hartford, Ltd."

"The walls listen, Milan."

"Yeah, that's what I'm told."

Chapter Twenty-Six

ANDREW RELAXED AT THE TABLE in my office, reading an old book from our library. He handled the bound edition with more respect than I suspect its first owner gave back in a time when books were common. The elementary classroom where I student-taught had nothing but books for the not very appreciative eight-year-olds. He rose as I walked in.

"Sorry I wasn't here," I started. "Clarissa wasn't on the short list of those in the know about Milan. I wanted to say good-bye before he left." I sat back in a chair and rested my hands on the edge of the table. "It's so great to have you all here. What's on your mind?"

"Faith." His hair looked shaggy, his eyes tired with worry about Phoebe. "Is this a bad time?"

"Busy, but not bad." I tuned down Milan's criticism, concentrated on my son.

"You know she wants to study law."

I indicated that I knew of her interest in becoming a lawyer. "We've spoken about it. The conversations haven't been very productive because we are concerned that corporate sponsorship of colleges dramatically reduces the quality of education."

"We agree on that, Mom. My graduate advisor is now a dean at McGill University in Montreal. The Canadian government doesn't condone corporate sponsorship. We've been communicating recently and I forwarded Faith's academic credentials. If Faith does well on their entrance exam, my advisor is willing to sponsor her in their blended program—some distanced learning, some residential-based. Probably take Faith about five years to be ready to stand for the bar."

"Would a McGill law degree be accepted in the United States?" Excitement for Faith studying at such a prestigious university pushed Milan from my thoughts. "The Canadians are so protective that we didn't consider Faith for their schools." Some economic facets like Canadian protection of jobs and borders resisted all kinds of global pressure.

"My father's family had a tradition of attending McGill. There's a scholarship program for high-achieving women funded by the Smithsons." He gave the information casually. "I offered to see what my brother might be able to do for her at a British college, but Ashwood is strong in her blood. She'd like to visit England, but wasn't keen on a trans-Atlantic commitment."

"And most of what I hear Faith talk about is getting away."

"She's a teenager." Andrew checked his communicator. "I offered her a trip to Montreal before I return to work. I assume she has travel credits available."

"Of course." The thought of our youngest moving from estate-school student to university candidate needed time to settle. "Thank you."

"My pleasure. She's my only sister and she keeps me connected with being young." He stood. "You've got a business to run and too many distractions. It's good to be of help."

"Right now I'm due to leave for Giant Pines. Ride with us?"

"Thanks for the invite, but I was asked to work with the students in conversational Chinese. The only thing more painful that learning how to speak Chinese is to listen to rookies plod through it."

David joined us. "You and Phoebe could talk your way around most of the globe with your knowledge of languages. We thought we were ready for the future by having a second or third language." He chuckled, then continued. "Unless you count your mom's ability to talk with foreign business people in educated Spanish and Ashwood's workers in American español."

STANDING IN THE MIDST of Giant Pines' sixty-person day shift, the melting pot workforce could be heard questioning Deshomm's goal and Ashwood's ability to stay intact. From Max's German accent to African-tinged English and urban slang, the crew spoke in a soup of mostly untaught languages with common understanding of words like continued employment, food allotments, funding for the Ashwood clinic, support of our estate education program.

That was where I began when Max and I sat in his office, a dish of fresh berries from Giant Pines between us on the table. Our crew valued berries as a seasonal treat. At least half of the metro population knew strawberry only as a chemical flavor or a dried particle in some mass-produced food.

"It is premature to be totally open with the employees about changes that are in the works for Giant Pines. I want to tell you what this part of Hartford, Ltd., will look like in the near future because you're important to that future and it is time to draw you into the new venture." With Max's full involvement critical in transitioning Giant Pines into a research and production facility as well as supporting John's development, I outlined how we would sidestep Deshomm's reach. Legalese was easy, but Max and John would have tough work ahead to sort through land use and all the operational implications.

"I don't know how we'll title your new role," I said as we wound down the discussion for that day. "It's not like you're giving up any responsibilities and you'll wear hats in both the estate side of the business as well as the research foundation. You say you feel you've been treated well from a compensation angle and I want to keep you feeling that way. So I suggest we talk about that in six months when we both have a better understanding. In the meantime, the human asset folks are supportive of putting a two-part bonus in place for your involvement in the planning and transition. Is that fair?" Max extended a hand and we shook.

I knew where David spent the time when I stepped into the transport for our trip home. "Is everything good with the herd?" I teased.

He nodded. "More important, how did Max react?"

"I wasn't concerned, but now I'm excited. He's got good ideas and is pleased to be a mentor for John." We notified security as we left Giant Pines. "It seems natural that you might stay on top of this effort?"

The Bureau escorted us back to Ashwood, which meant David could almost sleep in the driving seat, but his hands gripped the steering stick, and his jaw tightened. "It might not be good timing, Annie. There will be plenty to do when Dad passes and Phoebe's setup needs the attention of a research scientist."

Milan's last comment about preparing David to head Hartford, Ltd., sounded in my head at the lukewarm response.

"I'm executor of the estate," I reminded him, "and Phoebe might be better supported by someone who has current experience with research lab requirements." His lips pressed together. I chose to think that David wasn't able to think beyond his father's approaching death.

Chapter Twenty-Seven

PAUL DIED AT A RANCHER'S favorite time of day—in the quiet of early morning, not long before dawn. The time of day when he might have been sipping his first cup of strong coffee and walking to the barns.

The call came as I was washing my face. David was still sleeping, and I knew what Otis would say as soon as I heard his voice. "Mr. Paul just passed." He inhaled, a long wet sound. "I helped him sit up then went to get him a glass of water and when I returned he was gone. I'm very sorry, Ms. Anne."

I put down my washcloth, saw the tension muscles in my reddened face slacken. "Thank you, Otis, for everything you've done for Paul and the family these past months." He coughed on the other side, perhaps covering emotion. I pushed my own words out before sadness might choke them. "Please contact Dr. Frances while I tell David and the family."

"Will do. I'll comb his hair and shave him before everyone comes."

The rituals of death slipped over Ashwood. The return to economic stability gave us time for grieving. No more hasty disposal or abandonment of our loved one's remains. We would have our day of public mourning after Frances notified the officials.

"Mr. Paul and I had an agreement so you'd all remember him looking good." Otis remained loyal. "He thought everything of you. Thought you should be ruler of the world, I think he said."

"Thank you, Otis. I'll be there as soon as I wake David."

I drew the now cool cloth one more time across my face, washed away my tears. Quickly I brushed my hair and slipped on a soft shirt and linen skirt instead of my normal work clothes. In Paul's honor I inserted the South Dakota agate earrings he gave me to celebrate John's birth. The same earrings he gave each of his daughters-in-law.

David lay on his back in a state of semi-sleep, his way of easing into the day after I left bed. Before my asthma began, we would run together in the cool mornings three times a week. Now he ran alone.

"Honey." I touched his shoulder gently. "David, you need to wake up."

His eyes opened, a seamless transition from sleep to alert.

"Otis just called."

David pushed himself upright. "Dad?"

"He woke early and they spoke. He passed when Otis went for a fresh glass of water. No pain."

We had made the run from our room to Paul's many times in the past months. David sprinted ahead in his sleep clothes and I followed. Our bare feet thwacked against wood then tile floors. Frances would be on her way and Terrell would take responsibility for notifying people in Ashwood who needed to know.

At his father's door, David stopped and looked back for me. I held out my hand.

"I'm not ready for this." Sleep coated his early grief. David waited for assurance from me, an orphan for almost thirty years.

"We'll say good-bye together." I opened the door. Dawn's promise of sunlight came through partially open blinds.

Paul looked more like himself in death. His smooth face, still pale, no longer showed the struggle of breathing with a heart drowning in his body's fluid. His work-hardened hands rested along his sides. David touched one, his lips moving without sound. He lifted his fingers to smooth his father's hair. I stood at David's side, prayed for Paul's soul. Old religion brought simple comfort at the dark void of death.

"Did you call the kids?" David's eyes absorbed all that could be still be seen as living from his father's body.

"I wanted to give us time with him first."

"I would like it if they could be here." He reached for me, turned away from the bed and lowered his head to mine. "I'd like to stay with him. Just call them."

Frances knocked as she entered. "David, Annie, I'm so sorry."

"I'm going to tell the children in person." I kissed David's cheek and left.

The walk to the old manager's house was the longest distance to cover. I went there first to wake John and Noah. As I approached, I paged John, a light sleeper.

"It's Grandpa." His sleep-heavy voice didn't hesitate.

"Yes, about fifteen minutes ago. Dad's with him."

"Noah and I'll be there. Are you okay?"

"Sad."

I turned to the consultant quarters where Andrew was housed. As I walked up the stairs, I paged him.

"Mom?"

"Andrew, we're all gathering in Grandpa's room. He's gone." I heard Phoebe's gasp, stopped advancing.

"We'll be there in five." Andrew's words came clouded with Phoebe's emotional eruption.

"Of course, Andrew. I have to wake Faith."

Knocking on Faith's door, I waited for a greeting. She would be asleep at this time. I opened the door to her comfy small room. Daylight teased around the corners of her drapes. She slept so quietly her blankets looked untouched. At her side I took in all I could, knowing there were no assured future opportunities to capture the innocence my daughter still held while sleeping. Then I knelt at her side and broke the news.

David, Paul, Sarah, and I all raised the five adult children who stood around Paul's deathbed that morning. Andrew was the first to embrace David, two men now bound by their fatherless status. Noah, John, and Faith all hugged David with what looked like equal willingness to comfort and hunger to be comforted. Phoebe came to my side, put her wiry arms around my shoulders.

"I don't think I can bear this," she whispered near my ear. "You are the ground that keeps my feet steady, but Grandpa was the rock I need for strength and support." She smelled of coffee and the faint scent of the British soap Andrew received from his London-based half-brother. We stood together, arms around each other's bodies. "How are you, Mom?"

I couldn't answer. David, my fellow architect of a very good life, had held a difficult and demanding job. Being married to a frequently absent government intellectual worker meant I turned to Paul as a business confidante as well as father-in-law. I knew the world of bureaucrats and classrooms. Paul understood fields and barns and people who worked with their hands. Together we navigated the redevelopment of a free economy.

When my father died during my college years, I cried mostly out of fear of a future without his strength. Standing next to Paul's body, I grieved for what we'd lost. And something I could not name more elegantly than knowing that David and I were no longer young. A prediction Milan made when our children were young had come true—retired was a word that described old machinery, and we would all work until we died.

Phoebe leaned against me and I supported her weight, but emotionally I crumbled. Tears traveled from my eyes down my face, and I did nothing to hold them back. David moved Phoebe from my side so that he and I could be together. His hand gentled my back; I rested against his chest and quieted.

"Grandpa looks peaceful." Faith had moved near us. David stretched out an arm to bring her closer. "It's good to be with him and not hear him struggle to breathe." Her beautiful blonde hair draped down my arm. "I'll miss him."

THE REGAN EXTENDED FAMILY had used their travel allocations to visit Paul before he passed away so they would attend his memorial service via hologram in their South Dakota Catholic church. While David's older brother stood as patriarch for the South Dakota family branch, the scarcity of travel resources in the twenty-first century created two very separate Regan clans. On Ashwood Paul had stepped out of Hartford, Ltd., in his seventies, but it was hard to predict who would absorb the connective role he played in our family—both blood and extended.

The Death Society appeared within ninety minutes of official notification and prepared Paul's body to lie in state at Ashwood. Phoebe's presence ruled out the courtyard so we brought his body to a tree grove near the front gates. News traveled through surrounding communities where he had friends and was known by many who once worked on the estate or had family who spent time in the fields. I wished we could allow the drones to carry these human images to their owners.

Bureau protocol didn't allow Phoebe to be outside Ashwood's inner gates so she watched from the screen porch. We stood around him, accepting kind messages and hugs, comforting others. Giant Pines, the estate he loved, sent trucks of employees and their families to honor the man who understood nature in all its forms. True to Paul's heritage, carafes of hot coffee stood next to the fruit, breads, cookies, and pies on tables along the waiting line. He reminded me regularly that the bounty of the land was meant to be shared, to nourish, and comfort.

A formal memorial service would be held later, but that was the day Paul would have cherished. The South Dakota rancher with silver hair and weather-wrinkled skin belonged to the air and sun and people.

Chapter Twenty-Eight

ASHWOOD SETTLED INTO A WEEK of hard work following Paul's death. David spent long days relocating his herd from Giant Pines to new acreage adjacent to our land. Noah participated in medical school prep sessions and studied. Andrew and Phoebe were together whenever possible, exploring Ashwood with adult eyes and curiosity.

The threatened Deshomm hostile takeover turned into a settlement process with lawyers and accountants arguing the value of obtuse items like loss of executive direction, disruption of product development, and the very real costs of damage to our engineering systems and weeks of additional security.

The actual business of running Hartford, Ltd., devoured my days. Giant Pines redevelopment filled late afternoons. Faith finished her studies early enough to join the meetings. She asked questions that were surprisingly insightful. The child who always studied on my office table had not only absorbed what she'd heard or read over a decade, but also had opinions. John, with a tendency to be intense about focusing on the subject, showed limited patience for Faith's presence.

"I think the next generation's Hartford, Ltd., CEO is sleeping in a peach-colored bedroom," I shared with David after the first week. "Our child understands the interconnections of operations and asks damn good questions. Low residency college studies might be wonderful for both Ashwood and Faith. I intend to involve her in whatever she wants to learn."

Even with his back to me as he slid on a clean shirt for dinner I read his disagreement, knew I had rubbed against his romantic plan that spared Faith from the work-driven pace of our economy. He wanted to carve a space for her to enjoy school, make friends and live like an old-world college student. Corporate titans managed to make a 2050 version of that happen for their offspring. We didn't have that amount of money or influence. Regans might live without money worries, but not without working.

"Don't push her, Annie." He hung his dirty shirt in our cleaning cabinet. "Looks like there's enough in here that I'm going to run a load, okay?"

"Go ahead."

He pressed the start button, turned. His skin had tanned with working in the barns and fields. Beyond his size, his features were more his mother's than Paul's, including beautiful dark eyes which held that tired look of grief. "If we work it right, she can fulfill her community service time during her college years like Noah and John instead of working in some metro hell hole." There was nothing new in his plans for Faith's near future, but I listened. "I'm hoping she can spend a year or two at McGill with other young people. She'll work her whole life. I'd rather we didn't tie her down before she turns eighteen."

David chose to remain separate from long days with key managers and consultants about the transformation of our corporation. I broke our tradition of not talking business in our bedroom. "Please spend the next two days with me. We're turning Hartford, Ltd., into a more organized corporation that will outstrip the capabilities of our current team. You are exactly the right person to provide new leadership."

"My time is committed to establishing the herd right now."

Milan was right, David now led perhaps the easiest life in our family—bare minimum hours required by the DOE to maintain his working status, the hobby herd, a small acreage farm. He volunteered at harvest times, kept an eye on a handful of insignificant subsidiaries of Hartford, Ltd.,

"Max has good folks involved with the herd. Trust them." As I expressed the truth, a touch of my frustration crawled into the words. His resistance frustrated me, tainted other parts of our relationship.

"This could be the best time for you to totally leave the DOE and bring all your great people and project management skills full-time to Hartford, Ltd." Persuasion skills that employees, vendors, and other businesses admired didn't faze David. "You could make the next iteration of the corporation happen while preparing John or Phoebe or Faith to step in."

"You want to plug me into that open box on the organization chart called president?" David's consultative method of responding with questions began.

I fidgeted instead of protesting this behavior I found so annoying. "Yes."

"Why now?"

"Because for Hartford, Ltd., to change, it needs to have a leader not so tightly bound to its operations." The company needed its founder to step aside. I couldn't say that out loud quite yet. "Maybe we should finish this conversation in the office tomorrow. We can look at the reports and the Deshomm agreement and keep everything more business-oriented."

"Only if you promise to keep your shirt unfastened."

I looked down, kept my voice all business as I raised my face. "Too many listening devices in that building for mixing pleasure and succession planning."

"Annie, I love how you can act like we're still young enough to take those kinds of risk." David put an arm around my shoulder for our walk to the dining room.

Chapter Twenty-Nine

Family dinner conversations that summer changed our relationships from the level of parents and children to the richness of adult friendships. We spoke about politics, work, the economy, friends, and dreams in between light-hearted matters. Faith matured during unfiltered conversations about life that replaced typical teen chatter with topics that demanded thought. One night she talked about McGill University and what she hoped to do with a law degree.

"I think you should go to England for college," Phoebe challenged during a break in Faith's monologue. "I loved England. It's the closest to Europe without language challenges. Terrific science labs. It's not too late. Andrew or I can pull strings and land you a place."

"Funny, but I remember pathetic calls from you about how the Brits drove you crazy." Noah pointed his empty fork toward Phoebe. "I was concerned you were going to take after Tia Regan and almost cashed in all my travel allocations to save you."

"That had nothing to do with England. I had other issues and horrible jet lag. Why are you bringing that up? Feeling insecure about something?" Like many coddled intellectual elite, Phoebe had limited social grace in the flow of how regular people lived.

Noah, her self-appointed tether to the real world, didn't smile. "It would be nice if we could all show support for Faith's decision. Today college admission without making a corporate commitment is pretty difficult." He tilted his head and waved the fork again. "You have dominated everyone's attention for weeks, now give our little sister her share of attention."

"It's the lifestyle I'm used to, Noah. You could have lived it also."

"Not really, Phoebs." Noah returned the fork to his plate. "I couldn't give up an opportunity at living a normal life with ordinary people. I loved the witty intellectual conversation, but hated the elite environment. This is where I belong."

"You threw away the chance to do something big for the world." Phoebe's commitment to that mission anchored her words. "Squandered the intellectual potential you were given."

"I walked away from the intellectual elite lifestyle, not from challenging work. Do you feel the same way about Andrew's choice of work?"

Phoebe opened her mouth, but made an odd growling sound instead of speaking. She flushed, closed her mouth, and pushed her chair back from the table. Andrew moved faster to help her stand, and then supported her as they left the dining room. She beat one hand against her hip and the other pressed against the side of her head.

The five of us watched before turning back to each other and our meal.

"I'd like to permanently install something in Ahlmet's head." Noah pushed his plate away. "Andrew says she seldom sleeps more than forty-five minutes without an attack by that animal."

"What happens when Andrew leaves?" Faith asked. "Will he take her with him?"

"Her medical leave requires that Phoebe remains here or returns to a supervised setting in Chicago." I gazed down the hall where the two could be seen. They were heading to the back of the residence, probably out to the lower yard to sit by the pond. "I'm pretty sure Phoebs doesn't want to be in Chicago."

Dishes were passed around the table. Pasta from the wheat fields of the Regan South Dakota farms tossed with fresh vegetables from our gardens, cheese from our dairy cows, a new slaw recipe the Hartford, Ltd., kitchen was testing. Some of us sampled the first of the summer ales. Noah and John had gained weight since arriving. Noah's heavy study schedule kept him pale while John's wandering of Giant Pines gave him the light golden skin of a healthy farmer.

"Dad, you'd be really interested in the first research grant we're hoping to land for Giant Pines. The Italian animal geneticists you and I discussed are looking for a collaborative partner for a feeding project." John's enthusiasm lured David out of a pensive state. Faith lost interest in Phoebe. Amber and I chatted about a school picnic for families.

Out of the corner of my eye I saw Faith stand up. The sound of her chair hitting another chair underscored her horror as she screamed.

We all turned to the hall, to the sight of a blood-spattered Phoebe weaving toward us.

"Andrew's hurt." She wobbled. "He's hurt."

David and I pushed back from the table. I fingered my communications alarm, blocking all entrance or exit from our lands and activating emergency protocols. John was the first to Phoebe's side. Noah grabbed Faith.

I bolted past them, followed their earlier path down the central hall, out the back doors, David and Terrell close behind, to my son's side. With adrenalin fueling my own strength I pulled him from the pond, pushed the crisis alarm a second time as Terrell reached my side. Stopped as Andrew gasped. Stopped as I saw blood dripping from a wound in his chest.

Terrell pushed me aside, performed a physical assessment of Andrew, and gave directions to the lead of his kitchen team to get the estate medical kit. Security backed everyone away. I only watched Andrew, hovered as close as an umbrella over Terrell's back, dropped back to my son's side.

"Where's Frances?" I carefully picked up Andrew's hand. His eyelids fluttered open, then closed. "Hold on, Andrew." Bending around Terrell, my lips touched Andrew's wet forehead. "Help him, Terrell." I straightened, kept my voice low. "For God's sake do something."

Alarms buzzed or clanged from every corner of our land, warning the criminal that they would not escape and telling all others to not even dream of entering. Terrell ripped open Andrew's shirt as Lao drove Frances over the lawn in a small cart.

She waved me aside and I saw my bloodied hand. Frances motioned to Terrell to serve as her second in assessing Andrew's condition. In the background, coming from the house, the sound of Phoebe's keening cry accompanied the alarm. Winged insects created a subtle buzzing.

"I killed him." The blood on her face may have been her own, may have been Andrew's. Her arms flailed against her father's capturing grasp. "Mom, I'm so sorry. Someone hold me." She leaned against David's arms, her voice escalating into a screeching garble of confession and confusion.

Andrew's lids opened, closed over eyes like mine. My firstborn stretched on the rock and grass patio with thick auburn hair above a white-gray face. Frances plunged a needle into his chest near the wound, too close to the wound for my sensitivity. His legs rose from the ground, his torso moved. I cried out loud, surprised at the sound.

David held his daughter. John supported Faith. Noah rushed to the water's edge. Lao came to my side, stopped me when I would have pushed my way back to Andrew's side, held me up when my son turned his head to vomit pond water and groan.

Flies approached. "Why isn't the bug protection working?" My question carried no further than a dragonfly near Terrell's head.

"We need air transport to Abbott." Frances threw the command to Lao. "Tell them we have a gunshot wound to the chest. No exit wound. He needs a surgical suite, stat." Her small hands packed dressing to staunch the bleeding, placed a large clear bandage over the site. She looked up again. "Order it *now*. And get these bugs away from us."

"Milan must be contacted first." Lao raised his chin toward Phoebe. "Intellectual Corps protocol." His voice hardened. "You understand?"

I remained still in his strong hold. "We will not risk my son's life to honor a crazy protocol. Call air services." He shook his head and turned away, calmly voicing a code I didn't recognize. "Frances, please, make Lao understand."

She didn't turn, concentrated on Andrew's care. Noah joined Terrell, drew on gloves at his direction.

"Otis, take Phoebe to her room and make sure she doesn't leave." I projected my voice over Frances's terse questioning of Andrew. "You best make sure she isn't armed. No one beyond the family, Lao, or Dr. Frances should have access to her." Hysterical wailing and yipping added more torture to the unimaginable scene. "Assign watch until I change orders." Fighting for control, I lowered my voice. "Terrell, let Noah help Frances and do something to make Phoebe shut up."

"Mom, she's not herself." No scold accompanied Noah's words.

"Let's hope not." Color began chasing pallor from Andrew's face. "Using a gun against another person is a felony. She could serve time." I reached to swat an insect approaching Noah and he ducked away from my bloodied fingers. "You have a bug on your neck." I waved it off. Noah knelt next to Frances. "How is Andrew doing?"

"He needs air transport. We can't know where the bullet settled." Frances checked his heart and blood pressure. "Use a wipe, then you can hold his hand. He's conscious."

My hands shook as I wiped away blood and pond residue. I folded my knees to one side, sat by Andrew and gently picked up his fingers. My thumb felt for the bump on the side of his forefinger where he was deeply cut while working with the cattle. A fly circled his head. I waved it away. His eyelids flickered. Frances urged him to stay quiet.

"Speak to us, Lao." I called my friend and turned away from the bloody packing Frances removed. Terrell filled in a fresh packet without a word. Finally David joined us, put his hand on my shoulder.

"We're both here, son." David laid his palm on Andrew's thigh, applied light pressure, and removed it. A two-inch wasp like bug approached then fell to the ground and began crawling toward us.

Before Lao turned to speak, Otis ran from the residence carrying a sealed bag containing a small handgun. It was old-fashioned, the kind occasionally found in the estates of elderly who risked the possibility of time in prison for the forbidden comfort of a gun in their residence. I hadn't seen any guns like it since the depths of the great 2020s depression.

"This was in her pocket, Mr. Lao." Paul's former aide extended the bag.

Buzzing insects, bubbling water, Andrew's ragged breathing amplified as Lao finished his conversation to accept the compact weapon. My groan grounded us back into crisis management.

"A portable surgical suite will be here in ten minutes." It was clear that Lao's statement could not be questioned. He looked our way, a commander leading weaker civilians. "This is best."

"Best for Andrew or best for Phoebe or best for the Bureau?" David stood. "Who made the decision?"

"Dr. Frances is in agreement."

"I didn't hear Dr. Frances say anything after you started that conversation, Lao. What do you think, Frances?"

"I've never treated a gun wound. Have not seen one in twenty years. I can't make that call." She brushed a supersized fly with the wingspan of a monarch butterfly away from the wound. "Damn it, what's with the bugs? We need protection."

"Milan can't trade my son's life for Phoebe."

Lao did not answer me, just gave his assistant directions for location of the portable hospital suite. Listening to their conversation, I understood that unless he died, Andrew would not leave Ashwood.

"Sounds like you're setting up a field hospital unit back here." David's hand rested lightly on the top of my head. "The cost of doing that is insane." Insects ceased their attacks, our perimeter re-instated.

Lao carefully laid each word among us. "Phoebe's safety is a matter of national security."

"Then someone should take care of the criminal in Chicago dominating her brain." David waited for response from Lao who appeared to be following protocols beyond our estate. "I want Anne to speak with Milan. Taking this risk with Andrew's life makes no sense."

"The best field surgeon has been assigned to Andrew." Noah sat back on his heels, reading his communicator. "My advisor has access to assignment rosters. She says someone cherry picked the best out of rotation. He'll be in good hands."

Andrew's eyes fluttered and I felt his fingers tighten. Frances bent low, her stethoscope pressed to his chest. She motioned for Terrell to hand her something from the medical kit.

"What's happening?" I asked Frances, Terrell, maybe God.

"Andrew's blood pressure is dropping. He's bleeding internally." Terrell moved items to Frances without looking at me. "He's holding his own, Anne."

I reached toward Lao. "Get Milan."

He tapped his earpiece, spoke to someone, and then nodded toward me.

"Anne." Milan's voice brought me back from emotion to action. Releasing Andrew's hand, I got to my feet and moved away. From around the corner of the residence an Ashwood transport carried a load of field tenting materials to an entry near our lower level storage facilities and safe room. "Andrew will have the same medical field team that would be sent if a government official needed high level care."

"Tell me that Ahlmet's been taken into custody." I looked to the sky, impatient for the copter's arrival."

"Special protection has been ordered for Phoebe and your entire family. Ava Smith will arrive with the medical field unit." I heard the buzz of other voices from his side of our conversation. "Phoebe must be kept safe."

"I won't sacrifice either Phoebe or Andrew."

"You are all in my thoughts, Anne. I have to go."

The sound of a med copter ended our conversation. I turned back to Andrew understanding that we were immersed in a crisis created by a brilliant madman in a lab.

"How's he doing, Frances?" A medical blanket had been pulled over Andrew.

"No change." She looked up to the sky. "They'll have him in surgery in five to ten minutes."

"I want to greet the team, make sure they have everything they need."

"You're looking at everything they need." Using her chin, she pointed to the med copter hovering above our lower yard where the younger kids' soccer field had been merged with a grassy area to create Ashwood's "parkland," the only unplanted acreage on the estate.

"What you can do right now is bend low over Andrew while they land. Plenty of dust and debris is going to be churned up. We need to keep him covered." Frances gestured for David to join us.

We formed a human blanket above my son. The med copter blades tossed dust and recently mown grass our way while shutting down. I looked over Terrell's back at medical staff running our way and knew fear instead of relief. A stocky man trotted first to Lao.

David pulled me back as the first medical crew reached Andrew. One conferred with Frances, two began assessment and inserted an IV line, others brought a gurney to his side. Frances introduced Noah, worked him into the team caring for Andrew.

Leaving Ashwood

"Ms. Hartford, I'm Chief Medical Officer Rizzi." A stocky man separated from the crew. He had blue eyes, a shaved head and did not smile. "Your son will be in good hands. We'll let Dr. Frances and Noah observe but need to have you remain outside. Dr. Frances will keep you informed. The wound appears clean, we'll have to see what the bullet has done internally. The pond water is being analyzed for contaminants."

I wanted to walk with the gurney, but Andrew was nearly to the med copter with crew performing procedures and prepping him as they moved. Rizzi nodded and was gone. The side doors closed. My legs shook.

"Easy, Annie." David spoke next to my ear. "We can sit here by the pond or go in the house."

Inside seemed too far away. To sit by the pond meant waiting next to medical refuse and Andrew's blood. Neither choice felt right.

Terrell followed my eyes over the pond-side scene. "We'll move chairs and a bench where you can keep that big bird in your sight," he offered and gestured for Lao and David to help. I pitched in, fear giving me energy and strength. David, Terrell and I sat. Lao excused himself. John, Faith and Amber joined us.

We had few experiences with family medical emergencies. Beyond the large field, sunshields waved slightly in an evening breeze. Our bug zapping system once again offered protection. Faith sat on the ground, her head resting against my leg. I ran my fingers through her hair until I couldn't sit still. "I'm going to walk around the med copter. I have to move."

Faith slid her hand into mine. "We'll walk together. I saw an interesting wildflower in this field a few days ago. It might be a mutant, but it is pretty. Come see it."

Terrell excused himself, kissed my cheek, and headed back to the residence. Blood on his pants made me look away.

David finally stood, walked on Faith's other side. We paced the width and length of the field area, sometimes exchanging small talk about a bird or what we knew little about guns. Twenty minutes, then thirty minutes passed. The early evening light changed. The family dinner table discussion about Faith's college choice drifted through my mind to be chased away by Dr. Rizzi's page to the copter's door.

"Andrew was fortunate." The surgeon did not waste words. "No major internal organs damaged, small knick in a vessel, which we closed. His right lung collapsed, but should respond to post-surgical care."

Noah remained with Andrew, but Frances joined us. Her smile, while genuine, didn't match her eyes that darted back to the residence as Rizzi described Andrew's post-care. I thought she was looking for Terrell, tried not to be distracted by her behavior.

"Excuse me," David interrupted. "I'm being paged from inside the residence."

Rizzi looked toward Frances. She nodded and excused herself. I watched her hurry to catch up with David. "Ms. Hartford, we've put together a temporary recovery suite in the old sick room of your residence. Andrew will be moved there within the half hour."

"There's a medical suite attached to the clinic at the end of the drive."

"We're following Intellectual Corps protocol, which requires we house the patients in the residence." He rolled his shoulders.

"Andrew isn't in the Intellectual Corps."

He rubbed one hand across a hairy forearm. "We've been ordered to remain for a procedure on Phoebe Regan. Following that, we'll leave a professional here to manage patient care for approximately seventy-two hours."

David matched his stride to a large man carrying a limp Phoebe. Frances accompanied the group, spoke to a woman in medical scrubs then with David. They advanced slowly, taking each step with care.

"I understand there's a nano chip implant located near the base of her skull which must be removed." Rizzi shifted weight, ready to return to his surgical suite. "That's what I know. This could be a relatively easy procedure, or we could be searching for a nearly invisible speck." He began walking. "Your son will be moved to recovery in a sterile box to free space for the next procedure. I'm not in favor of this expedited transfer for a chest wound, but we have orders. Keep everyone out of the way of the team."

Rizzi's words didn't prepare me for the clear coffin-like unit eased from the med copter and onto a self-propelled gurney. Four medics accompanied Andrew with Noah leading them to the lower level entrance to Ashwood. My feet moved toward him, my eyes ignored Noah waving me to stay back. Faith followed me, young enough for no one to suggest she not cry in fright.

"He's okay, Mom. Both of you stay here with Dad." Noah held up both hands. "Stay there. I'll come for you."

Terrell, my greatest support after David, grabbed Faith's hand. He extended his other hand for me, but I would not be drawn away from Andrew. I followed the box, kept my distance, heard the sounds of unseen equipment monitoring his heartbeat, his blood pressure, and whatever stats Rizzi needed. Ashwood's door opened, Andrew's escorts lifted the gurney and entered. The door closed. Blinds covered each window. I was reminded that even with the multi-corps dominating our economy, Uncle Sam held even tighter to its precious human resources.

"He's healthy and strong. He will be okay." David came up behind me.

Leaving Ashwood

I turned away from the blank windows to face him and Phoebe's situation. "Tell me what happened inside. You look so collected and I'm a complete mess. Why was Phoebe being carried?"

He looked over my shoulder at the med copter's now closed door. I followed his eyes and wished I had a way to demand someone give me entrance. David's hand closed around my elbow. "Let's sit down."

Faith joined us, eyes puffy with more tears. She slipped next to David on the bench. "John went back to be with Phoebe. When Otis found the gun in her pocket, she began talking to herself. John said her behavior became extreme. Then she collapsed."

In a flash I remembered Faith asking if Phoebe would still fit in with Ashwood. Instead of alarm at news of another collapse, I felt weariness. Weeks of the drama of Phoebe's life distracted everyone at the core of Ashwood. I listened, waited for some new detail to come from this episode, some piece of information that would change my mind from growing concern about the price of sheltering this brilliant woman and all her eccentric behavior in the midst of innocent people who could be hurt.

"Mom." Faith tugged at my shirt edge.

"I am listening." I put my hand over hers. "And thinking. Aside from shooting Andrew, the man who says he loves her, this is all the same pattern caused by that damn chip. How is it that the nano chip location is now known and who is giving orders?"

David stared forward, finally responded. "Call Milan? He usually directs the game."

But I shook my head. "He'll call if he wants me to know something. This is between him and Phoebe. He has a watcher among us who probably tells him if Phoebe stubs a toe."

"What's that supposed to mean?" David's question was fair.

"Only that I'm not sure we can keep Phoebe safe any longer without endangering more innocent people. Maybe she should be with Milan in hiding." I wanted to lift my blood-spotted shirt and ask who would be next. "The people protecting him should be able to deal with the Ahlmet issue."

"This is her home, Annie. Do you know how important we are in this situation?"

Faith didn't look at either of us as emotions shifted. From experience, she expected her parents to deal logically with conflict. The med copter's low drumming and the sight of drones held harmless by powerful jamming of the government vehicle chilled me.

"Ashwood is home to many people, David, which is exactly why I am concerned about Phoebe's condition. Under this madman's influence, she used a gun to shoot Andrew. Next time that attack could be against you or Terrell or me or anyone who happens to be in the area at the wrong moment."

"Don't jump to conclusions, Annie." His voice had an edge, anger that I hoped wasn't directed at me. "She will be okay after this operation. No need to make plans to send her away."

"That's what I hope."

"If they can't find that chip, I agree with Mom." Faith didn't turn as she spoke. "Each time she visits school, I worry she'll lose it and frighten the kids." She sighed, a choppy sound hinting of tears and stress. "You saw her room, Dad. She's destroyed everything at that guy's direction. She's afraid he might kill her."

I hadn't been in Phoebe's suite for a few days, but saw David's head nod slightly in acknowledgement of Faith's observations.

"What's happened in her room? When I visited there last time everything was normal."

They exchanged a look before Faith took the lead. "All the dresser drawers are busted up, the wooden chair is smashed, and the comforter got ripped apart. Amber had stuff replaced yesterday, but it was all crazy again after dinner."

"My God, our poor girl." Tears came to my eyes, evaporated in the heat of the anger I carried. Faith leaned her head on David's shoulder and cried. I envied the comfort of his arms as he pulled her to his chest.

Summer's long evening was fading. Small garden lamps turned yellow. Faith's sobs quieted until crickets became our background noise. Terrell left to care for his kids. John and Amber brought out water, insect repellent shirts, and a brief message from Lao that Ashwood was secure. They moved chairs next to me. I lowered my head into my hands, my thoughts churning through the moment and dreading the future.

In the metro area families might still gather in hospital waiting rooms while loved ones underwent treatments or fought for their lives. I dimly remembered being taken to a hospital with my parents when my grandfather had heart surgery. For hours I worked on school assignments, walked with my mother through the halls to purchase lunch we would bring back to the family.

With less invasive procedures and downsizing of the business of healthcare, many of the old rituals disappeared. Babies were born in clinics, bones set in a transport unit, diagnostics conducted remotely. Yet here we were reconnected with the human experience of filling anxious minutes and hours with our own thoughts and prayers while waiting for news of our loved one.

Leaving Ashwood

Noah sent me updates from Andrew's side and as I passed the news to everyone, we made small talk. As forty minutes stretched to sixty then seventy-five, my thoughts fixated on the unknown of who'd ordered Phoebe's surgery and why. David and I agreed that he would continue to wait with the others if I received the call to visit Andrew.

Fatigue accompanied Frances when she walked down the med copter's ramp. Her head came up and she saw the five of us. David and I were on our feet to meet her midway as if even five seconds of additional wait could not be tolerated.

"You should go inside," she said. "The surgical team is holding Phoebe in a light state of sedation while communicating with a Bureau medical representative in Chicago." She removed her head covering. "I think everyone has a better idea of what they are looking for, but because of the structure and size of the chip, there is reluctance to do extensive work without additional information. Phoebe was able to tell Dr. Rizzi what she remembers about how Ahlmet might have planted it, which is somewhat contradictory with what the Chicago people believe."

"What condition is she in?" Frances heard my question and appeared to evaluate our emotions.

"I can answer that on many levels." Her eyes rested on Faith first, then David, before resting on me. "She is lucid at times, she is frequently out of control requiring the doctors to use sedation. Her vitals are being monitored at all times and have been erratic."

My communicator signified I could visit Andrew in ten minutes. "I need to be with her," I responded to Frances. "She must be so frightened."

Frances took one of my hands. "I knew you would feel that way." She squeezed my fingers gently. "The medical team are tops. They are doing everything possible to keep her physically comfortable and stable. As an Intellectual Corps member, Phoebe is very used to others caring for her needs regardless of the nature. They care for her body so her mind can be free of everything but work. She is more comfortable with strangers in this condition than with family." Her factual tone didn't sugarcoat Phoebe's life. "Immersion in our normal life has been hard on her. Milan made sure this medical team had experience with Intellectual Corps."

"So he's calling the shots." I heard David's lifelong bitterness about government involvement with the lives of our gifted offspring. "These doctors will keep her body healthy as a holder for her goddamn brain. Like she's not a person."

"I'll be there as long as Phoebe wants me." Frances placed her arms around me, hugged me. "She asked me to tell you she's sorry and she loves you." Stepping back, Frances dropped an arm to my waist. "Let me walk you part of the way to Andrew."

We turned our back on the med copter. Frances's arm physically supported me. "Andrew should be able to talk with you," she explained. "The lung has been re-inflated, but he'll feel like he fought with a robo boxer for the next week or two. The bullet ripped tissue within the body that will need time to mend."

"Thank you for everything you're doing."

Frances smiled. "It's what I can do." The smile faded. "If we can end Ahlmet's tyranny of Phoebe, and she decides to stay to work in this new Giant Pines research corporation, she'll need psychological help through the adjustment to regular life. Or you can create some version of the Bureau's Intellectual Corps lifestyle and continue to support her brain through absolute support of her body. Keep me in the loop. Remember I'm her psychiatrist first."

"What about Andrew?" I knew my son would ask for her.

"Regardless of what Phoebe might say, right now she is not available for an emotional relationship with a person leading a normal life. She's a narcissist, not a partner."

Frances stopped walking. "I have to turn back. Give your boy a kiss and keep the conversation light. He should be debriefed about the shooting by now, but it's best for him to stay quiet." She straightened her shoulders and extended her short spine. "You know the drill, Anne. One step at a time. You concentrate on Andrew and your family. I'll give my attention to Phoebe."

Chapter Thirty

D**AVID TEASED ME THAT** if a three dimensional picture were taken of my brain, it would look like the world's smallest apartment building with big challenges forced into an amazing number of small compartments. I called that survival.

Noah met me at the door and ushered me through personal cleaning then into sterile garb. He assured me Andrew was doing well, but in an un-Noah way offered no jokes or small talk. I saw him step out of his role as the family's charmer into one as a member of the medical team.

Ashwood's old sick bay, a collection of beds and tables and easy chairs had been transformed into a modern mobile medical suite. The sterile transfer unit had disappeared. In its place, Andrew rested in a high-tech hospital bed that recorded his vitals without a visible cord or cable. He breathed in oxygen via nasal tubing. Another tube drained fluid from his chest. His eyes were closed and his face, while still pale, had more natural pink tones.

"He knows he was shot by Phoebe, but doesn't know anything happening with her. Keep it that way." Noah unfolded an old wooden chair. "You can touch his hands or arms or feet or legs or forehead. Stay away from any tubing areas and his chest. He has some badly bruised ribs, probably from falling."

All I had taken in about transforming the sick room and Noah's natural assumption of his new career fell into mental boxes for future consideration. And all those small compartments faded at Andrew's side. As a teen, he'd had a high tolerance for pain. I hoped that would help him through his recovery.

"Andrew, I'm so relieved to see you." I stood close, gently touched his hair. "You look a lot better."

A grunting sound came from his throat.

"Don't try to talk, Andrew." Noah was at his other side. "There was a tube down your throat. The longer you stay quiet, the sooner the tissue will heal. Just give Mom a smile. We're going to let her hold your hand."

With his large hand in mine, I sat and talked about small meaningless topics like the mutant flower Faith found and the sound of the crickets while we waited outside during his surgery. I told him how Terrell and I changed this space from a spare storage room into a place for sick or hurt child workers and that he was always willing to read to another kid who needed to spend time here. Someone handed me a moistened cloth and gel for his drying lips. I dabbed tenuously around the tube. My hand remained steady. My heart beat fast.

Fifteen minutes extended into thirty before they told me I needed to leave, Andrew squeezed my hand. I walked away with one compartment door refusing to close.

Chapter Thirty-One

IN THE SECOND HOUR, we moved our vigil to Paul's former room where the med copter could be watched from the windows. Terrell and Lao rejoined us.

I watched David, saw worry freeze his forehead into many small lines. Frances sent us short updates, but clearly the battle for Phoebe's sanity and survival took place 400 miles away in Chicago and in the halls of bureaucracy. Blankets and tea and food arrived. Faith studied. John, Amber, and Magda played a board game in silence. When Andrew slept, Noah left sickbay to sit next to David.

Looking like an alien ship with illuminated windows and low landing lights shining below, I wondered about the security system that kept the med copter's presence invisible to the drone swarm. Around two in the morning more of its windows lit up. I tugged on David's arm to be sure I wasn't imagining the change. Lao stood and signaled me to join him in stepping away from the group. I followed, certain the lack of an update from Frances about obvious activity spelled trouble.

"Is it Phoebe?" I kept my voice low. "Or has Andrew taken a turn?"

He put a finger to his lips, took my elbow to move us faster from the main residence and to the DOE building next door. I upped his speed, urging my feet to move faster than my mind. Instinctively I headed to my office.

Lao activated the hologram system. Milan, dressed in full business attire at this strange hour, joined us. He sat in a conference room that could be anywhere in the world although I assumed it to be a government office.

"You will hear news of significant disruption in the Bureau of Human Capital Management. I have been asked by President Hernandez to join her cabinet as Secretary of the Bureau." Milan removed glasses from a pocket. Lao and I sat frozen in our chairs, caught by the amazing announcement. "There are a number of implications for the Regans in this change which I must ask Anne to communicate to appropriate members of the family. I'll be brief because I know your attention is focused on Phoebe." He looked over his glasses at me.

"Congratulations, Milan." I tipped my head. "Correct that. Secretary Milan."

"There will be time for that later." His face softened. "You will always be a friend first, Annie, so let's not do the title." Emotion thickened his voice and he paused. "I have three imperative messages. To avoid a conflict of interest with my new responsibilities, I am relinquishing legal guardianship of Phoebe to you. We'll talk more about this when we've had a few hours of sleep, but if she is still interested in pursuing private research work she is free of any contractual obligations to the Bureau. And, in my first official action, I will be restructuring the Intellectual Corps citizens to work in approved private sector if their work is of value to advancement of the United States."

"Thank you. I look forward to telling her this good news." Sleep deprivation sharpened the sweetness of this development as well as fear Phoebe would not live to enjoy this freedom. "You must know how the medical team is struggling to keep her alive."

"I am monitoring reports and share your concern." Milan looked down, read from his pad. "Anne, this second piece of information is important for you on many levels. Deshomm has been implicated in supporting the research and activities of Ahlmet, including bureaucratic interference in the manipulation of Phoebe and two others."

Lao sat up straighter and responded. "They arrive in six hours to sign the settlement papers resulting from the takeover attempt. We have authorized temporary security for a small number of their people."

"They'll probably choose to do the settlement remote now that all possibility of opening discussions on a news deal have been killed. They've been barred from a number of activities related to expanding their economic influence within agricultural markets for one year." Milan looked my way.

"Thank you, Milan. One day I'd love to know the details. Right now I want to scorch their multi-corps asses." I wondered if Sadig's enthusiasm for Deshomm had been influenced long before his involvement with Ahlmet. Something else I wouldn't know without wasting time. "I'll have our legal counsel collect our compensation. Not for Hartford, but for Phoebe. Let's move to your third note. I'm eager to return to the family."

Milan pulled off his glasses. "I understand. My status report says surgery is underway to remove the chip." He put the now smudged glasses in a pocket and folded his hands on the table. "Lao, I asked you to be here as an official witness while I deliver a Presidential Executive Order under emergency government authority for activation of Ms. Anne Hartford for a period of up to one year to lead creation of an ethics board within the newly restructured Bureau of National Human Capital Management. Details of your service including financial considerations will be forwarded to you by noon today. I'll expect to see you in Washington, D.C., in twenty-one days assuming family health concerns allow travel."

"So witnessed," said Lao. He held out a hand. "Congratulations, Commissioner Anne."

As my hand accepted his across the table I looked at the hologram for clarification from Milan about what this whole proclamation meant. The seriousness of his plain face told me that whatever had transpired within the Bureau was a major disruption, one that might change the current administration and maybe the nation long-term. The governmental bartering of human capital could hardly become less humane.

"Media will receive details of the Bureau re-organization during their morning briefing. We will not disclose the ethics board formation until later in the week, by which time an information officer will be assigned to work with you at Ashwood or in Washington. Schedules will be coordinated with Clarissa. Now go back to your family. Please let them know I wish the best for Andrew and Phoebe."

His hologram disappeared. I spoke as Lao stood. "I want to remain focused on the kids until later this morning. Let me talk with David first."

"What I would give to know what happened in Chicago," Lao responded. "An information blackout went into effect when I left the pond area to work with the medical team. I overheard chatter in the crew that set up the recovery suite. This crew only travels at the direction of a very highly placed individual."

He opened the office door. "Which reminds me that communication scripts about tonight, for Ashwood's employees and the media, will be sent to your mail for review. Regardless of outcome, there's a staff meeting to be held at eight and we're required to stay on message." He put an arm around my shoulder, a gesture I valued from this friend and associate. "Nothing is to be said about your change until later."

Anne Hartford, concerned mother, rejoined the family and rejoiced at three twenty in the morning when Frances arrived with news that the chip had been removed from the base of Phoebe's neck and she rested peacefully. This time David and I walked to the med copter with Frances to see Phoebe and thank the crew.

The sun rose as we left the temporary recovery suite, and I told David about Milan's three messages. Cows and goats would be milked, produce harvested, eggs gathered. The workings of agriculture wouldn't change that day or the next because of who sat in the managers' desks or who lived or died.

Chapter Thirty-Two

Even old houses keep settling on their foundations sending hairline cracks in plaster unmarred for a quarter century. A skilled craftsperson can mud over the fissure, repaint and hide the imperfection, but a homeowner will always remember and watch for the line to re-appear.

The quakes that shook our marriage could be named—Paul's death, Phoebe's shooting Andrew, the Washington, D.C., appointment. The cracks were minute, maybe not visible.

"Imagine Ashwood without Annie Hartford standing at its front door," was David's response to the presidential assignment.

I wanted something stronger from him, condemnation of Milan's handiwork or an offer to help plan the twenty-one-day transition. Deciphering the silence between us as we entered our bedroom required a psychic force. David slapped his sandals on the closet floor, closed the closet door, and walked to the windows. He looked tired and worried and unhappy. Ditto for me.

"What is Milan dragging you into?" David finally engaged. He gestured to the reading chairs, ready to talk when both of us were also ready to drop. "Hernandez is unpeeling government programs faster than officials created them during the depression. They are naïve if they think the multi-corps will relinquish their role in determining U.S. economic policy. If we don't keep businesses happy, other nations will do so gladly."

"Something serious happened in the last twenty-four hours that the public might not be told." Thirty messages backed up in my mail. I turned my communicator face away. "I'm not being asked to consider this assignment, I've been commissioned by the president. This must be what you felt like when the DOE sent you to China for three months, except I'm not a federal employee." A giant yawn cracked through my jaw and caused popping sounds in my ears. "We have lots to talk about. Just not right now. Our first priority now is to bring employees news about the kids. Scripts have been prepared, and I plan to take the lazy route and use them."

"Well, I plan to take a nap."

"I'm going to shower and go to my office until breakfast. You'll be with me for our employee meetings?"

He nodded, stood, and began pulling off his clothes as he spoke. "I don't think I said congratulations, Annie. This could be a gigantic pain in the ass, but you know there was a tough vetting process before the commission. You are a rare person, Anne Hartford."

"It's odd to think that I was being investigated as everything here remained so normal."

A snort came through the shirt going over his head. "Since our daughter came home, little has been normal. Phoebe carries all kind of energy with her. Not all of it so good. Do you think Andrew understands what he's in for?"

"I think Andrew will have time to think that through while he recuperates and Phoebe will have big decisions about her future, which will distract her." I wrapped a robe around myself. "Take your nap. I'm too keyed up to sleep."

"Rightly so, Annie."

In the shower I thought through how to draw together an interim management team and knew David had to step in. *Enjoy your rest*, I thought as I walked around his sleeping form. *Tomorrow will be a very different day for me, and for you.*

Chapter Thirty-Three

DAVID AND I STOOD SIDE BY SIDE in the courtyard at eight. The med copter lifted from Ashwood as our first local employees began their shift, but members of the overnight crew stayed to hear if truth was more interesting than rumor. The morning suggested a hot day. Straight from visiting with Phoebe and Andrew, my adrenalin began sputtering. We stood where Clarissa placed us so that the crew at Giant Pines would have the best holographic image of our speeches.

"Good morning. Some of you have heard that there was a medical emergency here last night. Fortunately we are able to share positive news this morning.

"A Bureau employee who accompanied our daughter Phoebe to Ashwood brought a small handgun with her. Because she arrived directly from work within the Chicago labs campus where strict security protocols exist, we did not conduct a weapon search upon her arrival. I want to emphasize that we welcomed her into our residence in full compliance with all Intellectual Corps security practices. Yet, not searching this individual set up an unfortunate string of events that resulted in the accidental discharge of the weapon and injury of my son and Clarissa's nephew, Andrew Smithson. The med copter team performed emergency surgery late last night and he is resting comfortably right now with full recovery expected."

Lao and I fought over the Bureau's cover story for Phoebe's shooting of Andrew. Truthfully we weren't sure where the gun came from so the Bureau's fabrication of facts was as good as any. But I hated the slight sense of fault that colored Lao and his team. Like a loyal soldier, he accepted the slur without protest and insisted I practice delivery of the script until I could offer it to our staff with sincerity. He called this preparation for my Washington, D.C., stint.

"Some of you have witnessed our daughter Phoebe suffer a series of seizures. These incidents became serious enough to require her to take a medical leave of absence from the Intellectual Corps. Last night she suffered a particularly difficult episode, and with a med copter crew available, she underwent exploratory surgery because of suspicion that she had been the victim of corporate sabotage and might have a foreign implant in her body. That proved to be true. Her surgery was completed early this morning, hence two tired parents." I paused, hated this partial truth telling. "Andrew and Phoebe are resting and we're at work."

A few laughed. One hand flew up.

"We've been asked not to talk further about these two medical emergencies," I cautioned, "but what is your question?"

"Whose going to repair the garden damage?" The young field employee, a landscape designer in coveralls, asked his question tentatively. "Will you be accepting bids?" More felt able to chuckle.

"We'd like to get a few hours of sleep before bringing that to Amber's attention," David answered. People began to shift as if readying to return to work.

"There's one piece of business news I also need to tell you," Shuffling stopped, faces turned to me. I saw apprehension, perhaps fear that more work would be automated. "We were informed this morning that due to violation of federal laws, Deshomm has been banned from certain agricultural expansion in the United States or overseas within aligned nations. This is good news for us and definitely ends their hostile takeover activities."

"I heard Mr. David's private herd was up for sale." A woman from the Ashwood greenhouse crew spoke up.

"My wife might wish that was true, but it's not," David said lightly. "The herd has been moved to its own facilities to clear space at Giant Pines for other activities."

"I heard the talk in town. Two men were there looking for directions to Giant Pines this morning." She wouldn't budge.

"Well, it isn't true, but let's talk before you return to work," David said.

"Nothing else to report, except to thank you for your hard work and great camaraderie. Stay hydrated today." I ended our presentation and watched David and Lao move to the side with the woman. She was a long-term employee and good person, someone who I would trust.

My inbox of critical material filled before nine o'clock—Bureau memorandum, confirmation of Deshomm's withdrawal and issuance of compensation, a confidential White House presidential packet, my schedule for the next five days.

"Clarissa, I need to see you in my office."

"I'll be there in five."

Waiting for her I scanned the White House packet. Milan thought of most everything I would need. Except for David, our family, my friends. Many years ago I told him that what I really remembered about the best of life began here. A citizen could not turn down a presidential commission except for extreme considerations. Clarissa found me staring out a window, not truly seeing the familiar scene I could describe with my eyes shut.

"Did you get any sleep, Annie?"

"Too many things happening this morning." She closed the door behind her and sat in front of my desk.

"More important than the kids' recovery?"

"Of course not. But quite impactful." I rubbed my eyes, reminded myself to have them retouched. "You'll be contacted by the office of the Bureau of National Human Capital Management this morning to schedule a number of meetings over the next three weeks. I'll be going to Washington, D.C., to accept a commission that will last at least one year. I'll report to Milan who was appointed to President Hernandez' Cabinet as Secretary of the Bureau."

"Congratulations." Clarissa sat back in her chair. "My God, what an incredible turn of events. What will you be doing?"

"Establishing a Board of Ethics for the Bureau."

Most people would have the same look of disbelief that crossed Clarissa's face before she returned to calm. "What do we need to do?" was her response.

"There's a mountain of decisions that need to be made. Let me tell you what's going through my head and you jump in with your ideas. Lao and David are the only others here who know about this commission. I'm still trying to process the last eighteen hours."

Clarissa seldom mixed personal with business. She ignored my last comment and headed straight to planning. "If I am going to be selfish, I'd want to see Hartford, Ltd., prepared for your absence." She made a note. "John's too young to sit in your place. Will you still go ahead with the environmental research center at Giant Pines now that Deshomm is out of the game?"

"The answer is yes. You are going to be a busy person today, Clarissa. I need two hours with David, John, Noah, and Faith this afternoon. I wish Andrew and Phoebe could participate, but we can't wait. After that meeting, I'd like to visit with Raima. Maybe an hour. Don't let anyone get out of these sessions." I looked out the window, wondered what window I'd look out in three weeks.

"Last, protect me from any multi-corps contacts, anything that the management team should be able to handle, media snoops. Cancel me out of any regular Hartford meetings. A Bureau information officer will be arriving late this afternoon and need to spend time with me. You'll receive information about when. Please join us."

"When will you take a nap?"

"I'm going to visit the patients, then you'll tell everyone I'm unavailable until lunch."

"Even the president or Secretary Milan?" Clarissa asked, or maybe, teased.

The question took me by surprise. I wasn't a person used to reporting to others. "Let's hope we don't have to worry about that quite yet." I yawned, pushed myself up to my feet. "Want to go with me to sick bay?"

"No thanks. You should have time alone with them."

I walked outside to the back of the residence. Not twenty feet from the office building doors Lao fell into step with me.

"Clarissa says you have no time in your schedule today so I will be brief." How he managed to look wide-awake made me envious. "By end of day today you will share personnel assigned to Phoebe's protection. We have changed protocols around your security upon directions from the Bureau. You'll be able to identify some of the unit by their brown uniforms. Others blend in with Ashwood staff."

"That's amazing. Why do I need protection?"

Lao didn't mince words. "The battle for control of the Bureau has created some big winners and angry losers. Blood was spilled. Including a member of the Intellectual Corps by the name of Ahlmet. No chances are being taken."

He was not my son, but I felt a crippling moment of pain at the news of Ahlmet's death. An evening on Chicago's Michigan Avenue came to mind when he walked between Phoebe and me on our way back from dinner. His curly hair was tossed by a breeze and his hands waved in the air as he told us a story about his childhood. Phoebe laughed out loud. For that I thought he offered her a most valuable escape from the craziness of their lab-driven lives. The man who became my daughter's oppressor wasn't present. That night, Ahlmet was kind and charming. Maybe that was his true nature and genetic engineering triggered the behaviors that brought him to a violent end. Phoebe would be relieved, but I hoped she might also be saddened by his loss.

We rounded the corner. Apple trees stretched as far as a person could see to our right. A path of pavers with a hedge of hybrid pear-bearing bushes had been installed at the insistence of Paul to soften the rear of the DOE building. The morning sun was still pleasant even if the temps would hit ninety degrees later in the day. Summer mornings in Washington, D.C., would be oppressive.

"How did you find out about this?"

"Security briefing at seven this morning. Additions to Phoebe's protection unit were in place by the time you talked to staff."

"I meant the blood spilled and Ahlmet."

Lao nodded to an orchard laborer before answering. "Same security briefing. I've been granted wider access to appropriate government information." Two individuals in brown stood on the path between sickbay and us. "Clarissa now knows if I need access to you, I will receive access."

Apparently mornings on Ashwood could become oppressive as well.

Chapter Thirty-four

I NOTICED FIRST THAT THE TOP of Andrew's bed was slightly elevated and his mouth hung open without a tube taped to his lips. His eyes were closed, but his face looked awake. Under the sheets his legs moved. Someone had taken the time to partly conceal the drainage bags. Cameras monitored every action in the room.

"Should you be doing that?" Touching one foot, I broke his concentration. He opened his eyes, offered a weak smile.

"Doctors' orders." The words came out slurred and rough. He gestured for me to take the chair. "Noah's found his niche."

"I agree with you about that. And, I'm amazed at your progress in only twelve hours."

"Pain management, Mom." He pointed to a small pack strapped on his arm. "They tell me I'll heal better because I've eaten and slept well since I got home."

I thought of Andrew as the most professionally established of our kids. He owned small rest pods in the cities where his primary clients had headquarters. Each of his places had been well decorated with identical technical and entertainment resources. That he considered Ashwood home meant a great deal to me.

"Someone from the Bureau primed me this morning about how to talk about last night." He moved slightly, grimaced. "Truth is neither of us had any clue where that gun came from."

He licked at lips that were dry and cracked. I picked up a water glass and held it for him. He sipped, licked his lips again before finishing his thoughts.

"Phoebe said she found it under towels in the linen shelf. Maybe the cares planted it." He stopped, took a breath. "I wonder if the officials will take action against her." His facial color whitened, his hands clutched the covers.

"Can I get you anything?" I put one hand on his. Our orders were to stay away from the big stories of the night before—the bloody standoff in Chicago, Milan's rise to the Cabinet, Ahlmet's death, my commission. The space couldn't be certified as private as required by Milan's people.

"A magic carpet to take us forward a few days."

He didn't know that I had no days to waste. "Andrew, I'm calling for a family business discussion this afternoon. I wish I could wait for you and Phoebe to join

163

us, but there are developments that make that impossible. Don't answer me right now, but I have the sense you aren't interested in a career with Hartford, Ltd., Is there any way you would like to be involved with the business?"

"I've been thinking about that since I arrived." He stopped, tapped at the pain pack, took a shallow breath. "You know my father left me enough resources to provide for a family and have a nice life. I would appreciate some land here to build a house of my own." His eyes fluttered, probably from the medication. "If there's room on the board, I'd appreciate consideration."

"Consider it done. We'll work out details later. It'll be a plus to have your experience and instincts." His eyelids drooped. "You need to rest. I'll be back around lunch."

PHOEBE'S SURGERY, WHILE DELICATE, had been far less extensive. Years of poor eating, a lack of sleep and chemicals introduced by the Corps would suggest a longer recovery. Her beautiful curls contrasted with the white pillow cover. More premature gray hairs appeared in her hair and some thinning near the crown. She looked vulnerable.

"Mom?" One hand rose off the bed as she opened her eyes. A small groan followed as if any movement triggered discomfort. "I missed you this morning. I kind of hoped you'd be here when I woke up."

"I was here. You were pretty drugged and don't remember." I took her hand in mine, raised it to my lips for a small kiss. "You had a tough night."

Tears brightened her eyes and slipped down her cheeks like when she was an infant. I wiped her face and offered encouragement that she rest.

"Can you forgive me?"

"You weren't yourself, Phoebe. When you've recuperated, you'll be able to live without fear of Ahlmet's control. Just think of that. Better yet, go to sleep and dream about it."

"No one will let me see Andrew and I can't really rest until he comes to see me. Is he okay?"

Frances's words about Phoebe's narcissism pinged in my mind as I reported on Andrew's recovery with a reminder that he was barely a half-day out of surgery and still on a limited visiting schedule. She nodded and appeared to fall asleep. We would have to talk about the future of Hartford, Ltd., without her input.

Phoebe was used to life with cares and watchers and handlers, but I had much to learn about moving with others' eyes on me. I took the inside residence steps and headed toward our room for a nap. The world could be put on hold for two hours.

I folded my clothes on a chair and kicked my shoes underneath. The sheets felt cool, the pillow a perfect combination of soft and supportive. I rolled to my right and gazed across David's side of the bed at the table with his favorite picture of our kids taken when Faith was a toddler. I began a simple meditation to slow my mind when a small circle of a mismatched wall color came into view, a visual monitor.

Sleep was elusive. We had motion detection monitors in all our sleeping rooms instead of viewers. I wondered if a government tracking tag would be placed under my skin in D.C., tried for a more comfortable position and started the meditation process over.

The door opened. David, who knew I was asleep or just pretending, sat on the bed. "Annie, we need to talk before the family summit." He rubbed my shoulder.

"If you keep doing that I might fall asleep." I pulled an arm out from under the sheet and stretched. "After I saw that damn visual monitor I couldn't settle my mind. Let me pull on my clothes."

"Don't get up. I told Lao you wouldn't be happy about the visuals. We had them all over the house when you arrived."

"And the first thing I did in my rooms was turn it to motion only. Even then I couldn't sleep with a viewer." I stood, shrugged on a simple dress. "I suppose I'll need to upgrade my wardrobe for D.C. Maybe Faith and I can spend a night in the cities." Dressed, I sat in the reading chair so old it curved to my body's impression. "Let's talk."

"You were right about goading me into a larger role in Hartford, Ltd., but I balked for a lot of selfish reasons. Looks like I don't get to hang back any longer. How does chairman of the board sit on your shoulders if I slip into the CEO seat?" His tone was light, his face serious. "Is that what was on your mind?"

"I would add interim to CEO."

David shook his head. "I'm not comfortable with that. I want you to be free to consider other opportunities that might come out of this commission. If you decide to return to our business, Hartford, Ltd., can use a more active chairman with attention on strategic possibilities."

How would I permanently release the only responsibility more demanding than parenting? David watched as I thought through my answer. My husband was brilliant intellectually, led complex project teams working on different continents, grew up in agriculture and understood working with nature. He knew Hartford, Ltd., in ways an outsider could not quickly assimilate.

"Before this commission issue, the management model I had in mind was something more collaborative. I thought you might take over more of the operations side and I would stay connected to strategy and marketing." Organization charts in my top drawer might help us think a layer down the management ladder, but David's proposal met today's needs. "You are right. I will bow out of day-to-day management. As quickly as possible. Congratulations CEO Regan."

"It will all work, Annie. You'll still be my boss."

I laughed out loud at the thought of bossing my husband around on any level, then matched his seriousness. "I've been thinking it's time for Hartford, Ltd., to have a real board with external directors. Let's have lunch. I'm curious about what else you've been thinking."

He stood first and reached out a hand to me. "So you know, the visual imaging monitor can be turned off for half hour increments with a code that Lao left in my side table drawer."

"The CEO sleeping with the chairman of the board might be called nepotism and there would be a permanent record," I joked.

"That's why Hartford, Ltd., was set up as a private, family-owned business. So you could have the power to boss all of us at least forty hours a week."

Chapter Thirty-five

WE CARRIED LUNCH to the screen porch, both of us hoping fresh air might refresh our tired brains. Like his parents, David drank hot coffee all day all year round. We talked about the kids' recovery progress and Andrew's request for land and a directorship. Clarissa sent me six messages from Washington, D.C., during the first fifteen minutes.

"Who gets Clarissa," David said with an absolutely straight face. "It would be good for you to have a familiar person watching your back, but I'm not sure she'd be open to D.C."

"I think she needs to stay here. She knows where to find everything, the history of most purchases, how to get ordinary things done at the regional or state level. We agree she is a good judge of people, including the staff." I talked myself into leaving Clarissa behind. "Guess I'll be going it alone."

"There might be a few of my former DOE analysts who would jump at the chance to work close to the White House." David put down his coffee cup. "Do you think you'll be near the inner circle?"

"David, really. I'll be building a new ethics review for a bureau. If I meet the president, it'll probably be with a few hundred other people in a reception line."

He gave me a look that implied I was clueless about the months ahead. My previous time in Washington, D.C., was as a poor trainee in a federal program during the end of the depression. The closest I'd been to the White House was a private tour for David and I after his return from the Paraguay abduction. A savvy business owner, I suspected that I'd also be a country bumpkin in shark-infested political waters.

"Raima is reviewing a stack of paperwork." I yawned and felt my jaw might not close. "I think I read something about signing a Patriot Pledge and maybe a vow of celibacy."

"Phoebe wants to see us." David was on his feet before his communicator quieted. My joke stayed behind with the remains of lunch.

A brown suit drifted behind us as we made our way through the residence. I glanced back two or three times. The broad-shouldered security agent slowed when we slowed. "Why don't you just walk with us," I asked over my shoulder. "We may as well introduce ourselves and tell you where I'm going."

"Not protocol, ma'am. That would be a distraction."

"Well, you're not going to blend into the crowd in our home." David pulled on my elbow. "I'll get used to being protected from people I see every day."

"Don't make it difficult for the guy," David said in a low voice. "He's doing his job. They know more about how you live than you'd want to believe. Don't think about it."

People fed me, washed my clothes, and cleaned the rooms where I worked or rested. Not that many years ago I was self-conscious about having others do the fundamental work. I decided I could become comfortable with their protection, particularly if it meant I no longer had to drive.

Still weak and tethered to a hospital bed by oxygen tubes, Phoebe had improved. She pushed aside the tall cup held by an aide when we saw us. Her eyes widened as David picked up one hand and kissed it. "How's my girl doing?" he asked. She raised a shoulder, lowered it.

"You're looking better, Phoebs." I stood next to David. "Dr. Frances says you're doing well, but how do you feel?"

She held onto my hand, pulled me closer. "I'm very tired and I hurt."

To hear her thready voice, we had to bend close. "I have something I need to tell both of you." Her cracked lips pained me. "Noah told me you're having a family meeting about Hartford this afternoon. I want to do what we talked about within the foundation."

"Milan is now heading the Bureau and there will be changes in the Intellectual Corps. You can work in the private sector on work of value to advancement of the United States." I felt David staring at me as I spoke to Phoebe, upset I had not shared this with him earlier. "So you have choices. Things will be quite different with Milan at the helm." I used a tissue to gently wipe her face of a slow flow of tears. Again I held back news about Ahlmet.

"Amen." David's simple response sounded above the medical monitors and equipment.

Phoebe didn't ask for details. "That's good. Milan will have to approve the Regan research plan."

"No, your choice is in your hands, Phoebs." I dabbed more at her tears. "There have been deep changes. When you're stronger, you can read all about it."

"I'm too tired to talk. I needed you both to know I want in on the new venture. And I want a full research lab. I'll help pay for that, Mom. It has to be the best." She looked at David. "You know what a lab needs."

"I do. We'll take that into our planning."

"And, I'm not sure I want it to be here." Her eyes closed. "Somewhere on Lake Michigan. North. Far north. Nowhere near a big city." She raised one hand, dismissing us.

I leaned over and kissed her forehead. Her hand touched my chin.

"Thanks, Mom. Sorry, I got to sleep."

"Do that, sweetheart."

David headed out. I settled her hand back on the bed and followed him toward Andrew's corner of the large room. With the head of the bed elevated and pillows behind his head, Andrew sat propped up holding a covered mug. A tray with light foods straddled his body.

"Helluva routine," he said pointing to the tray. "I sleep, eat, sleep."

"Why does Phoebe want to live in Wisconsin?" David's lack of greeting surprised me, but Andrew took the question calmly. "She wants in the Giant Pines research plan, but with her labs on Lake Michigan. And, you want land here. What's up?"

"Better for a research group focusing on clean water to be located near a polluted great lake?" Andrew sighed. "Your small group that services clients using Tia Regan's technology is based in a place called Fish Creek. Phoebe said they tell her that she wouldn't have to fight to find good lab workers."

David looked ready to press for more understanding, but I reminded him that Andrew was in a hospital bed.

"Phoeb and I call Ashwood home and we'd like to build here." Andrew volunteered. "Think about it, she came here to continue her work. People don't have to be where their labs are unless they are lab scientists. She's not in any shape to fully articulate her plan."

"Of course." David murmured. He rubbed the back of his neck. "I got ahead of myself."

"We're going to get out of here and let you finish your lunch." I wiggled his big toe. "Every time I see you I'm more encouraged."

"The doctors say I'll be in here about a week and could be laid up for a couple of months after that." Fortunately he escaped serious internal injuries, but there was trauma and a lung that was causing concern. "They already notified my boss. Hope you don't mind an extended stay."

"Not at all." I thought about asking for an extension on my Washington, D.C., report date, but knew Andrew should be well out of physical danger in three weeks. "I'll be back later."

David waited for me in the hall, standing at a window with his hands in his pockets. He looked younger than his age, yet I wondered if he had ten to twelve hours of energy each day to keep up with Harford's demands.

Leaving Ashwood

"I don't understand their relationship or her demands." David kept his voice low in a hall famous for amplifying even a small sneeze. "Property on Lake Michigan's northern shore will cost millions, equipping a lab an equal amount, and we don't have a clue about what she wants to study or if it will be commercially viable."

"Here's something Frances said to me last night—the life that Phoebe leads feeds narcissism. Think of the Bureau doing everything necessary to keep her research and bodily needs satisfied." I paused to pull my next words together with care. "Andrew knows what he wants. I hope he understands the implications of Phoebe's situation."

"I'm with you on that. As much as I would love to see Phoebe spend her life with someone as decent and stable as Andrew, I also want our guy to have a peaceful life and family. She's a most unlikely candidate for parenthood. Kind of like her mother." He stopped talking. Should have stopped one sentence earlier.

We walked up the stairs to the residence's main floor in silence.

"Clarissa is asking me to review my mail," I said as we walked through the busy hall leading to the dining room. "I'll see you in about ninety minutes."

"Shouldn't we be going over business matters before the meeting?"

"I sent you the entire business file on re-organization as a refresher. For this level of discussion that's plenty. No reason to overprepare." I affectionately squeezed his arm.

"We can walk over together." I could tell by his voice that his mind was moving to other concerns.

"Sorry to throw you into this head first, David."

"No problem. I've been thrown into a lot of major projects in my career with a lot less knowledge. I'm more concerned about how we'll all get along without you here."

"Holograms, communicators, and mail. I'll be back for long weekends. That's more time together than during most of your foreign assignments." I activated the office door and waved him in first. A brown suit waited behind us. "It will be strange to have a place that is only mine."

"You'll love not having to share a bathroom."

"Spoken by the one who hogs the shower." I yawned, headed to pour myself a cup of coffee before sitting down to read mail.

Clarissa prioritized everything according to subject, marked time-sensitive, and items already handled. A new confidential folder appeared that I wouldn't be able to access until I accepted my commission by filing completed forms.

Raima's review of the White House forms was summarized in five sentences: "Congratulations. No way out. Make the best of it. Forms are sloppy, but non-negotiable with the exception of reimbursable expenses, staffing, and housing. Repeat, make the best of it." As directed in the original packet, she directly billed the White House vetting office.

Before our afternoon meeting I completed the White House packet and took my place on the federal government payroll as Special White House Commissioner Anne Hartford. In forty-eight hours I would be official with authorization to lease both office space and living quarters in Washington, D.C., and hire the first of a dozen staff.

Young people who don't want to spend their lives traveling, or may not have the best scores on annual achievement examinations, gravitated toward federal government jobs. Decent wages, wonderful benefits, and the possibility to climb your way up the wealthy rungs of the Washington, D.C., career ladder looked attractive to kids living in cramped multi-generational metro housing. Federal jobs provided the closest living to the old middle-class. Reviewing the compensation and fringe benefits offered for my one-year commission made me pause. The starting pay levels for my D.C. staff, beyond reflecting a ridiculous cost of living adjustment, would provide generous increases for quite a few of our Ashwood employees. I thought about options.

Chapter Thirty-Six

AS A CHILD I PLAYED schoolteacher with dolls and stuffed toys balanced behind shoebox desks. Not one person who knew Anne Hartford from before the Second Great Depression would recognize the corporate executive preparing to hand off leadership of a decent size corporation to accept a presidential appointment. The Annie they knew wanted a nice career as a teacher, time for her husband and children, a comfortable home. I had hoped to put my kids through college, see Europe, and travel the United States.

Many of those people are dead now. Some didn't survive the starving years of the depression. Some couldn't survive the grueling labor years of the recovery. Others gave up. The Bureau of Human Capital Management used psychological assessments to put people without needed skills back to work. They probably inventoried the potential jumpers or wrist slashers as well. No resources were used for the future of those who wouldn't return the investment.

I spent three years in a Washington, D.C., training center learning to manage an agricultural production facility staffed by assigned workers and children taken from their city homes. The bitter, solemn, and emotionally damaged Anne Hartford who walked down Ashwood's hall to her first meeting had no line of sight to the woman she would become. When I could dream about my future once more I repeated the pattern of my great-grandparents coming out of the first great depression and looked to build security for those I loved. The only way out of the government-assigned workforce was bona fide labor in a family business that contributed to the nation's security. That's what David and I built to offer shelter of good, honest employment to our kids.

With an acceptable education program and social service plan, Faith had five years before assignment and could chose Hartford, Ltd., an option not available when her siblings entered the work registry. This day was why I grew the company with David and Paul in support. If our children wanted to be part of Hartford, Ltd., they had a choice, a priceless freedom in our nation.

From grants given David and me twenty-seven years earlier in compensation for serious government infractions, we had built ourselves a tidy empire. In the bipolar economic structure of the mid-twenty-first century, we were on the safe side. Hartford, Ltd., was diversified across industries and flush with cash. Pre-second depression our children might have lived off trust funds. Post-second depression our children were given the gift of working in a healthier environment.

Deshomm and the president may have rushed the timing, but our children were ready to make decisions about their work futures. We sat around a large conference room table with Andrew on hologram. Clarissa was present to ensure the accuracy of our meeting's records and monitor incoming communications. I asked Terrell, Magda, Lao, and Max to be part of the group because they each headed significant parts of our operations. Raima and our external services director joined later as consultants.

"Much has changed in the last twenty-four hours, which is why I've asked all of you to change your schedules to make this meeting possible. I wish Phoebe were able to join us, but we can't delay."

Regardless of relationship, each person in the meeting looked professional, even Faith. I noticed Terrell studying me during updates on Phoebe. He looked tired. Losing a night of sleep wasn't easy on any of us so far past our twenties. I smiled at him as the small talk ended.

"You were all asked to accept a new code of confidentiality. Take it very seriously." I paused, slowed down what would be shocking to my children. "If you followed any media today you know that a difficult conflict occurred within the Bureau of National Human Capital Management. I don't have details to share except to tell you that last night our friend Milan was appointed Secretary of a restructured Bureau."

Small applause followed the news along with comments about being close to someone who was close to the president. David and Lao were quiet.

I drew in a breath. "In two days President Hernandez will be announcing that I have been commissioned to form a Board of Ethics within the new Bureau. This is very confidential."

All chatter about Milan's rise died. The kids and I had lived in the metro area for a few years while Andrew, Phoebe, and Noah attended a gifted offspring school. But our children thought of me as mom and a fixture of Ashwood.

"Congratulations, Annie. We're very proud." Fatigue lifted from Terrell's face as he smiled. "Milan's been trying to get you off Ashwood, and he finally got the president of the United States on his side." He nodded his head.

"Will you move to Washington, D.C., Mom?" Our youngest child, the only one who still saw me every day asked. "And could I come with you? Washington, D.C., would be so great."

Leaving Ashwood

"Will you be leaving Ashwood? What about Hartford?" Magda kept the meeting business-oriented.

Briefly I wondered how Magda would work with David. She ruled agricultural production. If she didn't have strong interpersonal skills with her management team down to common day laborers, I might have had to replace her. We were longtime friends, but that didn't stop her from being challenging and headstrong when convinced hers was the only right way to accomplish a goal.

"I'll answer your question on two levels." I felt freed. "I don't really know the full scope of the president's expectations for the Ethics Board. My contract stipulates that I will work an average of four days per week in Washington, D.C., through the first ninety days of my service, with air transport between Minnesota and the capital provided by the government."

"Will we contact you when there are questions?" Magda tilted her head, her lips closing tight after her last word.

"For Hartford, Ltd., this will be a time of change. We've decided to formalize the board of directors and look outside for appropriate industry members. I will limit myself to sitting as chairman of the Board and concentrate on Hartford's long-term strategy. David has agreed to step into the role of president and lead the day-to-day. All becomes effective at midnight."

Silence followed. I had thought someone might congratulate David or nod their head in agreement. Our kids looked thoughtful, Clarissa seemed to stutter in her note taking, and Magda appeared stunned. She and Terrell had been involved with some strategic planning in their functions, but the announcements showed how different Hartford, Ltd., was today than a half dozen years ago when everyone knew everything.

"How long do we have for transition?" Max had his calendar open plus a small notepad. "There are issues at Giant Pines because of new government regulations that I was hoping to discuss with you. Probably in two to three days."

"We're hoping you can shoulder additional leadership, Max." I moved us into grounds where Magda could be difficult. "I leave for Washington, D.C. in twenty-one days and my calendar is out of control. So fortunately David has been involved in almost everything at Giant Pines and a lot of the important issues of Hartford over the past few years."

"I have to object if we talk about splitting dairy and livestock from general agricultural operations." Magda tied her words too closely to the end of my sentence. "Whether we ship lettuce or eggs or milk or hamburger to market, it all requires Hartford labor. We'll have inefficiencies."

"Max might feel the same way." David stepped into his new role, offering Magda his perspective originating from long days at Giant Pines. She'd find him tougher to quarrel with because he had spent time in the fields and barns. "We'd like to see the Ashwood brand have more prominence in the livestock market."

"Does a Washington, D.C., move impact the environmental research center plans?" Andrew asked from his hospital bed.

David and I had agreed to use this question as a launching point for a wider discussion about the future of Hartford, Ltd., We had expected John to be the first to ask.

"Because of Paul's significant financial endowment, we'll continue with our plans to transition part of Giant Pines for the research foundation. John will be leaving consulting to head the foundation. Phoebe will head a second classic research lab in what we're now calling Hartford Futures focusing on water purification products and other projects with commercial potential."

"Where do I fit into the picture?" Everyone turned to look at Faith. "I am willing to complete college, but only if I can be part of growing Hartford, Ltd." She looked down at her data pad. "I am young, but I've worked in the greenhouses and barns. I read everything about our business that I'm allowed to see. This is where I want to be."

"Where do you see yourself in the business?" No one smiled around the table. Faith put herself into an applicant role in a crowd of people used to assessing skills and potential. David sat back after asking the question.

"Since I interviewed with McGill, I've been approached by a number of multi-corps. They would love to understand what we do here that makes Hartford, Ltd., so successful." She made eye contact with each person around the table. "Andrew's help made it possible for me to do a four-year law program that will only require me to live away six months each year. I want to work here during my remote study time to be exposed to everything I can so when Raima is ready to retire, I can be in-house counsel." With flair she sat back in her chair, lowered her eyes for a few seconds, then looked at the group with confidence. "She has agreed to have me clerk within her firm."

Andrew began clapping and others joined. Recovered from the shock that multi-corps reps were contacting Faith, I wanted to walk around the table and hug this beautiful daughter, but I didn't want to diminish her step into adulthood. David and I would talk later, both amazed at how Faith had developed.

I used her four-year program as a good timeframe for everyone to think about Hartford, Ltd., and led a robust discussion. Clarissa kept us on task until two hours ran out, then drew me away from the table.

Leaving Ashwood

"They want you in Washington, D.C., tomorrow to prep for announcing the ethics board." She didn't wait for me to absorb this schedule change. "You'll be picked up by air transport in the morning. Milan has you booked for dinner with a working session at the White House. It will be a long day." Then she paused.

"Really?" I thought that even if I went straight to bed now I couldn't make up the last two nights.

"Really," she replied. "Your credentials arrived about ten minutes ago. Only you can receive the packet so a government underling is waiting outside your office."

David stood on the far side of the room talking with Magda, Max, and John. The discussion appeared friendly, although I could see the defensive hold in Magda's shoulders.

"Clarissa, could you arrange a nice time in the city for Faith and me before I leave?" She looked surprised. "I know I don't have a lot of days to spare, but this one is important."

"We'll shoehorn that in." She shook her head, checked her communicator. "The courier is waiting, Ms. Commissioner."

"Call Milan, ask for clearance to tell the extended staff before I leave."

"Will do." She opened the door. Two brown suits fell into step behind me as I crossed the hall and entered the sunny space I had considered a refuge.

The courier bowed his head, old civil protocol. I did the same.

"I need a voice sample, finger print, and blood stick test, Ms. Commissioner."

"Here's my right hand." I held it out, let the serious young woman press one finger onto an inkblot, then jab the next finger.

She checked the fingerprint against her source and read data off the blood stick. "Everything is accurate." With her head bowed, she extended a thick packet closed with sealed wires. From her coat pocket she took out a small clipper and broke the seal. "Have a good day." She turned and left. One brown suit left. One remained outside my office door.

Chapter Thirty-Seven

WITH TYPICAL DRAMA, Phoebe developed an allergic reaction to residue from a surgical cleanser and ran a high fever throughout that evening. Instead of going to bed early, David and I split the hours between dinner and midnight. Thankfully medication brought her relief before one of us passed out at her side.

"Do you think I could ask my nice, inconspicuous bodyguard to carry me upstairs?" I joked with David as we shuffled our way toward the staircase. "Who built this place with such a long staircase anyway?"

"The feds. Nothing easy with those dudes." He tucked one hand into the corner of my arm and we swayed up the steps and down Ashwood's central hall toward our suite. For a moment I considered crawling into bed fully dressed or maybe fully nude. Then I remembered the motion monitors and changed into a sleep shirt. David snored on his side of the bed.

When David traveled for the DOE, his snoring was frequently a loud, noisy sound that pushed me into earplugs. Used to being the parent in charge of caring for our children and the estate owner awakened when things happened at Ashwood or Giant Pines, I had become a light sleeper. David's snoring disrupted my sleep when I had a sleep surplus or made falling asleep more difficult when my mind raced from thought to thought even though I needed rest. The unexpected Washington, D.C., preparation trip kept my mind busy. My sleep-deprived body could not find rest.

After two o'clock I got up, found a robe and went to our family room where I kept a pillow and blanket for these kinds of nights. I thought I saw Amber walking into the kitchen area. Settled on a sofa under a soft cover, my eyes closed.

"Ms. Hartford."

A stranger's voice called me from a dream about green walking shoes. A touch I didn't recognize jolted me upright. A young man, clad in brown, squatted by the sofa.

"Phoebe is asking for you and a communication has been initiated for the two of you with Secretary Milan."

"You're kidding." Allergies caused me to breathe through an open mouth so I sounded more like an old man than myself. "She was fine at two a.m. and it can't be much more than an hour or so later. Who originated a communication with Milan at this time?" But I was sitting up, reaching for my robe as I tried to speak logically. The young man held out soft house shoes that I kept in the foyer, a kind gesture that felt uncomfortable.

"Why didn't Phoebe just call me?" My question was rhetorical, just conversation to fill the awkward time until I felt steady and awake. We began to walk, the young man a step behind.

"They say she tried. You might have been sleeping deeply. By the way it is three thirty."

"What is your name?"

"Robert."

For a number of years in Phoebe's childhood, I abandoned sleep to comfort her through night terrors. How others stayed asleep while she screamed, I never understood. Small lights illuminated the central hall. The deepest part of the night was past. Sunrise would begin in sixty or seventy minutes. I held on to the railing as we made our way down the stairs, trailed one hand along the lower floor's wall. Half the sick room was dark, the rest half-lit.

"You look tired." People in her Chicago lab would recognize the quality of her raspy voice better than I could. "Sorry to drag you out of bed."

The nurse recording vitals pulled a chair to the head of Phoebe's bed. "She's much improved since you saw her at eleven. You should sit down." I obeyed. She shook a blanket open and tucked it around me as if I were an invalid.

"Milan isn't dressed for the public yet." Phoebe told me this unremarkable information as if sharing a significant discovery.

"You should both be sleeping," my confidante turned boss said as a hologram formed on Phoebe's bed tray. "But, I understand that Phoebe needs to know what is happening in Chicago and how that impacts her future."

I wondered how many times he answered Phoebe's odd requests as her legal guardian and who would provide her that kind of support in the new order. She sat forward. Her bony elbow, so close to my face, tugged at my maternal instincts even as I backed away from the view.

"My mother said Ahlmet could no longer control me and I overheard other comments about him. The implant is gone, but what exactly happened?"

"Ahlmet died in a fight outside the Chicago labs, Phoebe." Milan gave her facts, no empathy or emotion. "There has not been media coverage because of specific language in his employment contract."

"No national day of mourning?" Her voice became whispery. "No crowning of a new Intellectual Corps member? I guess you have two vacancies with my decision to join the family business."

"You haven't had access to mail, so you may not know that we've changed the rules somewhat around how the work of the Intellectual Corps may be done. If you continue to work on clean water and water reclamation research projects, you can do that within private industry with certain expectations around commercialization of your output."

Phoebe looked toward me. "I think Mom tried to tell me that. Good. I'd like to send someone to Chicago to pack my things when I'm ready to relocate. I'm thinking of Northern Wisconsin along Lake Michigan."

A yawn preceded Milan's response. "Take advantage of the technology corridor funding in that peninsula area."

"Exactly." She smiled, looked relieved and sleepy. "Is there anything else I should know, Milan? Will you still be here for me?"

"Only as a friend, Phoebe." He cleared his throat. "The legal guardian structure has been replaced. My new role is rather demanding."

"Congratulations." Her words and facial expression appeared contradictory.

"There is one important development with Ahlmet's passing. He's willed continued work on his implant technology to you—labs, patents, contracts." Milan paused, providing Phoebe and me time to absorb this news. "Of course most of that wasn't his to give away, but there will be handsome royalties in the future that will pass to you."

Her lips turned downward and she shook her head. "I'll want a voice in how that technology is deployed. I don't want money made by enslaving people's minds. You have no idea what that was like."

"That will be one of the issues Anne's new group will review. It certainly is a rare governmental ethics challenge." Milan waited while Phoebe yawned then put a hand to the incisions on her neck. "There's time for all this to be discussed when you are stronger. Go to sleep, Phoebe. No one expects you back at work for the next few weeks. And, let Anne go back to sleep or she and I will be yawning at the White House tonight." He disappeared.

"Sleep here, Mom." She pressed her call button. "That chair extends and I'll have the staff give both of us something that will give us a couple of hours of good zzz's." Someone entered her alcove. "Please don't leave me alone."

Chapter Thirty-Eight

I ESCAPED DAVID'S SNORES with a few hours resting on the chair-cot and a deep inhale of some medicinal smelling vapor. Before the lights dimmed, my eyes closed. I awoke with none of that sluggish feeling that accompanied sleep aids. Phoebe didn't stir as I left her side.

Resident workers showed surprise at the sight of me walking through sunlit halls upstairs in my robe and slippers. For a moment I thought of playing lady of leisure and stopping in the dining room for breakfast before dressing. But I wasn't a person with time to waste. Hartford, Ltd., needed a thoughtful transition and my government mail had to be read.

"Ms. Hartford." I turned at a stranger's voice. Another brown suit walked out from the formal gathering room. "Your stepson is waiting to talk with you in the family room."

"How many of you are wandering around?" I asked.

He smiled, shrugged.

"I know. That's classified." With brown suits, handlers, watchers, and cares, the federal government had built an army of secret support employees. I began to understand why there was constant pressure for Hartford, Ltd., to accept workers within our domestic positions. Our halls could be a training site for jobs that required unobtrusive behavior. Perhaps some of our trainees received their true pay from federal agencies. I swerved from the short hall to our suite and headed to the family room.

"They said you were visiting Phoebe," Noah said as he took in my attire.

"That is partly true." I sat down. "We had a conference with Milan around three thirty then I let the staff give me a little something so I could sleep for a few hours. And here I am, wandering about in my pjs when you are all up and working."

"Let me have the guy in brown bring you some coffee."

"I was just wondering if Ashwood had helped train people who became brown suits. Quite a job description--personal attendant, body guard, watcher." Noah did not respond to my comment. "What has Milan done?"

I called to the nameless shadow waiting in the hall. "Could you please get me a carafe of coffee and two cups? Maybe a muffin." He showed no surprise at being sent on an errand. "Thanks."

Noah moved toward a corner of the room. Faith's cat, the only one allowed above the lower levels in the residence, lounged on the back of a chair. He picked it up and sat down, holding the lazy animal in his lap. "You're not the only one to talk with Milan. That guy must never sleep."

"This sounds serious."

"They want me back in the Intellectual Corps. Different terms. This could change my plans at Mayo."

Growing up alongside Phoebe's brilliance, Noah's extraordinary intellect attracted less attention. Our family gentle soul, free spirit, comedian, and least predictable member had opted out of the Intellectual Corps without a second look.

"What does your father think?"

"I don't have to talk with him to know he'll be against it. You've both preached the dream of determining our own lives. I wanted to talk this one through with you."

A knock at the room's door gave me time to pull thoughts together as coffee and a complete breakfast tray was carried in by a regular Ashwood worker. Noah pulled a table closer. I poured us coffee, stirred cream into mine, and suddenly remembered my mother giving up this small treat while fighting weight and cholesterol. A different life.

"Tell me why Milan's invitation feels right." I took my first sip of coffee.

"If I want access to the best research facilities and staff, there are two or three ways possible. Intellectual Corps, multi-corps, or large university that is probably tied to one of the multi-corps. Even Mayo couldn't commit resources to research that wasn't commercially viable." Noah poured generous cream into his coffee. Ashwood would destroy his taste for the white liquid called cream in the metro. "I like the Mayo folks, and I understand the reality of today's economics, but I've become concerned that I'll be tracked into research that's on a corporate research agenda."

"You really don't want to practice medicine? The surgical crew thought you were a natural."

"Of course I'd like to practice medicine, but Phoebe and I were engineered to do more." He raised one eyebrow, a David gesture. "I need to accept my responsibility to make a difference. To find ways to keep people healthier longer. I've screwed away enough time."

Noah might not have worked to his potential, but he had scarcely led a leisurely life. "Tell me what Milan offered."

"Expedited med school wherever I choose, and support for establishing my own research connected to a major medical institution or contained within one of the

Leaving Ashwood

Bureau's centers." He paused, slowed his recital. "I have to sign a five-year post-doctoral agreement. Financials aren't a lot different than what Phoebe has described." His seriousness broke as he changed to typical Noah concerns. "Eight weeks vacation per year. Support if I choose to do research off-site. Housing not limited to Bureau barracks, limitations on handlers and watchers. Picking my own care. A personal transport and private jet travel."

"What, no king bed or dog?" We laughed. "Would you like Raima to review the proposal?"

"It's already in her office."

Breakfast waited, couldn't distract me from this conversation. "You've made up your mind. Will you still study at Mayo or head somewhere else?"

His hands connected behind his head as he leaned into his chair. The cat jumped off his lap. "I'm attracted to Stanford, but the geophysical situation is too threatening for long-term research facilities. It's down to Harvard and Mayo at this point. One has the prestige and I am attracted to the other because of its outreach facilities in many parts of the world. I'll let you know next week."

"Congratulations, Noah." I put down my cup and stood up to hug him. He threw his arms around me and patted my back. "Ashwood's school will become even better known for early education of two of the Intellectual Corps."

"If we could lure Andrew to the Corps, that would be three. You should become known for raising brainiac kids as rather ordinary people." He pulled away. "Well, relatively ordinary considering our genetic engineering."

"Talk with your father."

"Later." He winked. "First, I'll finish your breakfast."

Back in my room, I gathered clothes and locked myself in the bathroom where David assured me there were no monitors. As the shower dashed away the last of my sleepiness, I forced myself to think positively about Noah's decision.

Chapter Thirty-Nine

A Bureau air transport dropped me off in Ashwood's courtyard shortly before midnight after a day that included Washington, D.C., meetings and a press conference. The announcement served a fresh face to the media for its perpetual news cycle. By the time I boarded my ride home, everything known about my past had been turned into dinner table chatter with a few leftovers for the morning. Everything was open—David's years with the DOE, my surrogate status, the Paraguay abduction and occupation of Ashwood, Tia's career and death, the Stolen Children campaign, our children's careers, Phoebe's Intellectual Corps achievements, and slightly confused stories about the shooting episode. Many reporters pegged my long-standing relationship with Milan as the reason I accepted President Hernandez's invitation. Everyone seemed eager to gloss over the fact that I served under commission, not involuntarily. The political and media sharks waited in the waters hungry for more.

David greeted me from the screen porch, but suggested we relax with wine and cheese in our suite. I knew he was troubled.

"Tell me about your day," he invited with a tight smile. "I saw more bad pictures of us than I remember."

Accepting that others would now do for me, I handed my briefcase and suit bag over to an assistant and walked with empty arms to our room. David turned the monitor to blur while I slipped into clean pjs. I spread my toes on the cool wood floor, delighted to be out of dress shoes.

"I believe Milan wants ethics guidelines developed for the agency and has vetted good people." David looked interested, but not like he was listening. "I also believe Hernandez is willing to let Milan have his ethics group in return for his taking on a huge, shitty mess. She may not want much to happen out of the ethics work. Very mixed messages."

"What about housing and staff?" He poured himself a full goblet of white wine.

"I'll have a generous two-bedroom-plus-den apartment in a building that houses embassy and Congressional staff without permanent addresses. It's very secure. Staffing is a topic for tomorrow." I put my hand over my wine glass as he held out the bottle.

"Did you know Amber is preparing Dad's former rooms for Andrew and Phoebe?"

I thought he was upset because of Noah's decision and was surprised. "We didn't talk about it, but the space would work."

"And you're comfortable with housing them together?" He sounded confused, not angry.

"They're adults. They don't have to ask permission."

David concentrated on the wine he swirled in his glass instead of looking my way. "Andrew must recognize that Phoebe is in no shape to make personal decisions. His life will be hell, and when they separate, our family will suffer."

A sigh escaped, a tired sigh. Crop reports and investment decisions made easier problems than politics and bedfellows.

"They are adults, David. I have concerns as well. We'll talk with them but not until they're stronger. The shared room can always be talked about as part of the recovery strategy."

"Do you feel the same way about Noah's decision to throw aside medical school and join the corps?"

"Noah presented an impressive set of reasons for why he's made this decision. His terms are more flexible. I couldn't find anything outside my own hopes and fears to tell him this might be a mistake."

"Look at what's happened to Phoebe's life." He pointed my way with his wine glass. "Tell me that's the way you want another one of the kids to live."

"There is a new administration of the Intellectual Corps." I put my hand on his knee. "And Noah is a mature individual, not an impressionable teenager."

"He knows that I don't agree, but he signed the papers today. He'll be moving to Boston in August and doing some hocus pocus expedited medical training at Harvard."

"You didn't use those words with him."

David put down his glass, settled one hand over mine, and shook his head. "Of course not. We could have offered him financial support to set up a medical practice."

"I know."

"If this doesn't work out for Noah, it will be tough for me to forget how tight you've been with Milan."

"I know that also." We sat quietly. I glanced at a clock and saw I had only four and a half hours until my first Washington, D.C., weekly phone call.

"And I heard that Amber has been spending her nights with John." David drank the end of his wine, looked over the glass rim for my reaction.

I should have been shocked, but the day had stripped away most of that emotion. I giggled.

David groaned. "Our son is so good looking."

"So is she." Now I understood why she looked good even at two in the morning, sneaking into the kitchen.

"I may be getting older, but I still recognize a beautiful woman. She's also six years older than he is."

"Unless you want to go wake them up right now, I really need to get some sleep." My voice cracked. "I have a conference call at six thirty."

"I missed you." David tucked me under the cover and turned off the lights. "Go to sleep."

In the dark my body slipped into relaxation while my mind stuck on David's unhappiness about our children's choices. Andrew's love couldn't magically smooth over Phoebe's perplexing mixture of sweetness, narcissism, common sense and cunning. That mixture made her successful in school and work, but could be toxic in a marriage and parenting.

David snored lightly, turned on his back, and stretched his legs across the foot of our bed. He twitched then settled. I moved toward the edge of the mattress, closed my eyes, and meditated until distractions faded. The alarm sounded at five and decades of repetition pushed me along. Instead of heading to my office, I turned to the kitchen for coffee and companionship with Terrell and Amber.

"Ms. Commissioner is back in residence," Terrell teased. "Before the brown suits learn how you like your coffee, let me pour you a mug." For a moment the simple kindness of friends brought nostalgia stronger than the aroma of Terrell's heavenly brew. "You okay?" he asked as he handed me my favorite blue clay mug.

"Three very late nights after three intense days." Accepting the coffee, I brought it to my face and inhaled. "If the CEO of Hartford, Frances, and your wonderful kids don't mind, I'd like to make you my first Washington, D.C. hire." I laughed to assure him I was joking. "You'll be my second hire, Amber. A year in D.C. would teach you much about the world."

She smiled, but her deep brown eyes showed confusion. Usually easy with words, Amber had nothing to say.

Terrell watched the two of us. He probably knew what was happening in Amber's personal life. A woman wouldn't talk with the mother of her lover about such things. I sipped at my coffee, wondering what I was looking for in the kitchen.

"If you got a few minutes, let's grab you a breakfast bowl and eat in my office." Terrell picked up a tray marked for my office. "Unless the two of you need to talk?"

"We'll catch up later, Anne." Amber nodded and pulled out her data pad. "Have a good morning."

New packaging for high-priced cereals filled the conference table in Terrell's office, but we settled in our regular place for conversation, two overstuffed chairs in the corner. Here his kids sometimes studied, here Terrell handed out his worldly counsel.

"How was D.C.?" Terrell crossed one ankle over the top of his other leg. "Looked like the media goons want to party on this whole ethics board thing. You in for a rough ride?"

"It's murkier than working with the FDA on the organic wheat council. And the politics are crazy. The multi-corps have nothing on the federal government when it comes to wondering who is pulling the strings." The first bite of an egg and bacon croissant incited a small sense of wellness. "Dinner was a protein stick and a wrap of sweet o's on the transport. I'll pack fruit and nuts in the future."

I took another bite. "What's happening here? Phoebe and Andrew and the federal government seem to be distracting me from keeping on top of the people news."

"What are you fishing for, Annie?" His eyes twinkled.

"Something about my youngest son and the beautiful Ms. Amber."

"Something your husband discovered when he walked in on a personal conversation?"

"I thought she'd nab Andrew. They're closer in age and have always been so companionable."

"Age and companionship don't usually spark romance. John and Amber are definitely an item." He quirked his head. "You okay with it?"

"I'll have gorgeous grandchildren."

He held up a hand for a high five. "And David?"

"Lots happening in our personal world and he's not used to dealing with the messy side of parenting." I put my tray on the floor, kept the coffee close. "You're not that many years from kids thinking about what to do after finishing their schooling here. Maybe you hope one of them will be a doctor and they both decide to go for government jobs in the city."

"This about Phoebe and Andrew?" No twinkling eyes accompanied his words. A touch of sadness often entered our conversations about his favorite Regan child.

"Partially."

"We haven't really seen Phoebe as herself since she got here, Annie." He chewed on his bottom lip. "I know Fran thinks she's got Phoebe all figured out, but I'm sure that that young woman is more grounded than we all see. I don't know that they're a match made in heaven, but this world is more about practical than hearts and wishes."

"Well, Andrew certainly is practical."

"You opened that young man to laughing and singing and feeling safe, Annie. But your son also learned to depend on himself at a young age." He put a hand over mine. "Before the shooting he came to our house for a talk with Fran and me about Phoebe. His mind is as engaged as his heart."

My communicator hummed. "I've got to run." I bent to pick up my tray and he stopped me. "Keep your Saturday mornings free when I'm commuting to Washington. We'll have breakfast."

He'd find out later about Noah's decision to join the Intellectual Corps. That news could only be shared in truly secured space. The announcement ceremony would take place here with a nauseating amount of federal chest pounding about the dedication and patriotism of Noah in accepting this responsibility. Plans were underway to parade Phoebe, David, and myself in a show of our family's public service tradition. No one at Ashwood, not even Noah, knew of these plans.

Two brown suits appeared as I closed Terrell's door. I suspected that one of them would be all over Terrell's office by mid-morning to make sure the time I spent there was safe and clear of listening devices. Ms. Commissioner had come home.

Chapter Forty

PHOEBE ATTEMPTED TO KILL HERSELF at nine forty that morning. Her timing showed careful coordination of family members' schedules to take place during a pocket when everyone was engaged. David and John were halfway to a meeting in the metro. A visiting physician had started withdrawing Andrew's wound drains. Noah and I were in a secured conference room.

Frances, the only person outside the family given free access to visit Phoebe, was scheduled to assist with Andrew's procedure. Fortunately the visiting physician brought an associate, so Frances, who heard hacking sounds from Phoebe's alcove, left. She found Phoebe choking on the last of a small stash of miscellaneous pills.

Lao followed Intellectual Corps protocol and closed the estate's perimeter while on his way to collect me. He muscled past the brown suit of the morning to whisper "Phoebe" in my ear. I called the meeting to an end with Lao standing next to me inside the secured room.

"What's happened to Phoebe?" I asked as I pushed back my chair. Noah stood as well.

"Inadvertent medication." Lao spoke softly.

"Is she alive?" The other word could not be said.

"Frances found her in time." He opened the door. "A cart is waiting outside."

The self-fulfilling prophecy, begun by an unknown grandfather, carried through a mother, almost claimed my beloved stepdaughter. The nature versus nurture debate remained unresolved for another generation. The little girl who wished she was dead when her father was missing, the teenager screaming alone in a college dorm, a young woman standing on a chair on a Paris hotel balcony had actually acted on emotions. She waited until she had come home to try a date with death.

I held out a hand to Noah. "Come with me. David knows?" Lao nodded. "Who else?"

"John is in the transport. No one else outside the medical team."

"What about Andrew?" Noah's hand remained in mine, strong and cool.

"He's sedated for the transfer upstairs that's happening right now." Lao pointed to doors opening on the residence's lower level. "They're pumping Phoebe's stomach so you might not be able to enter her room, but Andrew has been moved."

Noah jumped to the ground before Lao stopped and ran in the door.

"Want me to stay?"

I accepted with a nod of the head. Inside the sick bay calm ruled. It was possible to hear a gagging sound and low voices. I returned to the hall, to stare out a window at the pond where this part of Phoebe's debacle began. Lao joined me, put one arm around my waist, a rare physical action.

"She will recover. Frances found her choking on the last pills." He spoke only facts, gave me a gentle squeeze, and then stepped away.

The July sun was hot over the orchards and open fields where the grass remained crushed from the med copter. We should have been having a family picnic lunch on the patio or planning a special dinner before everyone headed back to his or her work. My mind searched through what I knew for a way to respond to this crisis, to plan the words I would say when Frances pulled back the curtains.

"I don't understand why now?" Lao bent his head closer to me as I spoke almost to myself. "When Ahlmet was torturing her I expected something like this. She was in hell. Now her life is smoothing out."

"Maybe that's frightening." He crossed his arms, turned his back to the window and looked at me. "The lab routine ruled her life. Her mind lived larger than her soul. She may not be as strong as young people who have had to figure out the simple and difficult questions of life."

"She was too young when they took her." I lived in the metro for three years to keep her within the family until she was at least thirteen. Andrew and Noah were not sent to college until they were sixteen, but Phoebe was too bright. "All those emergency trips to Boston when no one could control her." Tears rolled down my face at the memories. I brushed them away. "Milan himself had to force them to let her come home for the holidays and a few weeks in the summer. She was a young girl studying with twenty-year-olds and faculty."

"You did what you could." He tipped his chin up. "Noah is coming."

I rubbed away the last tears as I turned. Noah's arms wrapped around me. "She'll be fine, Mom." He pushed my head into his shoulder, the comforter. "Don't cry." Over my head he asked Lao when David would be back and confirmed it could be an hour or more. "Want to see her now?"

We stepped apart and I patted my pockets for a handkerchief. "Sorry, I just lose all perspective when I think about what the Bureau's gifted offspring program did to her."

"If she stays here, she'll find her way. You and Terrell give her grounding." He pulled at my arm. "Please don't be generalizing and think that I'll go the same route as Phoebs. I'm in far more control."

Lao's head turned slightly. I held a finger to my lips. Noah flushed, hit his forehead with the palm of one hand.

"From here to the stairs, the hall is clear," Lao offered. "It's been scoured every fifteen minutes since the medical team began setting up sick bay. We've been monitoring their scour for any listening or watching devices. So talk. I think I need to know about this."

I took the lead, gestured for Noah to be quiet. "You'll have mail waiting for you regarding a conference call at three this afternoon about revisiting security for the announcement of Noah accepting appointment to the Intellectual Corps. That's tentatively scheduled for late next week."

"Congratulations." Lao held out his hand and they shook. "A family of honored individuals. My son should take note. And our future son."

"Congratulations to you as well. I know you wanted more children," Noah said and I wondered how they came to have that conversation. "I want to check on Phoebe. Maybe Frances can come out to give you an update."

The sick bay door opened. In the seconds before it closed I thought I heard the sound of weak crying. I leaned back against the window ledge, felt the warmth of the sun on my back.

"One of us should contact Milan," Lao suggested.

"Not really. They've terminated the extended legal guardian relationship. Milan is now merely a friend of the family. And my boss." Lao made a small sound. "I know, I've traveled across twenty some years to report to the same person."

"Regardless of the legal status, he will want to know that Phoebe is not doing well." He handed me his communicator, the only one on the estate that was always secure from external hacking or interference.

I held up a hand. "I'd rather you made the contact. I need to think."

While he left a terse message, I divided what had to be done into segments, made a few notes for myself on my data pad.

"After I see Frances and Phoebe, I'm going to talk with Andrew. He'll probably be out of sedation. I wonder if I should tell Faith or give her this study time?"

A brown suit approached, holding out a communicator. "Secretary Milan for Ms. Hartford."

"Anne, how are you holding up?" The kindness in his voice gave me permission to let my emotions come through. "I've been in touch with Dr. Frances and it sounds like Phoebe was a long way from successful."

"I haven't seen her yet. David has always been afraid this day would come and I really believed it wouldn't. Phoebe promised me that she would call for help." It was impossible to push aside guilt, but mostly I shook with anger at those who damaged the woman known as Phoebe. Lao put his arm back around me.

"She'll be okay, Annie." Milan spoke quickly. "Frances will be her constant companion and she has the family for support. This is an unfortunate medication mix up that someone should have noticed."

I handed the communicator to Lao, unable to listen as Milan spun lies to cover his Bureau. Lao stepped away. I waved the brown suit back. "You'll get your damn communicator back," I hissed. "Give us some space."

Lao spoke with Milan, ended the call, and pocketed the brown suit's communicator. "He directed me to have Frances give you a sedative."

"Don't you dare."

The sick bay door opened. Frances appeared, her usual calm physician exterior replaced with fierceness. She closed the door before walking the short distance to where we waited. I motioned toward where the brown suit lurked.

"Leave," she said pointing toward the guard. "I want you no closer to this door than the staircase or I will enter your name in the case notes as contributing to the stress of my patient."

He held up his hands, raised his shoulders as if caught in a lose-lose situation. She held her ground. With one more gesture of confusion, he wandered away.

"Phoebe is fine physically. Her throat and nasal passages are uncomfortable, her stomach upset. She is hysterical so she has been sedated and very gently restrained. Noah is with her now, but she isn't making sense." Frances exhaled loudly. "She did not take enough medication to kill herself. In fact the pills she had secreted were an assortment of painkillers, sleeping aids and antibiotics. Nonsense."

"Thank God you were here." I took her hands in mine.

She smiled, a little upturning of her lips, squeezed my hands then pulled hers back. "We'll keep someone on a twenty-four-hour watch of her as long as I feel that's necessary." Her hands slipped into the pockets of her physician coat. "I understand I'm being ordered to provide direct psychiatric care for ninety days and my regular clinic practice will be covered."

"Milan?" The plan was beyond common sense and I could see that Frances was angry. "Maybe in a day or so you can talk him into reason."

"Annie, I'm going to be straight with you." Frances brought her hands out, swiped one through the air as she spoke. "This was just another dramatic search for attention. All Phoebe's handlers jump when she wobbles off center. Something bothers her. She doesn't have to stop and think, she throws out flares and others figure out how to make her feel secure again. They've supported a whole set of rewarded dangerous behaviors."

David called us from farther down the hall. Frances reached for me. "She wants to see you. Go ahead. No sympathy, no tears. Be calm. Follow Noah's lead." She bent her head toward the sick bay door. "Go ahead. I'll update David and let him know that Phoebe will see him later, when she's ready."

The alcove had been cleared of everything except Phoebe's bed, a lamp, a monitor and two chairs. Noah leaned against the foot of the bed looking at his sister. He pointed for me to stand next to him.

"Phoebe, Mom's here. Talk to her. You scared her to hell." He spoke with authority as if directing a less-experienced sibling. "Wake up, Phoebe."

Her eyelids twitched, one hand clenched the edge of a blanket a bit tighter. Clearly she could hear her brother and didn't choose to acknowledge my presence.

"Frances said you wanted to see me, Phoebs." I left Noah's side and smoothed the blanket away from her hand. I said two things that would provoke reaction. "I only have a few minutes to make sure you're comfortable and check on Andrew before another meeting. You know how Clarissa manages my schedule."

Her eyes opened, all drugged and sad and irritated. "Not even life and death stop work."

"Harsh, Phoebe, you of all people," I responded. "The whole family is here to," the right word escaped my mind, "help you," I finished.

"What will you tell Andrew?" The words came out rugged.

"What would you like me to tell him?"

"The truth." She cleared her throat, her face showed discomfort. She reached for a cup of water.

"I don't really know what that is, sweet one, but I will tell him what happened here."

"Just pull the curtain." Again she swallowed water. "I'll tell him myself."

"He's been moved upstairs. Remember, that was the plan." I moved my hand to her thin arm.

She merely shook her head, tears rolling down her cheeks.

"Shhh, Phoebe." I gestured for Noah to hand me tissues, wiped her cheeks. She leaned into my hand in an odd, needy way that stopped me. "Dr. Frances says you need to sleep. We'll visit more later."

I handed the tissue to Noah, bent to kiss her forehead, then left. Outside the door I leaned against the wall, struggling with the emotional game of tug and run in my mind.

"How is she?" Sun shining through the window accentuated the lines and creases of my husband's worried face. I walked a delicate high wire between love of the mentally ill woman in the room behind me and this man who had already walked through the torture of a woman intent on ending her own life.

"Frances took good care of her, David." I told him nothing new while taking care to not poison the waters with my reaction to her finely tuned hooks into our emotions. "She's tired and kind of a mess. Noah is amazing."

"I'm going in to see for myself. I need to see her." David was through the door before Frances could step in.

She shrugged as the door closed. "Good a time as any. Everything is being monitored."

Lao and John were gone. Down the hall I saw the shadow of the brown suit guard. I lowered my voice. "This may have been the first time I felt a kind of revulsion to her naming me as the one who must be by her side. Tell me what to think about that."

"That's healthy, Annie. It will be good that this new Washington job demands your attention. You're her emotional cares in the absence of an assigned gofer." She checked her watch. "When David comes out I want you to return to whatever you planned to be doing. I'll be directing all future contact with her. I assume you'll tell Andrew?"

I nodded.

"Be honest with him. Tell him what physically happened. I wouldn't suggest you pass on your emotional response unless he asks." She checked her watch again. "Andrew is an insightful man who grew up with an emotionally impacted first mother. He'll ask whatever questions he needs answered. Now I've got to ask David to leave so I can take care of the patient."

Chapter forty-One

DAVID AND I WALKED SLOWLY down the long hallway, holding hands, but not speaking. I turned abruptly, waved the brown suit to join us.

"When we get upstairs, I am going to speak with my son. In private." I struggled to keep my voice polite. "I am not happy about your presence and will be filing a request to restrict the presence of the entire brown suit work group within this home. From discussions with other commissioners I understand there are alternative electronic security methods." I checked to see if he understood what I was asking from him. "So I'm directing you to monitor all entrances and exits from whatever building I might be in while we are in Minnesota, but to not in any way trail me inside the buildings."

"Ms. Hartford, I am following directives." His shoulders did not lower, his eyes bored into mine.

"Thank you, but I just told you that from what I have discovered, your crew is being overly intrusive in a perimeter already operating under Intellectual Corps security protocols. You need to back down."

I turned away. David squeezed my hand. "It's true. I've send Lao a bulletin distributed in Washington about potential abuse by this security group. I should have waited for him to take action, but this particular young man has been like an unnecessary shadow. I'm not in the mood to play along."

"I'd like to visit Andrew with you." David sounded uncertain.

"Of course. Then we'll have coffee in the secured conference room. By the way, Lao scoured Andrew's room so we can talk openly."

The suite where Andrew would recover was bathed in sun filtered through soft blinds. He rested on a recliner, covered by light blankets, and once again monitored. Otis, Paul's former medical assistant, recorded information by Andrew's side.

"Good timing," he said as we entered. "Andrew's doing well. There's a bit of drainage I'm watching, but that's expected. His temperature is a bit elevated, again the doctor said that would be normal." He closed his data pad. "I'll get out of here and come back in about thirty minutes. He can have water or juice."

I pulled over a stool to sit by Andrew. David brought a chair.

"Before you sit down, could one of you get me some water?" Andrew smiled, his eyes still dilated from medication. "Pulling the tubes out wasn't fun, and I've got a feeling the pain will be here for a few days."

"You've been a star patient." I patted his leg.

"Where's Phoebe? I thought I'd wake up in here and she'd be in the other bed."

"She's still in sick bay and will be there until Dr. Frances releases her." His eyes widened and I rushed to give him the facts. "She took a pile of pills this morning that she had been saving. Not enough to really cause harm, but enough that her stomach was pumped and an emergency medical plan has been dropped into place. The Bureau will call it a medication error."

Andrew drew in a long breath, his face showed how the effort hurt. "My fault. I thought we'd both rest better together here. She was enthusiastic, but probably not ready." David appeared ready to say something, but Andrew continued. "Having a relationship with Phoebe is difficult."

"That shouldn't be a surprise," David offered. "She's a complicated person."

"Maybe too complicated." Andrew's words settled in the quiet room. "I love her, thought I could bring stability into her life. Like you did, Mom. But she doesn't really operate independently. Being involved with her is like asking a hermit to throw a big party."

I smiled at the odd image, typical of Andrew's wide reading. "She does love you."

"I know she would say that, but I don't think she understands what loving another person means. It's like the concept of love to her is what others give. I looked it up. It's called narcissism."

Suddenly David, the one worried about a possible calamity if these two continued their relationship, backtracked. "Don't think too much about it right now, Andrew. Frances is going to work with her, and we'll be supporting her. Things will get figured out."

"Not in the time before I return to work, David. The stuff built into Phoebe will take a whole lot of undoing."

"What can we do to keep you comfortable?" I played mother and tried to turn the conversation to blankets and books and away from painful emotions.

"Music." I remembered introducing him to a piano teacher when he was eleven and his joy in practicing long hours. "If they want me to stay totally quiet for a couple of days, then I'd like company. Have Faith study in here. I'd love to help John work through the foundation's setup. Anything to put my mind back into operation while my body recuperates." His eyes closed then reopened, physical and emotional discomfort mixed in darkness.

"Rest, son." David gently squeezed Andrew's shoulder.

"I'm falling asleep. Sorry."

"That's the right thing for you to do. We'll leave." I lightly mussed his hair. "Love you."

Clarissa waited outside Andrew's door. "I've been looking for you. Lao suggested I clear your schedule through lunch. There's a priority conference including Lao and some Washington people about security at one, but almost everything else on your calendar has been cancelled or rescheduled."

She didn't ask about Andrew or question what happened. Maybe Lao gave her a brief explanation. Clarissa was one of those people who knew much more than she let on while displaying little interest in goings on.

"How are they doing?" The question could be based on the original plan that moved Phoebe and Andrew to this suite today or could reflect some knowledge of Phoebe's suicide attempt during Andrew's procedure.

"He's tired. Removing the chest tubes wasn't easy." I purposefully addressed just half of her question.

"Does he know about Phoebe's medication issue?"

David flinched at the Bureau's cover-up words, at the continued subterfuge of Phoebe's life. He still wondered every time Tia's death was mentioned if the person believed the Bureau's story about how she had been attacked in a dark alley or knew that she was found there with a hypodermic needle in her arm.

I wrapped us in the code language for now. "Yes, we told him. He asked why she wasn't with him and we gave him the facts."

She lowered her head, licked her lips, and nodded. "You know he loves her very much."

"I do know that." I put my arms around Clarissa, a woman who had lived without much affection. "We'll all be there for both of them. That's what we can do, you and I."

In the residence all moved like a normal weekday. Clarissa and I talked through the remainder of the day until Otis walked toward us with a thermal carrier for Andrew's lunch.

"He was finding it hard to stay awake, so we left," I said. "And, thank you, for accepting responsibility for his care. He mentioned he would like some music. If you look in the sound storage file, there should be some Mozart and Chopin. Those would be a good start."

Clarissa excused herself.

"Maybe you should take her to D.C.," David commented. "I never know how to read her."

"Think of the old bachelor Norwegian farmers who lived near your parents. No need to look happy or sad, just work to be done." I watched through the windows as she walked to her office. "I know nothing about her childhood and only a small amount about her marriage. I think we have given her a place to live and work, possibly a reason to live. She is as proud of Andrew as we are but as stiff as a broom." I turned back to him. "You need her here. People respect her and she understands the pressures you will face."

John waited in the DOE offices, his face tight with worry. "Noah says they're both okay. Anything else you can tell me?"

I opened the secured conference room door and waved them both inside. "The official story about this morning is that Phoebe suffered from an accidental medication incident. No one outside the immediate family should hear anything else from us. We just talked with Andrew. He'll be fine, but right now he's uncomfortable."

"We should talk." John stood behind a chair. "Do you both have a few minutes?"

David looked at me and I pulled out a chair. "Clarissa cleared our morning schedules for family matters. Sit down."

"This won't take long," he said as he lowered into a chair next to David. "I wanted you to be the first to know that Amber and I plan to get married as soon as we get registered and throw together a little party. It might seem rather sudden, but we've been close for a long time."

I raised an eyebrow. "Really? I thought she was missing a man she met in France when on vacation."

He agreed with a rueful half laugh. "We started talking about spending our future together a few years ago over the holidays. But I just couldn't see how to make it work with my travel. When you told me about the French guy, I knew she and I needed to make a decision."

"She's older than you and has almost nothing to her name." David inserted like fathers throughout the ages. "Plus you're barely twenty-five. You've thought about all of that."

"She's beautiful and intelligent and we love each other." John raised his shoulders, not his voice. "What more than that did Mom have when you decided to spend your lives together?"

David laughed and held out his hand to grab John's. "Touché."

"And she does have an acre of land on Ashwood plus some inheritance from Grandpa and a good job that she tells me pays well."

Tears came as we hugged. Death and troubles, love and promises.

"I want to take her to Washington," I mentioned. "She would learn so much and be a real help."

"That's her decision. I just want us to register the relationship before she leaves."

"Should we call her in? We can't exactly welcome her to the family, because that was done years ago. You will have gorgeous children."

Clarissa buzzed. "Dr. Frances ordered medication for you, Anne. Do you want to return to your room?"

"Send Dr. Frances a message that I am fine. I'll be working from this conference room the rest of the day." David gave me a questioning look that I waved away. "Please find Amber and have her join us as soon as possible.

Chapter Forty-Two

ASHWOOD'S PEOPLE CAME TOGETHER the next day to celebrate the relationship registration of Amber and John, what we used to call an engagement. A marriage would follow after harvest, a grand mixing of the most basic of the earth's rhythms. The impromptu party in the courtyard quickly diminished interest in Phoebe's health and soothed subtle discomfort between David and his first son. I noticed more shaved heads among young metro workers gathering in clusters, more long hair on college-educated men and women, very few multi-corps sleek styles.

In our Ashwood community, the brown suits stood out like ants before a storm and made themselves visible everywhere I went. Lao was unable to uncover who listened to their recordings or read their reports. They could be gathering information for Milan's people or the White House or an entirely different group with interests counter to the Bureau and the ethics board's formation.

Amber did become my first Washington hire, agreed to act as chief of staff for at least six months. She would hire a housekeeper, begin the vetting process for ethic board employees and work with Lao to screen brown suits with single loyalty.

In the following week, my attention would be split between coaching David and orienting myself to the Bureau's Washington missions, logistics, and politics from afar. I sidestepped each invitation to spend a day or two in D.C. using Phoebe's recovery as an excuse no one would question.

Frances dictated the speed of Phoebe's return to the household. Both raised a glass virtually at the registration party. Two days after the suicide attempt, Phoebe spent a first night in her totally restored suite of rooms. Frances found a young psychiatric health attendant to live onsite as a companion. I heard our daughter wanted a cares to attend to her every personal need, not a health attendant under the direction of Frances.

With sixteen days left before my departure, I drew together a group to present plans for Milan's visit in three days to welcome Noah to the Intellectual Corps. While offering Noah congratulations, mixed feelings were visible. I dragged the planning session to completion. Noah acted like a soldier thoughtfully enlisting in battle. Clarissa's lips remained pressed together as if she fought physical illness. Amber and Lao accepted long lists of assignments with their typical willingness.

Leaving Ashwood

Frances promised Phoebe would appear at her brother's side and deliver a short comment.

After the meeting I had my first conversation with Milan since the morning of Phoebe's attempted suicide. Strain in our family, exasperated by living within close confines, kept me awake at night and overly alert during the day. I prepared careful notes for our meeting—the hiring of Amber, vetting of potential ethics board members, readiness of Ashwood for his visit. Phoebe did not appear on my list. Time would not allow the family chattiness we shared for decades.

Milan, seated in the opulent Bureau Secretary office, looked like an accountant in a wealthy man's home. He wore an expensive suit and a shiny new wedding band.

"Annie, you look tired." He flipped a switch, dulled his surroundings. "I hope the people I care about at Ashwood are healthy? Want to catch up before we talk about Noah?"

"I'm short on time." True Minnesotans learn to avoid direct unpleasant behavior so I smiled instead of snarling. "Your chief of staff received plans about the Noah press conference and reception."

He refused to fall into formality. "Frances says Phoebe is ready to welcome Noah. It sounds like she is doing quite well."

"She isn't eating, and with the exception of Noah, none of us have visited with her since the crisis. But Frances says Phoebe will appear with Noah at the conference."

"It won't be easy for us to work together on this very important initiative if you hold me accountable for Phoebe's instability." Holograms can present crystal clear images or blur at the wrong moment. Milan's face fell in and out of shadows. "I've been her consistent protector since her birth. The most brilliant offspring in the first generation of genetically adapted individuals."

"Don't insult me, Milan. You're talking to the woman who changed her diapers, held her through night terrors, lived with five children in a small metro apartment to give her a few additional years of nurturing. Don't forget we sought a court injunction to block her Harvard start date."

"Annie, we built an appropriate support program for Phoebe. You and David chose to see only the child, not the national treasure. You are short-sighted about your children with those turn-of-the-century dreams."

"Phoebe's pursuit of freedom, the true American dream, was denied before she was born. We're not going to agree on this one, Milan." The sadness in Andrew's eyes as he distanced himself from the woman he loved, the worry David carried for all our children in the evolving societal control of the multi-corps hung over our home. Milan couldn't understand life at the daily level any more than I could live like a metro grunt. "We'll see you in a few days. Who would have known you would go from protected status to leader of the only federal government unit larger than the Pentagon?"

"If we had their budget, we could do so much." He paused before shifting the conversation. "My wife may be joining us. She hasn't seen the Regan crew for many years. I assume you can set one more place at the table?"

I wondered where his wife lived now. She was a decent woman who played on the floor with Noah and John, taught Phoebe to twirl a baton, knit a sweater for Faith's fifth birthday present. "It will be good to see her again. Now, we should go over plans."

While he read the file, I leaned my head back against my chair and stared across the room at pictures of Ashwood. Under my guidance, often pushed by David's foresight, the estate continuously changed. Leadership was like that. My father joked about the rightness of situational leadership, of knowing when the time arrived to change direction without apology. In ten minutes we were through and I sent Clarissa notes.

I didn't hear David come in. "How did it go with Milan?"

"He talks like a king bureaucrat. I feel like the kid who said the emperor had no clothes, but I think that's why Hernandez appointed me." I waved him to sit. "It's time for us to embrace Noah's choice. He could have joined the military or moved to Europe, but he's got purpose and good intentions. We have raised a responsible man."

"He's naïve," David replied, but I heard pride. "It won't be an easy life."

"Nobody's lives are easy. The Bible thumpers like to remind us that this is the punishment given to Adam and Eve."

"You sound like my mother."

"I'm just shooting the bull." I smiled, felt some happiness return. "Noah is going to be a big cheese. We raised two of the smartest people in the country. And John will do good stuff with his environmental business. Plus there's that whole marriage thing that will be fun for us." I saw David begin to let go of his disappointments. "Andrew will either get over Phoebe, or figure out how to accept her for what she is." I checked for agreement. "And we have an executive in the making leaving junk in her mother's office." I picked up Faith's hair clip as I stood. "I think we did good and now it's their turn to make the world better."

"If we can keep Phoebe from repeating Tia's mistake."

"Can't do that, David. Either she finds the way to make it in this world or there's a chance for incredible sadness. Tia had demons and memories of finding her father's body. Phoebe's got all kinds of insecurities, but I also think she's a strong person rebelling against the fancy padded cage the Bureau's built for her. She's a Regan and Regans are blazingly independent."

"Screw work. Let's ride over to Giant Pines and see the new calves."

"Why does that make sense?"

"Because when you're in D.C., you can think about the cows bellowing when the politicians start blowing hot air and try not to laugh out loud."

Chapter Forty-Three

Noah Bradford Regan took his place in the Intellectual Corps on a hot July day in front of the school building where he learned multiplication at three years of age, explained a complex chemistry experiment to a DOE engineering student, and stuck bubble gum to a young teacher's chair. John, his half-brother and best friend, stood right behind him on one side, while Phoebe stood on his other side. David and I stayed together, out of the direct camera.

"We were all disappointed when Noah decided to turn his back on clinical practice," Phoebe said, not reading from the script prepared by the Bureau. David tensed. I did the same.

"He would be a great doctor—smart and kind and very intuitive. It is a loss to every hospital that Dr. Noah Regan will not treat patients. But the world will be a better place because somewhere he will be directing research about childhood nutrition or repairing cell damage or some other life-threatening condition. So we will all live better with my brother working within the Intellectual Corps. Unlike our pioneer crew, Noah is the first adult to independently choose to join the Corps. I am so proud to welcome him to a life that is difficult, consuming and the greatest service that can be dedicated to our nation."

She stood tall, her curly hair a dramatic contrast to her black clothing. This was the Phoebe who spoke at international symposiums to the world's brightest researchers. She stepped away from the podium to shake Noah's hand then embrace him in front of carefully chosen media representatives. Her smile was so genuine that her face didn't look pale and thin.

Stepping back, she leaned forward. "If you will all excuse me, I have a conference in ten minutes and am about twenty minutes behind in preparing. Noah will soon understand that."

Another stray from the plan that would have had her join us while Noah spoke. I watched her walk away, not able to leave. Gazing around I looked for someone to fall in step with her. With the exception of Frances, everyone who knew about her attempted suicide and depression stood behind Noah and in front of the media. For once I hoped the brown suits would appear.

I listened to Noah, annoyed that Phoebe once again took a chink out of our family's ability to simply enjoy another member's success. The audience, the media, the Hartford staff present had no idea that David and I were worried about her even as we applauded Noah.

We deferred making statements in spite of Bureau pressure. David said he did not want to distract from Noah's day. I gave the same excuse. Fortunately the Bureau organized two interviews with very trusted media representatives so we were spared possible questions about the shooting or Phoebe's health.

Refreshments were served in a tented area of the courtyard. I skirted the serving area to check up on Phoebe. Like every key federal employee she had a special tracking chip in her body. But to call for a search would draw attention with so many politically critical guests on the estate.

Her rooms were empty, she wasn't with Andrew, and no one sat on the pond benches. The DOE offices surveillance didn't track her appearance. Lao searched monitors until we saw her sitting on the ground under trees in the oldest apple orchard section. I knew the place as a favorite from when she was a child wanting to get away from her brothers.

"Keep watching her," I instructed Lao, "but don't let anyone disturb us unless I call. Keep the brown suits back."

I took off my dress shoes and put on sandals as I walked out a side door the crowds would not notice. In five minutes I approached her.

"Sorry, I thought I would wander too far from script and just made up that whole story about a conference. Of course you know that no one expects to conference with me right now, but I think I pulled it off." Her heeled boots stood next to her, she had unzipped the top of her shirt. "You don't need to miss the party, Mom. Milan probably has people here that you need to know back in the swamp city."

"I'd rather you came back with me."

"Mom, this is my favorite spot on earth. I'll be fine here. Tell Frances I needed fresh air and nobody watching me for a half hour." She grinned. "I know the monitors are on us, but that's not the same as having an *attendant*."

"Do you mind if I stay for a few minutes."

"That linen will be destroyed if you sit on this grass," Phoebe said as she patted the earth next to her. "You'll catch eyes in D.C. with that outfit. I want to go shopping with you and help you pick out some real city clothes, some things that don't say Minnesota. It's a good thing you look fabulous in black."

Phoebe and shopping had nothing in common. Others shopped for her, clothed her.

"I know what you're thinking, but I decided this was the way I wanted to look. I didn't just let people put things in my closet. At least starting a few years ago I stopped letting people dress me." She giggled. "By the time a woman is twenty-three or twenty-four, she should have some idea of what looks good on her. The cares tend to buy brown and gray. Not good with my coloring."

"When I came to Ashwood I had to wear estate matron uniforms." Calling myself a matron always made our kids laugh. "Simple straight skirts and pants and tops and sweaters or jackets. I was proud that I had had mine tailored in Washington, D.C. I also picked out a few scarves, not uniform code, to show off my hair color."

"I have one of those scarves. Dad gave it to me when I was homesick."

I knew the drawer in her Chicago apartment where she kept her Ashwood tokens. Pictures, books, pine cones, cups, or whatever else she wanted to remind her that she had roots.

"Andrew will be gone in a few months. I don't know if we'll find a way to be together. I'm a mess." The homesick comment turned the conversation toward her insecurities.

"Phoebe."

She held up her hands. "Even before he leaves, you and Amber and Noah will be gone. The funny thing is that I want to stay here. I don't want to think about leaving. I'll work hard. I really do miss working. I've got to get out of my head and learn how to reconnect with life. I don't need Frances to tell me that." Her hands locked around her knees.

"Start now. Come back to the party with me. Noah would be pleased."

The tricky part about teaching smart people new skills can be their reluctance to look imperfect. I saw Phoebe process my simple request and stop at that possibility.

She shook her head. "No, but you should go or you'll be annoyed that I kept you away from Noah's big day."

I left her under the apple trees. As I walked away I thought I heard her humming, a cheerful sound like when she was a girl.

Chapter forty-four

My days at Ashwood trickled away. I became more convinced that the president had no appetite for tackling ethics in the Bureau of National Human Capital Management. On top of that disconnect, conversations with Milan's chief of staff uncovered large philosophical distances between the Bureau's leadership and myself in how to define the breadth of my work.

"The key difference between our government and the multi-corps is that one is elected with an obligation to represent the needs and protect the freedoms of a constituency, while the other exists to create wealth for its shareholders. The multi-corps have nothing in common with governments except hunger for a low-cost, appropriately skilled workforce." David listened as I tried for the fifth or twentieth time to describe the conundrum I faced. "So how do we reach consensus on something so intrinsic if we don't share common values."

"You're suggesting that the multi-corps aren't vested in the countries where they do business? That's kind of extreme." He fussed with a broken bootstrap as we talked.

"Let's not talk about it. Just leave the light on for me if Washington, D.C., doesn't like Anne Hartford asking value-based questions."

We laughed that night, but as I boarded the Washington transport a few mornings later I wondered if some conspiracy had been hatched to distract my attention from Hartford as the next Deshomm-style challenge developed. We landed with an hour before my first meeting with Congressional leadership. They claimed there was interest in holding hearings on severing a tradition of Bureau and multi-corps collaboration. For every success story, multiple failures could be told. Higher education controlled by former benefactors, public institutions turned privatized that became priced beyond voters' means. The increasing demand that low-cost, highly trained labor held communities hostage from developing strong, diversified industrial structures.

Hartford, Ltd., had trained close to a thousand young workers over the years and had educated even more children. In the beginning the government funded that effort, but for the past decade state or federal government units chintzed on paying their share. Where once city kids came to Ashwood for food, education, and protection, the typical student worker now came from a broken home or living on the streets and needed to be prepared for the work world. There was always pressure from multi-corps to equip older teens with training for specific industries.

Like China, India, and Russia, the United States brokered increasingly larger groups of cheap labor in transportation corridors near raw materials to international multi-corps. Limited voters didn't silence a swell of unhappiness. Some saw the labor assignment process developing into labor conscription as their kids were sent to jobs thousands of miles from home.

"Listen, Anne, the Bureau survived the surrogacy program scandals when your kids were young, and we have a vibrant system in place now to ensure generations of critical intellectual discovery." Milan and I had dinner in his office that night. The food was elegantly prepared and served as if we were at a four-star restaurant. An identity chip had been placed near my right shoulder blade that afternoon and I was distracted by its existence.

"We made the jump from government-sponsored work to private industry jobs with few hiccups by building a solid federal payroll system. This Bureau establishes competitive pay to protect workers." He leaned toward his plate and looked over his glasses at me. "The federal government ensures an office worker in Dallas that they are paid the same as someone doing the same job in Chicago or Manhattan by separating cost of living issues from the value of work. So the question of ethics should be limited to how Bureau employees conduct business with representatives of private industry." He speared a small tomato and raised his fork. "Issues like conflict of interest, accepting gifts, punishment for accepting bribes, nepotism, and such. That will keep you plenty busy. Stay away from Congressional politics. They'd have you bust this place apart."

I understood that a country where over fifty percent of the work force was unemployed in the 2020s would take pride in nearly one hundred percent employment. But my heart understood the stories state representatives and senators each told me that afternoon about the inability to protect communities and workers from giant corporations.

"The Congressional hearings will focus on policy matters related to ethical treatment of citizens bound to employers by the Bureau." I feared Milan's bloated Bureau wouldn't be pleased that I saw a need for new models. "They want this board to deal with issues like hours of work, forced relocation, withholding of wages for required tools, and work injuries. They would move the Bureau's role in genetic engineering away from that program's execution." I placed my palms on the table. "So expectations are miles apart. The president doesn't seem to have an opinion. The folks I met with today are preparing for elections with a message that she doesn't like."

"You brokered some great resolutions in the middle of fierce opposition on definition of agricultural products. And you aren't dealing with the Russians or Chinese here. This should be easy." Milan let the big bureaucrat façade fall away. "The president doesn't know what to think, that's why we're here. You can steer the conversation to specific areas within the Bureau and give her important platform wins for the election. Congress is asking to turn around a ship that's too far away from port. They want a way of life that can't be found again."

I wanted to get him out of this office and walk through the roads of Ashwood to have an honest talk about what he wanted from these final years of his own work. At his age, he could sit on boards, teach, work as a mentor. Instead he was giving away his health to sit on top of this administration.

"My plan is to listen before drafting the first ethics board mission statement. President Hernandez must sign off on that document. Then we'll vet members and develop a schedule." Fatigue dulled my mind. "We'll see how far we can go in the next eleven months."

"Enough work, Anne. Tell me how it feels to be mother of the bride and the groom?" He visibly relaxed as he steered conversation to the Regan family, and I realized that for all the bureaucratic histrionics, Milan had no clue how to steer the ethics conversation.

When I returned to my apartment late that night, Amber had created a small sense of home. We drank tea in cups brought from Ashwood. She went to bed, but I began writing the document that would make it to President Hernandez's desk months from now. Heads might roll, hopefully including mine because I believed this time the elected officials knew the issues of their districts better than those in the fortress known as the Bureau. The disconnect between the executive and representative parts of government had never been wider.

Chapter forty-five

BEFORE I RISKED WALKING the political suicide plank, David and I set out to safeguard Hartford, Ltd., and our family from what could turn into powerful fallout. We created a Minnesota land grant entity at Giant Pines to preserve the environmental research foundation for one hundred years. Raima worked long hours, and charged major dollars, to build legal walls around our businesses that used government regulations to keep the multi-corps away. Our personal wealth had long been separate from Hartford, Ltd., but we updated all documents. In the process we created walls around the children's trusts so they would also be beyond the courts.

I worked four days a week in the halls of Washington and continued working even harder over the long weekends as chairperson of Hartford, Ltd., On his way to Harvard, Noah spent a few days with Amber and me in the capitol.

As August ended and legislators headed home for their September break, I spent fourteen days in Minnesota. During his final days of sick leave, Andrew offered help in researching potential political minefields for the ethics board. Questionable relationships between Bureau managers and multi-corps individuals speckled the organizational chart he developed like mouse droppings in an unprotected cereal bin. Milan sat on top of the mess unblemished. The links were more tenuous among elected officials where the lack of funding disclosures made it impossible to identify hands pulling strings behind the curtains. Except for President Hernandez who attracted big donors from the biggest multi-corps.

Andrew and I had interesting discussions about those links. His experience as a consultant inside a few multi-corps tested my assumptions about their power. Phoebe joined us to tell her stories about multi-corps reviewers' sway in Bureau research projects and the large contracts frequently negotiated by agents for Intellectual Corps specialists in direct violation of their government agreements.

Frances approved Phoebe's part-time return to work. David watched as Phoebe kept to a schedule in the DOE labs. They spoke about her work and the hours she spent daily re-acquainting herself with personal maintenance activities. No one else would understand that Phoebe picking up a lunch tray in Andrew's room was an achievement. During my time home I didn't ask about her medications, but admired her thoughtfulness and calm exterior. Most late afternoons I saw her carry work out to the orchard.

Before I returned to the capitol, final information arrived on the individuals we hoped to invite to join Hartford's new Board of Directors. I began making calls, asking for their involvement in exchange for a combination of compensation, land, and organic food for their tables. Raima, our lead banker, Andrew, David, and three outside directors agreed to serve as the corporate board of Hartford, Ltd. I placed a communications consulting wizard on retention to manage Washington issues. The boutique firm specialized in crisis management.

Paul would have said that we had put our ducks in a row, and encouraged me to let all hell rip. We even paid Faith's McGill tuition in advance and secured private lodging in Montreal should it be necessary. But, as I sat in the transport on September eleventh, I felt neither adventurous nor brave. Suddenly I saw Milan's strategy that in advancing my name he trusted something big would happen purely because I found the status quo so unacceptable. He took a gamble that I might pull a trigger that would bring down a president or the largest government agency.

I delivered treats from Ashwood to Amber who had stayed in Washington to button down scheduling issues and explore the city. We chatted about home and the November wedding plans. With the good talk out of the way, I asked about our schedules for the week. She sweetly held one finger to her lips and pointed at a table lamp, the mechanical panel and the spare wooden arm of our small sofa. We walked to a noisy Indian restaurant for dinner, and I shared with her about my insight into Milan's choice of me for the ethic mess.

"That would explain who calls me back with open meeting times and who is stonewalling." Amber drew out her data pad. "You are booked through the next three days with three quarters of the representatives and senators we contacted. About eight senators not on our list would like time. Most are interested in serving on the ethics board if asked. Members of the Moderate party are hesitant. I think they're waiting for a signal from Hernandez's people."

Amber fit into the Washington, D.C., scene that always favored young, beautiful people. She wore her long hair up this evening and a sleeveless light yellow linen dress with a single fake-silver bracelet. No one dared wear real precious metals or gems on the street. Two men, senate staffers, stopped by our table to say hello.

After the second visitor left, she returned to her lists. "I'm not having much success attracting key Bureau managers. It might be time to ask Milan for support."

"First, I wanted to say how impressed I am with the way you have mastered this city. I had some pushback from Hernandez's staff about bringing someone unfamiliar with the capitol into this role. Of course, they didn't know you move mountains with government types in your Ashwood duties." She rolled her eyes. "I'll speak with Milan, but he may balk."

He did resist. Over the next weeks I held dozens of informal meetings, hired a handful of key staffers, and drafted the ethics board's first position paper while he remained quiet. By November first, three months into my twelve-month appointment, I gave Amber the green light to schedule a meeting with Milan to review the position paper and to send a formal request to the White House for a meeting with the president early in the new year.

His chief of staff required that Amber physically appear at the Agency's office three consecutive days before granting a meeting on the Tuesday of Thanksgiving week. The bureaucrat acted quite put out by managing Milan's schedule, but passed on his invitation to fly back to Minnesota in his government transport.

Milan had not responded to an invitation for the wedding when Amber and I flew home for an early November weekend. The formal signing of John and Amber's pre-nuptial agreement was the real reason for that trip. David and I acted as their witnesses at the regional register of deeds where the document was filed along with a marriage license application. A marble legacy from earlier in the century, the marriage hall was an odd mixture of solemnity and joyfulness. We partied at a dinner club in St. Paul and called a driver to take us home after a few bottles of wine.

Sitting in the family room Sunday night, listening to Amber describe final wedding details, I shut the door on my political life to be the Regan family's matriarch. We drove the men crazy with talk about wedding cake versus pie, hair ribbon color, and flowers. Under all the banter, I found myself thinking of extra precautions I needed to take with the first ethics position paper so a media leak wouldn't taint this family event.

"You wore a long dress and carried flowers Magda cut from the gardens." David pulled me next to him in bed that night. "We got married outside. It was perfect."

"I was pregnant with John and we were lucky the Bureau allowed you to marry outside the intellectual group." I relaxed, tried not to think about final packing and meetings in the morning. "Terrell managed to assemble an incredible spread of foods and pastries with only kids to help in the kitchen. He figured out I was pregnant because you kept insisting I sit."

"You were tired during those first months and I had no idea how to take care of you." Already sleepy, David softly snorted. "The circle is continuing with you and me standing where my parents stood." His body settled into the mattress, no tension left in any muscle. "Are we sure there's no one from Amber's family to invite?"

"No. Her father ran off when she was a baby and her mother died ten years ago. One brother is in the Marines and turns back any communication, the other was a baby the last time she saw him. He has a large family of his own in Los Angeles."

His breathing evened. In the dark, I worried about returning to D.C. without Amber the next day. When sleep slipped out of reach, I pulled on a robe and wandered the residence to clear my head. The moon illuminated an empty patio, the pond and lower orchards. Bare branches and twigs of apple trees performed a gentle dance against a clear dark sky. I could be that exposed to the political jackals by the next time I stood here. Mentally I summarized possible fallout and defensive steps Hartford should consider.

"Pretty isn't it?" Phoebe, looking young in old running clothes and a generous shirt, surprised me. "I've been staying up at night lately to watch the trees and look for stars." She had gained weight, her hair had shine. "Sorry if I scared you. Everything okay?"

"Just couldn't sleep. I can't stop thinking about the what-ifs of this damn ethics thing." I pulled my robe tighter.

"Want a cuppa? I've got a pot of calming herbal tea in my room."

I hated those teas, but for time with Phoebe would manage. "Sounds good."

We walked in silence past rooms six to eight child workers once called theirs, the small chapel that served as Ashwood's nursery when Phoebe was born. She opened her door. Covers on the large bed were folded back, two small lamps made warm light pools around a stuffed chair and a table covered with papers and books. Cool air freshened the space and pushed the herbal tea fragrance to greet us. Family pictures filled one shelf, a collection of postcard images from places she had traveled made a pretty display on another. A large picture of Stratford on Avon rested in one corner. A carpet I remembered from her Chicago apartment covered much of the floor.

She saw me recognize the carpet. "I had one of the cares send me a few items. Is it possible for you to swing through Chicago before the end of the year to help me clear out my place? We'd have help packing and sorting. I think I'll donate most of the furniture."

"Do you know where you want to live?"

The teacup Phoebe handed me was translucent English china, another item from her Chicago home. She filled her own cup and held it to her face, inhaling the tea's fragrance before naming her next home.

"Frances and I think Ashwood might be the best place to call home at least through next summer. I can move much of my research needs to the University of Minnesota's tech group and keep using the DOE facilities. I need time to raise additional funds for a Wisconsin lab. The Fish Creek research campus has signed a letter of intent to work for me." She sipped, closed her eyes, and breathed out. "Surprised?"

"Entirely delighted. Dad and Faith must be pleased to know you'll be staying here."

"We're running together Tuesdays and Thursdays. Dad misses you keeping him active. We try to have dinner together regularly." She sipped again. "This is part of my treatment—learning to live like a normal person. Make my bed, show up for meals, put clothes in the hamper." She wrinkled her nose. "I'm looking for a personal assistant instead of a cares. You did a good job of teaching me the basics, but it's taking more time than I expected to relearn what people really do who don't have cares."

A regular office employee would find this conversation unbelievable. If I hadn't spent time with Phoebe through the years, I wouldn't have full appreciation for how divorced she had become from her body and needs. "You'll stay in these rooms?"

She shrugged. "It's almost as much room as I had in Chicago. There are two small houses on the estate that I could move into, but Frances suggested I wait until I can plan and manage that kind of move on my own. That might never happen. These old teachers' rooms are far enough from the family quarters to give me breathing space." She smiled, a softness in her face making the gesture look genuine.

"Why are you unhappy, Mom?"

"I've been in difficult situations before, but nothing with national consequences. Think of the implications of the data you and Andrew and I reviewed. This is huge. If I am not careful, the combination of that information and the anger among elected representatives could take down the administration."

White noise filled in the silence while Phoebe thought. I ran my thumb over the handle of my teacup, stared at the blanket on her bed.

Her eyes followed mine. "It was yours. I found it in a box in the storage room and didn't think you'd mind. Your grandmother made it."

"That's right. She gave it to me when I got married the first time. Some of the flowers are made from scraps of dresses she made for my mother or me."

"You probably want to give it to Faith."

I shook my head. "I like seeing it here. It belongs to whomever will value it."

Phoebe extended a narrow foot to touch my leg. We called this "toe hugs" when she was a child. "Do what you think is best, Mom. We'll be here to support you. Milan picked the right person."

"You won't be saying that if I have to spend the rest of my life in a safe room."

"Not going to happen, Mom. People will probably want you to run for president."

"That is not going to happen, Phoebs." I put down my cup. "Thank you for this great tea and talk. I should try to get some sleep before I head out to battle the dragons."

We hugged, her arms offering comfort instead of clinging with need.

Chapter Forty-Six

MILAN ECHOED MY WORDS about taking down the administration when we finally met before Thanksgiving. He looked tired and I felt exhausted. The transport waited for our meeting to be completed. Had our discussion been about a less incendiary topic, we might have held our meeting during the ride to Minnesota. Instead we met in a secured conference room with no printed documents.

"These senators and representatives are suggesting we return to human capital management practices from decades ago," he pointed out. "A free market approach to labor threatens global competitive pay and our ability to attract multi-corps' projects. That's almost anti-American."

"The fact is that you know you're sitting on one of the most corrupt government agencies of all times, Milan. You want me to lead the charge because these changes will break the cronyism that binds the Bureau and multi-corps." With the dice now thrown in Milan's direction, I gave up control. He could make suggestions about changes before this first document went to Hernandez. He could reject the policy paper, ask me to write a new version or have the appointment withdrawn. He could do nothing and let the president be caught unaware.

We had minimal debate about the fine points contained in a questionable practices section of the report. Milan was surprised at the depth of corruption and the extent of the labor practices requested by the multi-corps that had become law. I couldn't detect how much he knew of widespread involvement of the multi-corps in restricting voting rights. His discomfort was obvious about the volumes of documentation we had uncovered about the corporate activities.

We were both somber on the ride back to Minnesota. Milan avoided talking about his holiday plans before falling asleep. I tried to catch up on Hartford, Ltd., reading.

"Tell Amber and John I wouldn't miss their wedding and please apologize for my late response. I'll be coming alone," Milan said shortly before we landed. At the airport, large snowflakes were beginning to fall. We stepped out into cold, damp air. He gestured for me to walk down the stairs first. We walked to the terminal together and wished each other a happy Thanksgiving.

Leaving Ashwood

Garlands trimmed the fences and gates of Ashwood. Small twinkling lights lit the drive and surrounded a stunning front entrance decoration. David opened the door as I exited my transport and waited for my packages to be unloaded.

His smile was welcoming, his arms comfortable around my shoulders. "Magda's crew outdid themselves," he said. "I wish my folks could be here to see the old ugly place all dressed up. If you put enough lipstick on a pig maybe it can be a fairy princess." He lifted one bag. I took my briefcase and his hand.

I understood David's combination of sweet and bitter at our decorated door. I squeezed his hand. "I suspect we'll both be thinking of our parents these next few days. I can hear Sarah making a case for more ribbons in the decorations."

David kissed the side of my face before he called to announce my arrival. Our children came to greet me with wine and treats. For that evening we were an American family, blessed to have each other and a life of plenty.

We kept our Thanksgiving meal simple and shared baskets of real foods with every Hartford, Ltd., employee. In the quarter century after starvation crippled the United States, no one was ever secure about food sources so the Thanksgiving baskets were valued. Terrell and his family, Magda and her partner, and Lao and his family joined us for our main meal. In a tradition started by a young thirty-something matron and a man who made himself into a cook, the meal featured food from Ashwood's crops with a few side treats of candies and nuts.

The Friday afternoon wedding was attended by two senators, a congressional representative, the mayor of our region, the Secretary of the Bureau of National Human Capital Management, a few prominent business leaders, our family and friends. Amber looked spectacular in a European-designed dress from a Washington, D.C., vintage shop. Phoebe and Noah stood as witnesses to the ceremony, and I found my thoughts wandering to the layers of bureaucracy built around the simple decision to become life partners.

I tried not to watch Phoebe and Andrew through the reception and festivities, but they were the most attractive couple moving among our guests. Andrew seemed to know nearly every VIP invited and Phoebe practiced the art of social small talk in the charming, if awkward, manner of many brilliant people. Still quite thin, she looked more like a ballerina than intellectual researcher.

MILAN CALLED TUESDAY MORNING as I stood in the dark courtyard waiting for my transport. "Check the Capitol Chatter," he said.

"Can you read it to me? My reader's in my briefcase and I can see the transport entering the gate."

"Anne Hartford, who has prepared more workers for the gristmill of life in government or multi-corps' ranks and two Intellectual Corps stepchildren, reportedly doesn't appreciate how the Bureau of National Human Capital Management does its business in protecting the people part of the nation's capital assets. Well-known for sponsorship of local educational programming, and a history of leadership in more than one agribusiness special interest group, Hartford reportedly is spending her time listening to legislators concerned about the state of American labor. Hard to discount a patriotic surrogate who began her post-Depression career as an estate matron and built a comfortable business empire on the concept of sustainable agriculture."

His voice, low and gravelly, stopped. "Welcome to the fish bowl."

"What do you want me to do," I asked. The transport driver lifted my bag into the vehicle. I motioned that I needed to finish this conversation.

"I hoped we could stay out of media attention until after the holiday recess." I could hear other voices on his side. "How about you work from Ashwood until January? Congress adjourns December seventh and you know they'll keep the White House staff busy."

"If you can free up that short list of Bureau directors for virtual meetings. Without those meetings, I can't vet board members." The driver pointed at her timepiece. I turned away. "Is that a deal?"

"You can count on four names. We'll run times through Clarissa." He coughed. "And, Anne, don't talk to the media. Use your assigned communications specialist."

"Thanks, Milan."

I had the driver carry my bags back to the residence's front steps and sent her away with a decent tip. Six in the morning and I could change into my estate wardrobe, have a decent breakfast, and look forward to working in my office and time with my family.

The Minnesota Post picked up the story by nine and ran an entire story stitching together old information and quotes from the two senators who ate at our table four days earlier, a congressional aide, and someone close to Milan. There wasn't a lot of meat to the Capitol Chatter snippet, but I wondered if there were writers and editors waiting for a way to open exploration of the American labor structure.

Brown suits were allowed back inside the residence to scour every room I entered. A lead suggested an inside tapping source. I spent two hours that afternoon in our safe room talking with a highly placed Bureau director, one with lots of dots on Andrew's chart, who spoke fluently about a classical definition of ethics while skirting any discussion of the future of American workers. By the time David, Phoebe, Faith, and I finished dinner, part of that conversation had been broadcast.

I passed a paper note to Faith before we left the table, asking her to find Lao and direct him to our stable conference room. Her puzzled look said she didn't understand, but she carried the paper away.

He showed up with Terrell, and unlocked the door. The room was cold, the air stale. "No one's been in here for months," Lao said and fidgeted with the air system. "Should have brought blankets or coffee."

"We don't need a lot of time. The brown suits scoured the safe room before I spoke with that Bureau director." They listened. "Two hours later an audio clip from our meeting is on national media. Who is listening to conversations at Ashwood?"

"Probably recorded within the Bureau." Terrell looked to Lao for confirmation.

"The brown suits are known for working for multiple agencies," Lao added. "You're under special protection because of the Capitol Chatter. We're better set up to handle issues onsite."

"I suppose the first director raising her hand to be interviewed, might see the contents of this interview as an opportunity to jump to the head of the class if Milan is asked to step down."

The sound clip made me uncomfortable that my words implied an assumption that the Bureau must be changed. White House communicators had to be buzzing. "The congressional recess and holidays should dampen this story. Lao, I'm nervous about security here, for everyone."

"Lao and I were talking about estate holiday plans when Faith appeared." Terrell took a deep breath. "With you and Phoebe in residence, it's impossible to stage the annual Ashwood holiday pageant. Too many temporary workers, too many undocumented visitors."

The pageant had grown from an effort to distract child workers who couldn't go home for Christmas to a loved community event held under a big tent inside the gates. There were a dozen ways cancelling this party could make for bad media coverage for Hartford, Ltd.,

"What about moving the tent to the Schneider farm acres? Except for David's herd, there's not much going on there. No one can enter Ashwood from that land and we could get away quickly if needed."

Terrell pulled at his chin as he thought through the proposal. Lao's communicator distracted him, but he was nodding his head by the time Terrell answered. "If David approves, we got a plan. All the public places we might have booked are in use that night."

"Let's engage the communications specialist I've got under contract to handle the announcement. We can claim family grieving time as an excuse, but absolutely no mention of the ethics board or Phoebe. I'll talk with David."

Media hits on the Ethics Board proposal filled my data pad news feed by the morning. Clarissa put an office assistant in charge of monitoring the file and running simple analytics. I became the name and face of the president's ethical dilemmas, a voice for oppressed citizen laborers. With inflation driving up the cost of food and threatening holiday season buying, the story snowballed.

Congressional leaders flooded anyone with connections to me—the small Washington office crew, Amber, Clarissa, our children—with their thoughts or demands. A significant minority of the messages prophesied that the U.S. economy would sink if the existing labor allocation and reimbursement systems were changed. Some of the messages offered personal insults, a few included threats to Hartford, Ltd. or me.

Clarissa shared dozens of speaking offers from legislators facing re-election and special interest groups, most offering generous honorariums. Heartbreaking testimonies from regular people nearly brought down the Washington, D.C., information system.

Milan was true to his word about opening the calendars of another three Bureau directors for meetings on the direction of the ethics board. They were polite, conversant and stayed on a common script about the importance to establish a narrow definition for board activities that would focus on internal compliance with federal anti-graft laws. Analyzing the interviews, staff found a couple dozen sentences using exactly the same language in support of the efficiency of the Bureau as a labor exchange for international multi-corps as well as main street America employers.

I waited for a summons from Milan or the White House as the week passed. Interest did not fade. In the absence of new legislative issues immediately prior to congressional recess, it became the central media story. Saturday morning Clarissa summoned me from a run with Phoebe inside Ashwood's fenced lands to prepare to be picked up in two hours for meetings with Milan, then President Hernandez. I asked her to add one additional passenger and notify Amber of our departure time. David was in the metro for meetings, so I left him a message that I would call later that evening.

"Let me come along." Phoebe made her request with no fanfare. "Politicians asking uncomfortable questions can become mean dogs."

"There have been threats." Lao and David knew of late-night intrusion attempts, but at my request told no one else. "Amber wants to clear some items out of our apartment so she is coming along. I'm too nervous about protection to add you."

"Milan plans to play you, Mom." Phoebe stopped me from moving forward. "I don't think he has anything to gain from this fight except to clear his conscience of how he's contributed to the chaos." We stood in the courtyard. I thought about her insight as a transport arrived to deliver kids for supplementary Saturday lessons. While cold, the air was dry.

"Don't go, Mom," Phoebe said. "My gut says you could be in danger. Remember that as powerful as Milan is, he was almost killed in June. I don't want you to become a martyr."

"Maybe I should take Lao and not Amber," I teased while checking my communicator for the time. "I have to pack."

"You're not listening to me. The multi-corps will think nothing of taking you out. Nothing."

Kids' voices carried from outside the school where a playful pushing and shoving game had developed. I wondered if our grandchildren would still attend this kind of school or if remote education would once again dominate.

"I am listening to you. I'll tell Amber she needs to stay here. What else would you like me to do? Short of refusing to appear at the White House?"

"Have Lao drive you to the airport and fly commercial. Don't trust anything arranged by anyone connected to the Bureau."

Her recommendations made sense. "Okay, I'll talk with Lao."

"And don't cancel the arranged transport. Talk to Lao in the secured conference room."

I balked, thinking Phoebe might be acting more intense than necessary. She tapped her own communicator, set orders in play without my acceptance, and then took my arm to lead me to the conference room.

Cued by Clarissa, Lao already planned flying me to Washington, D.C., on one of Hartford's vendor's transports. Neither of our names would appear on a passenger manifest. On Sunday I was to return on a commercial flight under an alias with a holiday shopping group. In Washington, cousins of Lao's sister-in-law contracted to provide ground transportation and a bed. Lao and a private bodyguard with White House clearance would be at my side throughout the twenty-four hours.

Though I understood their precautions, I felt frightened. David and I had damage control in place for our business as the national ethics debate expanded, but I had not anticipated how I would feel about such personal danger. Brown suits, now cleared for service by Lao, increased surveillance as threats mounted.

Anne Hartford and Ashwood were so synonymous that someone with a grudge or a multi-corps with evil intention had more than one target. I contemplated staying at my in-law's metro condo over the holidays to keep the family safe.

"If I can't stay at my D.C. apartment, I need to pack clothes." I jumped to the facts and away from the painful thoughts that Milan would walk me into danger. "I don't have a flak jacket." It was a weak attempt at humor.

"These folks don't use guns, Mom."

"We'll have clothes waiting." Lao stated without emotion. "Carry just your business briefcase. Meet me in the courtyard in forty-five minutes."

"Did we cancel the transport?" I asked Clarissa. She looked puzzled and shook her head. "Okay. Let's hope for the best."

Chapter forty-Seven

In flight, strapped into a jumper seat in front of tons of specialty measurement equipment for an East Coast manufacturer, Lao and I spoke little. I read through encrypted messages from Milan's office to reassure myself that he and I had common grounds in spite of the politics of his management team. Lao appeared physically to rest and monitor communications.

Crossing Lake Michigan, not far from Phoebe's intended lab site, news came of the crash of a Bureau land transport sent for Commissioner Hartford. The driver experienced mild injuries. A large piece of road equipment in transit from a work site crushed the passenger cab. We passed through mild turbulence, not unusual over the Great Lakes. For the first time in my life, I was sick.

"Creating a martyr will make this all more difficult." The sour taste of vomit lurked in my rinsed mouth.

"While people mourn or protest, backroom negotiators can broker agreements," Lao said. "You were right to leave Amber and Phoebe at home."

"David knows I'm safe."

He nodded. "Don't worry. When we land, we'll notify Milan that you used alternative travel plans."

Milan met us at the cargo transport station, a sign Lao's careful plan had been at least partially breached. They argued inside the hangar about how we should travel into the city, each pointing at the other's failures in this first section of the journey. Milan traveled in an armored transport with a police escort. Lao replaced the escort with his private security force and changed the route on file.

I assumed we would meet in Milan's offices, but he insisted we move to his private apartment within Bureau's headquarters. As we left the sunshine-filled December afternoon to enter the Bureau's underground garage, I saw two women pushing strollers and envied their simple freedom. Large metal doors opened ahead of the first escort vehicles. The doors closed behind us, my claustrophobia upping the tension. Milan moved from the transport into a mishmash of brown suits, federal security and private guards. Lao exited, checked with his lead person. His face resembled a warrior as he surveyed our surrounding. I hesitated. He extended a hand.

"Washington real estate prices and security requirements have become prohibitive so Cabinet members have the option of living within remodeled fallout shelters." Milan sounded tired, his explanation delivered like a tour guide. "This apartment was designed about six years and three secretaries ago, but it's comfortable." He glanced over his shoulder at me. "Anne, I apologize for submitting someone with a dislike of enclosed spaces to this setting. After the Minnesota transport accident, we felt you would be safest here."

The morning had set me off-kilter, suspicious of everyone, uneasy surrounded by strangers, exposed to unnamed dangers. The long, sloping walk probably moved us a story below the parking garage. In an elevator I wouldn't have noticed the lack of natural light and I wondered if Milan led us this route because of our entourage, or to keep me uncomfortable. I watched his walk, noticed the slight hitch explained away with a story of minor surgery back in June. The side of his face had dark spots, wrinkles covered the back of his head between the end of his thinning hair and collar.

"You're quiet, Anne." He must have sensed me watching him. "How are you doing?"

"There are a lot of places I'd rather be." My thoughts couldn't move far from accepting the fact that people wanted me dead.

A door ahead of us swung open, the sound of a water fountain gentled the beat of shoes on concrete. Milan waved us inside. "My home, please come in. Lunch is waiting."

At the mention of food I looked to Lao who did not provide a visual answer as we walked through a small foyer into a round room with upholstered chairs surrounding a cherry table. On a sideboard stood a soup tureen, basket of bread, a small wheel of cheese and serving utensils.

"We'll all eat from the same food. Please feel free to have any of it tested. I regularly do." Milan stepped to the table, pulled out a chair, and sat. I did the same. I remembered Milan visiting my small D.C. office, pouring himself a cup of coffee, and cutting a slice of pumpkin bread from the loaf Amber baked without a single concern. Five weeks of traveling a whole lot of political territory brought me to no place good.

"If we could have the security people wait outside this room," he directed. "You can divide yourself between the outer perimeter and the apartment. Nothing will happen to Anne while she is with me." Lao appeared ready to ignore Milan's request. "We have business to discuss, Lao. Business that is best kept in the smallest circle possible. Test the food, then please protect her from outside the door for two hours."

The testers were quick and in a few minutes we tasted our split pea soup, buttered our bread and stayed quiet.

"I saw Andrew a few days ago." Milan spoke informally, as if we were dining at Ashwood. "I noticed his name on those attending a lobbying event and invited him out for a beer. Sounded as if he planned to spend Christmas with the family. Any special plans?"

I shook my head. "The normal. What about you? Will you stay here or spend the holidays in Duluth?"

"To be determined." He sounded tired. "Let's talk about ethics and the president."

"Before we begin tell me why you placed me in this position? I've trusted you as a confidante and friend for almost thirty years. I could have died in the transport sent by your staff. Friends don't kill friends." I kept my voice detached, struggled to speak slowly.

"I understand this morning was traumatic." He looked at me, compassion in his eyes. "You're smart. You speak the truth. If anyone could get the conversation started without thought of personal gain, it would be you." He pushed bread around his plate. "This will be the perfect jumping point for you if you'd like to be in politics."

"Big players interested in this topic might kill me, harm my family." I gazed toward the door. "Have you played loose with my life to make a political point?"

"You'll be all right, Anne. Rough run for the near future, but this is a battle that fits you."

"That's not what I asked, Milan." An itchy feeling began in my throat. "I asked if you deliberately placed me and my family in jeopardy?"

"Your family is closer to me than my own, Anne. I've watched over Phoebe, Noah, and Andrew for decades. I am very fond of them." He sneezed. "The time I spent at Ashwood to untangle Phoebe's issues was not easily arranged, but I was there." He sneezed again then coughed, a tight air limiting sound.

I drank water as the itchiness continued. "And perhaps Phoebe's abuse helped fuel your takeover of the Chicago labs?" Under the table edge I pressed my communicator for Lao then exploded in a giant sneeze followed by another and another. "I have to get out of here. There's something in the air."

He raised a hand, held captive by a stuttering cough.

Between my own sneezing that began the quick turn into a wheeze I paged Lao again.

Milan pushed a key across the table, crippled by long wheezes. I held my sweater in front of my nose, reached into my bag for my asthma inhaler, and pressed it to my lips while moving to the door. The key slid into its hole, I turned it. Lao pushed the door open, pulled me into the hall and eased me to the floor. From inside Milan's wheezing had a desperate edginess.

Two brown suits ran in to help him out. My heart raced, breathing demanded attention. I held up a hand to my throat. "I can't . . ." was all I said before slipping into darkness.

Chapter Forty-Eight

Lao told me I would have died if one of the brown suits had not muscled her way past him, to sink an epinephrine injection into my thigh. During their physical struggle, she tried to let him know she had serious allergy issues and carried a prophylactic injectable. Emergency medical team said she saved my life.

Milan was not as fortunate. The allergen we inhaled raised havoc within his older, less healthy, body. Security agents took turns with CPR while waiting for the emergency technicians. The medical team revived him, stabilized him in transit, but damage was already done to his heart, lungs, and liver. Intubation made breathing possible, but he remained in shock. As the medics cared for me, I heard Lao fight with the medical respondents about choice of a small, private hospital. Hartford contracted security surrounded us through transit.

By the time we arrived at the hospital, Lao had activated private physicians and medical professionals to be present for our intake and treatment. I had severe cramping, nausea, dizziness, and blurry vision. My heart raced. I hallucinated and fought medical staff. Nothing convinced me that the trip to the cargo transport station was a good decision. I heard Lao authorize the push of sedation.

For our safety we were flown back to Minnesota. I remember nothing of the flight except a most awful feeling when we arrived that Milan lay dead on the next gurney. Phoebe told me later that I was not alone with that suspicion. I began crying as we landed, tears without foundation and, therefore, hard to stop. I cried even after the medical staff read his vital stats.

I wanted to go home, to feel Ashwood in the air. I clung to David's hand as they rolled Milan from the cargo plane, and then prepared to transfer me to an ambulance and travel to Abbott-Northwestern Hospital.

"They say you'll be okay, Annie." David spoke quietly, close to my face. I felt his fingers rub away the mysterious tears. "We won't leave your side."

"I want to go home, David." My hand shook. "I'm so sorry."

"Sorry about what? You were doing your duty as a citizen. You don't have to stay in this fight." I couldn't see his face clearly enough to understand the steel under his words. "Put the energy into fighting for your life. Someone will pay."

David and Lao told me that the story of the aborted assassinations of a key U.S. Cabinet member and citizen commissioner was carried around the world. My privately hired media expert assisted the White House team in what threatened to become a story about the laxity of national security when pitted against multi-corps strength. As Congress packed up for the holiday recess, the government trembled.

No one entered my room without permission of Lao and David, no food was delivered unless made in Ashwood's kitchen and delivered by Terrell or Amber, and no media had access. After the first twenty-four hours, the cramps lessened, the vertigo diminished, and I stopped crying. During the second day I woke from a nap to a quiet space and the ability to see the faces of David and Phoebe.

The third day, as weak as wet paper, I went home. My muscles hurt just sitting on the side of the bed and I needed help to walk the short distance to the toilet, but Lao insisted I would be safer at Ashwood. We were airlifted and set down in the field where the giant medical copter had landed that summer.

The doctors said I would regain mental clarity, my vision would return to normal, and energy level increase. Specialists didn't know about the long-term impact on my lungs. They had never encountered the use of the massive allergen mixed with pure oxygen that was used to take us down.

Faith served as my constant companion during the first week home. She studied at my side or spoke with me about holiday preparations and small family occurrences. I couldn't hold on to her stories from day to day, struggled to tell David what happened a half hour earlier. Somehow he managed to prop me up for a brief appearance at the holiday pageant.

Without Paul, Ashwood felt subdued during the week before Christmas. Amber and Phoebe assumed responsibility for the family holiday. David, working through his first fiscal year end as head of Hartford, Ltd., spent long days in the office. The seventeenth of December I woke from a nap and felt like a damper had been lifted from my mind.

"Faith?" I was restless. "Could we move to the family room and have," a word escaped my grasp only to be replaced by understanding that I wasn't sure if I wanted hot chocolate or hot tea. I smiled at my daughter, tried to erase the frown marks between her eyes. "I'm not sure if I want hot chocolate or tea. Maybe both?"

"You bet, Mom." I noticed her use my communicator to send a request to the kitchen. "Let me help you with your sweater."

"Maybe it's time I try to do this on my own." I swung my legs to the side of the bed and pushed my arms into the sleeves. I tired, but challenged myself to claim the small independence of dressing myself. Faith offered me an arm as I stood on legs that needed a moment to steady. "Okay, now we're making progress," I said in an even tone.

Leaving Ashwood

I pretended not to notice that Otis appeared from nowhere to gather up my oxygen tank, steroid inhaler and a small pouch of other medical supplies. When I felt strong, the door opened. The room stayed steady, my breath flowed without hitch. Faith walked by my side, pointing out holiday greeneries, a wall filled with get well wishes, the smells of fresh cookies cooling in the kitchen. My eyes teared in thanksgiving for the simple journey from bed to a sofa in our family's room. She helped me settle against pillows.

"Alleluia." My exclamation came out puny on volume and high with fervor.

"Agreed." Phoebe said entering the room. "It's a huge relief to watch you toddle down the hall." She unfurled a blanket and fussed with tucking it around my feet, legs, and up to my armpits. "I was a bit worried that by being here, I jinxed Christmas this year."

Faith stopped using my communicator and looked up with a puzzled face. I understood my narcissistic stepchild's thought pattern, but didn't feel strong enough to diplomatically explain Phoebe's thinking to Faith. At that moment the holiday began as David, Amber, John and Terrell joined us with a tray that carried a teapot, hot chocolate, sweets, cheeses, and fruit.

For a half hour, conversation ranged from the room's velvet ribbon trim to gifts waiting to be purchased and how wonderful the weather felt for December. I listened, spoke sparingly and relished the realization of being on the mend.

"Have we been able to convince Mom's doctors that a Christmas tree in the living room won't send her into sneezing and wheezing?" Phoebe asked after I admired a wreath cookie. "She didn't have a negative response to the garland in the bedroom."

"Don't be letting Frances or Lao know you snuck spruce in that room, or both our heads will be on a platter." Terrell's warning brought laughter from David.

"Having picnicked with you in the middle of the blue spruce grove, I thought we were safe with a small experiment," David said. "Still, we were probably lucky you didn't react to it."

John excused himself and pulled Faith out with him. Left with three people I could trust to tell me the truth, I asked about Milan.

Phoebe looked to David. "His condition is still critical but stable," he said. "He is older, not in great health, and didn't have the advantage of the timely antihistamine injection."

"I should talk to him." My words came out slowly. "Where is he?"

"In a private nursing facility," David answered. "Still needs a respirator. His heart, lungs, and other organs were impacted."

"Will he survive?" Phoebe sat at my feet, took both of them into her lap and rubbed my toes.

"His daughter told me the doctors say there's a fair chance that he'll be off the respirator by Christmas and sitting up by New Year's." David stopped. I could see him weigh words. "He won't return to work."

"He's always been a part of my world. Even before you, David."

"I know." David didn't elaborate on Milan's condition or future. "We'll invite Milan and his wife to spend time here when he's back on his feet. He's always loved Ashwood."

"How is this story being covered in the media?" For the first time I reached for news of the outside world although fatigue had begun to shorten my attention span.

"It's huge." Phoebe seemed to take leadership. "International story about attempted assassinations in the American capitol. Lots of good pictures of you. Lots of calls for investigations." She straightened the blanket, brushed off crumbs. "Your doctors have placed you off limits and there is enough security here to scare off even the craziest journalist."

"Has anyone claimed responsibility?" I coughed, remembered the first tickle in my throat that afternoon, reached for water.

David, Phoebe, and Terrell looked at each other. I sensed there was an answer, but not one I would hear today. "Nothing definite," offered David. Phoebe squinted and shook her head slightly. "I meant there's only speculation. You shouldn't be thinking about this."

I told myself I'd feel stronger tomorrow and would ask again. For the moment, I nodded and coughed and searched for my inhaler as I grew anxious that the cough would put me back into the cycle of losing my breath completely.

Chapter forty-nine

A NDREW AND NOAH MADE IT HOME for the holidays. I felt my fragility in their gentle hugs. For the first time, Ashwood's front door was closed Christmas Eve to all but family and close friends. We mourned Paul, we celebrated a marriage, and each other's presence. Although I had little appetite for the wonderful food set out, I sat at the table for brunch both days and listened to the flow of my family's story telling.

On Christmas Eve night we recreated our annual tradition and watched greetings from many of Ashwood's past workers in the dining room with Clarissa, Magda, Terrell, Lao, Max and their extended families. We chuckled at the chunky guys who had been skinny house staff, admired babies and husbands, felt proud of college degrees, knew we had supported the development of hundreds of good people.

We had a white Christmas and shared breakfast with all the staff that called Ashwood home, including the teen workers who had no other place to be that morning. I remembered Christmases when the residence's halls had been noisy with dozens of children opening two gifts each around a big tree decorated with a few strands of electric lights, ornaments from David's home, and homemade garland. The past hung close.

"So this is how your parents felt when they came to live with us," I said to David on Christmas night. "The older generation learning to let go."

"They didn't run a complex international company or head up a national commission at the president's request." He drew me close.

"But they were grandparents many times and pulled their family through a catastrophic depression." I wasn't sure where my thoughts wanted to go. "I don't feel as much part of the future as I did five years ago. It's not bad, just different."

"After January first I'm dragging you back to Hartford, Ltd. We've got lots of future to explore." He nuzzled my neck. "You looked beautiful today and we were all relieved to see you stronger." I felt a gentle kiss near my ear. "You are really loved, Annie."

My dreams that night were of Ashwood, of coyotes running across snow, of children playing in apple orchards fragrant with blossoms, of rooms filled with familiar faces. When I awoke I wanted to kickstart recovery, to understand what had happened in Milan's Washington, D.C., apartment deep in the Bureau.

After David and the guys went to Giant Pines I called Lao and Frances. We met in the sitting area of the bedroom where we wouldn't be interrupted.

"I need to know what happened and what's happening now." I knew they had anticipated this question. "Stop sheltering me. I'm ready to move on."

Frances nodded to Lao who took the lead. "In a nutshell, the vice-president has been implicated in cooperating with a powerful coalition of multi-corps to stop the ethics board. Hernandez has announced she will not run for re-election. There is significant instability in the capitol." He finished and looked at me.

"My God." I could barely whisper. "What did Milan and I do?"

My friend and medical caregiver took my hand. "A majority of Congress is united behind one of your Senate supporters to fill the vice-president vacancy. Hernandez has no choice but to follow their wishes. She'll be a hobbled lame duck with a strong watchdog in the room." Frances's fingers crossed my wrist, monitoring my pulse as she spoke. "Most Americans would say you and Milan are heroes who tried to stop wholesale power going to the multi-corps."

She turned my hand back over. "Breathe, Annie."

"I'll have to go back and finish my appointment." A small wheeze ended my sentence.

"You're not doing that." Lao made his sentence into a parental command. "Hernandez has decommissioned you and turned your work over to a Senate committee."

"But I didn't give my work to anyone." Again Frances and Lao looked complicit.

"There is language in the agreements you signed that allowed designated representatives of the federal government free access to all records and materials assembled by you under certain conditions." I listened to Lao's explanation and remembered Raima reading segments to me during a discussion. "Two criteria have been met—a significant threat of disruption within the government and your physicians have forbidden travel for an indefinite period of time."

A sense of responsibility for the national political storm stuck in my conscience. I took risks setting the congressional lions loose against the multi-corps defense of the U.S. labor market. I asked for the return of my data pad and communicator. Frances refused, but gave me a reader pad and permission to follow the outside world without becoming involved in its doings for another week.

Chapter Fifty

MANAGEMENT EXPERTS HAVE ALWAYS underestimated the wild element possible in changing the human condition. Sometimes change happens by accident, upsetting traditions that hold the pieces of fragile co-existence in place. It's comforting to graph out how a decision or action will topple obsolete behaviors. But people are multi-dimensional and when boxes are shuffled some of them will drag their feet while others run faster than expected.

Changing a democracy is even messier. Nothing happens unless trades are made between enemies as well as friends. My six months dabbling in the Washington, D.C., pond made me hungry to be where the big decisions about citizens' rights were being made. Healing at Ashwood felt like crawling to the moon. I could have been part of the big debate about the U.S. as a government for the people and by the people versus a broker of people, services, land, and resources. But I had no choice.

Illinois Senator Tyler Baye, a Democrat who became vice-president, wheedled permission from Frances to meet with me later in January. We talked about the ethics board's files, about the economic advisors' concerns over change, about the possibility of political failure. He was as persuasive as he was inquisitive. I wished him well.

From my office I watched the Democrats pick out small chinks in the massive Bureau machine like re-instating parts of the Fair Labor Standards and limiting the role of big business in public institutions of learning.

"Go for a walk, fire-breather?" Phoebe stopped by my office on one of the first warm days of March. She had a string of nicknames for my business and politic roles. "I've got time and I hear our mutual keeper wants you to get fresh air."

I took another look at news breaking about child labor laws before responding. "I've become a news media junkie." She laughed and held out my jacket.

"How does it feel to have your baby out of the house?" Phoebe had escorted Faith to Montreal in my place. "For someone who wanted to stay here and begin working, Faith is excited about eight weeks at McGill."

"She's ready to learn how to live on her own." I inhaled cool air, waited for a cough that didn't happen. "The past ten months have been extraordinarily stressful for all of us. It was her first spell of living with uncertainty."

"I talked with Milan this morning." Phoebe twisted her hair up on her head and jammed a pencil through the curls. "Did you know he turns seventy in June? I knew he was older than Dad, but seventy seems very old." She stretched her steps. I did the same. "I'm going to visit him this weekend. Want to come along? We have to use secured transit."

Tulips had pushed up inches through the ground near the residence. Impulsively I locked my arm through Phoebe's drawing one of the big laughs we all loved. "Sure."

"I'm proud of you, Mom." She hugged my arm to her body. "When I was young, you were always in charge of everything—the family, the business, parties, whatever. I was surprised back in June that you had become a true business exec and gave Amber total run of the residence and human resources management. That was a major change."

"Clarissa's been a good coach." Phoebe's eyebrows rose. "I knew that would surprise you. She challenged me over and over about using my time well and about giving people responsibility for their own issues." We separated as the path became uneven. "I didn't have any one to kick my butt about how I used time until she found her voice."

"Andrew sent me first designs for his house." She turned back toward the residence. "I said I'd help supervise the building since I'll be here for some time."

We walked peacefully, my thoughts jumping to the possibility Andrew and Phoebe would find a future together. Removed from the atmosphere of the Bureau labs, with the help of Frances, Phoebe was a fundamentally good person. She applied her intelligence and work talents to defining a good life.

"Do you think we'll have another depression if the Democrats get all the changes they want?" Her voice didn't ask for assurances.

"No. That's rhetoric to scare people." I believed what I said.

"Exactly." She loosened her hair. "I agree."

Before we went inside I assessed the big old stucco house, never made anything more than barely handsome over the years. But the red front doors were open. Pots of pansies lined the wide stone steps. People came to Ashwood for friendship, business, comfort, family. Some came for respite.

"Tell me about your research," I asked and listened to her vision of the future.

Leaving Ashwood

Acknowledgements

As the Ashwood trilogy closes, I am thankful to family, friends, readers and editors who have kept the story alive. For the third cover in this series, I thank Terrence Scott. For the major story editing, I am grateful for the work of Ben Barnhart. For their continued confidence in my work, North Star Press of St. Cloud is appreciated.